The New Century of South African Short Stories

For my mother who introduced me to stories

The New Century of South African Short Stories

Selected and introduced by
Michael Chapman

AD DONKER PUBLISHERS
JOHANNESBURG & CAPE TOWN

Published in 2004 by
AD DONKER PUBLISHERS (PTY) LTD
An imprint of JONATHAN BALL PUBLISHERS (PTY) LTD
PO Box 33977
Jeppestown
2043

ISBN 0 86852 227 9

This material is based upon work by Professor Michael Chapman, supported by the National Research Foundation under Grant Number 2054127. Any opinion, findings and conclusions or recommendations expressed in this material are those of the authors and therefore the NRF does not accept any liability in regard thereto.

Cover painting by George Pemba, *Korsten* (1961)
Cover design by Michael Barnett, Johannesburg
Cover reproduction by Triple M Advertising & Design, Johannesburg
Typesetting and reproduction of text by Alinea Studio, Cape Town
Printed and bound by CTP Book Printers, Duminy Street, Parow, Cape

CONTENTS

PREFACE

This is a new anthology. It is not a revised or updated version of the earlier *A Century of South African Short Stories* (1978). The selection ranges from the traditional oral tale to the written story of 'post-apartheid' times. Although the texts are in English, the stories include translations from Afrikaans and African languages. Many of the translations, including reworkings of earlier versions of oral tales, were commissioned for this anthology. The aim is to offer readers a fresh selection of what is arguably South Africa's most resilient and innovative form of literary expression.

The anthology does not seek a 'great tradition', or the canonisation of a relatively small number of authors. Rather, it regards the story as a protean form of communication. There are superb practitioners: Pauline Smith, Herman Charles Bosman, Nadine Gordimer, Can Themba, Abraham H de Vries, Bessie Head, Hennie Aucamp, and others. There are also storytellers who, in an occasional story, have struck a nerve, opened an insight or a perspective, or turned a style in a unique direction. *The New Century* is alert to both established and lesser-known voices. As a criterion of selection, the quality of the story supersedes the reputation of the author.

Indeed, consistency has resulted in my avoiding the usual practice of concluding the anthology with biographies of the individual writers. Suffice it to say that most contributors are connected to either university teaching or journalism. While Gordimer is a professional writer, Smith and Head had no occupation, the former living in modest family security in England, the latter in self-exile and poverty in Botswana. Alex La Guma was a political activist, while Es'kia Mphahlele and Can Themba both suffered the difficulties of being banned persons. The art of the short story is not an art of reputation. It is an art of the left hand.

The introduction discusses the character of 'story' in relation to the selection criteria. The arrangement of the material delineates an oral past, a restricted but important chronology of colonial to modern, and a shift of emphasis from the struggle years of the 1970s and eighties to our contemporary scene. The chronological Part Two concludes with a story from Gordimer's fifth collection (1972). (The author published her first collection of stories in 1953.) In Parts Three and Four authors are arranged alphabetically. Sources of the stories appear in the acknowledgements, where references to oral traditions are listed under the heading, 'Oral Past'.

Translators are acknowledged under the titles of the relevant stories. I wish to acknowledge, also, the invaluable assistance of research student Ashlee Lenta.

STORY: AN INTRODUCTION

The New Century of South African Short Stories suggests that the imaginative and intellectual climate after apartheid, after the ideological divisions of the Cold War, is conducive to a renewed interest in shorter forms of fiction. If apartheid in South Africa provided writers with a big theme, then the big narrative of the novel perhaps was the most appropriate response to the national question. With the novel we enter a big world; characters develop in interchange with society; there is a beginning, middle and end to the plot. With the story beginnings, middles and ends are not as decisive. We encounter instead the fragment, the irresolute moment; lyrical intensity intrudes upon prosaic matter; tone predominates over plot; action shifts almost imperceptibly from the social to the psychological realm; and value is granted not so much to character as to the storyable incident. Whereas the novel is equated with big ideas, big events, the story favours flexibility, ellipses, surprise, emotion, implication. With large, singular plots (the narrative of nationalism or socialism) discredited, the story permits us smaller, various, often unconventional insights. These find consonance in a country in the complexity of its transition from an authoritarian order to a civil imaginary. The multiplicity of voices in a collection of stories suggests the range and diversity of our possibilities.

My shorthand attempt to distinguish between the story and the novel could strike readers as rudimentary. The fact that criticism has not formulated any unique theory of the short-story genre according to which we might understand its unique kind of experience or the unique way it imitates and creates its experience, alerts us to the difficulties of defining the form. The qualification 'short' further complicates the issue. The term, 'short story', has come to be associated with the written, realist styles of late nineteenth-century Europe and America.

But storytelling returns us to ancient times. The short story, with its usual focus on a single event or single effect, has remained close to the primacy of myth according to which myth expresses the inner meaning of things by telling a story. If the novel is a syncretic form, the story is an elemental form: its origins are myths, fables, parables, folk tales, or the genre of the romance. In fact, the story of the early nineteenth-century united folk-tale material with the voice of the individual perceiver. As in the Romantic revival, the spiritual impulse yielded to secular concerns. It is Charles E May's contention that the modern short story has never quite lost touch with its romantic origins and that 'story' may be defined by a paradox: 'the reality of artifice'.

Paradox is the one constant factor in discussion of the genre: a paradox that is germane, too, to story in South Africa. Ancient tales – it is said – enacted, illustrated, and dramatised the moral lessons of communities (e.g. the African oral tale). At the same time, the story – it is said – captures the temper of insecure societies, outcasts, submerged population groups, or as Elizabeth Bowen phrases it, 'the disorientated romanticism of the age'. The latter is a fair description of the jazzy, gangster stories of Sophiatown in the 1950s, in which black writers such as Can Themba and Casey Motsisi reflected desperate affirmations amid desperate urban dislocations. If the realist novel requires a normal society, then the impressionism of the short story suggests the abnormal condition including frontier division, social and cultural heterogeneity, and rhythms of life that do not accord with the stability of a middle-class reading habit. It is no surprise that in Europe the short story initially found inspiration in both supernatural and bohemian cults, and in the United States in New World adventure. Despite the pre-eminence granted our novelists, conditions in South Africa favour shorter forms of expression. In the volume of its output, the short story is arguably our most resilient and popular literary form.

To continue to note the paradoxes, Edgar Allan Poe's influential early criticism suggested that the short story began not with plot construction, but with a 'certain unique or single effect to be wrought out': a reminder not only of the Gothic and ghost stories of sensation, but of the 'twist in the tail/tale' utilised by a host of late nineteenth- and early twentieth-century writers including Guy de Maupassant and O Henry. (It is a subtle mingling of single effect, anecdotal yarn, and surprise ending that lends to Herman Charles Bosman's stories a dual perspective of the local and the universal.) Unfortunately, Poe's observation tended to be adopted as the 'rule' of story by too many second-rate talents, resulting in the reduction of the substance of the tale to a formula. It is in this context that James Cooper Lawrence said, not outrageously, that a story could be anything one wanted it to be: there are stories of fact, stories of fancy, stories told historically, dramatically, and didactically. To which Frank O'Connor added that readers not schooled in theory would probably accept anything as a good story so long as it is vivid, illuminating, lends shock to the action, grants pleasure in its language-style and, above all, is plausible. Although it is difficult to decide at what point action or character behaviour becomes completely inexplicable – O'Connor continued – the story that defies explication as a whole is probably artistically defective. We are reminded here of debates in the political crisis of the 1970s and 1980s in South Africa as to whether the 'spectacle' of events had not overwhelmed the 'ordinariness' of human behaviour, or whether the long, discursive and didactic stories of Mtutuzeli Matshoba – stories too lengthy to be included in the present anthology – were politics talk or art talk. Whatever the subject or style, selection returns instinctively to the difficult-to-define quality of plausibility.

How long or short may a short story be? We may ask: how long is a piece of string? Nadine Gordimer's latest collection *Loot* (2003) includes a story of three and a half pages and a story of 84 pages. Norman Friedman, at least, avoids the dilemma by recasting the question: what is the size of the action? Is it comprised of a speech, an episode, a plot? Does the action involve a change and, if so, minor or major? But this assumes that the story is a complete entity unto itself: that it conveys its entire meaning to the passive reader. Many commentators have found a unity between ancient oral stories and modern written stories in that, to a greater degree than the novel, the short story invites the participation of its listener or reader. Its brevity and elusiveness challenge its audience to 'complete' its suggestion and to seek coherence even when the experience, or the style, signals dislocation. As H E Bates puts it, the story is something shaped also by readers, by social expansion. Or to quote Jorge Luis Borges, the story is finally more than a 'structure of experience'; it is also the 'dialogue' that it establishes with its reader, the 'intonation it imposes upon his voice', the 'changing and durable images it leaves on his memory ... This dialogue is infinite'.

One may test this proposition on one of the tales in Part One: Oral Past. The San/Bushman story, 'The Young Man who was Carried off by a Lion', has the lion sensing a mystical, creative/destructive attachment to the Young Man. It 'wants' the Young Man; it wants to devour him. As this is a special Young Man, the San/Bushmen throw other children at the lion. But the lion rejects the sacrifices or libations. Eventually the Young Man is devoured and the San hunter-gatherers, in turn, kill the lion. The mythic mode defies easy interpretation. But is the story simply evidence of Bushman barbarism, as colonial readers would have had it? Or do we enter Borges's 'infinite dialogue'? In beginning *The New Century of South African Short Stories* with the section Oral Past, I suggest that we have need of a common history and heritage.

Recovery, however, is not an easy matter. Our San/Bushman, Khoi and

African tales arrive through complicated passages of mediation. Most were collected in the mid-nineteenth century by European missionaries, administrators, anthropologists and linguists. The local narrators by the time had become colonised subjects, and in some stories one finds traces of European fairy tales (e.g. Cinderella). This notwithstanding, the situation is no different anywhere else in the world. To take the example of Cinderella, the version we know was stitched together from medieval remnants and given the gloss of the then contemporary manner by the sixteenth-century collector, Charles Perrault. In the medieval version Cinderella leaves home because as a result of her own mother on her deathbed having forbidden her father to love anyone less beautiful than his dying wife, the mother had at the same time left her husband with recourse only to incest with his beautiful daughter. The plague led to dislocated families; retributions were cruel. At the end, the evil stepmother is forced to dance in red-hot metal shoes until she drops dead. We do not encounter such details in subsequent rewritings. By the time of its Disney-fication, the story of Cinderella has become in its moral schema a middle-class Western fantasy.

San/Bushman, Khoi and African tales have all been recast as children's stories. I have returned, however, to our earlier sources. In the case of San/Bushman tales, this is the Bleek and Lloyd Collection. Briefly, the German linguist WHI Bleek and his sister-in-law Lucy C Lloyd persuaded the governor of the Cape Colony to release from the Breakwater gaol several Cape-Bushman prisoners who were serving sentences for stock theft. (Deprived of their hunter-gatherer way of life by Boer farmers, //Kabbo and others had resorted to stealing sheep.) These convict-narrators in the late 1860s helped Bleek and Lloyd learn the ancient click language as they recollected their myths, legends, and stories. The linguists duly, and dutifully, transcribed every word including repetitions, devised a script for the Cape San dialect, and then provided literal translations of the stories in English. (Aesthetic 'charge' was not Bleek and Lloyd's concern or interest.) The result is a curious mixture of 'authenticity' (the repetitions, disjunctions, and ellipses preserve the feel of oral utterance) and 'unreadability' (our modern impatience probably means that we do not complete our reading of any single story). There have been subsequent interventions: rewritings that have 'cleaned up' Bleek and Lloyd and, as I said above, rewritings that have transformed Bleek and Lloyd into contemporary children's stories. My approach has been to commission a prominent writer to keep as close as possible to Bleek and Lloyd (who are admittedly not the source; there is no original, written source) while making the stories accessible to the reader of today. I have included also intelligent and innovative recastings of the San/Bushman tale by Eugène N Marais and

Marguerite Poland. If we have an inheritance, the tradition – to quote HIE Dhlomo – must continue 'to live!'

Despite what I trust is a legitimate digression, we are no nearer to an all-encompassing definition of 'story'. Used loosely, story is everywhere: the newspaper story; your or my story (the subject of the glossy magazine). Even when used restrictively, the newspaper story and the story of the imagination are not necessarily mutually exclusive, especially in societies like South Africa where the 'facts' of public events have intruded upon subjective or private experience. Walter Benjamin's distinction between fact and experience, for example, cannot explain adequately the practice and status of prominent South African storytellers including Can Themba, Karel Schoeman, Antjie Krog and John Matshikiza, all of whom – in this anthology – infuse reportage with fictional qualities of character creation, the atmosphere of setting, and the resonance of moral consequence. Neither can we reduce 'your story' or 'my story' to the sexual proclivities of the popular magazine. My story – in a wider search – might encompass the most profound expression of the self in society. What is it to live in, and be, a citizen of a new South Africa?

Faced with story everywhere, the anthologist has the difficulty of delineating the field. There is a story in a 'Madam and Eve' cartoon (a narrative of incident, a twist of surprise in the closing frame). A single-frame Zapiro cartoon can expand in the mind: two shackland dwellers sit on the outer edges of the big (Johannesburg) city and read in the newspaper that the Mbeki government has the economic fundamentals in place. The single frame expands into a national narrative. Or, a (barroom) joke may wish to be a story:

> The dominee visits Hans and Hanna in Vrededorp [or wherever] and is asked, hesitantly, by Hans whether the Lord objects to couples having sex on Sunday.
>
> 'As long as you are a married couple,' intones the dominee, 'I cannot say that the Good Book objects.'
>
> Prompted by Hanna's whisper [jokes are usually sexist] Hans clears his throat, nervously: 'Dominee, may I ask if it is sanctioned to have sex in the standing position?'
>
> To which the dominee replies ponderously: 'Nee, nee, I think not, for this could lead to dancing on the Sabbath.'

It is difficult, philosophically, to disqualify this joke as a story. It employs recognisable fictional qualities: character interaction, dialogue, surprise. It situates itself in a wider cultural code. Indeed, this 'joke' is not confined to the dour world of pre-1990 Afrikaner Calvinism. It is repeated – characters replete in kilts – in a Mel Gibson film about the Scottish clans. The joke, however, usually does not exceed its own quick laugh or snigger. Not a storyable incident, it fails to evoke the resonance of a Bosman anecdotal tale. In 'Funeral Earth', for example, Bosman translates 'jokiness' into the sad humour of interracial and intercultural experience.

In sidelining the joke as story we may follow, usefully, Flannery O'Connor's elimination by negatives. The short story is not a mini-novel. It is not a simple tale, or incident. It is not a joke or lyrical rhapsody in prose. Not a case history, or a reported incident. 'The short story is none of these things,' says O'Connor, 'because it has an extra dimension.' This dimension is achieved when the teller or writer puts the audience firmly in the middle of an action. It is an action 'illuminated and outlined by mystery'. If this sounds vague, perhaps that is how it should be. I am obliged to consider, nonetheless, not only the story, but the South African story. My view is that we are not yet so free of our history as to privilege in an anthology designated 'South African', stories which ignore entirely the specific accents of this country.

My selection criteria invoke, accordingly, a three-point consideration. There is, first, an implicit social project that remains alert to the 'rule' of diversity in a culturally heterogeneous society. It follows, second, that there is a cultural purpose: although not reducing the aesthetic order to power relations or ideology, the stories are usable in their recognition of our shared humanity even as we recognise keenly our differences. There is, third, an ethic of truth telling. In a South Africa in transition, the obligation to moral action remains a binding force on story; indeed, on our collective story. Such a three-point consideration has already been suggested in my decision to begin the anthology with a selection of San/Bushman and African oral tales. As exemplification, I return to the story of the young man who was carried off by a lion. The story is at once social and mythic; at once strange and familiar; at once particular and universal. It invokes cultural heterogeneity as it appeals to infinite dialogue.

There are further consequences of my selection criteria. In expanding an African oral past, I have both complicated and curtailed the colonial past. We are reminded, in complication, that the recovery of oral tradition involved considerable colonial intervention. I have curtailed, in contrast, numerous stories by late nineteenth-century colonial administrators, magistrates, commissioners, and assorted birds of passage, in which native servants or wards were talked about, or parodied, as objects of curiosity. I have avoided, also, what I call the 'imported story': that is, the story of fortune or misfortune which without shift of character, accent or tone, simply transfers a Victorian world of dream and desire to a local setting. Such stories often involve a cad who, after 'going native', redeems himself (he strikes it rich on the diamond fields) and returns to the arms of his long-suffering but always faithful English fiancée. This is story reduced to stereotype, and is usually laced with racial slurs at Jewish sharp-dealers or, at the edge of the action, clownish kaffirs. I have included Sarah Gertrude Millin's astute variation of the theme ('Up from Gilgal'). Playing similarly on a stock situation, HW Nevinson's 'Vae Victis' turns the Boys' Own Adventure – a trait of numerous Boer War yarns – into a small drama of uncomfortable confrontation and illumination. There was always more than a single side to a war that affected not only men, but women.

Several stories in Part Two: Colonial to Modern convert the story of sensation into the challenges of transition from tradition to modernity. This is particularly evident in black writers. Here, I have had to be particularly selective. There are no stories by Alan Paton (his best stories, in my view, are his long stories, or romances, *Cry, the Beloved Country* and *Too Late the Phalarope*). The 'liberal' story of white guilt, or at least overture to black/white accommodation, has not travelled well, whether in Paton, Dan Jacobson, or Jack Cope. I have also omitted stories by the respected Afrikaans writers MER, J van Melle, Toon van der Heever and Boerneef. Their stories are so claustrophobically 'Afrikaans' as to be too little aware of the intrusions of a surrounding, less than homogeneous society. Afrikaans stories in translation, nonetheless, feature prominently in the anthology.

The same cannot be said, regrettably, about translations from African languages. Outside the oral tales there is only one story – by PT Mtuze – that was originally in an African language. Afrikaner political, hence cultural, capital in the 1960s encouraged large-scale translation projects in which Afrikaans literary talent was made available, to a wider audience. By contrast, apartheid policy directed African-language endeavours at the ethnic group: in terms of publishing viability, at the closely monitored school text-book market. An anthology of African-language stories in English translation, *The Rainbow Flute*, eventually appeared in 1997. Many of the stories, however, have a tang of pre-modernity. There is an over-reliance in the contents of stories written as recently as the 1970s and eighties on antiquity: stories of ancient communities, jealousies over chieftaincy, clashes of factions, superstitions, all without the critical, distancing perspective of the present day. The stories that deal with urban issues lack the impact of the *Drum* writers of the 1950s, or the immediacy of the post-1990 concerns of a writer like Rosemary H Moeketsi (the rape of a black schoolgirl by an older, influential black man). The liberation of an African-language literature from both apartheid's preordained tribal universe and the prescriptions of the classroom constitutes a major challenge.

Despite this, the reader by the end of Part Two will have been introduced to a range of voices. There is the yarn, the anecdotal tale and, in Nadine Gordimer among others, the scenic method or modern story of implication, in which less is said than is inferred and in which external action yields to the inner meaning of things. As in the oral tale so in the Gordimer story of South African suburbia, the audience is invited to participate in the completion of the experience. The years up to the 1970s witnessed, also, a major shift in the conventions of Afrikaans story-writing: from the dark, rural psyches of *plaas* stories (including, although she wrote in English, Pauline Smith's Little Karoo) to the satirical 'non-nationalism' of C Louis Leipoldt and the absurdist universe (European existentialism turned to South African demands) of Sestigers Chris Barnard and Abraham H de Vries.

Just as De Vries's stories are not confined to any particular division of the anthology – indeed, De Vries's career continues today – neither do the stories in Part Three: 1970-1990 denote historical limitation. Hennie Aucamp's 'The Coat without End', for example, is as much a story of post-apartheid South Africa as it is a story of an earlier decade. The story returns us, in fact, to an influential attempt to mark the character of the modern, written story. It is often said of Nikolai Gogol's attempt in his story, 'The Overcoat', to combine the fantastical event with realistic detail that all modern storytellers came from under Gogol's overcoat. The point is that Gogol created a new form that was neither satiric nor heroic. He took as his hero an ordinary copying clerk and imposed over his image that of a larger resemblance (in Gogol's case, the spiritual dimension of Jesus Christ). In Aucamp's case, it is the imposition on ordinary people of the larger abnormality of the society. The novel requires the big story and the character with whom we can identify. The short story has no hero but – I return to an earlier observation – a submerged population group. Aucamp points us beyond the heroism of liberation to the ongoing wretchedness of a poor life.

The years of the 1970s and eighties – to quote Gordimer quoting Gramsci – were the years of interregnum, in which the old order was dying and the new struggled to be born. These were the years in which André Brink, JM Coetzee and Gordimer herself granted pre-eminence to the novel: in the case of Brink and Gordimer, to the unavowedly anti-apartheid novel; in the case of Coetzee, to extended parables that captured what Gramsci had noted as characteristic of the interregnum: its morbid symptoms. Yet those years witnessed the talents, also, of several new short-story writers including Bessie Head, Ahmed Essop, Njabulo S Ndebele and Peter Wilhelm. Short stories were a main feature of the magazine *Staffrider*, and the 1970s saw attempts to chart maps of tradition, albeit tradition confined to English-language and Afrikaans stories respectively, in two influential anthologies: Jean Marquard's *A Century of South African Short Stories* (1978) and Abraham H de Vries's *Die Afrikaanse Kortverhaalboek* (1978). Again the paradox: the novel favours the big theme, the short story the elusive moment. Yet the novel desires the normal society; the story thrives in conditions of insecurity.

What writers of whatever genre found to be a challenge in two decades of severe conflict was the relationship of art and politics. In South Africa, there can be no easy separation, even today. Part Three does not avoid politics; instead, it attempts to reach beyond ideology to evoke 'aura'. Ndebele's 'Death of a Son', for example, is both a graphic reminder of police callousness and a subtle exploration of a marital relationship. Barris's 'The Questioning' is simultaneously so bizarre and so banal – Hannah Arendt's 'the banality of evil' – as to be a chilling truth of the old regime. Haasbroek's 'Departure' transports the military border wars, metaphysically, to the gates of hell, all in an understated, indeed a colloquial idiom. From the dumbed-down perspective of a British comprehensive school, Hope observes the tragicomedy of the other side of Empire. In Reddy's South Africa, the Indian family comprehends its entire world within either the claustrophobia or the security of its extended household. The difference between this self-absorption and the self-absorption of Afrikaans stories of the 1930s and forties is that Reddy permits the larger, contemporary scene to exert a contending pressure upon the old code of 'keeping it in the family'. Wilhelm's 'Jazz' in the miniature of a few pages reminds us of the fragility of the big issues: a white guy tries his luck with a white girl who is 'student-ishly' attracted to the glamour of black jazz culture, but remains victim of her middle-class suburban mores. The story ends in tragedy or farce, or in the recognition of our fallibility. The reader must decide.

Should not Wilhelm, a writer of distinction over three decades, have been granted more than a single story? The question bears upon the aims of the anthology. Given the constraints of space (more severe than in an anthology of poetry) the editor has difficult options: a 'great tradition' of the South African story; a middle way, in which several significant writers are permitted several stories, but not to the detriment of a reasonable spread; or a sheer miscellany of voices. The current anthology adopts the miscellany approach for reasons that have already been stated. The decision to favour translation and range was not confined, however, to the aim of seeking the storyable equivalent of a society in a phase of social expansion. We are returned, at the same time, to a consideration of the story as waiting to be told, sketched, reported, artfully written, received, everywhere. The inclusion of more than one story by Gordimer and De Vries acknowledges two careers that span forty years. To have included several stories by several writers (Aucamp, for example, has enjoyed a long and distinguished career) would have prevented my including a number of wonderful, one-off stories. Former editor of the magazine *Tribute* Maud Motinyane, for example, has no pretensions to being a Nadine Gordimer. Yet her single story, 'Two Minutes', opens a vista that is unavailable to Gordimer. To paraphrase HE Bates, the unknown writer appears with a great story, and in that one-off voice we are given something unexpected and new.

Part Four: 1990- features several writers whose work first appeared well before the 1990s, or even the 1980s or 1970s. The criterion is adaptation to new circumstances. We read of revisited white/black relationships, crises in Afrikanerdom, crime and insecurity, gay life, locals living abroad, the absurdity of the past, the African Renaissance with its challenges, wisdoms, vulnerabilities and hypocrisies; above all, the multiple identities either willingly assumed by or enforced upon contemporary South Africans. The colonial 'madam and maids' formula (in which madam spoke authoritatively to the maid) is given a gender twist in Van Niekerk's 'Labour'. The shibboleths of the past – racial possession of the land, bourgeois possession of the city – figure ironically in Venter's 'Tinktinkie' and Vladislavić's 'The WHITES ONLY Bench'. The complications, or muddles, of older separations and categories lend inventiveness to stories by De Vries, Gordimer, Gray, Jamal, Scheepers, and Wicomb. A continuing blurring of fact and experience, history and imagination, informs the stories of Krog, Matshikiza, Moeketsi, and Roberts. Isaacson's 'I Could Have Loved Gold' lends to a 'Western' story of capitalist consumption a compulsive Sophiatown parallel. Matshikiza satirically subjects Africanism to its own reliance on Western gadgetry and fashion.

Such a variegated landscape, or cityscape, is not suited to the novel. The variety is better captured in an anthology of individual stories: stories that grasp the future possibilities of what the past has made available to us; stories that help us think backwards (how did I arrive where I am?) while understanding ways forward (what shall I, or we, do next?). If Ruth Suckow is correct in her assessment that short stories offered the United States a way of making itself intelligible to itself amid its chaos, unevenness, newness and inexperience, then the same may be said of stories from South Africa. *The New Century of South African Short Stories* affirms the significance of the storyable incident.

Michael Chapman
University of KwaZulu-Natal
2004

Works cited in the Introducton

Benjamin, Walter, 'The Storyteller: Reflections on the Work of Nikolai Leskov', *Illuminations*, ed., Hannah Arendt, New York, 1963.

Borges, Jorge Luis, 'A Note (towards) Bernard Shaw', *Labyrinths: Selected Stories and other Writings*, ed., Donald A Yates and James E Irby, New York, 1975.

Dhlomo, HIE, 'Zulu Folk Poetry', *Native Teachers' Journal* (April 1948).

Jones, Steven Swann, *The Fairy Tale: The Magic Mirror of the Imagination*, New York, 1995.

May, Charles E, ed., *Short Story Theories*, Athens, 1976. See extracts from HE Bates, *The Modern Short Story* (1941); Elizabeth Bowen, 'Introduction to *The Faber Book of Modern Short Stories*' (1936); Norman Friedman, 'What Makes a Short Story Short?' (1958); James Cooper Lawrence, 'A Theory of the Short Story' (1917); Frank O'Connor, *The Lonely Voice* (1963); Edgar Allan Poe, 'Review of [Hawthorne's] *Twice-Told Tales*' (1842).

May, Charles E, *The Short Story: The Reality of Artifice*, New York, 2002.

Ndebele, Njabulo S, 'The Rediscovery of the Ordinary: Some New Writing in South Africa', *Journal of Southern African Studies*, 12:2 (1986).

O'Connor, Flannery, 'Writing Short Stories', *Mystery and Manners*, ed., Sally and Robert Fitzgerald, New York, 1969.

Suckow, Ruth, 'The Short Story', *Saturday Review of Literature*, 4 (1927).

Perrault, Charles, *Perrault's Complete Fairy Tales*, New York, 1961 [1697].

PART ONE

ORAL PAST
Myths, fables, legends, tales/stories suggesting ancient or olden times

SAN/BUSHMAN TRADITION

The Sun is Thrown into the Sky

Translated from click language/dialect by WHI Bleek and Lucy C Lloyd; reworked by Elana Bregin.

The First Bushmen, the men of the Early Race – [!Kwi-an told her son //Kabbo] – were those who first inhabited the earth. Their children were the ones who worked with the Sun. The people who came later say that it was those children who made the Sun ascend, for their mothers had told them that they should throw the Sun-person up into the sky, so that he might warm the earth for them; so that they might sit in the Sun and feel its warmth. Until that time, the Sun was a man who lived on earth. In the beginning, he gave forth brightness only in the space around his own dwelling. The rest of the country remained very cloudy, as it looks now when the Sun is behind thick clouds. The sky was dark and black. The shining came from one of the Sun's armpits, as he lay asleep with his arm lifted up. When he put down his arm, darkness fell everywhere; when he lifted his arm up again, it was as if day had come. In the day, the Sun's light used to be white, but at night, it was red, like a fire.

The children of the Early Race gently approached the Sun-armpit to lift him up while he lay sleeping. Their mothers had spoken to them and told them to do this. An old woman was the one who had instructed them. She herself had no young male children, so she spoke to the children's mothers. For she saw that these were clever children, who would understand nicely what to do when they went to that old man, Sun-armpit. The old woman spoke to the children through their mothers, telling them to tell their children that they should throw the Sun-armpit up into the sky, so that the Bushman rice might become dry for them. So that while the Sun moved along across the whole sky, it would make all places bright. This is what the mothers said:

'O children! You must wait till the Sun-armpit lies down to sleep. Then, you must gently approach him while he lies asleep. Take hold of him all together, and lift him up so that you can throw him into the sky.'

This is what the old woman had told the mothers to say to their children.

The children came and the children went away again. The old woman said: 'You must sit down and wait. You must look to see whether the Sun's eyes are still open or whether he sleeps. You must go and sit down and wait for him to fall asleep.'

And so the children sat down and waited, as they had been told to do. The Sun lay down; he lifted up his elbow. His armpit shone upon the ground as he lay sleeping. The children took hold of him and threw him up into the sky the way they had been instructed to do. The old woman had said:

'O children going yonder! You must talk to the Sun when you throw him up. You must tell him that he must altogether become the Sun, so that he can go forward as the proper Sun – the Sun which is hot, which stays hot in the sky as he moves along high above us; so that as his heat shines down, the Bushman rice can become dry.'

This was the old woman's message to the children, the old woman whose head was white. And so, when the time was right, the children arose and stealthily approached the Sun. They all took hold of him together and lifted him up while he was still hot and threw him up into the sky.

'O Sun!' they said to him, 'you must stand firmly there, you must go along in the sky and remain there while you are still hot.'

Then the children returned to their mothers. One of them said: 'I and my younger brothers and their friends and their friends' brothers all took hold of him. I told them: "You must grasp him firmly – grasp the old man firmly, and throw him up."'

Another youth spoke and said: 'O my grandmother! We threw the Sun up, we told him that he should properly become the Sun, which is hot, for we are cold. We said: "O my grandfather Sun-armpit! Remain in your place in the sky. Become the sun that is hot, so that the Bushman rice may dry for us. Make the whole earth light, give heat, so that the whole earth may become warm in the summer. Shine properly, taking away the darkness; you must come, so that the darkness will go away."'

And so it is thus. The Sun comes, and the darkness goes away; the Sun sets, the darkness returns and the Moon comes out. The day breaks, the Sun comes out again and the darkness goes away as the Sun moves across the sky. At night, the Moon comes out to brighten the darkness; the darkness departs. The Moon shines, making bright the darkness as it goes along. The Moon sets; the Sun follows it, driving away the darkness. The Sun takes away the Moon. As the Moon stands in the sky, the Sun pierces it with the Sun's knife, and the Moon decays away because of what the Sun does with its stabbing rays. Therefore, the Moon pleads with the Sun, saying: 'O Sun! Leave for my children at least the backbone!'

And so the Sun does this. It promises to leave the Moon's backbone for the Moon's children. And so the Moon goes painfully away. Painfully, he returns home, moving along the sky. The Sun desists from cutting him further. For the sake of the Moon's children, he leaves the Moon's backbone behind. Because of this, the Moon again goes on to become another Moon, which is whole again. He lives again, even though it seemed as if he had died. He becomes a new Moon. He again puts on a stomach; he becomes large. He becomes a Moon which is whole again. He goes along at night, for he is the Moon which goes by night. He feels that he is a shoe, therefore he walks in the night. For once, the Mantis, inconvenienced by darkness, took off one of his shoes and threw it into the sky, ordering it to become the Moon.

The Sun is here and all the earth is bright. The Sun is here, and the people walk about while the place is light. They perceive the bushes, they see the other people, and the meat which they are eating, and the springbok. They hunt the springbok in summer, and also the ostrich, while the Sun shines down on them. They shoot the springbok, they steal up on the gemsbok and the kudu, while the Sun makes the whole place bright for them. They also visit each other, while the Sun shines upon the path. They travel in summer, hunt in summer, spy the springbok in summer; they go round to head off the springbok and lie down in a little house of bushes, while the springbok come.

Since that time when the Sun was thrown up into the sky, it became round and never was a man afterwards.

The Girl who Made Stars*

Translated by WHI Bleek and Lucy C Lloyd; reworked by Elana Bregin.

My mother was the one – [said //Kabbo] – who told me about the girl who made stars out of wood ashes. This girl arose from where she was lying in her little hut. She put her hands into the wood ashes of the fire and threw them up into the sky. She said to the wood ashes: 'These wood ashes which are here must become the Milky Way. They must lie white along the sky, so that the stars may stand outside of the Milky Way – the Milky Way which used to be wood ashes. The wood ashes must fully become the Milky Way and go around the sky with the stars, lying across the sky while the stars sail along'.

And so it is this way. When the Milky Way stands low upon the earth, it turns across the front of the sky, waiting for the Stars to turn back. The Stars wait for the Sun, until they feel that he has turned back; for he travels on his own path. Then the Stars also turn back and go to fetch the daybreak, so that they may sink nicely to their rest, while the Milky Way goes to rest with them.

The Stars sail along upon their footprints, which they follow across the sky. They know that they are the Stars which are meant to descend. The Milky Way continues to lie along the sky as it travels back to its place, to the place where the girl threw up the wood ashes. It travelled the sky while lying along it. It went around the sky while lying along it, waiting for the stars to turn around as they passed over the sky. The sky lies still. It is the Stars which move, sailing along as they feel that they are meant to do. The Stars begin to set, following their footprints as they sail along. They become white when the Sun comes out. After the Sun sets, they stand all around in the sky and turning, follow the Sun. When the darkness comes out, the Stars wax red, whereas before they had been white. They stand brightly around, sailing along in the night. Then, the people can walk by night, while the ground is made light, while the Stars shine a little.

Darkness is upon the ground. The Milky Way gently glows. It glows because it still feels that it is wood ashes. It obeys the girl who said that the Milky Way should give a little light for the people, so that they might return home by night, even in the middle of the night. For the earth would not have had any light had not the Milky Way been there, the Milky Way and the Stars. The girl thought that she would throw up *!huin* roots into the air, in order that the *!huin* roots should become Stars, the red, old roots making red stars and the white, young roots making white stars. But first, the girl gently threw up wood ashes into the sky, so that she might presently throw up the *!huin* roots to become the Stars.

The girl was angry with her mother, because her mother had not given her enough roots so that she might eat abundantly; for she could not go out of her hut to seek food for herself. So she was hungry while she lay in the hut. The mothers were the ones who went out. They were the ones who sought for food. They were bringing home *!huin* to eat. The girl lay in her little hut which her mother had made for her. Her stick stood there in the hut; because she was not yet a woman, she did not yet dig out food with the other women. She had to stay in the hut and wait for her mother to bring her food, which she ate lying down in the little hut which her mother had built for her. Her mother had closed her into the tiny hut because she was about to become a woman. During this time, she could not go far from her hut or walk about freely. She could not eat the game killed by the young men. She could only eat the game of her father, who was an old man. For if she ate the young men's game, their hands would become cool. Their arrows would become cool. The arrow head would become cold. The arrow head would feel that the bow was cold, while the bow would feel that the young man's hands were cold. The girl feared to eat the young men's game lest, while eating, she put her saliva into the springbok meat. This saliva would then go into the bow of the hunter, and the inside of the bow would become cool. Therefore, the game hunted by her father was the only game from which she could eat. For her father's hands had been properly worked by her, to take the coldness of her saliva away from them. During the time that she was waiting to become a woman, she must not look at the springbok, lest they should become wild. If she went out of her hut, she had to keep her eyes upon the ground, and not go far. When presently she became a 'big girl', then she would be allowed to leave the small hut, to walk around like the other women and look about again.

But this girl was disobedient. Because she was hungry she arose and went out of her hut and threw up wood ashes to become the stars, so that her father and the other hunters would have light to return home by. This girl is said to have been one of the people of the Early Race (*!xwe-lna-ssho-!ke)* and the 'first' girl, and to have acted wrongly. She was finally shot by her husband.

*See Marguerite Poland's 'The Wood-ash Stars', [ed.]

The Young Man who was Carried off by a Lion

Translated by WHI Bleek and Lucy C Lloyd; reworked by Elana Bregin.

A young man of the Early Race – [said Díä!kwain] – while out hunting one day, ascended a hill to look for game. While he sat there, he became sleepy. He felt the need to lie down, for he was very sleepy. What could be wrong with him today? He had not felt such sleepiness before.

He lay down and closed his eyes. While he slept, a lion came. It was on its way to a water pit. The oppressive noonday heat had made it very thirsty. The lion saw the man lying there asleep, and it took him up in its jaws.

The man awoke in fright and found himself being carried away by the lion. He kept very still, knowing that if he moved, the lion would bite him and kill him. He waited to see what the lion intended to do, for it appeared to think that he was dead.

The lion carried him to a zwart-storm tree and carefully placed him in its branches. It still needed to drink, for its thirst was very great. It decided first to go to the water, and then come back and eat him.

It pressed the man's head between the branches of the zwart-storm tree, and turned to go to the water pit. The man moved his head, just a little. The lion caught the movement; it looked back suspiciously – why had the man's head moved? The lion was sure that it had fixed the man's head firmly between the branches. But it had apparently not been firmly enough, for the man fell over. The lion came back and once more pressed the man's head between the branches of the zwart-storm tree, this time very thoroughly. It licked the tears from the man's eyes. For the man was weeping. The man felt a sharp stick piercing the hollow at the back of his head. But he dared not stir, for he saw that the lion suspected that he was alive. Finally, since the man did not move again, the lion concluded that it had pressed him firmly enough into the tree. It went on a few steps, then looked back towards the man. The man kept still, pressing his eyelids together, looking through his eyelashes to see what the lion was doing.

The lion went away. It ascended the hill and began to descend it on the other side. The man gently turned his head to follow its movements. He saw the lion raise its head, peering at him over the top of the hill, wanting to make sure that he was not just feigning death. When it saw that he was still lying as it had left him, the lion ran off quickly to the water, intending to slake its thirst and then return so that it might eat this man. For it was very hungry.

The man watched the lion disappear. It seemed as if this time, it had gone for good. Just to be sure, the man continued to lie still for a time, in case the lion again came back to check on him. For he knew that the lion was cunning. It might deceive him into thinking it had really gone away, only to return to catch him the moment he stirred. A long time passed. Still the man waited; finally, when there was still no sign of the lion returning, he concluded that it had really gone away.

He remained cautious, however. He did not leap up and flee immediately, but got up carefully, and sprang away to a different spot. His intention was to confuse the lion, so that it would find it more difficult to locate his trail from this new place. Then, instead of heading straight for home, the man ran off in a zigzag direction, hoping by this means to throw the lion off his trail. For he knew that if the lion detected his footsteps, it would follow him and seek him out where he lived.

Finally, he emerged at the top of the hill near his home. He called out to his people, telling them that he had been 'lifted up', he had been 'lifted up' by a lion. He instructed them to bring out many hartebeest-skins, and roll him up in them, for he had been 'lifted up' in the middle of the day, while the sun stood high. He knew that the lion, when it came back and found him missing, would resolve to seek him and track him down. For that reason, he wanted the people to roll him up in hartebeest-skins, so that the lion would not be able to scent him and get to him. Everyone knew that the lion does not forget its prey. Once it has killed, it will never leave its prey uneaten.

So the people rolled the young man up in mats and hartebeest-skins. They covered him over with sheltering bushes from around the homestead, so that the lion, when it came seeking him, would not be able to find him. For this young man was their hearts' young man. They loved him, and they did not wish the lion to eat him.

The people went out to seek a special edible root; they dug it out and brought it home at noon and baked it. An old man was one of those out gathering wood for his wife so that she could make a fire to roast the root. He was the one who saw the lion as it came over the top of the hill, exactly where the young man had walked, following the young man's trail. He shouted to the others, 'Look – look at the hill! There at the top where the young man came over – see what's there.'

The young man's mother said, 'You must not allow the lion to come near the houses. You must shoot it dead before it comes here.'

The people quickly slung on their quivers and went to meet the lion. But when they shot at this lion with their poisonous arrows, it would not die.

Another old woman spoke, she said, 'You must give the lion a child, so that it will go away from us.'

But the lion said that it did not want a child. It wanted the person 'whose eyes' tears' it had licked; he was the one that it wanted.

Other people said to those who had shot at the lion: 'How was it that when you shot at the lion you could not manage to kill it?'

Another old man said: 'Can't you see? This lion must be a sorcerer. It will not die when we shoot at it, it insists upon having the man whom it carried off.'

The people threw children to the lion; but the lion ignored them, still seeking the young man. The people continued to shoot at it. But their arrows had no effect. They said, 'Bring us spears, we have to kill the lion.' They stabbed it with spears, hoping to stab it to death, but their spears, too, had no effect. The lion continued to seek the young man, saying that it wanted the young man whose tears it had licked. He was the one it wanted. It tore things apart, breaking the people's houses to pieces, seeking the young man out.

And the people said, 'Can you not see that the lion will not eat the children we have given to it?'

And the people said, 'Can you not see that it must be a sorcerer?'

And the people said, 'You must give a girl to the lion, we'll see if the lion will eat her and then go away.'

But the lion did not want the girl either. It only wanted the man whom it had carried off.

And the people didn't know what else to do. They had been shooting at the lion since morning, and it would not die. It had refused the children whom they gave it, it had refused the young girl. It wanted only the man whom it had carried off.

So finally the people said, 'Tell the young man's mother that, although she loves the young man, she must bring him out. She must give the young man to the lion, even if he is the child of her heart. For she can see that the sun is about to set, and that the lion is still threatening us, it will not leave us, it insists on having the young man.'

The young man's mother wept and said, 'You may give my child to the lion. But you must not allow it to eat my child and live. You must kill it while it is upon my child, so that it dies as my child dies.'

So the people took the young man out of the hartebeest-skins in which they had wrapped him, and they gave the young man to the lion. And the lion bit the young man and killed him. And while the lion was biting the young man to death, the people shot at it and stabbed it.

The lion spoke: 'Now I will die,' it said to the people, 'for I have finally found the man I have been seeking.'

And so it died, lying dead with the young man that it had killed.

AFRICAN TRADITIONS

Nkulunkulu, the One Who Came First

Translated from isiZulu by Henry Callaway.

The ancients say that Nkulunkulu, the One Who Came First, is God, because they say he was the first to appear; they say he is the people's reed, from which the people were broken off. The ancients say that God exists; he made the first people, the ancients of olden times. Those ancients died but there remained other people generated by them - their children. From them we heard that there were ancient people of olden times who knew about the breaking off of the world from the reed. However, even they did not know God; they had not seen him with their own eyes, but they had heard that God existed and had appeared when people broke off from the reed bed. It was God who generated the people of old, and they generated others. It is our ancestors who have told us the stories about God and about the old days. Today's people pray to the ancestral spirits; they praise their ancestors so that they may come and save them.

How Death Entered the World

Translated from isiZulu by NN Canonici; reworked by Elana Bregin.

Long long ago, people did not die. They lived for years and years and years without dying. The One Who Created Everything looked out and saw that it was good. It was good that people should not die. It was good that people should live until they were bent over, without ever dying. He called Chameleon to him. Slowly, Chameleon came and stood in front of the Creator.

The Creator said to Chameleon: 'Chameleon, I am sending you on an errand; I am sending you to the people. You must go to them and tell them that I say that they are not to die. Do you understand?'

'Yes, Lord, I understand,' said Chameleon trembling. Its eyes looked first forward then backwards. Finally, Chameleon turned. Its leg shook and went forward; it put it down. It lifted another leg; this too shook as Chameleon put it forward. There is Chameleon, moving now, constantly lifting its shaking legs, with its eyes looking forward and then backwards.

After walking for a long time, Chameleon saw some wild berries. Its eyes saw the berries. Its mouth started watering. It said: 'I'll get to the people, it does not matter when. There is no reason to rush. Let me branch off here for a little while. For I am hungry, and I have no food. The Creator won't see me.'

And so Chameleon made for the berries. It shifted itself; forgetting that it was on an errand. The Creator saw it, however, and was angry. He called Lizard, which came swiftly. The Creator spoke to Lizard, saying: 'Lizard, take off at full speed and go to the people. Tell them immediately that I say they must die. I sent Chameleon, but it is wasting time with wild berries on the way.'

Lizard set off, shaking its tail as it ran. Dust blew up behind it. It did not even try to pluck food on the way. It passed Chameleon still busy with the berries. It hurtled by at great speed and disappeared. When Chameleon saw Lizard it was struck by fear. It remembered that it had a message to deliver. It stopped eating the berries. Shaking, it followed Lizard.

Lizard arrived among the people and said: 'Listen, all of you, listen to the message I bring from the Creator. All of you listen.'

The people listened in silence, setting aside their tasks. All wanted to hear the Creator's message carried by Lizard. 'Listen all of you. The Creator says, people must die!'

Then Lizard turned and went back home. The people stood there talking about Lizard's words. They were still talking when Chameleon appeared, breathing heavily. It kept shaking as it slowly approached them.

The people saw it and said: 'Look at Chameleon! It looks as if it wants to speak.'

Chameleon spoke: 'Listen all of you. Listen to the message coming from the Creator. All of you listen.'

The people said: 'Chameleon also says it carries a message from the Creator. Let's hear what it says.'

The people listened carefully to what Chameleon had to say. Chameleon went on: 'Listen all of you. The Creator decrees that people should not die.'

The people said: 'Away with you! Why are you telling us this? Where were you wasting your time just now? We have already received Lizard's message.'

Chameleon was upset; it turned back and slowly went off again.

Today there is still a proverb which goes: 'We have heard the lizard's message', meaning, we are holding onto what we already know. This is how it originated.

Maqinase, the Wily One

Translated from isiZulu by NN Canonici; reworked by Elana Bregin.

Children: Grandmother, please tell us a story.

Grandmother: Are you asking for a tale now? Don't you know that you'll grow horns if you are told a story in the daytime?

Children: Yes grandmother, we beg for a story now. We won't grow horns.

Grandmother: All right, I'll tell you one. If you grow horns it's your business. Don't come crying to me. Have you finished your jobs around the house?

Children: Yes, we have finished them. We ask for a tale now.

Grandmother: All right, my grandchildren. However, before I tell you a story, you'd better repeat after me:

Horn Horn, don't grow here (On the head)
It's as hard as a rock here (Head)
It is soft here (Ground)

Children: (Repeat line by line)

Grandmother: *Kwesukesukela* ... Once upon a time...

Children: *Cosi, sampheka ngogozwana!* We cook her in a small pot! [i.e. We have got her in a tight corner. Now that she has pronounced the initial formula *'kwesukesukela'*, she must go on with the story.]

There once was a mother pig with five children. One of the children was very fond of wandering about on his own. This child was truly pig-headed. His name, Maqinase (the Wily One), fitted him perfectly. The mother pig did not like her children to go out of her sight. Maqinase, however, was restless. When all the other pigs were sitting at home, he would suddenly disappear. He would go off on his own and return whenever he felt like it. His mother kept scolding him sternly, but it did not make any difference to Maqinase.

One day it was very hot. Maqinase's mother was overcome by the heat and fell asleep. Maqinase realised that his mother was asleep. He looked at his brothers and sisters and saw that they too were asleep, overcome by the heat. He smiled to himself. He got up and tiptoed away, so as not to awaken the sleeping ones. He went to the door and opened it slowly, without making any noise. He told himself: 'When they wake up I will be gone!'

As soon as he was out of sight of the house, Maqinase started walking straight ahead, moving quickly, as if showing off. The way he walked drew attention to him. There he is, over there!

On the way he met a donkey. Donkey said to him: 'Where are you heading for, Maqinase?'

Without even stopping, Maqinase answered: 'Leave me alone! Do I look like a person who should be addressed by one with ears as big as yours?'

Donkey was upset to hear Maqinase answer in such a way. He said: 'What an arrogant child you are! Why do you insult me when I addressed you nicely?'

'It must be the hot sun that gives rise to such strange happenings,' answered Maqinase still walking fast ahead. 'Do I insult you when I tell you the truth? Have you ever noticed how long your ears are? Do not bother me, when the sun is so hot!' And on he went.

As he walked further, he came across a tortoise. Tortoise said: 'Where are you heading for, Maqinase? You are walking so fast!'

Still walking, Maqinase answered, 'Am I having hallucinations today?' He raised his little nose and said: 'Do you drag your feet so as to delay on the road and ask me such stupid questions?'

Tortoise was hurt and answered back: 'Oh, Maqinase, why answer me with bad manners when I asked you politely? What an arrogant child you are!'

'I am used to being called arrogant by now,' Maqinase shot back. 'That fool over there with long ears also called me that. You leave me alone; mind your own business.'

And Maqinase was off, leaving Tortoise open-mouthed in astonishment.

Maqinase then met a frog. Frog said: 'My goodness, look at Mr Wily in person! Where are you going with such a swinging gait?'

Maqinase was upset by this and answered: 'Today must be my unlucky day. First the donkey, then the tortoise and now you, all asking me questions. Why do you gurgle at me as if too tired to breathe, wasting my time by asking me where I am going? Furthermore, are you so well acquainted with me as to address me as Mr Wily?'

Said Frog: 'Yes, indeed, Maqinase, you are really arrogant. Let those who have eyes see what you are!'

'Let them first see that enormous mouth of yours and leave me alone!' answered Maqinase, walking on ahead.

After passing Frog, he left the main road and crept through a fence. He said to himself: 'Better turn off the road lest others see me. These fields look really beautiful. I shall easily fill my stomach today. Let those who sleep eat their sleep!'

However, Maqinase had been seen as he came into the field. The farmer called his dog: 'There is Maqinase, he is back. Get him!' He had hardly finished speaking when the big dog made straight for Maqinase.

Maqinase was heard crying: 'We ho … ho … ho …! We … ho … ho … ho …!'

The dog was not silent either; it kept barking: 'Heyi heyi heyi! Heyi heyi heyi!'

When Maqinase went through the fence again, it tore his skin. He took to his heels, still crying. Seeing Frog he called: 'Frog, frog, please rescue me!'

But Frog answered: 'Sorry, I am still fixing my mouth!'

Maqinase went on at top speed with the dog at his tail, often nipping him with its teeth. He saw Tortoise and shouted: 'Tortoise, tortoise, please rescue me!'

Tortoise answered: 'How can I rescue you, I who can only drag my feet?'

Maqinase went on, always running. He saw Donkey and said: 'Donkey donkey, please rescue me!'

Donkey answered: 'Sorry, I have no time, I am still fixing my ears.'

The dog bit him one last time, then turned back and went home.

'Where have you been?' asked Maqinase's mother.

'Nowhere in particular,' Maqinase answered.

His mother was angry at that: 'Nowhere in particular, and you are squeaking and panting?'

Maqinase denied it: 'I was just running around on my own, amusing myself, since you were all asleep.'

'And why was that dog chasing you?' his mother asked.

'No, it wasn't chasing me, it was just accompanying me.'

Said his mother: 'So, you think you are clever do you? Remember that no clever person can lick his own back.'

It is finished.

The Bird that Made Milk

Translated from isiXhosa by G McCall Theal; reworked by Elana Bregin.

It is said that there was once a great town in a certain place which had many people living in it. They lived only upon grain. One year there was a great famine.

Now in that town there was a poor man, by the name of Masilo, and his wife. One day, they went to dig in their garden, and they continued digging the whole day long. In the evening, when the digging gangs returned home, they returned with them. Then there came a bird which stood upon the house which was beside the garden, and it began to whistle and said: 'Masilo's cultivated ground, mix together.'

The ground did as the bird said. After that was done, the bird went away.

In the morning, when Masilo and his wife went to the garden, they were confused and said, 'Is this really the place where we were digging yesterday?'

They saw by the people who were working on either side of them that it was indeed the place. The people began to laugh at them, and mocked them, saying, 'It is because you are so lazy that your ground remains undug.'

Masilo and his wife continued to dig again that day, and in the evening they again went home with the others.

Then the bird came and did the same thing as before.

When Masilo and his wife went back the next morning, they once more found their ground altogether untouched. Then they believed that they were bewitched by some of the others. They continued digging that day again. But in the evening, when the digging gangs returned, Masilo said to his wife, 'Go home; I will stay behind to watch and find the thing which undoes our work.'

Then he went and laid himself down by the head of the garden, under the same house on which the bird always perched. While he was thinking his thoughts, the bird came. It was a very beautiful bird. Masilo was busy looking at it and admiring it, when it began to speak.

It said, 'Masilo's cultivated ground, mix together.'

Then Masilo caught the bird and said, 'Ah, it is you who eats the work of our hands!'

He took out his knife from its sheath and was going to cut off the bird's head, when the bird said, 'Please don't kill me! I will make some milk for you to drink.'

Masilo answered, 'You must bring back the work of my hands first.'

The bird said, 'Masilo's cultivated ground, appear,' and it appeared.

Then Masilo said, 'Make the milk now,' and, behold, the bird immediately made thick milk, which Masilo began to drink. When he was satisfied, he took the bird home. As he approached his house, he put the bird in his bag.

After entering his house, Masilo said to his wife, 'Wash all the largest beer pots which are in the house.'

But his wife was angry on account of her hunger and she answered, 'What have you got to put into such large pots?'

Masilo said to her, 'Just listen to me and do as I command you, then you will see.'

When his wife was ready with the pots, Masilo took his bird out of his bag, and said, 'Make milk for my children to drink.'

Then the bird filled all the beer pots with milk.

They commenced drinking, and when they were finished, Masilo warned his children, saying, 'Beware that you do not tell anybody of this bird, not even one of your companions.'

The children swore to him that they would not tell anybody.

Masilo and his family then lived upon the milk of this bird. The people were surprised when they saw him and his family. They said, 'Why are the people at Masilo's house so fat? He is poor, but now that his garden has appeared he and his children are so fat!'

They tried to watch and see what Masilo was eating, but they could never find out at all.

One morning, Masilo and his wife went to work as usual in their garden. Around the middle of the day, the children of that town met together to play. They met just in front of Masilo's house. While they were playing, the others said to Masilo's children, 'Why are you so fat while we remain so thin?'

Masilo's children answered, 'Are we then fat? We thought we were thin just as you are.'

They would not tell the others the cause of their good nourishment. The others continued to press them, saying, 'We won't tell anybody.'

Then the children of Masilo said, 'There is a bird in our father's house which makes milk.'

The others said, 'Please show us the bird.'

Masilo's children went into the house and took the bird out of the secret place where their father had placed it. They ordered it as their father did to make milk, and it made milk, which their companions drank, for they were very hungry.

After drinking the children said, 'Let it dance for us,' and they set it free from the place where it was tied.

The bird began to dance in the house, but one of the children said, 'This place is too confined for it.' So they took it outside the house. While they were laughing and enjoying themselves, the bird flew away, leaving them in great dismay.

Masilo's children said, 'Our father will kill us this day; we must go after the bird.'

So they followed it and continued going after it the whole day long. For when they were at a distance, the bird would sit still for a long while, but when they approached, it would fly away.

When the digging gangs returned from digging late that afternoon, the people of the town cried for their children, for they did not know what had become of them. When Masilo went into the house and could not find his bird, he knew where the children were; but he did not tell any of the other parents. He was very sorry about the bird, for he knew that he had lost his source of food.

When evening set in, the children wanted to return to their homes, but there came a rain storm with heavy thunder, and they were very much afraid. Among them was a brave boy, named Mosemanyanamatong, who encouraged them and said, 'Do not be afraid. I can command a house to build itself.'

The children said, 'Please command it.'

Mosemanyanamatong said, 'House appear!' and it appeared, and also wood for a fire. Then the children entered the house and made a large fire and began to roast some wild roots, which they dug out of the ground.

While they were roasting the roots and making merry, there came a big cannibal, and they heard his voice saying, 'Mosemanyanamatong, give me some of the wild roots you have.'

The children were afraid; the brave boy said to the girls and the other boys, 'Give me some of yours.' They gave him some, and he threw the roots outside.

While the cannibal was still eating, the children stole out of the house and fled. The cannibal finished eating the roots and then pursued them. When he approached, the children scattered more roots upon the ground, and while the cannibal was picking them up and eating, they again fled.

At length, they came among mountains, where trees were growing. The girls were already very tired, so they all climbed up into a tall tree. The cannibal came there and tried to cut the tree down with his long sharp fingernail.

Then the brave boy said to the girls, 'While I am singing, you must continue saying, "Tree be strong, Tree be strong!"'

Mosemanyanamatong sang this song:

It is foolish,
It is foolish to be a traveller,
And to go on a journey
With the blood of girls upon one!
While we were roasting wild roots
A great darkness fell upon us.
It was not darkness,
It was awful gloom!

While he was singing, there came a great bird which hovered over them, and said, 'Hold fast to me.'

The children held fast to the bird and it flew away with them, and took them to their own town.

It was midnight when it arrived there, and it sat down at the gate of Mosemanyanamatong's mother's house.

In the morning, when that woman came out of her house, she took ashes and cast them upon the bird, for she said, 'This bird knows where our children are.'

At midday, the bird sent word to the chief, saying, 'Command all your people to spread mats on all the paths.'

The chief commanded them to do so. Then the bird brought all the children out, and the people were greatly delighted.

The Child with a Moon on his Chest

Translated from seSotho by SM Guma; reworked by Elana Bregin.

It is said it was a great chief, Bulane. He had two wives. Now one of them did not have any children, while the other one had them. This chief had a moon on his chest. One of these women was very much loved by Bulane; it is the one who had children. He ill-treated the one who was without children.

After a short while, the childless woman conceived. A few months passed and it was time for her to be confined. The woman who had children came and helped her. She gave birth to a child who had a moon on his chest. Now the midwife took it, and threw it behind the pots in the cupboard. A mouse quickly took it, and went into its hole with it. The baby's mother was unconscious. The midwife quickly went outside. She found a puppy in a hen's nest, and quickly returned with it and put it next to the child's mother. Then she shook her. 'Wake up and see; you have given birth to a dog.' And this childless woman was disappointed when she found she had given birth to a dog.

Then this midwife quickly went outside to Bulane and said, 'Your wife has given birth to a dog.' Bulane was greatly disappointed. He said, 'Go and take that dog and throw it away.' They took it and threw it away. And the poor little woman came out of her hut disappointed.

A few days passed and Bulane's (senior) wife came to that hut. She found the mouse having taken out the child with a moon on his chest and playing with it. She was shocked and said, 'I thought that child had died!'

Then she quickly went out and said to her husband, Bulane, 'You can see, my lord, I am really ill. Divining bones say before I can get well, you must burn down your wife's hut, this one who has just given birth to a dog.' Bulane answered his wife and said, 'It is well that it should be burnt down,' because he loved her very much. Now this woman thought that if the hut were burnt by the fire, the child would die, the mouse would also be burnt by the fire, and she would no longer see this child with a moon on his chest, because she wanted to destroy it.

The mouse overheard the secret of the senior wife and the chief, and quickly left the hut with the child with a moon on his chest, and went into a donga with it. The chief went out the next day and burnt that hut. The *mofumahadi* was convinced she had destroyed the child and the mouse, and would not see them again.

A few days passed and the *mofumahadi* went to get cow-dung from the cattle kraal. She found the child with a moon on his chest sitting under a cow. She was shocked and said, 'What can I do to kill him?' When she left the cattle kraal, she moaned aloud and said she was very sick. The chief asked her, 'What are you suffering from? What can I do that you should be well again?'

She said, 'Divining bones say you should pull down your cattle kraal. It is only then that I shall get well.'

The mouse overheard the secret of the chief and the senior wife. It went out with the child and took him to a house of traders, *bahwebi.* When the cattle kraal was pulled down, the child with a moon on his chest was not there. The mouse parted with him there, and went to its home. One day certain people went to exchange goods, *bapatsa.* Now a certain man from Bulane's village also went there to buy. He found this young man, who had something shining on his chest. He returned home and told Bulane about the handsome young man he had seen with a moon on his chest. Bulane left there and then to go and see him. On arrival, he asked him, 'Whose child are you? How did you come here?'

The young man with a moon on his chest explained to him and said, 'My mother gave birth to me, and my father's wife threw me into a cupboard, *mohaolwana.* Then the mouse received me, went with me into its hole and there looked after me. My father's wife took a dog, and said my mother had given birth to it.' Bulane started examining him closely, *qamakisisa,* and remembered that his senior wife had said the other wife had given birth to a dog. Now the child with a moon on his chest told him how he had gone to the cattle kraal, until the mouse fled with him, and took him to the house of traders.

Then his father opened his chest, in order to see whether he was really the child with a moon on his chest. He found that it was the child with a moon on his chest. He took him and went home with him. He hid him in his hut. He called a big *pitso,* and invited all his people to it. Cattle were slaughtered and numerous pots of beer brewed. He said they should spread mats on the ground from where he had hidden the child with a moon on his chest. Then he took him out and brought him to this great *pitso.* He showed him to the people and explained how his senior wife had treated him (Bulane) in a treacherous way. Then the mother of the child with a moon on his chest was made to take off her rags and was dressed in beautiful clothes. And the child with a moon on his chest was made a chief by his father. As for the woman who had children without a moon on the chest, it was said she is a wicked person, *molotsana.* She was given her belongings, *thepa,* and it was said she must leave and return to her original home.

The Man who Threw Away his Bread

Translated from isiZulu by Henry Callaway; reworked by Elana Bregin.

This is the tale of a man who was going on a journey carrying his bread with him. He set out, having already eaten at home; and not knowing how to provide sufficient bread for himself, he took a large quantity. He thought he would eat it all. He ate, until he could eat no more. He could not tell what to do with the rest of the bread. He did not say to himself: 'Let me carry it; perhaps in front there is hunger, and I shall want food; perhaps I may meet a man who is hungry.' There were no such thoughts. But through being satisfied, the thought of taking care of the bread became lost; he did not wish to carry it, because he was then full; he saw one thing only that would enable him to go easily. He threw the bread on the lower side of the path, and so went on no longer burdened. He did not return by that path for many days. Mice took the bread, and ate it all up.

It came to pass when the land died, it being killed by famine, as he was going by that way, going and digging up roots (for there was no corn left; roots only were now eaten), the path made him remember the bread. He saw it still there; a year was as it were a day of yesterday. He was at once summoned by the place by merely seeing it, and said, 'This is the very place where I threw away my bread.' He arrived at the place; he saw where the bread had fallen; he said, 'It fell yonder.' He ran to find it. But he did not find it. He began to look earnestly in the long grass, for it was very thick; he searched, feeling with his hands in the thick grass until some time had elapsed. He rose up, and thought, saying: '*Hau!* What happened after I threw away the bread? For I say, I do not yet forget the place where I threw it. No, surely; there is no other; it is this very place.' He stooped down and searched. For whilst he is thus seeking he has gained strength, and is now strong through his efforts. 'Though I am hungry, my hunger will end; I may find my bread.' At length he was confused, he went up again to the path, he found the place where he first began to stand, and he said, 'I passed over all this place before I threw it away.' For where he threw it away, there was an ant heap; he saw that, and said, 'Ah, when I was here, I did thus!' He said this, imitating with his arm; the arm goes in the direction in which he threw the bread. And now he runs quickly, following the direction of the arm. He came to the place, and at once felt about; he did not find the bread. He went back again, and said: '*Hau!* What has become of it? Since I threw it exactly here; for no man saw me, I being quite alone.' He ran. At length the time for digging roots had passed; he went home without anything; he had dug no roots. He now became faint again, because he had not found the bread.

And that man is still living, yonder by the sea. The man told the tale when the country was at peace, and the famine at an end. It was a cause of laughter that conduct of his, to all who heard it, and they said: 'So-and-so, sure enough famine makes a man dark-eyed. Did you ever see bread, which was thrown away one year, found in another, still good to eat?'

He said: 'Sirs, famine does not make a man wise. I thought I was seeking wisely, and should find it. But famine takes away wisdom. And for my part, through my hunger, I believed – in truth – that I should find it; for I was alone, there being no man with me. But in fact that was the means of increasing my want, until I was nearly dead.'

PART TWO

Colonial to Modern
1800s-1970

//KABBO

'A story is like the wind'

Translated from the click language/dialect by WHI Bleek and Lucy C Lloyd; reworked by Elana Bregin.

CAPTURE AND JOURNEY TO CAPE TOWN

[*On being accused by a white farmer of having stolen a sheep*] [ed.]

My wife was there, I was there, my son was there; my son's wife was there, carrying a little child on her back; my daughter was there, also carrying a little child; and my daughter's husband was there. We were like this in number. Therefore, the Kafirs [African policemen] took us when we were like this, while we were not numerous; the Kafirs took us while we were not numerous.

I was eating a springbok when the Kafir took me; he bound my arms. My son and I, together with my daughter's husband, were put into the wagon while the wagon stood still. We went away, bound, to the magistrate. We who were in the wagon ran along swiftly upon the road while our wives walked along upon their feet. We ran, leaving them; we altogether ran, leaving them behind.

We went to talk with the magistrate; we remained there with him. The Kafirs took us away to the gaol at night. We had to put our legs into the stocks; another white man laid a piece of wood upon our legs. We slept, stretched out in the stocks. The day broke, while our legs were in the stocks. Early, we took our legs out of the stocks to eat meat; then we again put our legs into the stocks; we sat, while our legs were in the stocks. We lay down, we slept, while our legs were inside the stocks. We arose, we smoked, while our legs were inside the stocks. The people boiled sheep's flesh, while our legs were in the stocks.

The magistrate came to take our legs out of the stocks, because he wished that we might sit comfortably while we ate; for it was his sheep that we were eating.

The Korannas came to join us. They also came to put their legs into the stocks; they slept while their legs were in the stocks. They were put into another gaol's house. While we were eating the magistrate's sheep, the Korannas also ate it with us. We all ate it together, we and the Korannas.

We left that place and went to Victoria. On the way, we ate sheep. Our wives ate their sheep on the way too, as they came with us to Victoria. We came to Victoria to roll stones, as we worked on the road. We lifted stones with our chests. We rolled great stones. We carried earth with a big handbarrow that needed many Bushmen to lift it. We loaded the wagon with earth and we pushed it. Other people – Bushmen people – walked along with us. We were pushing the wagon's wheels; we were pushing. We poured the earth down and we pushed it back. We again loaded it, we and the Korannas. Other Korannas were carrying the handbarrow. Bushmen were with the Korannas; they were also carrying earth upon the handbarrow.

We again had our arms bound to the wagon chain; we walked along to Beaufort, fastened to the wagon, under the hot sun. Our arms were set free on the road. We got tobacco from the magistrate; we smoked it in a pipe of sheep's bones as we went along. We came into Beaufort gaol. The rain fell upon us while we were there. Early the next morning, our arms were made fast and we were bound again. We splashed into the water; we splashed, passing through the water in the riverbed. We walked upon the road. We walked, following behind the wagon until, still bound, we came to the Breakwater [prison]. On the way there, we ate sheep again. We came to work at the Breakwater.

Intended Return Home

[*After being entrusted by the Cape governor to the 'guardianship' of the linguists Bleek and Lloyd who, having learnt the oral click-language of //Kabbo and other San prisoners, created a written script and then translated the stories told to them into English. //Kabbo, who in the records of Cape authority remained a Bushman convict, had no hope of attaining the hunting gun on his return home.*] [ed.]

You know that I sit waiting for the moon to turn back for me, so that I may return to my place; so that I may listen to all the people's stories when I visit them – the Flat [plain] Bushmen's stories from their own place and other places too. These are the stories which they tell while the sun grows warm. I want to return to my place so that I may sit in the warm sun listening to the stories which come from a distance. Then, I shall get hold of a story from yonder, because the stories float out from a distance, while the sun is a little warm. I feel that I must visit there, so that I can talk with my fellow men. For I do work here at women's household work. My fellow men are those who listen to stories which float along from afar; they listen to stories from other places. But I am here; I do not obtain stories because I do not visit, I do not hear the stories which float along. I feel that the people of another place are here; they do not possess my stories. They do not talk my language. They visit their like, for they are 'work's people'; they are those who work to keep the houses in order. They work at food, so that the food may grow for them, so that they may get food which is good, which is new food.

The Flat Bushmen go to each other's huts and sit smoking in front of them. They obtain stories there, because they are used to visiting each other; for they are 'smoking's people'. As for me, I am waiting for the moon to turn back for me, so that I may set my feet forward on the path. I only await the moon; then, I will tell my Master that this is the time when I should be sitting among my fellow men, those who walking meet their like. I ought to visit; I ought to talk with my fellow men; for I work here together with women; I do not talk with them, for they merely send me to work.

I must first sit a little, cooling my arms so that the fatigue may go out of them. I must merely sit and listen, watching for a story that I want to hear, waiting for it to float into my ear. Those are the people's stories to which I will listen with all my ears, while I sit silent. I must wait, listening behind me along the road, where my name floats; my three names (Jantje, /Uhi-ddoro and //Kabbo, meaning 'Dream') float behind me along the road to my place. I will go and sit down there and, listening, I will turn my ears backwards to where my feet's heels have stepped, and wait for a story to travel to me along the road. For a story is like the wind. It is wont to float along to another place. In this way, our names pass through to the people of that place, even though they do not perceive our bodies going along. For our names are those which, floating, reach a different place.

The mountains lie between the two roads. A man's name passes behind the backs of the mountains, those names with which he returns. The road curves around his place, and the people who dwell at another place hear him coming. Their ears go, listening, to meet the returning man's names. The people know all his names. He will examine the place he returns to. For the trees of that place will seem to be handsome, because they have grown tall while the man of the place was not there to see them and walk among them. For he, //Kabbo, came to live at a different place; his place it is not. For it was this way with him that people brought him to another place, so that he should first come to work there for a little while. He thinks of his own place, and longs to return there.

He only awaits the return of the moon. He waits for the moon to go around, so that he may return home, so that he may examine the water pits, those at which he drank. He will work, putting the old hut in order, gathering his children together, so that they may work, putting the water in order for him; for he went away, leaving the place, while strangers were those who walked there. Their place it is not; for it was //Kabbo's father's father's place. And when //Kabbo's father's father died, //Kabbo's father was the one who possessed it. And when //Kabbo's father died, //Kabbo's elder brother was the one who possessed it; then //Kabbo's elder brother died, and //Kabbo possessed the place. //Kabbo married when he was grown up, bringing !Kuobba-an to the place, because he felt that he was alone there; thereafter, he grew old with his wife at this place, the place that is called //gubo, or Bitterpits. His children's children now were married. They fed themselves without help, they talked with understanding. //Kabbo's children placed huts there for themselves. They made their huts nicely; my hut stood alone in the middle, while my children dwelt on either side.

Because my elder brother's child Betje married first and my own children married afterwards, their cousin's child grew up first. She married, leaving me; she who had come to me from afar. It was I who brought her up and fed her. Her father was not the one who fed her. For her father died, leaving her. I was the one who went and fetched her when her mother also had just died; I brought her to my home. I had not seen her father die or her mother die, I only heard the story. And then I went to fetch Betje to come and live with us. For at that time, I was still a young man, and I was fleet in running. So I thought that she would get plenty of food, which I would be able to give her. She would eat with my own child, who was still an only child. And they would both grow well, going out to play near the hut, because they were both eating the game I shot for them. For I was young and fresh for running; I could catch things by running after them.

I used to run and catch a hare. I brought it to my home in my bag while the sun was hot. I had not seen any springbok, but I saw a hare. First, I used to shoot my arrows to send up a bustard. I would put it into the bag and bring it home. My wife would come to pluck it at home. She boiled it in the pot so that we might drink the soup. The next day, I would hunt the hare. I would be peeping about in the shade of the bushes and I would flush it out by shooting arrows, so that the children might eat. I would make it spring up from its form where it was lying and run away so that I could chase it. For the springbok were all gone away. For that reason, I was shooting hares. By chasing them, I would force them to run about in the noonday sun until they died from the heat, until they were 'burnt dead' by the sun. For I remembered that the hare does not drink; it eats dry bushes and does not drink, putting its own water upon the dry bushes which it crunches. Therefore, it remains thirsty where it dwells. It sits in the summer heat and does not drink, because it does not understand water pans, so it does not go to the water to drink. It waits, sitting in the sun.

Therefore, I chase it in the sun, so that the burning sun may kill it for me; so that I may eat it, dead from the sun. For it was I who chased it, while it ran along in fear of me. In fear it lay down to die in the sun, because it saw me following it and it ran about in the sun until it became dry. It did not stop to walk, so that it could look behind it. It ran about when it was tired; it was obliged to run about even at the point of death. Therefore, it went to lie down to die, because fatigue had killed it while it ran about in the heat; for this was the summer sun, which was very hot. The ground was very hot and burned its feet.

I would go and pick it up as it lay dead. I laid it in the arrows' bag. Then, I would look for another hare. This too would spring up running into the sun; being afraid, it would run through the sun while I ran following it. I would have to keep going until the sun could kill it by burning it. Then I would go and pick it up when it lay dead. Sitting on the ground, I would break its four legs and put it in the bag. It seemed that another hare might dwell in its vicinity. And so I would go to search around the neighbourhood of the hare's form. For the first hare had seemed to be married. Seeking around, I must now look for the female hare, so that I might also chase that. When I had unloosened and laid down the bag, I would chase it with my body, running very fast. If I felt myself becoming thirsty, I would know that I could go and drink at home. For the children would have fetched water for me. My wife used to send them to the water, knowing that I had walked about in the sun when the sun was very hot. I did this because the children needed meat, because I was worried that too much *gambro* would kill my children.

After the rain fell, I would look around for a pair of ostriches which like to seek the water along the Har Rivier. Going carefully around them, I must descend into the Har Rivier and, stooping low, steal up to them inside the riverbed. I must lie on my stomach in the riverbed; so that I may shoot my arrows at them. For the western ostriches, seeking water, come back to drink the new water after the rain has fallen.

And so I must sit waiting for the Sundays to pass that I remain here, on which I continue to teach you. I will not wait again for another moon; for this moon is the one about which I told you. Therefore, I desire that it should do as I have said and return for me. For I have sat waiting for the promised boots, that I must put on to walk in, which are strong for the road. For the sun will go along above me, burning strongly. And the earth will become hot, while I am still only halfway. I must go together with the warm sun, while the ground is hot. For a little road it is not; it is a great road and it is long. I should reach my place when the trees are dry. For I shall walk there, letting the flowers become dry while I still follow the path.

Then, autumn will quickly be upon us there, when I am sitting at my own place. For I shall not go to any other places; I must remain at my own place, the name of which I have told my Master; he knows it – he knows, because he has put it down. And my name is plain beside it. It is there at my place that I will sit waiting for the gun; he will send the gun to me there, in a cart which, running, will bring the gun to me. He must know that I have not forgotten; he must send the gun so that my body may remain quiet, and not hungry, as it was when I was with him; so that I may shoot to feed myself. For starvation was the reason that I was caught and bound. It was on account of starvation's food that I was caught when, starving, I turned back from following the sheep. Therefore I have lived with my Master, in order that I might get a gun from him, that I might possess it. So that I might shoot and feed myself, and not eat my neighbours' food; with a gun I would be able to eat my own game.

A gun is that which takes care of an old man; a gun is that with which we kill the springbok which go through the cold wind. We go to eat in the cold wind. Satisfied with food, we lie down in our huts in the cold wind. The gun is strong against the wind. It satisfies a man with food in the very middle of the cold.

PULVERMACHER [AG DE SMIDT]

Prayer of Titus Tokaan

Translated from the Dutch/Afrikaans by Sharon Meyering.

Hallelujah! ... Lord; you have behaved very well recently. Look at the grass! ... Look at the calendula! ... Look at the plentiful water in the ditch! ... Look at the cattle! ... They all want to burst out of their skin with happiness. Look how they run, kicking their back legs high in the air; just like young girls dancing energetically.

People are looking at their corn, their oxen, their potatoes, their sheep, their beans, their pumpkin, their peas. Everything is in abundance, and their children are pot-bellied from the fat of the earth. Yes, everyone, except for Jeremiah, his children are not!

We want to acknowledge, Lord, that you carried out your plans well, and that you did your best this year; yet Lord, you did not keep your word with Jeremiah. Jeremiah, he has behaved well recently. He gave up swearing, and has avoided women, every week he puts his three pence in the church plate, and he hasn't given you any trouble in a long time. And look what you did, Lord? ... You sent your lightning and struck dead all Jeremiah's milk goats. Jeremiah, Lord, he doesn't feel good about these things. When he was in trouble, you let his best lead ox die! It was not at all nice to reprimand him in such a fatherly manner, and for his ungodliness you let his small Lukas die quietly in the soap pot. Now, that was also unmannerly; and look now? ... There, the vultures are eating all his milk goats. Now just imagine, Lord, that Jeremiah was in your place: What would he do? Would he let your children and your goats die? ... But Lord we must continue under your rules and above all else we must forgive all mistakes. Hallelujah!

HW NEVINSON

Vae Victis

It was one of the happiest evenings in our lives, for after a year's campaigning we were ordered home. The orders had reached us in Pretoria, and a terrible journey we had made of it so far – riding our starved horses through stinging hail and blue lightning over the high veldt to Johannesburg; stuck up there for days and nights because the train would not start for fear of De Wet; then crawling slowly down the line, feeling at every bridge lest it should plunge us into death; camping out all night by Viljoen's Drift, with nothing to eat but the plunder of an old Scotchwoman's store of onions and tinned milk; brought up sharp next day by a patrol, who told us the train in front had been wrecked and we must wait, just in the centre of nothingness, till the sappers had cleared the line. Then at last we had crept into Kroonstad and jolted on through another night and day to Bloemfontein. There our troubles had ended, and we four had secured a carriage in a corridor train that was thought sure to get through to the Cape. We had shelves to let down as beds, and a smug little conductor in uniform to be tipped. It would still take us two days and nights to reach Cape Town, but what did it matter? The line was clear, and we were going home. So the war correspondent, 'You'll have to marry me now', the artist threw the baggage about for joy, the invalided 'Death-or-Glory Boy' smoked our cigarettes to show he had no nasty pride, and I kept ringing for the conductor. His pasty face, form, his expectant servility, delight; for they were tha assurance that civilisation was not far off.

As we kept on telling each other, we were 'fair fed up' with campaigning life. 'No more corrugated iron!' 'No more barbed wire!' 'No more horse and water!' 'No more cantering Colonials!' 'No more Loyalists on the make!' we cried in turn.

'Never again shall I sleep in a puddle with a family of enteric germs using my mouth as a shelter from the cold!' 'Never again will my mare chew a horse's tail for hunger, while another devours her mane!' 'Never again shall I lie rubbing my nose in the sand, afraid to wipe it for fear of the bullets!' 'Never again shall I ask a lord to dinner and give him half a teaspoonful of sugar for a treat!'

'Think of whisky and soda, bucketsful, with ice!' 'Think of several meals a day on board!' 'Think of getting into a bed with sheets!' 'Think of seeing a woman again!'

'Well, I saw some at Durban about six months ago, after the siege, and they seemed to me irrelevant, as the girl said of reading.'

'Poor old boy! How you must have suffered in that siege! You didn't think Mrs What-was-her-name irrelevant on the ship coming out!'

'You mean that woman with the scent-bottles? Yes, I remember. I used to break one wherever I sat down.'

'Yes, and poor old Price worshipped her down to the heels of her open-work stockings. Good thing for him he got shot, after all.'

'Only hope there's a lot like her on the ship going back. None of your long-range women for me!'

'No, not like those Boer girls at Pretoria, stuck over with the Transvaal colours like Christmas trees.'

'Curse them all! How superbly they detest us!'

'I can't for the life of me see why – the women, I mean.'

'It does seem against nature, doesn't it? You'd think we ought to be a pleasant change after those hairy Boers. Never mind, we'll have it all our own way at home.'

'Won't we do ourselves proud! Buck too, buck like Hades!'

We all laughed again, and the correspondent began driving his joy into the artist's head with the butt end of his revolver.

'Safe to take off your putties and breeches tonight,' said the 'Death-or-Glory Boy', as I climbed up to my shelf above his bed, and wrapped myself round with a plaid and a kaross of jackal skins. Outside it was freezing hard, and I watched the waning moon moving up from the bare horizon of the veldt among the unknown African stars. The world seemed full of glorious light, for I was going home, and thought only of the welcome that awaited me. Taking some letters stained and worn from my pocket, I read them through till I came to one which I could read without the light. So, drawing the green shade across the lamp, I pulled the end of the plaid well over my head, and fell softly down and lower down into the bottomless sleep, while the train went rumbling on the immense plateau towards the sea and home.

It must have been some hours later that the engine drew up suddenly at a wayside station, and the shriek of the brake against the wheels called me up from the depth of sleep. Into it I should have fallen again, listening to the unequalled silence of a train that has stopped, had not a girlish voice suddenly cried out at the opposite window, 'Where is de Boer prisoner? Where is de wounded Boer?'

She spoke in that distinct and childlike staccato with which most Boer women speak English. At the same time I heard fingers tapping at the windowpane. Then came the tread of the flabby conductor along the corridor.

'There ain't no bloomin' Boer here,' he began, 'so you can just clear.'

'What's that?' shouted the correspondent, throwing off his rug. 'There is a Boer here! There's that wounded prisoner on that shelf!'

'So there is. I quite forgot,' said the conductor, entering at once into the joke. 'Be quick round by the door, my girl, and you can have a look.'

Too sleepy to think, I listened dreamily, and next moment I felt the girl enter the carriage, bringing the frosty air in her clothes. Then I felt her fingers quickly – but, oh, so gently disentangle the dark plaid over my head and draw it down. Turning round, I looked at her. She had put her feet on the berth below, and in the dim light was peering into my face quite close. The ordinary type of Dutch girlhood, broad of feature and strong of bone, her mass of straw-coloured hair not to be hidden even under the enormous construction of her sun-bonnet, a marvel of washing and starch. But at the moment I only saw the wide grey eyes so near to mine.

In them lived the passion of unsure and uncertain hope that dare not trust its joy; the passion of pity, and of an affection too entire for reserves. It was a look with which at the resurrection a lover's soul, careless of its proper grave, might watch for the beloved's body as it formed again from dust. It endured but for one of those crowded seconds which last indefinitely, and then one by one I saw them die – the affection first, the pity next, and last of all the hope, so much the last that it seemed to have grown old with lingering. Then indifference came, and hatred, and the cold darkness which is not living despair, but only the death of hope. The fingers still clung to my plaid, but one by one they moved, so that they might not touch my neck.

'I'm very sorry, but there's no Boer here,' I said.

'Oh, damn! Oh, damn!' she cried in her quick staccato, slid down to the carriage floor, and was gone. Along the corridor I heard her voice: 'Where is de Boer prisoner? Where is de wounded Boer?'

The engine whistled. 'Come, clear off,' shouted the flabby conductor, 'or I'll have to heave you out.'

'Oh, hell!' said the gentle little voice from a distance, and the train moved on.

We all laughed. 'That's a good joke,' said the correspondent. 'I say, old man, she took you for one of your hairy Boers. Oh, damn! Oh, hell!'

He imitated the girl's voice exactly, and we laughed again.

'That's the language they catch from the cultured Colonial.'

'Not a bad-looking girl either. I wish she was coming on the ship.'

'Oh, we'll do better than that. Chuck me a cigarette, somebody. I can't sleep a curse.'

I let down my window and looked back along the line. The little station was already far away, but on the platform I could see the figure of the girl in the great white sun-bonnet, standing immovable. Then the solitary porter turned out the single station lamp, and she disappeared. The waning moon was now far up the sky. Not a house or sign of a farm was anywhere to he seen. All around us stretched the desolate veldt, and a few low kopjes of barren rock rose far in front. They were the beginning of the great Karoo desert, and I remembered again that I was going home.

EUGÈNE N MARAIS

The Grey Pipit

Translated from the Afrikaans by Annie Gagiano.

The small girl Nampti, the grey bird, was so tiny that the tame baby goats would push her over as they played.

The grandmother was *so* old that she scarcely remembered to gather wood every day. Nampti had to set the fire, cook food, and guard the goats. And the others in the yard treated these two badly. When there was meat, they got nothing, and the young girls would mock the granny for not walking upright and for being lame in one leg. They called her the old Wolf.

And on the plain Nampti found the small nest of a grey bird, and she led the goats past it and she sang to the mother:

Gampta, my little grey sister!
All I have in the world
Besides my old grandmother.
As you sing up there in the sky
You can see all the wondrous things below:
Where the small hare hides
And the steenbok has his hiding place.
And the maidens cannot touch you,
For you're stronger than everyone,
Even though you're weaker than I,
Even the mountain lion who frightens us
When he roars at night
Cannot touch you.
I will guard you, my sister,
Until all your little ones are grown.

And the small grey bird sang over her head:

My grey sister Nampti I see you!
I shall tell you something important:
Last night when the female Ostrich

Took shelter with her chicks,
The mountain lion, who scares you,
Set off the poison trap in the fountain gorge,
And he lies dead in the big ghwarrie bush.
The one who inserts a hair of his beard under their skin
Becomes a lion, as long as the female Ostrich grazes
In the wide veld with her chicks.

And she rolled up her small grey kaross over one arm and she ran quickly to the fountain gorge; and in the ghwarrie bush she saw the dead mountain lion who had for so long terrorised the yard. And she pulled out the longest hair of his beard and inserted it under the skin of her arm.

And the mother bird sang above her head in the sky: 'Nampti, my little grey sister! Now she is stronger than everyone; and outshines all the girls who mock her granny.'

And that evening, when she arrived at home with the goats, her granny said: 'Why are the eyes shining in the dark like that?' And Nampti laughed.

And when the moon rose, she stood up from her sleeping mat and went outside. And when she entered the yard, the dogs howled, and the goats started bleating behind their shelters. And she saw that her shadow was the shadow of a mountain lion. And softly she walked towards the shelter of the headman, Okiep. They were sitting by the fire, roasting meat, and around them were many calabashes with milk. And Nampti blew through the branches of the shelter, and all of them jumped up and ran into the straw house slamming the door, and she heard the women screaming inside. And she took the fattest pieces of meat and the biggest calabash of milk, and she carried these to her granny. And as they were eating, the old woman, who was blind in the dark, said: 'Why does my little one lick with the tongue to drink her milk? A person doesn't drink like that.' And Nampti laughed out loud.

And every night when the female Ostrich was in the mountain Nampti went out, and she brought all the best food in the yard back to their shelter.

And by day the young women would say: 'Why is the little grey bird getting so fat and good-looking and big? Where does the crook-backed old Wolf get the food to give to her?'

And Nampti would only laugh.

And when she grew up, all the young fellows said: 'There is no girl in our yard who can touch Nampti!'

And young Okiep, the son of the headman, brought ten goats to her granny to ask to marry Nampti. And Nampti said: 'As long as you'll guard my Grey Sister while her nest lies in the grass, you may have me.' And he promised.

And this was the biggest wedding that they had ever had in their yard.

When the food had been shared out, Nampti brought a fat reed-buck from her shelter. And young Okiep said: 'What kind of wife have I taken? Where does a maiden get the power to catch buck at night?'

And Nampti only laughed; but the bridegroom felt his heart shiver. And when Nampti walked in the veld that day, the grey bird sang above her head:

Nampti, my Grey Sister, never take a drink at night;
and if she wakes up, she must pull the skin blanket
over her head.

And that night when Nampti was sleeping in the new straw house, she woke up, and she got up to take a drink from the large calabash on the food platform. And young Okiep saw her, and he hid trembling under the bedding.

And when day dawned, he went to consult with the elders and the councillors and he said: 'In the night her eyes glow like green fire, and when she drinks water she licks it with her tongue.'

And the councillors said: 'This is something deeply wrong. Tonight we shall stand guard outside and peep through the smoke-hole, and if it is as you say we'll rid our yard of this monster.'

And Nampti, listening behind the shelter, heard what they were saying.

And as soon as the grass was dry, she went to the veld and she called: 'Oh, my Grey Sister, the heart of your little sister is sore. You have helped me and now your advice has led me to disaster!'

And the tears ran down her face.

And the grey bird sang above her head: 'Where is the danger? Is it not the task of the husband to rub *buchu* on his bride's arms?' And Nampti laughed as she returned to the yard.

And when night fell, she said: 'My husband, is it not the custom that the husband should rub *buchu* on his wife's arms? Why then is this custom not maintained in our home?'

And young Okiep took the ground *buchu* from the veld bag and he rubbed her arms, and it began to get dark, and behind the shelter lurked the councillors.

And young Okiep said: 'Why do my Nampti's eyes glow green in the dark?' And Nampti laughed. And he said again: 'Why are my Nampti's nails growing longer and curved?' And Nampti laughed.

And his voice trembled and she said: 'Rub the *buchu*; let us keep the custom.'

And his heart weakened; and he said: 'There's a thorn here in my Nampti's arm.'

And Nampti said: 'Is it not the task of the man to extract it?' And he rubbed with the *buchu* and felt her arm turning into the forepaw of a lion, and heard her voice deepening. And he extracted the beard-hair and then called to the elders: 'It's a lion! Help me, my Dad, or I am done for!'

And in they ran with knives and lights, and when the inside of the straw house was lit up, they saw Nampti sitting in the centre, and young Okiep rubbing her arms with *buchu*. And they said: 'Where is the lion?'

And young Okiep blushed and he said: 'I was scared in the dark. I was dreaming.' And they greeted Nampti courteously.

And she always remained the foremost woman of the entire yard.

SARAH GERTRUDE MILLIN

Up from Gilgal

It was night, and there was dancing on the ship sailing from Cape Town to Southampton. The wooden bar that divided the first class from the second class was away, and passengers from both classes were dancing together, and on rows of deck chairs reclined the people who were not dancing.

In the second row of deck chairs on the first-class side sat Mrs Elder with three other women. The four of them sat there every night, watching. They would have liked, very much, to dance too: they danced at home, for they could at least depend on their poor grumbling old husbands to dance with them. But now they were travelling, for one reason or another, without their husbands, and they were of no interest to any other men. So they listened to the bad music, and commented on the dancers, and felt how melancholy it was to be getting old, and remembered with yearning and humility and gratitude their husbands, who, they could see now, were the only human beings on whom they could depend – through the power of habit and pity and an ancient loyalty – for everything.

Mrs Elder had not dreamt it would be like this. She came from a Transvaal town which had a white population of five thousand, and her husband was the magistrate, and, of course, a man of great importance. The Elders lived at the Residency, the best house in the town; and if any influential person came there he had dinner with them – even the administrator of a province or the Prime Minister of the Union. And then Mrs Elder distributed the school prizes and ran the various committees. It would have been strange indeed if, at a dance, she had lacked partners.

Besides, she was not really so unattractive. It was true her skin was burnt and dried and wrinkled by the African sun, and there was a piece of flesh joining her neck to her chin which grew taut when she turned her head, and she was a little too stout. But she was not so old as one would have expected an Englishwoman to be who looked like that: she was thirty-seven; and she had big candid grey eyes, a straight, short nose, and richly brown hair. It wasn't, after all, a serious misfortune for a man to dance with her.

Yet here she had sat night after night, throughout the voyage, and it had never even entered any man's head that she could *want* to dance, that she was *entitled* to dance. She had sat with these three other women whose husbands had been left at home, and they were looked on – if they were looked on at all – just as four middle-aged women to whom one sometimes said a word or two, and there was an end of it.

She should not have linked herself with these women. She saw it now. They were women of forty-eight or fifty, and when she joined their group she became automatically one of them: she partook of their quality of dereliction, she was no more than the fourth side of a shut-in square.

No one even asked her to play deck tennis. She did not expect it of the jolly young ones. But the elderly bald men, whose white flannels opened at the pleats and were strained about their large waists – why did they not invite her to join them in a mixed doubles? What right had they to be so indecently convinced of their invincible maleness?

She played bridge every afternoon with her friends; and often they gossiped; and in the nights they sat here and commented on the dancers, and noticed who the people were who strolled away after the dances with their partners to make a little love, because, if their husbands or wives were on board, that was really the only chance they had.

And there was a pain in her heart when she thought that this voyage to England was the great event of her life – even although it had come about only because her mother was so seriously ill in England. For her husband's salary was not so grand as his magisterial position – there were three children – they had never been able to save enough to go on such a voyage together.

Out of sheer loneliness she wrote to her husband every day. She told him what a glorious holiday she was having – except, of course, for her anxiety about her mother, and her longing for him and the children. Her husband was greatly moved by her letters. He had not known she loved him as deeply as all that. 'And who do you think is on board?' she asked in her very first letter. 'Charles Devenish. In the first class. Naturally, I haven't spoken to him.'

No, she hadn't spoken to him. But then neither had he spoken to her. He was dancing now with quite a young girl.

* * *

Mrs Elder had first met Charles Devenish fifteen years ago. At that time her husband was magistrate of a little town called Gilgal, the centre of a diamond-digging district. Since then they had been transferred five times; and, although they were now higher in the service, they possessed hardly a household article that did not show the marks of all this moving about, and their children were in lower classes than they should have been, and they were still very poor.

They had been as happy in Gilgal as anywhere. It was a hot, dry, yellow, sandy, treeless, iron-roofed, ugly little town near a river which was often dry in the winter, for then no rains fell in the Transvaal. It had been called Gilgal because the first diggers had encamped near twelve large stones and, thinking of the dry river they had just crossed to get there, a man had laughingly asked if these were not the stones of the Jordan, and this not the Gilgal of God's command.

Gilgal, however, had not grown beyond one street. In that street were two hotels where men came to drink, the bank, the chemist's shop, several general stores, the school, and the magistrate's court. Yet the Elders were young in those days, all life seemed young, there was a sort of little society, and they were important in it.

To this society Charles Devenish was an event. He had come to Gilgal no one knew why, and he never did the prospecting of which he vaguely spoke. But people did not ask many questions in Gilgal, and he was thirty, he had manner and an accent, and his clothes were good.

The ladies invited him to afternoon tea and tennis, and he made love to several of them.

They told one another, in a competitive spirit, about this love he made, and they exaggerated his advances and their withdrawings – as if it were quite easy for a Gilgal woman to find personable admirers; as if they all knew what it was to keep a man's passion at bay. It was at this time it became customary for the Gilgal people to wear evening clothes at one another's dinner parties. For, without any warning at all, Mr Devenish had arrived at his first dinner in Gilgal – dressed.

And so things went on for nearly two months. And then one day a sum of money came for him through the bank, and immediately everyone understood the sort of prospecting Mr Devenish did, and why he was in Gilgal. He was in Gilgal just because he happened to be in Gilgal, and because he did not much care where he was so long as he could get what he wanted.

And that was, it seemed, a very large quantity of drink. As soon as his money came Charles Devenish went to the bar of the Empire Hotel and drank with and against everybody. He arrived at the bar early in the morning, and he stayed there all day, and all next day, and the whole week through, and as long as he had any cash, and as long after that as the barman would let him. It was as if he had had just enough control over himself to await the coming of this money.

Then, for a while, he disappeared.

When he showed himself again he still had his manner and his accent, but people looked at him now with different eyes. They forgave him his lapse – for every one in those digging districts knew of men who had drinking periods and then, for months afterwards, stayed sober – only they no longer acknowledged his superiority over them. And when the ladies asked him to their houses they did it as if they were being kind.

Even Mrs Elder, who often, without any sense of disloyalty to her husband, wondered if the love of a good woman couldn't reform him, was kind in that way. But he looked at her with careless, indifferent, unashamed eyes that, in some unaccountable way, transferred the consciousness of any misdemeanour from him to her; and sometimes he came to her as to the other people who had forgiven him, and sometimes he did not. It didn't seem, really, as though he wanted all this forgiveness, or the love, just romantically unhallowed, of a magistrate's wife.

And then, one day, another thing happened. Mr Devenish was due at Mrs Elder's for tea, and he went for a walk with her cook instead. There was no secrecy about it. Down the only street of the town they strolled, and he was a little more deferential towards her than, in these days, towards her mistress. He was carrying a parcel for her too. The day's meat, the people said.

It was an insult to all Gilgal, yet most of the ladies could only laugh to hide their chagrin. The doctor's wife, however (who was like that), declared that to bring the doctrine of true knighthood to its foundations, why should not a gentleman assist a housemaid with her pail, or a washerwoman with her bundle, or Mrs Elder's cook with her parcel of meat? Was chivalry, and ladies first, and all that sort of thing, only a matter of class? For her part, she said, she was prepared to receive Mr Devenish as if nothing had happened.

But Mrs Elder was not. For she wasn't, like the doctor's wife, fifty, she was twenty-two, and she was unhappy because he had touched her feelings more than a little, and it was, finally, to her he had forgotten or neglected to come, and with her cook he had walked instead.

She wanted to dismiss the cook. But Mr Elder wouldn't allow it. 'What should she have done?' he demanded. 'Refused to let him carry her meat?'

'Yes,' said Mrs Elder, her throat tight and sore.

'Oh, nonsense,' commented Mr Elder. 'Do you expect a Gilgal poor white to know more than an English gentleman? If you want to kick anyone out, let it be Devenish.'

But no one was henceforth given the opportunity to kick Mr Devenish out, for he spent too much time with the Elders' cook. The doctor's wife suggested that he found her, perhaps, more amusing than Gilgal society; but she could not really believe it. And when she saw him one day walking with the cook under the thorny mimosa trees just outside Gilgal, the mimosa whose scent was so clean and wistful in the hot, still air – like a longing never to be fulfilled – then even she could no longer laugh.

All Gilgal dropped Mr Devenish, and Mr Elder allowed his wife to dismiss the cook.

* * *

And now there came another phase in the Gilgal career of Mr Devenish. The hotel proprietor said he could not keep Mr Devenish in his hotel unless he paid for his accommodation. Mr Devenish explained that he was expecting money again next month. The hotel proprietor, however, asked him why he had not given him any of the money he had received last month. Mr Devenish answered pleasantly that he, the hotel proprietor, had had all of it. 'But, as to that, there's money owing in the bar too,' said the hotel proprietor. And he looked very disagreeable.

Mr Devenish stared at him a moment.

'I'm arranging to leave your hotel today,' he said in a manner that implied he had found the hotel not very satisfactory.

So now he bought himself a tent and cooked his own food. He bought things at one of the stores, and would have managed quite well if the storekeeper had not, like the proprietor of the Empire Hotel, talked so much about accounts. Why, asked the storekeeper, in due course, had he not been paid out of the new money that had come to Mr Devenish and all gone into the bar of the Royal Hotel?

Mr Devenish said he was not in the habit of bandying words with his tradesmen.

He spoke in these days, to the people he casually met, of leaving Gilgal. And yet he did not leave. For, just about this time, an awkward thing happened. No money came for him to the bank.

This was really a terrible period. He was no longer getting credit anywhere. For a while he did a little borrowing from the diggers who had drunk with him in the bars. Then he exchanged his watch for groceries. Occasionally he had a meal at the home of Mrs Elder's ex-cook. There were a lot of poor-white children about who made a disrespectful noise when he came.

Presently he sold his tent.

One morning an elderly prospector, who made Gilgal the headquarters of his unsuccessful expeditions, found him sitting, dazed, on the bench under the verandah of the Royal Hotel.

The bar was not yet open. The prospector looked carefully at Mr Devenish.

'You come home with me,' he said.

'Home' was a room made of corrugated iron with a window that was a single pane of glass. A dirty mattress lay on the floor, with several old blankets tumbled about on it. There were also a few pieces of crockery on a box turned upside down to make a table; a fork, a knife and a spoon; a smaller box with groceries in it; a chair, a saucepan, a kettle, and a paraffin stove.

'We'll have breakfast,' said the prospector.

He opened a tin of sardines, and made some coffee. The eyes of Mr Devenish grew more bloodshot.

'I'm expecting some money any day now,' he murmured.

'That's all right,' said the prospector. 'You can stay here till it comes.'

It did come, and then they both went to the bar and drank. For, the prospector, too, had not arrived at his present pass through excessive praying. And, in future, whenever money came, they disposed of it together in the bar of the Royal Hotel. For, as Mr Devenish had never stayed at the Royal Hotel, and had consequently never had any discussions about accounts there, he preferred it to the Empire Hotel. Only when there was no money was Mr Devenish ever again something like the Mr Devenish who had once been so pleasantly received by the ladies of Gilgal.

He had not, of course, visited their houses for many months, but they were now able to speak to him when they met him. They were able to speak because it no longer mattered whether they spoke or not. Mrs Elder alone could not bring herself to do so – because of those romantic feelings of hers he had once touched and then shamed.

But this stage, too, passed. Perhaps, before he came to Gilgal, he had lived with people who had done for him what they could, and so that was why he had arrived there no worse than he was. Now, however, he lived with the old prospector, and they went downhill together. Mr Devenish was not even clean in these days. His wardrobe consisted of what he wore, and he wore it a long time. His very manner was only a mirage of his old manner. All he kept intact was his accent.

One day the prospector found some asbestos. He naturally sold his claims for too little – other men afterwards made tens of thousands of pounds out of that asbestos field, but he was not dissatisfied. He added another room of corrugated iron to the first, took a half-caste woman, bought some fowls, and was very happy. He said Mr Devenish could remain with him, and Mr Devenish did so. Mrs Elder's cook married the driver of a transport-wagon.

* * *

Mr Devenish was not greatly affected by the coming of the Great War. Eighteen months of it passed without agitating him. Then, so it was reported, he got a letter to say that two of his brothers had been killed. A week later he was gone from Gilgal. No one was very interested in his going, not even the doctor's wife (the Elders had left Gilgal by that time) or the prospector. The prospector had given up drink and was deeply domesticated now, and, in his heart, he was relieved about the departure of Mr Devenish, because, in a two-roomed house, and with a new yellow baby, it was more comfortable without him.

So he went, unsped, and was forgotten …

Until, one day, towards the end of the war, Mrs Elder saw something about a Captain Charles Devenish, MC, in a newspaper.

'Captain!' said Mrs Elder, and thought of the days when he had come to Gilgal and the days when he had left. 'MC! Impossible! It must be another man.'

But it was not another man. The war had resurrected Charles Devenish.

And here it was ten years after the war, it was over twelve years since he had left Gilgal, and what, thought Mrs Elder passionately, as she sat there on the deck chairs of the left-behind and cast-aside watching him dance with that young girl, what had happened to them both during that time? Nothing to her, a virtuous woman, except decay and degeneration – at least, so it seemed, now, here on the ship. But to him, who had snuffled in the slime, soaring life.

She had not felt like this when she had met him on board the first day. She had walked past him with the old contempt of Gilgal; with the contempt of the magistrate's wife for her cook's lover, for the drunkard who had lived with a man who lived with a coloured woman. And he had walked past her – he still did – as if he had no memory of her.

But could that be, she now asked herself, agonised, could he truly have forgotten her? Had she become unrecognisable in twelve years? Was her essential being gone with her youth so that a man might look at her and see not a trace of it left?

Her mind returned to the beginning of the voyage when she had looked forward to having an exciting – even a possible romantic – voyage. How often had she not heard from women of their exciting and romantic voyages! Every one went a little mad on ships, they said. There was no time or space or past or future or success or failure on ships, they said. Things just happened. They happened wildly to anybody.

It seemed, however, that they did not happen always. The days had passed and no adventures had come to Mrs Elder. What did she, a middle-aged woman going to see a sick mother, a virtuous woman with a husband

and children, want of romantic adventures? What, indeed? she asked herself bitterly, sitting here, because of her loneliness, with these three women who also sat with one another because of their loneliness.

'Yes, a man of forty-five or fifty and a woman of forty-five or fifty are very different things,' said one of the three as she watched Charles Devenish dancing with his pretty girl. 'Would that man come to me for a dance – and I'm no older than he is? Of course not! Why should he? He can get any of the young girls to dance with him. Only too happy – a popular man like that!'

Mrs Elder opened her mouth to speak of Gilgal. But there was a rancour and a sadness in her heart that would not let her. It was as if she could not betray a something in herself. She remembered how he had once touched her feelings. She wished with a longing that pressed against the walls of her being like an instrument of the Inquisition, that he would come to her now and lift her out of the cast-aside and left-behind. For she could see now: without the small-town dignity her husband gave her, without his affection and support, that was all she was: in her own right, nobody wanted her.

But this man, she had known him in his degradation, she had felt herself infected by his shame – had she no meaning even for him?

The dance ended, and he passed her, chatting with his partner. He found her a seat, and went to fetch her some refreshment.

Mrs Elder had not thought of doing it, but she did it: she followed him hastily through a door. She touched him on the arm.

'Don't you remember me, Mr Devenish?' she said. 'Mrs Elder, of Gilgal.'

'Why, Mrs Elder, why, of course,' he said, as if at a revelation. 'Of Gilgal. And how is Johanna?'

Johanna was the name of Mrs Elder's cook of fifteen years ago.

She wanted to remind him passionately that they had long since been moved up from Gilgal, and how should she know anything of Johanna? But she could not.

He smiled at her – a still sort of smile.

She faced him in a profound silence.

She understood. The magistrate's wife, and the magistrate's wife's cook – he meant that they were equally behind him. What he wanted her to understand, in the bravado of his hatred of the past, was that she and Johanna and Gilgal and himself in Gilgal, were all linked together in his mind as part of an old shabbiness he had outlived and now chose to ignore.

'May I get you something to drink?' he asked her, too politely, and still smiling.

She hated him so, she would have liked the ship to go down with both of them, with all the happy young people, and the elderly cheerful people, and the three women with whom she sat and sat watching the dancing of others.

Her heart ached with the sorrow of being outside things. 'Will you?' she said, and self-contented, returned his smile.

PAULINE SMITH

The Sisters

Marta was the eldest of my father's children, and she was sixteen years old when our mother died and our father lost the last of his water cases to old Jan Redlinghuis of Bitterwater. It was the water cases that killed my mother. Many, many times she had cried to my father to give in to old Jan Redlinghuis whose water rights had been fixed by law long before my father built his water furrow from the Ghamka river. But my father could not rest. If he could but get a fair share of the river water for his furrow, he would say, his farm of Zeekoegatt would be as rich as the farm of Bitterwater and we should then have a town-house in Platkops dorp and my mother should wear a black cashmere dress all the days of her life. My father could not see that my mother did not care about the black cashmere dress or the town-house in Platkops dorp. My mother was a very gentle woman with a disease of the heart, and all she cared about was to have peace in the house and her children happy around her. And for so long as my father was at law about his water rights there could be no peace on all the farm of Zeekoegatt. With each new water case came more bitterness and sorrow to us all. Even between my parents at last came bitterness and sorrow. And in bitterness and sorrow my mother died.

In his last water case my father lost more money than ever before, and to save the farm he bonded some of the lands to old Jan Redlinghuis himself. My father was surely mad when he did this, but he did it. And from that day Jan Redlinghuis pressed him, pressed him, pressed him, till my father did not know which way to turn. And then, when my father's back was up against the wall and he thought he must sell the last of his lands to pay his bond, Jan Redlinghuis came to him and said:

'I will take your daughter, Marta Magdalena, instead.'

Three days Jan Redlinghuis gave my father, and in three days, if Marta did not promise to marry him, the lands of Zeekoegatt must be sold. Marta told me this late that same night. She said to me:

'Sukey, my father has asked me to marry old Jan Redlinghuis. I am going to do it.'

And she said again: 'Sukey, my darling, listen now! If I marry old Jan Redlinghuis he will let the water into my father's furrow, and the lands of Zeekoegatt will be saved. I am going to do it, and God will help me.'

I cried to her: 'Marta! Old Jan Redlinghuis is a sinful man, going at times a little mad in his head. God must help you before you marry him. Afterwards it will be too late.'

And Marta said: 'Sukey, if I do right, right will come of it, and it is right for me to save the lands for my father. Think now, Sukey my darling! There is not one of us that is without sin in the world, and old Jan Redlinghuis is not always mad. Who am I to judge Jan Redlinghuis? And can I then let my father be driven like a poor white to Platkops dorp?' And she drew me down on to the pillow beside her, and took me into her arms, and I cried there until far into the night.

The next day I went alone across the river to old Jan Redlinghuis's farm. No one knew that I went, or what it was in my heart to do. When I came to the house Jan Redlinghuis was out on the stoep smoking his pipe.

I said to him: 'Jan Redlinghuis, I have come to offer myself.'

Jan Redlinghuis took his pipe out of his mouth and looked at me. I said again: 'I have come to ask you to marry me instead of my sister Marta.'

Old Jan Redlinghuis said to me: 'And why have you come to do this thing, Sukey de Jager?'

I told him: 'Because it is said that you are a sinful man, Jan Redlinghuis, going at times a little mad in your head, and my sister Marta is too good for you.'

For a little while old Jan Redlinghuis looked at me, sitting there with his pipe in his hand, thinking the Lord knows what. And presently he said: 'All the same, Sukey de Jager, it is your sister Marta that I will marry and no one else. If not, I will take the lands of Zeekoegatt as is my right, and I will make your father bankrupt. Do now as you like about it.'

And he put his pipe in his mouth, and not one other word would he say.

I went back to my father's house with my heart heavy like lead. And all that night I cried to God: 'Do now what you will with me, but save our Marta.' Yes, I tried to make a bargain with the Lord so that Marta might be saved. And I said also: 'If He does not save our Marta I will know that there is no God.'

In three weeks Marta married old Jan Redlinghuis and went to live with him across the river. On Marta's wedding day I put my father's Bible before him and said: 'Pa, pray if you like, but I shall not pray with you. There is no God or surely He would have saved our Marta. But if there is a God as surely will He burn our souls in Hell for selling Marta to old Jan Redlinghuis.'

From that time I could do what I would with my father, and my heart was bitter to all the world but my sister Marta. When my father said to me: 'Is it not wonderful, Sukey, what we have done with the water that old Jan Redlinghuis lets pass to my furrow?'

I answered him: 'What is now wonderful? It is blood that we lead on our lands to water them. Did not my mother die for it? And was it not for this that we sold my sister Marta to old Jan Redlinghuis?'

Yes, I said that. It was as if my heart must break to see my father water his lands while old Jan Redlinghuis held my sister Marta up to shame before all Platkops.

I went across the river to my sister Marta as often as I could, but not once after he married her did old Jan Redlinghuis let Marta come back to my father's house.

'Look now, Sukey de Jager,' he would say to me, 'your father has sold me his daughter for his lands. Let him now look to his lands and leave me his daughter.' And that was all he would say about it.

Marta had said that old Jan Redlinghuis was not always mad, but from the day that he married her his madness was to cry to all the world to look at the wife that Burgert de Jager had sold to him.

'Look,' he would say, 'how she sits in her new tent-cart – the wife that Burgert de Jager sold to me.' And he would point to the Zeekoegatt lands and say: 'See now, how green they are, the lands that Burgert de Jager sold me his daughter to save.'

Yes, even before strangers would he say these things, stopping his cart in the road to say them, with Marta sitting by his side. My father said to me: 'Is it not wonderful, Sukey, to see how Marta rides through the country in her new tent-cart?'

I said to him: 'What is now wonderful? It is to her grave that she rides in the new tent-cart, and presently you will see it.'

And I said to him also: 'It took you many years to kill my mother, but believe me it will not take as many months for old Jan Redlinghuis to kill my sister Marta.' Yes, God forgive me, but I said that to my father. All my pity was for my sister Marta, and I had none to give my father.

And all this time Marta spoke no word against old Jan Redlinghuis. She had no illness that one might name, but every day she grew a little weaker, and every day Jan Redlinghuis inspanned the new tent-cart and drove her round the country. This madness came at last so strong upon him that he must drive from sunup to sundown crying to all whom he met: 'Look now at the wife that Burgert de Jager sold to me!'

So it went, day after day, day after day, till at last there came a day when Marta was too weak to climb into the cart and they carried her from where she fell into the house. Jan Redlinghuis sent for me across the river.

When I came to the house old Jan Redlinghuis was standing on the stoep with his gun. He said to me: 'See here, Sukey de Jager! Which of us now had the greatest sin – your father who sold me his daughter Marta, or I who bought her? Marta who let herself be sold, or you who offered to save her?'

And he took up his gun and left the stoep and would not wait for an answer.

Marta lay where they had put her on old Jan Redlinghuis's great wooden bed, and only twice did she speak. Once she said: 'He was not always mad, Sukey my darling, and who am I that I should judge him?'

And again she said: 'See how it is, my darling! In a little while I shall be with our mother. So it is that God has helped me.'

At sundown Marta died and when they ran to tell Jan Redlinghuis they could not find him. All that night they looked for him, and the next day also. We buried Marta in my mother's grave at Zeekoegatt ... And still they could not find Jan Redlinghuis. Six days they looked for him, and at last they found his body in the mountains. God knows what madness had driven old Jan Redlinghuis to the mountains when his wife lay dying, but there it was they found him, and at Bitterwater he was buried.

That night my father came to me and said: 'It is true what you said to me, Sukey. It is blood that I have led on my lands to water them, and this night will I close the furrow that I built from the Ghamka river. God forgive me, I will do it.'

It was in my heart to say to him: 'The blood is already so deep in the lands that nothing we can do will now wash it out.' But I did not say this. I do not know how it was, but there came before me the still, sad face of my sister Marta, and it was as if she herself answered for me.

'Do now as it seems right to you,' I said to my father. 'Who am I that I should judge you?'

RRR DHLOMO

The Death of Masaba

'Fellows, what do you think of this business of Masaba?'

'Yes, just tell us what happened.'

'Men, the boy is dying. I heard from Stimela, the boss-boy of the lashers, that Masaba fainted twice in the mine today. Stimela he ran to tell Boss Tom, who did not even want to listen to him, but only said: "Get away, there are lots of boys in the compound."'

'But what made Masaba faint in the mine?'

'Well ... I saw that there was a mistake in his ticket. It was not stamped *ten days' light underground work.*'

The others they laughed when they heard the word 'mistake'.

'Clear out,' they cried, 'there is no *mistake* there! We old boys know well that if Masaba had been a white man there would have been no *mistake.* Didn't Boss Tom say "there are lots of Kaffirs in the compound"? "If one dies," meaning Masaba, "the Government will bring more." He said that after Stimela had told him, "Masaba is fainting, he cannot lash."'

The others were silent; each was busy with his own thoughts.

This affair was worrying their hearts a great deal. These men – they were five, sitting round a glowing bucket fire – had left their kraals for the mines, forced to do so by hunger and want. They left their homes knowing of the terrible accidents that occur below the surface of the mines. Their only hope was that the always-wise white people would be true to them and treat them well: safeguard them from underground dangers, and work them as people with equal feelings though their skins were black.

The working place where they were stationed was deep down on the 18th level. The heat on that level was terrible; so intense that unacclimatised boys were liable to get heatstroke. Behind them a yawning, dreary shaft threatened their lives; while in front a naked, creaking rock rose sheer above them. From its grim, muddy face trickled drops of dirty, poisonous water.

Under these disabilities, with death everywhere beckoning, Boss Tom made them lash as though the Furies were after them. Here their half-naked bodies were bent unceasingly over the shovels. Even old lashing hands were seen staggering under the heat, and through the pangs of hunger. As these were their daily lot in life, they did not mind it at all, for they had infinite trust in their masters.

But today, when they saw Masaba, the victim of callous indifference, yes Masaba, their young fellow countryman, who was not even supposed to be placed on the lashing gang, their hearts were filled with blood. The first incident happened when they were shovelling madly. Masaba suddenly dropped down … and fainted.

Boss Boy Stimela ran and told Boss Tom: 'Nkosi, the boy Masaba has fainted. He can't lash.'

Boss Tom was greatly surprised when he heard that a 'Kaffir' could not do the job for which he was solely created, the handling of the shovel. He said to Steamer: 'What! Masaba can't lash? A bloody Kaffir … can't lash?'

'I know, sir,' replied Steamer, 'that Masaba faints as soon as he stoops to lash. I think he's not used to it yet.'

'Oh, kick him, Steamer.'

Steamer was, however, one of those fast-dwindling Boss Boys who, instead of 'waking up' Masaba with a kick, according to orders, went to him and said, 'Try and lash, boy. The Boss will hit you, say you're loafing.'

Poor Masaba went and threw himself at his master's feet.

'Nkosi, I am not used to lashing yet. I get so tired, sir, and my head aches so. My eyes get clouded and misty when I stoop to lash, sir. I beg you, sir, my good Boss, my father, give me another job until I'm used to this job of lashing. I will work well, sir. I will do anything for you, Boss. But lashing kills me, Boss, please.'

And he burst into tears, while his fellow workers muttered ominously under their breath.

It is difficult for a boy and his Boss to come to quick understanding down there. Because in the mine their language is different from ours. There their speech is made up of all those naked and revolting phrases that would shame the Prince of Darkness. Still muttering amongst themselves, they said, 'Masaba, isn't your ticket stamped?'

'I don't know,' sobbed Masaba. 'This is my first time to work in the mine. I began work yesterday.'

'Hey, what's up there?' bawled Boss Tom, drawing nearer. 'If I get you talking again, Masaba, there'll be hell for you.'

'He is dying, sir,' cried Stimela in a strained voice.

It was then that Boss Tom uttered words seemingly innocent in his thoughts, but to natives' minds full of damning meanings. This thoughtless ganger who did not know the working of a native's mind said: 'There are lots of Kaffirs in the compound!'

The boys having digested these words bent once more over their shovels. A piercing cry stopped their labours. For, with a heartrending cry, Masaba fell with a sickening thud, knocking his head against a jagged piece of rock on the stope. Without delay he was carried to the surface and from there was hurried to the hospital. When his fellow countrymen heard that Masaba was seriously ill, they brooded.

'Lord Jesus, please save Masaba for his poor mother's sake. She will be left alone in this world.'

The next day, as they were changing from their wet clothes, a mine police boy entered their room: 'Er … er … Madoda, the manager said I should come to tell you that Masaba is dead.'

When an inquiry was held over the death of Masaba, it was found that Boss Tom was guilty. For he had caused a new boy to lash before putting him first on light undergound work, as was the rule with new boys. Through his carelessness and indifference he had caused the death of Masaba.

'I say, fellows, if Masaba had died accidentally, it would not have mattered. But I hold that he was murdered. For his ticket was stamped: *Not to be employed on lashing*.'

'*Hau*, didn't you hear that Boss said to Stimela, "There are many Kaffirs in the compound"? Ho! Ho! You don't know the white people!'

And they went out to dig Masaba's grave.

HERMAN CHARLES BOSMAN

Funeral Earth

We had a difficult task, that time (Oom Schalk Lourens said), teaching Sijefu's tribe of Mtosas to become civilised. But they did not show any appreciation. Even after we had set fire to their huts in a long row round the slopes of Abjaterskop, so that you could see the smoke almost as far as Nietverdiend, the Mtosas remained just about as unenlightened as ever. They would retreat into the mountains, where it was almost impossible for our commando to follow them on horseback. They remained hidden in the thick bush.

'I can sense these kaffirs all around us,' Veldkornet Andries Joubert said to our seksie of about a dozen burghers when we had come to a halt in a clearing amid the tall withaaks. 'I have been in so many kaffir wars that I can almost *smell* when there are kaffirs lying in wait for us with assegais. And yet all day long you never see a single Mtosa that you can put a lead bullet through.'

He also said that if this war went on much longer we would forget altogether how to handle a gun. And what would we do then, when we again had to fight England?

Young Fanie Louw, who liked saying funny things, threw back his head and pretended to be sniffing the air with discrimination. 'I can smell a whole row of assegais with broad blades and short handles,' Fanie Louw said. 'The stabbing assegai has got more of a selon's rose sort of smell about it than a throwing spear. The selon's rose that you come across in graveyards.'

The veldkornet did not think Fanie Louw's remark very funny, however. And he said we all knew that this was the first time Fanie Louw had ever been on commando. He also said that if a crowd of Mtosas were to leap out of the bush on to us suddenly, then you wouldn't be able to smell Fanie Louw for dust. The veldkornet also said another thing that was even better.

Our group of burghers laughed heartily. Maybe Veldkornet Joubert could not think out a lot of nonsense to say just on the spur of the moment, in the way that Fanie Louw could, but give our veldkornet a chance to reflect, first, and he would come out with the kind of remark that you just had to admire.

Indeed, from the very next thing Veldkornet Joubert said, you could see how deep was his insight. And he did not have to think much, either, then.

'Let us get out of here as quick as hell, men,' he said, speaking very distinctly. 'Perhaps the kaffirs are hiding out in the open turf-lands, where there are no trees. And none of this long tamboekie grass, either.'

When we emerged from that stretch of bush we were glad to discover that our veldkornet had been right, like always.

For another group of Transvaal burghers had hit on the same strategy.

'We were in the middle of the bush,' their leader, Combrinck, said to us, after we had exchanged greetings. 'A very thick part of the bush, with withaaks standing up like skeletons. And we suddenly thought the Mtosas might have gone into hiding out here in the open.'

You could see that Veldkornet Joubert was pleased to think that he had, on his own, worked out the same tactics as Combrinck, who was known as a skilful kaffir-fighter. All the same, it seemed as though this was going to be a long war.

It was then that, again speaking out of his turn, Fanie Louw said that all we needed now was for the kommandant himself to arrive there in the middle of the turf-lands with the main body of burghers. 'Maybe we should even go back to Pretoria to see if the Mtosas aren't perhaps hiding in the Volksraad,' he said. 'Passing laws and things. You know how cheeky a Mtosa is.'

'It can't be worse than some of the laws that the Volksraad is already passing now,' Combrinck said, gruffly. From that we could see that why he had not himself been appointed kommandant was because he had voted against the president in the last elections.

By that time the sun was sitting not more than about two Cape feet above a tall koppie on the horizon. Accordingly, we started looking about for a place to camp. It was muddy in the turf-lands, and there was no firewood there, but we all said that we did not mind. We would not pamper ourselves by going to sleep in the thick bush, we told one another. It was wartime, and we were on commando, and the mud of the turf-lands was good enough for *us*, we said.

It was then that an unusual thing happened.

For we suddenly did see Mtosas. We saw them from a long way off. They came out of the bush and marched right out into the open. They made no attempt to hide. We saw in amazement that they were coming straight in our direction, advancing in single file. And we observed, even from that distance, that they were unarmed. Instead of assegais and shields they carried burdens on their heads. And almost in that same moment we realised, from the heavy look of those burdens, that the carriers must be women.

For that reason we took our guns in our hands and stood waiting. Since it was women, we were naturally prepared for the lowest form of treachery.

As the column drew nearer we saw that at the head of it was Ndambe, an old native whom we knew well. For years he had been Sijefu's chief counsellor. Ndambe held up his hand. The line of women halted. Ndambe spoke. He declared that we white men were kings among kings and elephants among elephants. He also said that we were rinkhals snakes more poisonous and generally disgusting than any rinkhals snake in the country.

We knew, of course, that Ndambe was only paying us compliments in his ignorant Mtosa fashion. And so we naturally felt highly gratified. I can still remember the way Jurie Bekker nudged me in the ribs and said, 'Did you hear that?'

When Ndambe went on, however, to say that we were filthier than the spittle of a green tree toad, several burghers grew restive. They felt that there was perhaps such a thing as carrying these tribal courtesies a bit too far.

It was then that Veldkornet Joubert, slipping his finger inside the trigger guard of his gun, requested Ndambe to come to the point. By the expression on our veldkornet's face, you could see that he had had enough of compliments for one day.

They had come to offer peace, Ndambe told us then.

What the women carried on their heads were presents.

At a sign from Ndambe the column knelt in the mud of the turf-land. They brought lion and zebra skins and elephant tusks, and beads and brass bangles and, on a long grass mat, the whole haunch of a red Afrikaner ox, hide and hoof and all. And several pigs cut in half. And clay pots filled to the brim with white beer, and also – and this we prized most – witch-doctor medicines that protected you against goël spirits at night and the evil eye.

Ndambe gave another signal. A woman with a clay pot on her head rose up from the kneeling column and advanced towards us. We saw then that what she had in the pot was black earth. It was wet and almost like turf-soil. We couldn't understand what they wanted to bring us that for. As though we didn't have enough of it, right there where we were standing, and sticking to our veldskoens, and all. And yet Ndambe acted as though that was the most precious part of the peace offerings that his chief, Sijefu, had sent us.

It was when Ndambe spoke again that we saw how ignorant he and his chief and the whole Mtosa tribe were, really.

He took a handful of soil out of the pot and pressed it together between his fingers. Then he told us how honoured the Mtosa tribe was because we were waging war against them. In the past they had only had flat-faced Mshangaans with spiked knobkerries to fight against, he said, but now it was different. Our veldkornet took half a step forward, then, in case Ndambe was going to start flattering us again. So Ndambe said, simply, that the Mtosas would be glad if we came and made war against them later on, when the harvests had been gathered in. But in the meantime the tribe did not wish to continue fighting.

It was the time for sowing.

Ndambe let the soil run through his fingers, to show us how good it was. He also invited us to taste it. We declined.

We accepted the presents and peace was made. And I can still remember how Veldkornet Joubert shook his head and said, 'Can you beat the Mtosas for ignorance?'

And I can still remember what Jurie Bekker said, also. That was when something made him examine the haunch of beef more closely, and he found his own brand mark on it.

It was not long afterwards that the war came against England.

By the end of the second year of the war the Boer forces were in a very bad way. But we would not make peace. Veldkornet Joubert was now promoted to kommandant. Combrinck fell in the battle before Dalmanutha. Jurie Bekker was still with us. And so was Fanie Louw. And it was strange how attached we had grown to Fanie Louw during the years of hardship that we went through together in the field. But up to the end we had to admit that, while we had got used to his jokes, and we knew there was no harm in them, we would have preferred it that he should stop making them.

He did stop, and forever, in a skirmish near a blockhouse. We buried him in the shade of a thorn-tree. We got ready to fill in his grave, after which the kommandant would say a few words and we would bare our heads and sing a psalm. As you know, it was customary at a funeral for each mourner to take up a handful of earth and fling it in the grave.

When Kommandant Joubert stooped down and picked up his handful of earth, a strange thing happened. And I remembered that other war, against the Mtosas. And we knew – although we would not say it – what was now that longing in the hearts of each of us. For Kommandant Joubert did not straightway drop the soil into Fanie Louw's grave. Instead, he kneaded the damp ground between his fingers. It was as though he had forgotten that it was funeral earth. He seemed to be thinking not of death, then, but of life.

We patterned after him, picking up handfuls of soil and pressing it together. We felt the deep loam in it, and saw how springy it was, and we let it trickle through our fingers. And we could remember only that it was the time for sowing.

I understood then how, in an earlier war, the Mtosas had felt, they who were also farmers.

C LOUIS LEIPOLDT

The Tree

Translated from the Afrikaans by Philip John.

Time and again the missionary was vexed by his converts. It was all good and well. They were lovely, soft-hearted people who regularly attended catechism classes and who earnestly allowed themselves to be placed under censure. In general he had nothing to remark against their conduct. Only this *one* problem vexed him a little too much.

In the forest stood a big tree, the trunk branchless for the first fifty feet, and from there gigantic branches spread, forming a canopy over the small grass-covered spot where the tree grew. It was, according to the heathens in the area, a holy tree. In it were evil spirits, idols, the personification of everything evil, cruel and inhuman, as well as of everything that was simply good and inclined to love. The malicious and the loving spirits lived between trunk and bark, emerging in the dusk of late afternoon with the setting sun and the green forest pigeons on their way to their sleeping places.

The missionary naturally didn't believe any of it. That heathens could believe it, that he could well understand. They were not yet enlightened, he thought, and in his pride he forgot that the light of his own little candle flickered as that of a firefly shimmering against the strong glittering blaze of age-old tradition, fed by the experience of innumerable repetitions of the spirit of being. But for him his surroundings were heathenish. What he couldn't understand and comprehend was simply not worth understanding and comprehending.

For his converts, it was different. They, at least, should know better. They, at least, could see that apart from the sole grace-giving creed that they had to repeat in the catechism class, there was nothing else that could bring solace and relief, salvation and deliverance. This he always emphasised in his two-hour-long sermons in the small church which they had built for him and his doctrine. With unsurpassable emphasis he showed that his faith, and nothing else, was the one, true faith. In this manner he converted many.

Even so, amongst the converts were some who apparently still believed in the nonsense about that old tree. Now and then, when he went for a promenade in the forest and reached that place, he could see that fruit and flowers had been placed next to the tree. Even more disgusting, sometimes there were figurines, cut out of soft wood or made of similarly soft clay, placed in worshiping rows around the tree. When he encountered such outrageous things, he always kicked them away, in the most public and demonstrative manner. Usually there was no one to witness the public but vicarious punishment, but every now and then he saw a loincloth hiding in the depth of the virgin forest, and then he was particularly satisfied.

'At least they can see that I am not scared of it,' said the missionary, half aloud, and he walked home pleased. Duty accomplished affords one the right to feel contented.

But despite his reprimands and vicarious punishment, the disobedience of his converts persisted. Sometimes he tried to reason with the enslaved heathens – with his converts naturally he didn't want to, because a Christian should believe without needing the support of reason.

'It is ridiculous,' he said, 'it is completely ridiculous that you should fear that old rotten tree.'

It was a figurative exaggeration of which he was very aware because the tree was definitely not rotten, but rather sturdy and healthy. He spoke thus to express his contempt.

'Yes, Master,' said the heathens, because they were always polite and friendly and never gave offence, even when he ridiculed their faith. The kind of people who don't respect themselves.

'A dead tree' – once again an exaggeration, a manner of speaking – 'which is worth nothing and can do nothing for you. Shame.'

'Yes, Master,' the heathens said once again, and added: '*Him* has the angry spirits, Master; *him* hurts when you don't appease him.'

'Ridiculous,' said the missionary, half passionately. 'A tree can hardly hurt you if you stay out of it. What is the matter with you people?'

'We appease him, Master,' said the heathens. 'Those clay figurines, we make sacrifices for him, so that he doesn't hurt us.'

It is a strange lot that can be so superstitious, the missionary thought, and once again forgot that he spoke in a similar superstitious manner in the catechism class. I have to put an end to it.

That evening he said to his servant, 'Abdoer, sharpen the axe well. Tomorrow I am going to cut down your … your tree.' He had wanted to say, damn tree, because he was very angry, but a missionary must be an example, so he restrained himself.

The next morning, after the church service – where he had told the converts about the wonderful ship that contained all the animals of the earth, together with their food – he arrived home cheerful and invigorated. Abdoer had his midday meal ready and the missionary thoroughly enjoyed the curry and bananas. Then he read a psalm for Abdoer and his own edification and took up his axe. First he had wanted to take Abdoer along, but he possessed enough humanity not to do it. Thus, he walked alone down to the forest.

It was a beautiful afternoon because he had waited until the rainshower was over. The whole forest was glimmering with the last rays of the setting sun. Big butterflies, a glory of pitch black and bright red, fluttered over the fragrant geranium flowers. In the branches the cicadas were in tumult, and high above the green doves cooed a harmonious choral which reverberated softly in the expanse of the forest. The shiny leaves of the fan palms were still wet from the rain, and he smelt waves of the strong fragrance of jasmine. Here, at the tree, it was peaceful and quiet except for the droning of the cicadas and the song of the doves, both muted by the thick forest wall which surrounded him. It was nearly dark here with the greenish-brown darkness of the virgin forest, where shadows appeared purple and lost rays of light, falling from above through the great canopy of leaves, rested like small flecks of silver on the carpet of grass. Dark and quiet it was, and the thick tree trunk stood like a beige giant against the background of dusky green.

The missionary removed his jacket and rolled up his sleeves. The tree trunk was thick, and he would have to work, work hard, to cut through it. Even then the tree would not topple. The creepers and surrounding tree branches would support it solidly. Only months later, after rain had fallen on it and ferns had grown on it, after small beetles had eaten off the bark, and the fungus which grows so abundantly in the virgin forest and consumes everything had destroyed the inside of the trunk, would it tumble, piecemeal, like an old king who has been dethroned and sinks decrepitly into his grave. The quiet and the attractiveness of the place made an impression on the mood of the missionary. He let go of his little axe and sat down on the grass, even though it was still wet.

Strange, wasn't it? That the people continued to honour this old tree. Naturally, nothing of it was true – all the sayings and superstitions about the evil spirits and the good spirits living between the bark and the wood. It would surely be ridiculous to give to this the slightest credence. Especially for someone who was a Christian and opposed to idolatry.

And still? Transmitted tradition, sustained by the experience of circles of lives – should one disregard this? Should one withhold respect from that which everyone else honours, or should honour, if they are human, a thinking human being standing in a normal relation to his surroundings?

No, it would be ridiculous to agree even to this. What then would be the point of everything that he had to tell his converts in the catechism class? About his own faith? About his own experience and the life he had lived?

The thought gave the missionary new courage, new strength. He stood up and didn't even notice that he had sat on the wet grass. With determination he held the little axe in his right hand and walked to the tree.

But the tree trunk was very big and he could see that he would not be able to chop through it in one afternoon. To chop halfway through, especially if there were no one to see him chopping, wouldn't mean much. His objective was to destroy the idol, just as the Iconoclasts had destroyed idols in Catholic churches in the Middle Ages, as an example to and as edification of their fellows. It is true, they destroyed many works of art, but about that they hadn't thought or concerned themselves. Just as little as the missionary would concern himself with the tree.

The tree was a masterpiece, a magnificent artwork of nature. Hundreds of years of slow growth were needed to let him rise up so high, so impressively beautiful. The dampness of thousands of days through years that were constantly summer had invigorated him and brought his roots a store of life provisioned by the decomposition of thousands of lives in his vicinity. A complicated system of transmutation worked in his tissue, diligently, patiently, through thousands of days, until the colourless metal was changed into the sparkling green of leaves and the unseen gases into solid wood and bark. Against this the best chemical workshop thought out by people was like a heap of children's toys. A miracle was the tree, something in front of which humans should kneel, humbly, in the silent amazement which, in reality, is sister to worship.

The missionary thought nothing about this aspect of the issue. To him the tree was an ordinary forest tree which vexed him because it was a stumbling block to his converts.

He took his axe and started chopping at the tree trunk.

And he continued chopping until there was a deep gash in the side of the tree trunk. The wood was hard and durable and the axe wasn't too sharp. After half an hour's work he was tired.

'Enough for one day,' he said. 'Tomorrow I come again.'

Then he walked home.

And nothing happened.

* * *

That evening, lying on his bed, the missionary could not sleep. Usually it wasn't difficult for him to fall asleep. Usually, his head barely touched the pillow and he was asleep because he was healthy and not weakened by the fever. He swallowed his quinine pills regularly and his conscience had never bothered him.

But *this* evening he was restless, awake as never before. There was something – what, he couldn't make out – which prevented him from falling asleep. He could hear his heart beating and, much more unpleasantly, he was conscious of the fact that he had to breathe. Quite natural, in fact. Everyone has to breathe, but it is such an ordinary process that no one is conscious of it, and if you do become conscious of it, you experience it as a personal insult. Such a thing you would never forget.

It wasn't long before the missionary became conscious of something else. His breathing wasn't regular anymore, it was fitful, with long intervals accompanied by a nauseous feeling in the upper part of his chest. Breathing in was close to how it always was, but breathing out was more difficult, and low down in his throat it sounded as if there were a little whistle which whistled irregularly. A thin, sickly sound was produced by the whistle, just like the small sugarbirds in the geraniums when they were looking for small insects in the flowers. Definitely not pleasant – on the contrary, highly unpleasant and uncomfortable. The missionary had never before experienced anything like this and it didn't please him one bit.

I believe I am going to experience an asthma attack, he thought. I don't know what the correct treatment is. Maybe a few quinine pills ... Then he stood up and swallowed half a dozen pills. It made his head buzz, but it didn't alter the noise made by the whistle. The whole night the missionary turned from the one side of his bed to the other without finding relief. The old general who had been victorious at Waterloo had the habit of immediately rising after he had turned once in his bed. 'Tossing time is rising time,' the old Duke had said, and he had always practised what he said.

Thus the missionary also rose. He lit his lamp and tried to read under the mosquito net. But he could barely read anything, because the whistle in his throat drew his attention away from his reading matter. At the crack of dawn he called his servant.

'Make coffee,' he said, and his voice was hoarse because he had difficulty in breathing.

Abdoer made the coffee and stared at his master.

'Why do you look at me like that, Abdoer?' the missionary asked.

'Master had ...' said Abdoer, embarrassed, because he was a convert and would be confirmed soon, if he managed to recite the creed fluently.

'I had done what?' the missionary asked curiously.

'They all get it who ... malign the tree,' Abdoer answered. 'It is the spirit under the bark, Master, which gives it ...'

'Insanity,' said the missionary, more and more irate. 'All clear insanity –

pure hogwash. How many times do I have to repeat it to you, Abdoer, the stories are all fairy tales? Shame. And you call yourself a Christian.' Abdoer left the room shamefaced with an empty cup and the missionary took up his medical book and read up about asthma. His reading consoled him, because asthma was an affliction which didn't last long and which usually only happens at night. The causes – well, he was a fool not to have thought about it.

'It is the wetness of the grass. I am glad that I didn't get rheumatism in addition,' the missionary said to himself. 'I will now take a little bit of lobelia tincture and potassium bromide, and in a few hours it will all be over.'

But the remedies that he used – and in the course of the day he tried everything that the medical book suggested – didn't help. He couldn't conduct the service and in the catechism class he was so hoarse that he could barely utter a word. But what he found worse and even more unpleasant was the manner in which the catechism class, from Abdoer to the youngest, looked at him and whispered amongst themselves. Their interest was extremely unpleasant, but he didn't want to give attention to it. Even so, their interest wasn't only because of curiosity. His catechism class held the white man in extremely high regard. He was higher, more reasonable, more knowledgeable than they. He could read two, three languages, and could talk with experienced priests about what transpires in the hereafter. Not an ordinary man. Someone, on the contrary, who stood high above them, and who deserved a measure of deference and respect.

But all of them knew about the hoarseness and that strange noise coming from their master's throat with every breath. They knew where it came from. It was the punishment of the tree.

And the only remedy against it was to placate the tree spirits.

But they were too scared to give their master this advice.

That night the missionary had an even more restless and uncomfortable time. He thought nothing about the chopping down of the tree. His thoughts were concentrated solely on his own physical condition. The whistle now went berserk and he had to get up repeatedly, because it was as if he couldn't breathe and suffocated when he lay his head on the pillow. Even the few drops of chloroform on his handkerchief – the last, and most dangerous remedy, according to the medical book – brought no relief. How he survived the night, no one knows. But when Abdoer came in with the coffee the missionary was a broken man who had just about given up all hope of recovery. Asthma is a terrible illness, especially when it continues for days.

With a barely audible voice the missionary whispered: 'What do you do when – when it whistles like this in your throats?'

Abdoer turned his eyes to the other side of the room because he was too embarrassed to meet the gaze of the missionary.

'We – we make sacrifices to the spirits of the tree, Master,' he eventually said. And he first had to swallow hard before he could utter the words.

'Shame,' the missionary whispered. 'And you are Christians ... I will stay home today and the class will have to wait until tomorrow.'

The missionary spent the whole day reading his Bible and his medical book, and made diligent use of the armoury of a servant of the gospel.

But the whistle continued blowing and by midday he went out for a short walk.

Involuntarily he walked in the direction of the tree, and shortly arrived at the tree. Here everything was quiet, but he could see that there was a heap of flowers around the tree, and a whole row of figurines. It was the work of his converts, who had made vicarious sacrifices for him, to placate the spirits of the tree. Seeing it vexed him immensely. The flowers he kicked away and the figurines he simply stood upon. The last one which he destroyed in this manner was a passable representation of his own figure, with hat and walking stick. The sole of his shoe pressed the head askew, so that the face carried a satiric expression. But he didn't even notice this, because what grabbed his attention was that the cut in the tree trunk where he had worked with the axe was almost completely filled up with hardened sap.

'You wait,' he said, between his teeth, 'you I will still cut down. It is all complete insanity.'

Back in his house, he could barely breathe. The whistle had now multiplied into dozens of smaller whistles squeaking everywhere in his chest, and the noise which they kicked up in unison when he had to breathe in, was unbearable. He wildly swallowed a handful of quinine pills, but it made him nauseous and for a few minutes he thought he was dying.

'As well,' he said, 'because I cannot bear it anymore. A torment like this – it is unbearable.'

But still he had to bear it, because he couldn't lie down. He couldn't even sit, because as soon as he bowed his head forward it was as if he were being throttled and he wanted to choke. Now and then he became lightheaded, and it brought a measure of relief, but as soon as he regained his composure, the suffering was as severe as before.

In the middle of the night he got up and went to Abdoer's hut. But he didn't reach the hut. Abdoer was next to the door outside his room, on his knees on the ground and it was clear that he had kept vigil the whole night. Because Master was not just an ordinary person, and such a person deserved a measure of deference and respect.

'Abdoer,' the missionary whispered. 'What are you doing here?'

'O Master,' the servant replied, 'the tree spirit acts like this … Master, we all know … the axe … what Master has done …'

'Yes, Abdoer. I wanted to chop down the tree, chop it up …'

'We know, Master. But the spirits … they will not allow … and Master is … not one of us … The illness …'

'Will it kill me, Abdoer?' asked the missionary, because he had thought: Well, the people know more about the local illnesses than I do … and one can only ask.

'No …' said Abdoer, and the missionary was astonished to hear something sad in the sound of Abdoer's voice … 'Never … it doesn't kill. But it … more than kills. Syma … she bothered the spirits …'

With a shudder the missionary understood what Abdoer referred to. Syma was a middle-aged woman, but seemed very old. And she had the mind of a baby … a lunatic, whose cough and unnatural behaviour were familiar to all in the camp.

'Syma was Goeniang's wife when Goeniang died of smallpox, Master,' said Abdoer, 'and in her sorrow she cursed the tree. The same evening she began to whistle, and four days later, she was … Syma, like she is today, Master.'

'Couldn't she … couldn't she,' the missionary whispered, and he was too ashamed to ask the question, but Abdoer knew what he wanted to know.

'It was too late, Master,' he said. 'After the third day the spirits do not want to be merciful … That is why I am here now, Master … please Master …' And with hands shaking he handed the missionary a basket full of fruit and flowers and a little cooked rice. And on top of the fruit was a clay figurine with a hat and a walking stick in his hand – a figurine which, in a small comic form, represented the missionary.

'What must I do?' asked the missionary, and he could nearly not utter the words because of the loud squeaking of the whistles in his chest.

'Master must go to the tree … with the axe,' replied Abdoer. 'I will go with Master. We make a big fire … burn the axe … come on, Master. And Master places the fruit … where we always put it, and puts the figurine on top … to … to …'

'Yes … to?' asked the missionary, and his whisper was barely audible, because he was close to choking.

'To remain and to pray, Master,' said Abdoer, and he didn't want to look at his master.

'And what happens then?' the missionary asked again, and took the figurine and studied it.

'Master just becomes healthy again,' said Abdoer enthusiastically.'It happens a lot ... I myself saw ... And then Master can ... again become Christian ... just like us in the catechism class.'

The missionary stood motionless for a moment. Then he took the basket and said curtly, or rather he whispered, because he couldn't speak: 'Come Abdoer ... you know the way in the dark.'

In the indigo above, the stars sparkled in their multitudes and in the virgin forest thousands of fireflies lit up the trees. The small monkeys groaned monotonously and innumerable frogs sang in a choir, a roaring harmony, which went up and down as if the singers had moved closer and then further away. The night was deliciously cool with a little damp of the morning dew and with the smell of the earth everywhere. On the tree shone spots of green light where big candle bugs were clamped like lanterns against the mast of a ship.

'Here, Master,' Abdoer whispered, 'Master, not too close ... the figurine here ... and the fruit there. And now Master has to – please, Master ... now Master has to pray.'

It was a nightmare for the missionary and he couldn't gather his thoughts because in everything there was one thought, one concept that coloured everything. He wanted to be rid of the terrible constriction in his chest, the terrible burden of a death that constantly threatened, but didn't want to come. His pride and his faith were both broken ... relief and deliverance: that is what he wanted.

'Deliver me ... deliver me from this illness,' he managed to say ... 'I ... I regret that I ... that I disturbed the tree.'

The words were barely uttered than the missionary found that his breathing was easier. Yes truly, he could draw his breath in without hearing the whistle. But he was tired, tired and sleepy, and before he could prevent it he tumbled over, right next to the tree. Abdoer picked him up, carried him home and lay him down on his bed.

Late in the afternoon of the next day the missionary awoke. He was still tired and weak, and with a shudder of indignation he thought back to the events of the previous night.

Then he stood up, went to his table, and immediately began to write. The letter ended: 'Because I can no longer serve as example, I herewith tender my resignation.'

Now he farms and Abdoer is his first foreman. On the tree there is a scar.

In the lounge of the farmer's house stands a small shrivelled clay figurine.

'My remedy against asthma,' says the former missionary, now free from asthma attacks.

HIE DHLOMO

The Barren Woman

The Bantu love of children is well known. This love is partly natural, just like that of other human beings. It is partly the result of a social system in which lobola, the demands and difficulties of labour, and a man's prestige and status in society all put a premium on the size of the family. Because of lobola girls are considered as valuable as boys. Perhaps more. Whatever may be said about the evils of the system today, in tribal society lobola enhanced the status of a woman and gave her protection and a high niche in a society where men held autocratic powers, and great value was placed on boys as potential military power.

Barrenness in women was a stigma and disgrace. Even today most Bantu people spend large sums of money and endure many hardships to fight it.

In the past African women were also reputed for their remarkable powers of surviving antenatal, actual labour and postnatal troubles. Just as warriors regarded death as a matter of course, women took giving birth in their daily stride, as it were – not as an exceptional event requiring special preparation and associated with anxiety.

Of the two modern social evils reported from time to time, child stealing (although unknown in Bantu communities) is more in line with the tribal tradition of love for children, and the abandonment of unwanted babies, foreign to it. But neither child stealing nor adoption as we know it was practised in tribal society. That is why barrenness was such a tragedy.

The story of Mamkazi Zondi is interesting because it involves most of the elements above. It is simple, has no dramatic climax, and no element of surprise. She lived in the remote but thriving and, therefore, well-populated village of Manzini. As in many other rural areas part of the population was tribal and 'heathen', and part 'Christian' – meaning anyone who wore European clothes, sent their children to school, lived in square houses no matter how humble and dilapidated, or did not conform to tribal patterns one way or another.

Mamkazi belonged to the 'Christian' group, had been married for three years, and would have been happy and her story not worth telling but for one curse.

She was barren.

She and her husband had gone to great trouble and wasted a fortune trying to get a baby. European doctors and African herbalists and witch-doctors had been consulted without success.

The couple were unhappy. Temba Zondi, her husband, loved her and was kind and devoted to her. Except on three or four occasions when they had had exceptionally violent quarrels, he never blamed her for her defect. However, the curse hung over their house and life. She was reminded about it frequently and in many ways. When her husband silently stared at her or took more than usual interest in a neighbour's or visitor's child, it hurt her deeply for she felt he was chiding and blaming her bitterly, if silently. Garrulous or unfeeling and spiteful neighbours gossiped about it. Innocent visitors and old, distant acquaintances who meant no harm hurt her when they asked if she had no child yet.

Of all her friends and neighbours, the best and most intimate was Ntombi Mate. But Mamkazi did not know whether to regard Ntombi as a blessing or a curse, a solace to her soul or a thorn in her flesh.

Unlike most 'Christian' women of her age in the village, who could only read and write (the younger generation were more progressive), Ntombi was considered 'educated'. She had passed Standard Six, had travelled to several big towns, and had worked for some time in a large mission hospital where she acquired a rudimentary knowledge of midwifery. Although she had not been out of Manzini village for years, was married and had a big family, she still retained her reputation and status. She was the unofficial, unqualified, but useful district midwife of the place. Whether she thought and believed it was professionally necessary or she was too lazy (and had grown fat) and too snobbish (was she not above others?), she insisted that those who needed her help must come to her 'clinic', which was a large hut with four beds. She never answered calls to homes, no matter what happened. Homes were far away and had no comforts, the way was rough, and calls came at inconvenient hours of the day and night. Well known and never without work, she was yet never inundated with cases because most women were strong and healthy enough to give birth successfully in their homes, and the others did not care about clinics and hospitals except in cases where there were complications.

The snag in the deep and warm friendship of Mamkazi and Ntombi was that whenever the latter referred to her work, Mamkazi was reminded of her plight. Otherwise each woman could do almost anything for the other. And Ntombi had done all to help her friend.

During the fourth year of her marriage, Mamkazi conceived. The fact lifted her to the seventh heaven of ecstasy, pride and expectation. But there were times when she was slain by doubts, fears and worse. Doubts and fears about miscarriage, stillbirth, and other accidents. Worse? Possibly. There was the sad case of the Kozas where the coming of a child after five years of barren marriage completely wrecked their home because of the allegation – supported by some and denied by others, and not open to proof or disproof in that backward society – that Koza's wife had been unfaithful and the child was illegitimate.

Mamkazi's fears were unfounded. Zondi was intoxicated with joy, and treated her with poignant tenderness and devotion. Doctors and hospitals were very far away. But urged by their own gratitude and caution and Ntombi's strong advice, Mamkazi paid four visits to the nearest town to consult a doctor. When the time came she, of course, placed herself under the care of her friend who was determined to display to the utmost her knowledge and experience on this occasion.

The baby came without trouble. It was a girl. Mamkazi was so fit that she could have returned home the next day and gone about her business. Two other women were in the clinic at that time. The same night they, too, had children, one a girl, and the other twins – a boy and a girl. The twins were not identical – but at the time this struck no one, not even Ntombi, as being significant.

The following night Mamkazi's heaven changed into hell. Zondi had almost been overpowered with joy and pride, and had found it difficult to leave the clinic even for a few moments or to return home in the night. Ntombi and Mamkazi had congratulated one another a dozen times. Many friends had come and stood amazed at the 'miracle'. Ntombi had openly given special attention to her friend. Expensive and lovely things had been bought for the baby. Everything was in striking contrast to the two other poor women, one of whom was a 'Christian' and the other – the mother of the twins – a tribal person.

Ntombi insisted on cleanliness and on what other 'modern' professional rules and methods she knew. One of these was not to cover heavily with blankets the new arrivals (and other sick persons), as fond mothers and relatives were inclined to do.

In the still hours of the second night, Mamkazi, who could hardly sleep for joy, woke up to find that her precious child had been smothered to death! It was impossible! A thousand-to-one-chance accident! And of all people, this to happen to her! No. God would not let it happen!

'O God, Almighty Father! It cannot be! Give life to my child! Restore it back to me! How can God be so cruel, mock with such evil! After years in hell, to lift me into heaven for a moment, only to plunge me back into deeper hell! Hear, Holiest Father, hear. I kiss and beg at Thy feet!'

Thus she prayed silently and insanely. But the ways of God are unfathomable. The child was dead. Demented, she had no power to cry out aloud or rave. After trying gently but excitedly to stir and suckle the baby into life, some demoniacal spirit descended upon her, making her cool and determined, and propelling her to some devilish scheme. There is no God! Why stand in the way of the Devil, then! In a flash, the evil plan was born and executed. Mechanically, rapidly, and with mad courage and precision, she undressed her dead baby, exchanged it with the scantily attired twin girl whom she dressed as her child, wrapped up the twin boy and the dead child heavily in a blanket as she had found them and retired to her bed in a state of nervous and insane anxiety.

'I have done it! Who will find out! Who dare accuse me! Three of us have girls – and how can they tell? I have the right to the living baby! It is mine! She does not need it. She has many other children. Come close to me, my dear one. Live and thrive! There is life in you, and your life is my life, hope and light. Let us sleep in peace.'

A raving maniac, she could not sleep, but managed to lie still.

As if by some evil spell, she had carried out her plan without disturbance. Hardly an hour later, a piercing cry rent the clinic. Soon there was bedlam. The mother of the twins had awakened and made the tragic discovery. Her lamentations were broadcast far and wide. The clinic was soon filled by the agitated Ntombi, members of her family and people who lived close by. The rare 'accident' left everyone dumbfounded and mentally paralysed. The mother of the twins could not be consoled.

The next day the whole village knew about the strange happenings. The husbands of the three women had rushed to the clinic early to stand by and comfort their wives. So did others. The tragedy was discussed excitedly, if in whispers.

After some time, the excitement and sense of grief subsided, and life in the village and in the families directly concerned took its normal course. No one had the least suspicion about foul play. The women of the village were amazed and impressed that Ntombi's constant and seemingly unnecessary and irritating warning about wrapping children in heavy blankets – advice she gave purely on 'hygienic' and snobbish grounds – had been justified so tragically. The old tribal superstition that giving birth to twins is bad luck was revived for a time. It helped seal the matter as 'natural' and in accordance with hoary tradition and sacrosanct custom.

The three women's agitation, sallowness and wild behaviour were considered natural and excusable under the circumstances. This was especially true of Mamkazi who received special and universal sympathy as her rare blessing coincided with such a misfortune. Of the three women, she was the most pitied and 'understood' for whatever strange behaviour and attitude she adopted. Her husband and friends repeatedly congratulated and consoled her with the words, 'Thank God, it did not happen to you!'

The excitement subsided and life in the village and in the families concerned took a normal course. No one had the least suspicion of foul play. Not so! Nature is 'scientific', omniscient and deeply jealous and revengeful when her course and ends are disturbed.

One person was keenly suspicious about the whole episode. It was Ntombi. Instinctively and intuitively the truth was revealed to her through a glass darkly. However, as a rational human being and a realist, she held her peace. But there was conflict, not peace, within her. She had carefully taken notice of Mamkazi's unnatural behaviour and agitation on the fateful day and after. More experienced, observant and trained than others, including the three mothers, she could tell the difference between newborn babes – in weight, behaviour, and even in physical features that would be imperceptible to others. Besides, she was the only person who had seen and handled all three girls. She was sure that there was something wrong. But was it possible? How could mediocre-minded and nervous Mamkazi have conceived and executed without help and discovery such a foul act?

What was she to do! The knowledge that, in bigger and more accessible centres, the thing would have led to an embarrassing, and even incriminating investigation, added to her uneasiness and inner conflict. It might be a sin in the eyes of God, also.

Thus, while the rest of the village had forgotten about the occurrence, two women – Mamkazi and Ntombi – remained restless, unhappy and guarded.

Time heals, makes us forget and helps solve problems. Pleasant but deceitful philosophy! Time festers old wounds, opens patched-up scars, complicates and increases problems, and makes us remember and grow afraid at every turn. Time plagues, derides, incapacitates.

Far from achieving happiness and triumph, Mamkazi found that she had set herself a problem that became more complicated as time went on. If someone spoke of Jabu Buthelezi, the mother of the twins, her child or her family, she became apprehensive. If she herself met one of the family, it was worse.

The passage of years had wrought many changes in Manzini village. The population had increased rapidly. With the opening up of new roads and the introduction of a bus service, there was more progress. A European district surgeon now visited the village on certain days of the week. He had a trained nurse assisting him. Ntombi's 'clinic' was a thing of the past. There was a fine, large new school, and the local store had been expanded and the goods improved in quantity and quality. There was no need for children and adults to trudge many weary miles to the distant school or the better store. Some tribal families – among them the Buthelezis – had become 'Christians'.

Mamkazi was reminded of her act at every turn.

'Ma! I met Zidumo Buthelezi and his mother at the store,' her daughter Simangele would report innocently and excitedly. 'His mother said "I love you as much as my boy. You look like one another." She kissed me and gave me sweets.'

Returning from a beer-drinking party her husband would blabber, 'And there was Buthelezi who said that he would be disappointed if our little Simangele did not marry into his family when she grew up. He is crazy about the child, just like the others. Ha! Ha!'

On such occasions she would weep, burst out into a violent temper or behave in some inexplicable manner. And remarks and incidents of this kind came every day.

She had quarrelled with her husband when she tried arbitrarily to restrict the movements of the little girl; when she said the child must be sent to the distant not the local school; when she suggested that they should go and live in another district. Zondi could not understand all this, and they became increasingly unhappy.

Mamkazi and Ntombi were hardly on speaking terms now for the latter had tried to discover the truth by subtle and friendly hints at first, but, at last, had bluntly demanded to know the truth.

'We are the best of friends. You can rely on me. We are growing old and must not die with certain secrets. Let me know the truth if only to ease my conscience. You can trust me not to tell. It would serve no purpose,' Ntombi had implored.

'Inquisitive spy! Blackmailing informer! Nagging cheat! It would wreck you as completely as myself! Of course, you dare not tell! It was your clinic. You are more educated! You should have known, and it was your responsibility. I can also blackmail you! The police and the people would believe it was done with your connivance. In fact, that it was your evil idea and scheme. For how else could a convalescent, ignorant, grieved woman like me have succeeded in carrying out the thing without your help and knowledge! Know then that your suspicions are true. I "switched" the two girls! I did! Simangele is her twin child! But she is forever mine! Mine, you hear! Go and tell! I hate you! Get out of my sight!'

Mamkazi aged rapidly. She cut herself off from society almost completely. Old villagers talked about it but, unsuspecting, gave the wrong reason for the change. Newcomers and the young did not care. Her husband drank heavily and more frequently. From being one of the most loving and happy couples, they became one of the most unhappy in the village. She had done all this for her husband's and her own triumph and happiness. Instead, she had wrecked both. Retreat was impossible. She clung to her tragic secret and followed her deadly course as if for life.

* * *

It is summer. The grass is green. Birds sing. Wild flowers gently sway everywhere. Near a humming stream rest two shy young lovers, Simangele Zondi and Zidumo Buthelezi. They are nineteen years of age, good-looking and in the full bloom of health. It is college vacation time. Although they grew up together, they have had little time to see each other in the past three years for they have been attending different and distant colleges.

'In youth when we were always together, we did not care whether we were together or not. Now that we crave always to be together we cannot always be together,' said Zidumo.

'Always speaking as if you were a full-grown man. I like to stay young,' laughed Simangele.

'I am a man. You will always be young.'

'But you were right. And mother would be raving mad to know that I have been seen with you, let alone that I am in love with you!'

'I cannot understand it. It has always been so, I am told, since we were tots. But I never noticed it. Did you?'

'I knew it. Perhaps some silly old family feud.'

'Possibly. But I doubt it, for my people love you and have nothing against your people. They seem just as puzzled. There is one solution. As soon as I complete my degree studies next year, I will elope with and marry you!'

At this, they laughed and kissed.

* * *

Tormented and vigilant, Mamkazi had heard of their meeting and of their being in love. The climax followed rapidly.

Zondi's largest room was soon crowded with distressed, puzzled and expectant people. The audience had been carefully selected. They had been hurriedly and secretly summoned at the persistent and intolerable ravings of Mamkazi who appeared to be near death and wanted to say something.

There was Ntombi and her husband; Buthelezi, his wife and Zidumo; the priest and his assistant; the Zondis.

Aware of impending tragedy, the priest had prayed for peace and guidance. But Mamkazi could not wait or be controlled. She groaned and raved in her bed. Supported, she sat up and spoke. There was mingled supreme triumph and utter despair, joy and bitterness, sanity and madness in her words and visage. She wept and laughed, defied and implored.

'Silence! Who dares! Ha! Ha! Listen to me. They shall not, cannot, marry. Yes, you two! The Buthelezis shall not have my daughter. Foiled? Indeed, you are! Ha! She is mine and I will have my way. Mine, I tell you, forever mine! O God, O Evil, the daughter you gave me! What? Yes, I stole her from you – your girl twin. Your child lives forever mine! How can brother and sister be married? Can't you leave her – me – alone! Ask her – ask my nagging, evil friend, there – the midwife. She knows! She will ...'

Mamkazi collapsed. Jabu Buthelezi wept aloud and sank on the floor. There was amazement, incredulity and confusion.

But the priest was equal to the situation. He called for and restored some measure of order, sent his assistant to call for the doctor at once, asked for God's help in a sentence, and finally commanded Ntombi to speak and explain. Trembling and old, she wept and stammered.

'It is true. It happened long ago in my clinic ...,' she began.

ES'KIA MPHAHLELE

Down the Quiet Street

Nadia Street was reputed to be the quietest street in Newclare. Not that it is any different from other streets. It has its own dirty water, its own flies, its own horse manure, its own pot-bellied children with traces of urine down the legs. The hawker's trolley still slogs along in Nadia Street, and the cloppity-clop from the hoofs of the over-fed mare is still part of the street.

Its rows of houses are no different, either. The roofs slant forward as if they were waiting for the next gale to rock them out of their complacency and complete the work it has already started. Braziers still line the rocky pavement, their columns of smoke curling up and settling on everything around. And stray chickens can be seen pecking at the children's stools with mute relish. Nadia Street has its lean, barking mongrels and its share of police beer raids.

Yet the street still clings to the reputation of being the quietest. Things always went on in the *next* street.

Then something happened. When it did, some of the residents shook their heads dolefully and looked at one another as if they sensed a hundred years' plague round the corner.

Old Lebona down the street laughed and laughed until people feared that his chronic bronchitis was going to strangle him. 'Look at it down the street or up the street,' he said, 'it's the same. People will always do the unexpected. Is it any wonder God's curse remains on the black men?' Then he laughed again.

'You'll see,' said Keledi, rubbing her breast with her forearm to ease the itching caused by the milk She always said that, to arouse her listeners' curiosity. But she hardly ever showed them what they would see.

Manyeu, the widow, said to her audience, 'It reminds me of what happened once at Winburg, the Boer town down in the Free State.' She looked wistfully ahead of her. The other women looked at her and the new belly that pushed out from under the clean floral apron.

'I remember clearly because I was pregnant, expecting – who was it now? Yes, I was expecting Lusi, my fourth. The one you sent to the butcher yesterday, Kotu.'

Some people said that it happened when Constable Tefo first came to patrol Nadia Street on Sunday afternoons. But others said the 'Russians' – that clan of violent Basotho men – were threatening war. Of course, after it had happened Nadia Street went back to what its residents insisted on calling a quiet life.

If Constable Tefo ever thought that he could remain untouched by Nadia Street gossip, he was mistaken. The fact that he found it necessary to make up his mind about it indicated that he feared the possibility of being entangled in the people's private lives.

He was tall and rather good-looking. There was nothing officious about him, nothing police-looking except for the uniform. He was in many ways one of the rarest of the collection from the glass cage at Headquarters. His bosses suspected him. He looked to them too human to be a good protector of the law. Yes, that's all he was to the people, that's what his bosses had hired him for.

The news spread that Tefo was in love. 'I've seen the woman come here at the end of every month. He always kisses her. The other day I thought he was kissing her too long.' That was Manyeu's verdict.

It did not seem to occur to anyone that the woman who was seen kissing Tefo might be his wife. Perhaps it was just as well, because it so happened that he did not have a wife. At forty he was still unmarried.

Manyeu was struck almost silly when Constable Tefo entered her house to buy *maheu*, the sour mealie-meal drink.

'You'll see,' said Keledi, who rubbed her breast up and down to relieve the burning itch of the milk.

Still Tefo remained at his post, almost like a mountain: at once defiant, reassuring, and menacing. He would not allow himself to be ruffled by the subtle suggestions he heard, the meaningful twitch of the face he saw, the burning gaze he felt behind him as he moved about on his beat.

One day Keledi passed him with a can of beer, holding it behind her apron. She chatted with him for a while and they both laughed. It was like that often; mice playing hide-and-seek in the mane of the lion.

'How's business?' Tefo asked Sung Li's wife one Sunday on the stoep of their shop.

'Velly bad.'

'Why?'

'Times is bad.'

'Hm.'

'Velly beezee, you?'

'Yes, no rest, till we get over there, at Croesus Cemetery.'

She laughed, thinking it very funny that a policeman should think of death. She told him so.

'How's China?'

'I'm not from China, he, he, he. I'm born here, he he, he. Funnee.' And she showed rusty rotten teeth when she laughed, the top front teeth overtaking the receding lower row, not cooperating in the least to present a good-looking jaw.

Tefo laughed loud to think that he had always thought of the Sung Li's as people from China, which from what he had been told in his childhood conjured up weird pictures of man-eating people.

When he laughed, Constable Tefo's stomach moved up and down while he held his belt in front and his shoulders fluttered about like the wings of a bird that is not meant to fly long distances.

When her husband within called her, Madam Sung Li turned to go. Tefo watched her shuffling her small feet, slippers almost screaming with the pain of being dragged like that. From behind, the edge of the dress clung alternately to the woollen black stockings she had on. The bundle of hair at the back of her head looked as if all the woman's fibre were knotted up in it, and that if it were undone Madam Sung Li might fall to pieces. Her body bent forward like a tree in the wind. Tefo observed to himself that there was no wind.

One Sunday afternoon Tefo entered Sung Li's shop to buy a bottle of lemonade. The heat was intense. The roofs of the houses seemed to strain under the merciless pounding of the sun. All available windows and doors were ajar and, owing to the general lack of verandahs and the total absence of trees, the residents puffed and sighed and groaned and stripped off some of their garments.

Madam Sung Li leaned over the counter, her elbows planted on the top surface, her arms folded. She might have been the statue of some Oriental god in that position but for a lazy afternoon fly that tried to settle on her face. She had to throw her head about to keep the pestilent insect at bay.

Constable Tefo breathed hard after every gulp as he stood looking out through the shop window, facing Nadia Street.

One thing he had got used to was the countless funeral processions that trailed on week after week. They had to pass Newclare on the way to the cemetery. Short ones, long ones, hired double-deckers, cars, lorries; poor insignificant ones, rich snobbish ones. All black and inevitable.

The processions usually took the street next to Nadia. But so many people were dying that some units were beginning to spill over into Nadia.

Tefo went out to the stoep to have a little diversion; anything to get his mind off the heat. He was looking at one short procession as it turned into Nadia when a thought crossed his mind, like the shadow of a cloud that passes under the sun.

Seleke's cousin came staggering onto the stoep. His clothes looked as if he had once crossed many rivers and drained at least one. He was always referred to as Seleke's cousin, and nobody ever cared to know his name.

Seleke lived in the next street. She was the tough sort with a lashing tongue. But even she could not whip her cousin out of his perennial stupor.

Keledi's comment was: 'You'll see, one day he'll hunt mice for food. The cats won't like it.' And she rubbed her breast. But Seleke's cousin absorbed it all without the twitch of a hair.

'Ho, chief!' Seleke's cousin hailed the constable, wobbling about like a puppet on the stage. 'Watching coffins, eh? Too many people dying, eh? Yes, too many. Poor devils.'

Tefo nodded. A lorry drove up the street, and pulled up on the side, almost opposite the Chinaman's shop.

'Dead men don't shout,' said Seleke's cousin.

'You're drunk. Why don't you go home and sleep?'

'Me drunk? Yes, yes, I'm drunk. But don't you talk to me like these pig-headed people around here. Their pink tongues wag too much. Why don't they leave me alone? There's no one in this bloody location who can read English like I do.'

'I'm sure there isn't.' Tefo smiled tolerantly.

'I like you, chief. You're going to be a great man one of these days. Now, you're looking at these people going to bury their dead. One of these days those coffins will tell their story. I don't know why they can't leave me alone. Why can't they let me be, the lousy lot?'

A small funeral party turned into Nadia Street on a horse-drawn trolley cart. There were three women and four men on the cart, excluding the driver. A man who looked like their religious leader sang lustily, his voice quivering above the others.

The leader had on a frayed, fading purple surplice and an off-white cassock. He looked rather too young for such a mighty responsibility as trying to direct departed souls to heaven, Tefo thought. The constable also thought how many young men were being fired with religious feelings these days …

The trolley stopped in front of a house almost opposite Sung Li's. Tefo looked on. The group alighted and the four men lifted the coffin down.

Tefo noticed that the leader was trembling. By some miracle his hymn book stayed in the trembling hand. He wiped his forehead so many times that the constable thought the leader had a fever and could not lift the coffin further. They obviously wanted to enter the yard just behind them. He went to the spot and offered to help.

The leader's eyes were wide and they reflected a host of emotions Tefo could not understand. And then he made a surprising gesture to stop Tefo from touching the coffin. In a second he nodded his head several times, muttering something that made Tefo understand that his help would be appreciated. Whereupon the constable picked up the handle on his side, and the quartet took the corpse into the house. Soon Tefo was back on the Chinaman's stoep.

It must have been about fifteen minutes later when he heard voices bursting out in song as the party came out of the house with the coffin. Again, Tefo noticed the leader was sweating and trembling. The coffin was put on the ground, outside the gate. The others in the party continued to sing lustily, the men's voices beating down the courageous sopranos.

Tefo sensed that they wanted to hoist it onto the lorry. Something told him he should not go and help. One of these religious sects with queer rules, he thought.

At the gate the leader of the funeral party bent forward and, with a jerky movement, he caught hold of the handle and tilted the coffin, shouting to the other men at the same time to hold the handles on their side. Tefo turned sharply to look.

A strange sound came from the box. To break the downward tilt the other men had jerked the coffin up. But a cracking sound came from the bottom; a sound of cracking wood. They were going to hoist the coffin higher, when it happened.

A miniature avalanche of bottles came down to the ground. A man jumped into the lorry, reversed it a little and drove off. The trolley cart ground its way down Nadia Street. Tefo's eyes swallowed the whole scene. He descended from the stoep as if in a trance, and walked slowly to the spot. It was a scene of liquor bottles tumbling and tinkling and bumping into one another, some breaking and others rolling down the street in a playful manner, like children who have been let out of the classroom at playtime. There was hissing and shouting among the funeral party.

'You frightened goat!'

'Messing up the whole business!'

'I knew this would happen!'

'You'll pay for this!'

'You should have stayed home, you clumsy pumpkin!'

'We're ruined this time!'

They had all disappeared by the time it had registered on Tefo's mind that an arrest must be made. More than that: a wild mob of people was scrambling for the bottles. In a moment they also had disappeared with the bottles, the corpus delicti! A number of people gathered round the policeman.

The lousy crowd, he thought, glad that a policeman had failed to arrest! They nudged one another, and others indulged in mock pity. Manyeu came forward. 'I want the box for fire, sir constable.' He indicated impatiently with the hand that she might have it. It did not escape Keledi's attention, and she said to her neighbour, rubbing her breast that was full of milk: 'You'll see. Wait.'

'Ho, chief! Trouble here?' Seleke's cousin elbowed his way to the centre of the crowd. He had been told what had happened.

'Funerals, funerals, funerals is my backside! Too bad I'm late for the party! Hard luck to you, chief. Now listen, I trust these corpses like the lice on my shirt. But you're going to be a great man one day. Trust my word for that. I bet the lice on my body.'

Later that afternoon Constable Tefo sat in Manyeu's room, drinking *maheu*. Keledi, rubbing her breast, was sitting on the floor with two other women. Manyeu sat on a low bench, her new belly pushing out under her floral apron like a promising melon.

Somewhat detached from the women's continuous babble, Tefo was thinking about funerals and corpses and bottles of liquor. He wondered about funeral processions in general. He remembered what Seleke's cousin had said the other day on the Chinaman's stoep. Was it an unwitting remark?

Just then another procession passed down the street. Tefo stood up abruptly and went to stand at the door. If only the gods could tell him what was in that brown glossy coffin, he thought. He went back to his bench, a figure of despair.

Kaledi's prophetic 'You'll see' took on a serious meaning when Tefo one day married Manyeu after her sixth had arrived. Nadia Street gasped. But then recovered quickly from the surprise, considering the reputation it had of being the quietest street in Newclare.

It added to Kaledi's social stature to be able to say after the event: 'You see!' while she vigorously rubbed her breasts that itched from the milk.

CASEY MOTSISI

Kid Playboy

Every time a hick job comes around in the office I get saddled with it. Now the editor pushes this folded white card at me and says to find out what I can get out of this here invite. I walk out of the office and read the card once more. According to the gold-lettered words a certain Kid Mabothobotho stays out Dube is getting hitched to an Alexandra cherrie.

On Saturday the wedding will take place at the cherrie's place in Alex. I decide I'd rather wait for it to come around to Dube on Sunday because I'm somewhat scared of hopping off to Alex especially on weekends on account the bright boys over there have turned the place into a gunsmoke and knife-happy township.

On Sunday I haul out my top hat and tails to make ready to go to Dube. I expect it to be one of those high society shindigs, as you know how hoity-toity these Dubeheimers can get when they want to. I get a good look at myself in my landlord's son's wardrobe mirror as I put on the tie he lent me, and I see that my eyes are unusually clear – sure sign among the boozing fraternity that I've been keeping shebeen queens, especially Aunt Peggy, waiting.

I get to Dube and don't have any difficulty spotting the place where this wedding is taking place on account of the half-a-dozen beribboned convertible cars parked in front of the house. A guy who meets me at the door looks scornfully at my not-too-well pressed trousers, whereupon he gives me the VIP treatment. Only he reckons the 'I' in VIP stands for 'Inconsequential'. He tells me to go and sit in the tent at the back of the house. I tell him who I am, whereupon he smiles and ushers me into the room.

This girl this guy's getting married to is so beautiful that I can't take my eyes off her for a pretty long time. After a while I manage to pull my eyes away from her to look at the groom. Cripes! It's none other than Kid Playboy. I feel the blood revolting in my veins. This is the same Kid Playboy who took away from me some time back the only girl I ever loved. He promised this girl of mine everything in the world and crowned the long list of promises by telling her that he would build a fire under the ocean just so's she can swim in winter.

And like all starry-eyed girls, this girl of mine went and believed every word he told her. Maybe if she hadn't been so gullible she would still have been alive today. As it turns out, Kid Playboy gives her the bird after stringing her for a month on account another foolish cherrie falls for his sweet talk. So what does she do, but commit suicide!

Kid Playboy's eyes meet mine and I pull out my tongue at him. He turns coal black and his Adam's apple starts moving up and down like someone who's seen a ghost. The guy looks real scared, and I am just beginning to hate myself for having scared the boy by sticking out my tongue at him when I realise that it's not me who's the cause of his sudden jitters. There's a girl who's sitting a few feet behind me who is proving to be the why for Kid's jaded nerves.

I turn around and look at this girl to see what it is about her that can cause so much panic in a satanic soul. But all I can see is that she's an ordinary homely girl, and the small sleeping child she's holding in her arms is the sweetest thing I ever did see.

I'm still busily occupied at looking at this fear-instilling girl and hoping that she's not a ghost, when a voice that sounds like a constipated ostrich's booms, 'Ladees and gentlemen, all those who have presents for the bridal couple may now see the "mabalane" (the MC of the wedding).' The 'mabalane' stands up, breaks into a toothless grin, bows and sits down again.

I thought they had invited us to a wedding, now they want to fleece presents out of us! But seeing as the announcer man said 'ladies and gentlemen', I reckon he has left me out on account nobody ever accused me of being a gentleman, let alone a lady. So I happily ignore him.

A few folk get away from their eats and drinks with parcels of varying sizes beneath their armpits. They stand in line before the 'mabalane', who jots down the name and address of each and everyone who dumps a parcel on the table. Some guys who had decided beforehand that it would be much better to save the few pennies they have for paying their rent instead of buying presents for Kid Playboy and his spouse – and perhaps a few others who have a needle against him, like yours truly – suddenly discover that the room is too hot and march out.

After some time the last name and address is written down, and I can see the 'mabalane' hinting at the groom's people for his payment for services duly rendered – a nip of hooch. But he doesn't get the hooch. Instead, the girl with the baby, who had so disorganised Kid Playboy a short while ago, stands up and walks to the 'mabalane'. She dumps the child, who is now awake and bawling his young head off, on the table and says, 'Here's my present to the bride and groom. My name is Maisie.' She gives a Mapetla address somewhere in Site and Service. She winds up by saying Kid Playboy's the pop of the child.

All of a sudden, there's a bang of a hullabaloo going on. Kid Playboy is making a hurried exit out of the house, and the bride is tearing at her bridal dress and hurling all sorts of names at Kid Playboy and his family, including the late ones. After every burst of unprintable words she keeps chorusing that she's got a lawyer that's going to show them what makes the grass green.

Up to today nobody ever hears a word about Kid Playboy. But Mr Rumour goes around the townships telling all and sundry that Kid Playboy is in his hometown somewhere in the Tanganyika Territory, although the folks from there pronounce it 'Tananika Torrotoro'.

I reckon the next time the editor tells me to go and cover a 'wedding', I'm gonna take an advance on my salary and hightail it to Aunt Peggy's joint and cover a bottle of hooch with Kid Playboy's ex-bride on my lap, as she now frequents this place ever since her lawyer proved not to be as hot as she had thought him to be.

CAN THEMBA

Crepuscule

The morning township train cruised into Park Station, Johannesburg, and came to a halt in the dark vaults of the subterranean platforms. Already the young of limb, and the lithe and lissom had leapt off and dashed for the gate that would let them out. But the rest of us had to wade ponderously, in our hundreds, along the thickening platforms that gathered the populations disgorged by Naledi, Emdeni, Dube, Orlando, Pimville, Nancefield, Kliptown, Springs, Benoni, Germiston. Great maws that spewed their workership over Johannesburg.

I was in the press that trudged in the crowd on the platform. Slowly, good-humouredly we were forced, like the substance of a toothpaste tube, through the little corridor and up the escalator that hoisted us through the outlet into the little space of breath and the teeth of pass-demanding South African Police.

But it was with a lilt in my step that I crossed the parquet foyer floor and slipped through the police net, because I knew which cop to pass by: the one who drank with me at Sis Julia's shebeen of an afternoon off. It was with a lilt, because it was spring as I walked out of Park Station into a pointillist morning with the sun slanting from somewhere over George Goch, and in spring the young ladies wear colourful frocks, glaring against the sunlight and flaring in the mischievous breezes. I joyed as I passed into Hoek Street, seeing the white girls coming up King George Street, the sunlight striking through their dresses, articulating the silhouettes beneath to show me leg and form; things black men are supposed to know nothing of, and which the law assininely decrees may not even be imagined.

Funny thing this, the law in all its horrificiency prohibits me, and yet in the streets of Johannesburg I feast for free every morning. And, God, if I try hard enough, I may know for real in Hillbrow every night.

There is a law that says (I'm afraid quite a bit of this will seem like *there is a law that says*), well, it says I cannot make love to a white woman. It is a law. But stronger still there is a custom – a tradition, it is called here – that shudders at the sheerest notion that any white man could contemplate, or any black man dare, a love affair across the colour line. They do: white men *do* meet and fall in love with black women; black men do explore 'ivory towers'. But all this is severely 'agin the law'.

There are also African nationalists who profess horror at the thought that any self-respecting black man could desire any white woman. They say that no African could ever debase himself as to love a white woman. This is highly cultivated and pious lying in the teeth of daily slavering in town and in cinema. African girls, who are torturing themselves all the time to gain a whiter complexion, straighter hair and corset-contained posteriors, surely know what their men secretly admire.

As for myself, I do not necessarily want to bed a white woman; I merely insist on my right to want her.

Once, I took a white girl to Sophiatown. She was a girl who liked to go with me and did not have the rumoured South African inhibitions. She did not even want the anthropological knowledge of 'how the other South Africans live'. She just wanted to be with me.

She had a car, an ancient Morris. On the way to Sophiatown of those days, you drove along Bree Street, past the Fordsburg Police Station in the Indian area, past Braamfontein railway station, under a bridge away past the cemetery, past Bridgetown Memorial Hospital (known, strangely, for bringing illegitimate non-European children into the world), up Hurst Hill, past Talitha Home (a place of detention for delinquent non-European girls), past aggressive Westdene (sore at the proximity of so many non-white townships around her), and into Sophiatown.

So that night a black man and a white woman went to Sophiatown. I first took Janet to my auntie's place in Victoria Road, just opposite the bus terminus. It was a sight to glad a cynic's heart to see my aunt shiver before Janet.

'Mama' – in my world all women equivalents of my mother are mother to me – 'Mama, this is my girl. Where is Tata?' This question, not because my uncle might or might not approve, but because I knew he was terribly fond of brandy, and I was just about to organise a little party; he would not forgive me for leaving him out. But he was not there. He had gone to some meeting of *amagosa* – church stewards, of whom he was the chief.

'Mama, how about a doek for Janet.'

The doek! God save our gracious doek. A doek is a colourful piece of cloth that the African woman wears as headgear. It is tied stylistically into various shapes from Accra to Cape Town. I do not know the history of this innocuous piece of cloth. In Afrikaans, the language of those of our white masters who are of Dutch and Huguenot descent, doek meant, variously, a tablecloth, a dirty rag, or a symbol of the slave. Perhaps it was later used by African women in contact with European ideas of beauty who realised that 'they had no hair' and subconsciously hid their heads under the doek. Whatever else, the doek had come to designate the African woman. So that evening when I said, 'Mama, how about a doek for Janet', I was proposing to transform her, despite her colour and her deep blue eyes, into an African girl for the while.

Ma dug into her chest and produced a multi-coloured chiffon doek. We stood before the wardrobe mirror while my sisters helped to tie Janet's doek in the current township style. To my sisters that night I was obviously a hell of a guy.

Then I took Janet to a shebeen in Gibson Street. I was well known in that particular shebeen, could get my liquor 'on tick' and could get VIP treatment even without the asset of Janet. With Janet, I was a sensation. Shebeens are noisy drinking places and as we approached that shebeen we could hear the blast of loud-mouthed conversation. But when we entered a haunted hush fell upon the house. The shebeen queen rushed two men off their chairs to make places for us, and: 'What would you have, Mr Themba?'

There are certain names that do not go with Mister, I don't have a clue why. But, for sure, you cannot imagine a Mr Charlie Chaplin or a Mr William Shakespeare or a Mr Jesus Christ. My name – Can Themba – operates in that sort of class. So you can see the kind of sensation we caused when the shebeen queen addressed me as Mr Themba.

I said, casually as you like, 'A half-a-jack for a start, and I suppose you'd like a beer, too, my dear?'

The other patrons of the shebeen were coming up for air, one by one, and I could see that they were wondering about Janet. Some thought that she was coloured, a South African mulatto. One said she was white, appending, 'These journalist boys get the best girls'. But it was clear that the doek flummoxed them. Even iron-coloureds, whose stubborn physical appearances veer strongly to the Negroid parent, are proud enough of whatever hair they have to expose it. But this girl wore a doek!

Then Janet spoke to me in that tinkling English voice of hers, and I spoke to her, easily, without inhibition, without madamising her. One chap, who could contain himself no longer, rose to shake my hand. He said, in the argot of the townships, 'Brer Can, you've eaten caustic soda. Look, man, get me fish-meat like this, and s'true's God, I'll buy you a *vung* (a car)!' That sort of thawed the house and everybody broke into raucous laughter.

Later, I collected a bottle of brandy and some ginger ale, and took Janet to my room in Gold Street. There were a few friends and their girls:

Kaffertjie (Little Kaffer – he was quite defiantly proud of this name) and Hilda, Jazzboy and Pule, Jimmy, Rockefeller and a coloured girl we called Madame Defarge because day or night she always had clicking knitting needles with her. We drank, joked, conversed, sang and horse-played. It was a night of the Sophiatown of my time, before the government destroyed it.

It was the best of times, it was the worst of times; it was the age of wisdom, it was the age of foolishness; it was the season of Light, it was the season of Darkness; it was the spring of hope, it was the winter of despair; we had everything before us, we had nothing before us; we were all going direct to Heaven, we were all going direct the other way – in short, the period was so far like the present period that some of its noisiest authorities insisted on its being received, for good or for evil, in the superlative degree of comparison only.

Sometimes I think, for his sense of contrast and his sharp awareness of the pungent flavours of life, only Charles Dickens – or, perhaps, Victor Hugo – could have understood Sophiatown. The government has razed Sophiatown to the ground, rebuilt it, and resettled it with whites. And with appropriate cheek, they have called it Triomf.

That night I went to bed with Janet, chocolate upon cream. I do not know what happened to me in my sleep; the Africans say *amadhlozi* talked to me – the spirits of my forefathers that are supposed to guide my reckless way through this cruel life intervened for once. In the mid of the night I got up, shook Janet and told her we got to go.

'Ah, Can, you're disturbing me, I want to sleep.'

'Come-ahn, get up!'

'Please, Can, I want to sleep.'

I pulled off the blankets and marvelled awhile at the golden hair that billowed over her shoulders. Then she rose and dressed drowsily.

We got into her ancient Morris and drove to town. I think it was the remembrance of a half-bottle of brandy in her room in Hillbrow that woke me and made me rouse her, more than the timely intervention of the *amadhlozi*. We saw a big, green *Kwela-Kwela* wire-netted lorry-van full of be-batonned white cops driving up Gold Street, but we thought little of it, for the cops, like fleas in our blankets, are always with us. So we spluttered up Hurst Hill into town.

Later, I heard what had happened.

I used to have a young Xhosa girl called Baby. She was not really my class, but in those days for what we called love we Sophiatonians took the high, the middle and the low.

Baby was pathologically fond of parties, the type of parties to which tsotsis go. They organise themselves into a club of about half-a-dozen members. On pay-day they each contribute, say £5, and give it to the member whose turn it is. He then throws a party to entertain all the members and their girlfriends. Almost invariably guys trespass on other guys' girls and fights break out. Baby liked this kind of party, but it soon became clear to me that I was risking the swift knife in the dark so long as I associated with her. So I talked it over with her, told her we should call it a day and that I did not want to clash with her tsotsi boyfriends. She readily accepted, saying, 'That-so it is, after all you're a teacher type and you don't suit me.'

So far as I was concerned that had been that.

But that star-crossed night, Baby heard that I was involved with a white girl. She went berserk. I gathered that she went running down Gold Street tearing out her hair and shrieking. At the corner of Gold Street and Victoria Street, she met a group of tsotsis playing street football under the street lamp with a tennis ball. They asked her, 'Baby, whassamatter?' She screamed, 'It's Can, he's with a white woman,' and they replied, 'Report him!'

Africans are not on the side of the cops if they can help it. You do not go to a policeman for help or protection or the which way to go. You eschew them. To report a felon to them, good heavens! It is just not done. So for a tsotsi to say about anyone, 'Report him!' means the matter is serious.

Baby went to Newlands Police Station and shouted, 'Baas, they're there. They're in bed, my boyfriend and a white woman.' The sergeant behind the counter told her to take it easy, to wait until the criminals were so well-asleep that they might be caught *flagrante delicto*. But Baby was dancing with impatience at 'the law's delay'.

Still, that sergeant wanted to make a proper job of it. He organised a lorry-full of white cops, white cops only, with batons and the right sadistic mental orientation. Or, perhaps, too many such excursions had misadventured before where black cops were suspected of having tipped off their brethren.

When we went down Gold Street, it was them we saw in the green lorry-van bent on a date with a kaffir who had the infernal impertinence to reach over the fence at forbidden fruit.

I understood they kicked open the door of my room and stormed in, only to find that the birds had flown. One white cop is reported to have said, wistfully, 'Look, man, there are two dents in the pillow and I can still smell her perfume.' Another actually found a long thread of golden hair.

I met Baby a few days later and asked her resignedly, 'But you said we're no more in love, why the big jealous act?'

She replied, 'Even if we've split, you can't shame me for a white bitch.'

I countered, 'But if you still loved me enough to feel jealous, didn't you consider that you were sending me to six months in jail! Baby, it could be seven years, you know.'

'I don't care,' she said. 'But not with a white bitch, Can. And who says that I still love you? It's just that you can't humiliate me with a white bitch.'

I threw up my hands in despair and thought that one of these days I really must slaughter a spotlessly white goat as a sacrifice to the spirits of my forefathers. I have been neglecting my superstitions too dangerously long.

Funny, one of the things seldom said for superstitious belief is that it is a tremendous psychological peg to hang on to. God knows the vehement attacks made upon the unreason and stark cruelty of superstition and witchcraft practices are warranted. Abler minds than mine have argued this. But I do want to say that those of us who have been detribalised and caught in the characterless world of belonging nowhere, have a bitter sense of loss. The culture that we have shed may not be particularly valuable in a content sense, but it was something that the psyche could attach itself to, and its absence is painfully felt in this white man's world where everything significant is forbidden, or 'Not for thee!' Not only the refusal to let us enter so many fields of human experience, but the sheer negation that our spirits should ever assume to themselves identity. Crushing.

It is a crepuscular, shadow-life in which we wander as spectres seeking meaning for ourselves. And even the local, little legalities we invent are frowned upon. The whole atmosphere is charged with the white man's general disapproval, and where he does not have a law for it, he certainly has a grimace that cows you. This is the burden of the white man's crime against my personality that negatives all the brilliance of intellect and the genuine funds of goodwill so many individuals have. The whole bloody ethos still asphyxiates me. Ingratitude? Exaggeration? Childish, pampered desire for indulgence? Yes – yes, perhaps. But leave us some area in time and experience to be true to ourselves. It is so exhausting to have to be in reaction all the time. My race believes in the quick shaft of anger, or of love, or hate, or laughter: the perpetual emotional commitment is foreign to us. Life has contrived so much, such a variegated woof in its texture, that we feel we can tarry only a poignant moment with a little flare of emotion, if we are ever to savour the whole. Thus they call us fickle and disloyal. They have not yet called us hypocritical.

These things I claim for my race, I claim for all men. A little respite, brother, just a little respite from the huge responsibility of being a nice kaffir.

After that adventure in Sophiatown with Janet, I got a lot of sympathy and advice. I met the boys who had said to Baby, 'Report him!' I was sore because they had singled me out like that and made me the pariah that could be thrown to the wolves. They put their case:

'You see, Brer Can, there's a man here on this corner who plays records of classical music, drinks funny wines and brings white men out here for our black girls. Frankly, we don't like it, because these white boys come out here for our girls, but when we meet them in town they treat us like turds. We don't like the way you guys play it with the whites. We're on Baby's side, Brer Can.'

'Look, boys,' I explained, 'you don't understand, you don't understand me. I agree with you that these whites take advantage of our girls and we don't like the way our girls act as if they are special. But all you've done about it is just to sit and sizzle here at them. No one among you has tried to take revenge. Only I have gone to get a white girl and avenge with her what the whites do to our sisters. I'm not like the guys who procure black girls for their white friends. I seek revenge. I get the white girls – well, it's tough and risky, but you guys, instead of sitting here crying your hearts out, you should get yourselves white girls, too, and hit back.'

I got them, I knew.

One guy said, 'By right, Brer Can's telling the truth.'

Another asked, 'Tell me, Brer Can, how does a white woman taste?'

That was going too far. I had too great a respect for Janet, the *woman*, to discuss that with anybody whether he was white or black.

I said, 'You go find out for yourself.'

The piece of advice I got from the mother of a friend of mine who stayed in the same street, Gold Street, was touching.

She said to me: 'Son, I've heard about your trouble with the white girl. It's you that was foolish. People know that your white girl is around because they recognise the car. If they see it parked flush in front of your house, they say, "Can has got silver-fish." What you should do is to drive the car into my yard here, right to the back of the house so that nobody could see it from the street, and then they wouldn't suspect that you have the white girl in your room down there.'

It seemed to me to be excellent, practical advice.

So the next time I got home with Janet, we drove the car into the yard of my friend's mother, right back behind the house, and walked down in the dead of night to my room.

In the middle of the night, my friend came clattering on the window of my room and shouted, 'Can, get up, the cops!' We got up, got dressed in breathless time, rushed to the car at his mother's place and zoomed out of

Sophiatown on a little-used route past St Joseph's Mission through Auckland Park into Hillbrow, where in the heart of the white man's flat-land we could complete breaking the white man's law as, apparently, we could not do in Sophiatown.

Later, I heard the sordid details of what had happened that night. My friend came home late, and overheard his mother and sisters discussing the Morris we had left in their yard. The mother felt that it was not right that I should be messing around with a white woman when she had unmarried daughters of her own and my eligibility rated high. So she sent one of her daughters to go and tell Baby that I was with the white woman again and that I had left the car in their yard. My friend felt that he did not have the time to argue with his family, that his job was to warn us as quickly as he could to get the hell out of there.

As it turned out, I need not have bothered. The darling Afrikaner at the desk told Baby, 'Look here, woman, every time you have a quarrel with your boyfriend, you rush to us with a cock-and-bull story. Clear out!'

ALEX LA GUMA

A Matter of Taste

The sun hung well towards the west now so that the thin clouds above the ragged horizon were rimmed with bright yellow like the spilt yolk of an egg. Chinaboy stood up from having blown the fire under the round tin and said, 'She ought to boil now.' The tin stood precariously balanced on two half-bricks and a smooth stone. We had built the fire carefully in order to brew some coffee and now watched the water in the tin with the interest of women at a childbirth.

'There she is,' Chinaboy said as the surface broke into bubbles. He waited for the water to boil up and then drew a small crushed packet from the side pocket of his shredded windbreaker, untwisted its mouth and carefully tapped raw coffee into the tin.

He was a short man with grey-flecked kinky hair, and a wide, quiet, heavy face that had a look of patience about it, as if he had grown accustomed to doing things slowly and carefully and correctly. But his eyes were dark oriental ovals, restless as a pair of cockroaches. 'We'll let her draw a while,' he advised. He put the packet away and produced an old rag from another pocket, wrapped it around a hand and gingerly lifted the tin from the fire, placing it carefully in the sand near the bricks.

We had just finished a job for the railways and were camped out a few yards from the embankment and some distance from the ruins of a one-time siding. The corrugated iron of the office still stood, gaping in places and covered with rust and cobwebs. Passers had fouled the roofless interior and the platform was crumbled in places and overgrown with weeds. The cement curbing still stood, but cracked and covered with the disintegration like a welcome notice to a ghost town. Chinaboy got out the scoured condensed-milk tins we used for cups and set them up. I sat on an old sleeper and waited for the ceremony of pouring the coffee to commence.

It didn't start right then because Chinaboy was crouching with his rag-wrapped hand poised over the can, about to pick it up, but he wasn't making a move. Just sitting like that and watching something beyond us.

The Port Jackson bush and wattle crackled and rustled behind me and the long shadow of a man fell across the small clearing. I looked back and up. He had come out of the plantation and was thin and short and had a pale white face covered with a fine golden stubble. Dirt lay in dark lines in the creases around his mouth and under his eyes and in his neck, and his hair was ragged and thick and uncut, falling back to his neck and around his temples. He wore an old pair of jeans, faded and dirty and turned up at the bottoms, and a torn leather coat.

He stood on the edge of the clearing, waiting hesitantly, glancing from me to Chinaboy, and then back at me. He ran the back of a grimy hand across his mouth.

Then he said hesitantly: 'I smelled the coffee. Hope you don' min'.'

'Well,' Chinaboy said with that quiet careful smile of his. 'Seeing you's here, I reckon I don' min' either.' He smiled at me, 'You think we can take in a table boarder, pal?'

'Reckon we can spare some of the turkey and green peas.'

Chinaboy nodded at the stranger. 'Sit, pally. We were just going to have supper.'

The white boy grinned a little embarrassedly and came around the sleeper and shoved a rock over with a scarred boot and straddled it. He didn't say anything, but watched as Chinaboy set out another scoured milk tin and lifted the can from the fire and poured the coffee into the cups.

'Help yourself, man. Isn't exactly the mayor's garden party.' The boy took his cup carefully and blew at the steam. Chinaboy sipped noisily and said, 'Should've had some bake bread. Nothing like a piece of bake bread with cawfee.'

'Hot dogs,' the white boy said. 'Huh.'

'Hot dogs. Hot dogs go with coffee.'

'Ooh ja. I heard,' Chinaboy grinned. Then he asked: 'You going somewhere, Whitey?'

'Cape Town. Maybe get a job on a ship an' make the States.'

'Lots of people want to reach the States,' I said.

Whitey drank some coffee and said: 'Yes, I heard of money and plenty to eat.'

'Talking about eating,' Chinaboy said, 'I see a picture in a book, one time. 'Merican book. This picture was about food over there. A whole mess of fried chicken, mealies – what they call corn – with mushrooms an' gravy, chips and new green peas. All done up in colours, too.'

'Pass me the roast lamb,' I said sarcastically.

'Man,' Whitey said warming up to the discussion. 'Just let me get to something like that and I'll eat till I burst wide open.'

Chinaboy swallowed some coffee: 'Worked as a waiter one time when

I was a youngster. In one of that big caffies. You should've seen what all them bastards ate. Just sitting there shovelling it down. Some French stuff too, patty grass or something like that.'

I said: 'Remember the time we went for drunk and got ten days? We ate mealies and beans till it came out of our ears!'

Chinaboy said, whimsically: 'I'd like to sit down in a smart caffie one day and eat my way right out of a load of turkey, roast potatoes, beet salad and angel's food trifle. With port and cigars at the end.'

'Hell,' said Whitey, 'it's all a matter of taste. Some people like chicken and others eat sheep's heads and beans!'

'A matter of taste,' Chinaboy scowled. 'Bull, it's a matter of money, pal. I worked six months in that caffy and I never heard nobody order sheep's head and beans!'

'You heard of the fellow who went into one of these big caffies?' Whitey asked, whirling the last of his coffee around in the tin cup. 'He sits down at a table and takes out a packet of sandwiches and puts it down. Then he calls the waiter and orders a glass of water. When the waiter brings the water, this fellow says: "Why ain't the band playing?"'

We chuckled over that and Chinaboy almost choked. He coughed and spluttered a little and then said, 'Another John goes into a caffie and orders sausage and mash. When the waiter bring him the stuff he take a look and say: "My dear man, you've brought me a cracked plate." "Hell," says the waiter, "that's no crack. That's the sausage."'

After we had laughed over that one Chinaboy looked westward at the sky. The sun was almost down and the clouds hung like bloodstained rags along the horizon. There was a breeze stirring the wattle and Port Jackson, and far beyond the railway line a dog barked with high yapping sounds.

Chinaboy said: 'There's a empty goods going through here around about seven. We'll help Whitey, here, onto it, so's he can get to Cape Town. Reckon there's still time for some more pork chops and onions.' He grinned at Whitey. 'Soon's we've had dessert we'll walk down the line a little. There's a bend where it's the best place to jump a train. We'll show you.'

He waved elaborately towards me: 'Serve the duck, John!'

I poured the last of the coffee into the tin cups. The fire had died to a small heap of embers. Whitey dug in the pocket of his leather coat and found a crumpled pack of cigarettes. There were just three left and he passed them round. We each took one and Chinaboy lifted the twig from the fire and we lighted up.

'Good cigar, this,' he said, examining the glowing tip of the cigarette.

When the coffee and cigarettes were finished, the sun had gone down altogether, and all over the land was swept with dark shadows of a purple hue. The silhouetted tops of the wattle and Port Jackson looked like massed dragons.

We walked along the embankment in the evening, past the ruined siding, the shell of the station house like a huge desecrated tombstone against the sky. Far off we heard the whistle of a train.

'This is the place,' Chinaboy said to Whitey. 'It's a long goods and when she takes the turn the engine driver won't see you, and neither the rooker in the guard's van. You got to jump when the engine's out of sight. She'll take the hill slow likely, so you'll have a good chance. Jus' you wait till I say when. Hell, that sound like pouring a drink!' His teeth flashed in the gloom as he grinned. Then Whitey stuck out a hand and Chinaboy shook it, and then I shook it.

'Thanks for supper, boys,' Whitey said.

'Come again, anytime,' I said, 'we'll see we have a tablecloth.' We waited in the Port Jackson growth at the side of the embankment while the goods train wheezed and puffed up the grade, its headlamp cutting a big yellow hole in the dark. We ducked back out of sight as the locomotive went by, hissing and rumbling. The tender followed, then a couple of box-cars, then some coal-cars and a flat-car, another box-car. The locomotive was out of sight.

'Here it is,' Chinaboy said pushing the boy ahead. We stood near the train, hearing it click-clack past. 'Take this coal box coming up,' Chinaboy instructed. 'She's low and empty. Don't miss the grip, now. She's slow. And good luck, pal!'

The coal-car came up and Whitey moved out, watching the iron grip on the far end of it. Then as it drew slowly level with him, he reached out, grabbed and hung on, then got a foothold, moving away from us slowly.

We watched him hanging there, reaching for the edge of the car and hauling himself up. Watching the train clicking away, we saw him straddling the edge of the truck, his hand raised in a salute. We raised our hands too.

'Why ain't the band playing? Hell!' Chinaboy said.

ABRAHAM H DE VRIES

The Girl with the Bra-pistol

Translated from the Afrikaans by Martin Trump and Abraham H de Vries.

Seated against the multicoloured cushions on the divan, the girl's face and arms have an olive hue. But where she is not tanned, her skin is as pale as milk under the electric light that reflects off the ceiling and showers on everyone like invisible rain. Her long blonde hair hangs restfully on either side of her oval face.

'Insane!' the woman beside her shrieks as Van Schaikwyk, the art teacher, whispers something in her ear. 'Insane!' and she spills her drink on the floor. The girl smiles and turns her glass slowly so that its curved surface seeks the light. Without anybody noticing it she adjusts her bra with the wrist of her goblet-hand. She drinks slowly.

'It's a problem,' says Cloete, a small little man with a pair of thick-lensed glasses, to the coloured man beside him. 'Their kind of imperialism. They seem to be unable to grasp all the nuances of the problem. Look for generalisations, easy ways out. And you people have been given the short end of the stick.'

The man shrugs and smiles, puzzled. (Why does everyone always have to help him remember?)

'Yes, it's difficult, isn't it?' he replies with nervous caution.

'Are you buggers still talking politics in my house?' Markus asks with a glass of red wine in one hand and his bent stem pipe in the other. Markus is the host, but because he and his wife occupy separate rooms, he is also rather like a guest at her parties. His hypersensitive movements continually incline to moments of confusion.

'I'm on the Church council,' Cloete says. 'And I can assure you the problems are not as simple as you think, Markus.'

'Would you then rather have sat on Jan van Riebeeck's?' Markus lights his pipe, pressing the tobacco down with his thumb.

'Meaning?'

'Everything was so uncomplicated. Simple. Jannie's times knew none of our problems, as you call them. Remember Cloete, you are the person who sees all the problems in every situation. But, problems might just be the stones out of which we build our own Tower of Babel.'

In the corner of the room, the record player reaches the end of the record, the stylus scratches in the last groove. Markus quickly walks over, changes the record, then straightens a row of books on the shelf.

'Markus always makes me think of someone who opens your bedroom door, curses you, and then, gone, away on tiptoes down the passage to the next room,' says Pieterse, the publisher, who has just joined the conversation.

'Insane!' shrieks the same woman on the divan.

'Just bloody hysterical,' comments Pieterse without looking in her direction.

'Out with it, Pieterse,' – it's Markus again – 'Are you going to publish Hein Hansen's latest book now that he is a political exile from his land of birth? No? Cowards!' and he sniggers behind his pipe. 'Don't look so bloody guilty. I'm only teasing you. You are all so damned serious tonight! Why?'

'And he's the one to talk!' Pieterse retorts. 'He who has of late invited women to his home who walk around in his castle with bra-pistols.'

'Who?'

'That girl over there on the divan. Don't you know her?'

'No, I don't. What about her? She's innocent and beautiful.'

'And she's wearing one of these new gadgets. A bra-pistol.' And talking behind his hand: 'Did you imagine in all your naiveté that her tits alone could be so big?'

'Look, Pieterse, I don't know what the hell you're talking about,' Markus says seriously.

'I'll show you. Do you see that piece of string hanging out of her sleeve? There! Now, within that little piece of string there is another one, and that is the pistol's trigger. She simply hooks it round her forefinger, opens her hand, and she spits fire. That, dear Markus, is what I'm talking about.'

'I don't know the girl. Ag, perhaps she's just afraid or something. Where do you find these bullshit stories?'

The coloured man has walked over to the window. He peers out. And he is no longer smiling as he turns back.

'Klaas brought her with him. She's nursing in Paarl. Klaas told me about the pistol. He knows her well. She takes lessons at one of those shooting schools which they now have for women. Bloody good shot with the thing, I hear.'

'It must be fun to coach them when they're wearing those pistols,' Cloete says with his hands in his blazer pockets. 'I made my auntie join a club too. She often returns home quite late from work. It's dangerous.'

'Ag, that girl is completely harmless,' Markus says as if to close the conversation. 'Tell her to take a few pot shots at the telephone pole behind the house if she feels the urge. John, what about another drink?' It's only when Markus speaks to him that the others become aware of the coloured man in their presence. He nods. 'I'll take one for the road when we leave. I have to be at the office again tomorrow.'

'Excuse the others; they're a bunch of boozers!'

⋆ ⋆ ⋆

Later as he steps out onto the veranda, the man notices that it's overcast. Behind the Cape-Dutch houses hangs a veil of grey rain. Dark and heavy fir trees bend as if they're trying to drag themselves free. He looks attentively through the glass doors at the people in the room. Then he takes three darts from the board against the wall and starts throwing them. His face is taut, expressionless. But his knuckles show up white on the hand with which he clasps the darts.

Markus walks across to the girl on the sofa. Klaas sits next to her, prods her bra with his fingers.

'Shoot the clown!' Markus says to her, and then, extending a hand: 'We've not yet met.'

'She can shoot a coin off the top of a bottle,' says Klaas with hazy pride. 'Just like that, *pienggg* …'

'Give it a miss, Klaas!' the girl says.

'But it's true,' he argues. 'You shoot it, *pienggg*.'

Markus laughs, but his eyes are unnaturally dark beneath his thick eyebrows.

'You have to work late into the evenings, I suppose?' he enquires gently.

'No,' the girl answers.

'It's at me. She fires at me,' Klaas says, and he starts to sing: 'Three blind mice, see how they run … Give us another dop, Markus old chap. Before we're all blasted to hell and gone.'

The girl places her hand over her glass. 'No thanks, no more for me,' she says.

'Strange lady,' Markus jokes somewhat uncomfortably. 'Doesn't drink, but carries naughty firearms!'

'Three blind mice,' Klaas sings. Everyone else in the room has suddenly stopped talking.

'Show us how you shoot with that thing,' Cloete says. 'So my wife can see that it's a good thing …'

The girl looks embarrassedly at Klaas. He says unhelpfully: 'Ja, come on, show them. Show how you can shoot a coin *pienggg* …!'

'Ja, come on ...'

'Ja, come on ...'

The girl looks out at the veranda. 'I can't shoot inside the room,' she says.

'Outside on the veranda then?' Markus asks uneasily.

'OK.' She stands up, pulls down the string and fastens it around her wrist with a leather thong. She hooks the eye of the inner thread about her forefinger.

Outside, on the veranda, she poises herself against the wall. The coloured man removes the darts from the board and joins the other guests.

Markus removes the dartboard from the wall, searches in his blazer pocket for a pencil and draws a circle on the worn plywood. 'One shot only,' he says. 'Otherwise somebody's going to get hurt here tonight. Guns are not toys.'

'Boeeeeee!' the others respond in a chorus.

The girl stands at ease with her feet a few inches apart. She holds her right hand stiffly at her side, then turns with a quick movement of her wrist. A dull crack sounds.

'That's it!' Klaas shouts out. 'Bull's-eye!'

'Hooray!' Cloete says and he staggers over to the low wall of the veranda. His wife joins him there.

'Insane!' shrieks the woman with the low-necked dress and she holds her glass out in front of her. 'Let's drink to the security of the Republic!'

Klaas staggers forward, draws another line on the plywood and quickly steps back. He signals with his hand.

With breaks of varying length, four shots crack out. Four little holes appear on the line.

'Insane!'

'Let's call it a day now,' Markus says. 'Somebody is going to get hurt here tonight.'

But Klaas says, 'Don't worry, I'm her instructor. I know what can happen.' The girl nods her head in agreement.

'She'll – you know what – she'll shoot your silhouette out against the wall if you go and stand there,' Klaas says. 'Ja ... And it won't be the first time she's done it either. It's the way we teach them. Best method to get rid of their fears.'

Once again, a silence falls.

'She's had a few drinks, Klaas. Damn it, don't be obstreperous now. Come on chaps, let's go and top up. Hell, miss, but ...' Markus walks towards the door.

But everyone remains standing.

'It's just like the circus trick with the knives,' Klaas explains.

Markus stands in the doorway with his hand against the frame. 'Go and stand there yourself. Loud mouth!'

No one has seen the coloured man stepping forward.

He positions himself against the board. His eyes are dark and big, but his face shows no emotion. He stares straight at the girl in front of him. She shifts her feet.

Then she bends forward and releases two swift shots. On either side of his hips two holes are smashed into the wood.

'Crop his candle!' Klaas chortles.

The man looks down, smiles broadly. As he lifts his gaze, the girl turns away and presses past Markus into the room.

No one follows her.

Everyone gazes at him.

He lifts his glass off the low wall. 'To the security of the Republic,' he says and his mouth is smiling. But his eyes are not.

JAN RABIE

Maiden Outing to Rondebosch

Translated from the Afrikaans by Wally Smuts.

The day after the *Vogelsang* dropped anchor in the bay the commander gave all the Netherlands women an opportunity of travelling to the *ronde bos* [circular patch of bush]. Never before had any of them gone farther than a mile or two into the interior of the strange, perilous land, but all were only too eager for a chance of getting away from the fort.

At crack of dawn the five matrons and the three young girls, whispering and giggling, settled themselves on the wagon. Amid the laughter and cheers of the escorting soldiers and infantrymen the commander dashingly swung himself onto his horse and raised his hand as a signal. A gun-salute boomed from the walls of the fort, the echo rebounded from the Table Mountain, and the sound died away over the bay which was lightly brushed by a gentle breeze from the west. At once the drivers shouted to their oxen and the creaking wheels began to turn.

The clumsy wagon of Cape wood and the rugged road had the women frequently clutching at each other or hastily disposing their dresses. The stately Mevrou de Stael, especially, seated up in front beside her sister-in-law Maria van Riebeeck, was hard put to hold firmly onto the luncheon basket *and* maintain her dignity. Yet it was a real pleasure excursion. The sallies of Antjie die Boerin who was holding her latest scion of many, the six-week-old Dirkie in one practised arm while indicating the scenery with the other; the excited exclamations of the girls, Cornelia Boom and Christina and Petronella Does; the fresh summer morning smelling of aromatic herbs; the unfamiliar cornet-shaped flowers as large as saucers growing on the slopes of the Windberg; and perhaps, too, a subconscious awareness of the significance of the outing, had made each woman there experience a glad tingling as never before in all their four-and-a-half years at the Cape, the hard, hungry years of struggling to get a foothold on the southern tip of Africa.

More than the others Maria sensed that this was an exceptional day. After so many nights of lying awake and hearkening she knew all about her husband's cherished plan: that now, after the blessing and providence of God, the Dutch settlement should be established even more securely with the aid of free-burghers – the first colonists.

A smile lit up and softened her face every time she noted how her husband would spur impatiently ahead and then ride back again at a gallop to point out something they ought certainly not to miss. His slight, vibrant figure, impeccable in fine broadcloth set off with silver cord above the rich garters and stockings of Napolese silk, reassured her and confirmed her thoughts: he has a right to be proud of what he has achieved so far, and to feel optimistic about what lies ahead.

Beside her Mevrou de Stael spoke: 'If only Jan does not need to spoil his fine clothes again by having to embrace the greasy, sooty Hottentots!'

'Yet I should like to see the commander cutting capers with them,' Antjie quipped irreverently.

Mevrou de Stael's disapproving eye quickly changed the girls' suppressed laughter into hasty speculations about other possible dangers. Such as lions, for instance, or the hyena that was shot as recently as the Saturday before last. With stealthy glances and delicious tremors they observed the armed soldiers before and behind the wagon, and then asked whether they might get down and walk a bit. But their mothers refused curtly, and made them pull their skirts down even more decorously.

For the troops and foot soldiers, mostly young and unmarried, it was also an out-of-the-ordinary day. One of them, Elbert Dirksen, had such goggling calf's eyes for the elder of the two Does maidens, the sixteen-year-old Christina, that his mates began to chaff him, till the corporal sent him ahead to roll rocks out of the road.

Whenever they paused to give the beasts a breather and allow the men a draw at their pipes, Christina was blushing with crimson cheeks. The worst part was the teasing of the mischievous Cornelia who was no older than she and would be marrying the second gardener in four months' time. Even the commander's wife had to lean over and, under the pretext of settling Petronella's headband, chide the girls, yet softly so that the menfolk shouldn't hear.

Noon was still far off when they came to the new lands close to the *ronde bos*. Here the soil was richer and the mountain even more beautiful, romantic and crenellated like a castle wall with deep, craggy battlements. At the little guardhouse everyone got off.

The commander immediately led the ladies off to view the wheat and tobacco fields within a sturdy paling. He drew attention to everything: the clover field where three men were making hay, the young apple and orange trees, the luxuriant Turkish and Roman beans, the full heavy ears of wheat which the harsh south-easter could never blast here in the shelter of the mountain.

'And all this has been accomplished in only six months. Just imagine what a number of industrious farmers could produce here,' he exclaimed enthusiastically and gestured with his Gouda pipe, that had long since gone out, to embrace the whole valley of the Liesbeek River.

'The honourable Company could really not do better than lay out permanent farms here.'

Beside him his wife nodded approvingly, but half distracted like the other women, enchanted by the splendour of the bushy landscape and the luxuriant golden corn below the mountain's flanks.

'Indeed, it is more beautiful even than in the fatherland,' one of them sighed dreamily – Janneke Boddys who had arrived at the Cape only recently.

'For the young children this is already their fatherland,' someone else said.

'Well now, I don't know,' Janneke objected, 'what about all the savage natives that ...' But her words were swallowed by the commander's laugh. The roguish and daring Cornelia had come from behind and placed her hands over his eyes as he was trying to relight his pipe, and in a high falsetto voice she now demanded that he should guess who it was otherwise he would remain 'blind-man's-buff'. The commander good-naturedly entered into the spirit of the prank.

Wherever they went the corporal and his six men followed at a short distance. Herry [leader Khoi/Hottentot band] and his treacherous minions were still skulking around here somewhere, near the Bush Hill, though, in truth, shivering with fear like a lady's lapdog whenever he saw a Dutchman, but a guilt-ridden Hottentot is also a dangerous one. When the girls kept straying off carelessly the corporal respectfully asked them please to keep close to the party.

It was Maria who finally persuaded her husband to return to the thatched watch-post, where Antjie Boom was expertly arranging the picnic luncheon. The two sentries had betimes gathered green branches and erected a cool shady bower against one of the turf-built walls. While the commander in his restless way was still supervising elsewhere and giving instructions, the women spread cloths, laid out the cutlery, and seated themselves serenely in the shade. Antjie die Boerin detracted somewhat from the genteel scene, by loosening her clothing and beginning to suckle her baby. Mevrou de Stael found it expedient to direct the sentries' attention to their duty of standing somewhat farther off to watch out for advancing hordes of Hottentots.

The portly Antjie looked after the men and sighed: 'The poor things, they do not see a baby every day.'

The women were so convulsed with laughter that quite a few dress fastenings had to be unobtrusively slackened.

The commander arrived at last and smiling at his wife he asked: 'Well, well, and are the ladies enjoying the day out?' Satisfied with the reply, he turned to the soldier who had come to stand ramrod stiff as a sentinel near him: 'No, no, Dirksen,' he said, 'go and relax: for you and the others today is also a holiday.'

'All men are as blind as moles,' the daughter of Janneke Boddys whispered to Christina, and was given a little pinch in reply.

Everything went merrily, except for a troublesome wasp that made Janneke sit rigid with tightly closed eyes while she asked repeatedly in a trembling voice: 'Is it still there?'

After the repast the commander led them higher up to see the mountain stream and the work of woodcutting in the forest.

It was hot: still, balmy warmth like the feel of a sleeper's skin. The young women were constantly running ahead, but the older women were slower, quieter and more sedate, as if the sight of the men's activity all around to tame the new rich earth made them realise more acutely that they were women and mothers of children.

The mountain stream whispered its soft urgency through the languid summer afternoon, and in the bush the doves cooed and the echoes of the axe strokes resounded from the nearby crags. Once some foresters passed close to them with two ponderous, straining oxen hauling a baulk of timber for the pier. Later on and higher up they were able to overlook the glorious landscape, far out to beyond the neck between Bush Hill and the mountain, where they could just descry tiny cattle grazing near the little brown hive-like huts of the Cape-men.

Jan van Riebeeck explained everything: where a mill to grind the wheat could be erected beside the stream, and which of the sturdy yellowwood trees they would try to preserve. His wife listened as attentively as possible but the faint smile hovering about her lips wavered at times to betray some trepidation, especially when the growth of trees began to draw in more densely and the close, dank odour of moss enfolded them.

'We've come far enough now, Jan,' she warned gently. 'See, the others are getting tired.'

But now a search had to be made for two of the girls who had strayed farther ahead, accompanied by one of the soldiers. The commander sent two others to call them back, and the women sat down to rest. Only poor

Mevrou de Stael remained standing in order to conceal a torn stocking beneath the stately tent of her dress.

A flower had been the cause of this interruption. The soldier, Elbert Dirksen, had told the girls about a waxen red flower growing just off the narrow track, and of course they had to go and examine it. Awkward and trembling he had plucked one for Christina and she scolded him for his vandalism. And then her younger sister had to run to a great yellowwood tree, after borrowing his knife, to carve out her name.

'This will remain here very, very long,' she said, pouting prettily, and proceeded to add the date: 5 December 1656.

Suddenly Christina gave a little scream. Framed in the wild foliage were two brown faces staring open-mouthed at her.

Elbert immediately reached for his flintlock, but the Hottentots laid down their bundles of spears and with expressions of crafty pleading made signs with their hands.

When the girls backed away the Hottentots emerged from the shrubbery, their mantles of oxhide draped proudly over their shoulders, and their necks and wrists glistening with copper circlets. They did not look at the soldier, only at the young girl. Then there was a thrashing in the bush where the blue tunics of more soldiers appeared, and suddenly one of the Hottentots began to stammer in broken Hollands: 'Why you drive us away?' And in hesitant, apprehensive pride he called again to the girls: 'Why you want to take our land?'

Then the two soldiers came up with levelled muskets, and he and his companion sprang round and vanished into the bush.

'Wh … what … why did he … talk so to me?' the girl stuttered.

'They often plague us like this, ever since we began the fields and the watch-posts here, but we only wish to raise food for ourselves …' Elbert began to explain.

But his fellow-soldiers laughed: 'Oh, forget the savage heathens. Eh, Christina, you lovely thing?' And boldly they wanted to touch her and Petronella. Giggling and coy, the two sisters warded off their eager hands and ran back to the little path where the others were waiting.

A little while later, after the girls had been thoroughly reprimanded by their mother, and the commander had praised the soldiers for not acting over-hastily, the stroll back to the guardhouse was resumed. No afternoon could possibly be more beautiful, and more soothingly evoke obliviousness to care.

When the shadow of the mountain began to lengthen Maria became restless to return to the fort where her youngest had been left in the sole care of a young slave girl. Antjie's sleeping infant, who had been carried a while by an embarrassed soldier, now also awoke protesting loudly.

Tired yet satisfied they all gathered by the wagon. But before they left, the commander celebrated the memorable day by distributing tobacco and broaching a small vat of Spanish wine. Those of the ladies who wished were given some, as also the male escort, who jubilantly proposed a rousing toast to this maiden journey of the ladies, the founders of the nation.

Finally the commander clapped his hands for silence and called: 'We're leaving now. Think well whether we've forgotten anything!'

Nobody had; only Christina looked perplexed for a moment as if she were trying to think.

Then a box was placed beside the wagon to enable the older women to ascend. The soldiers fell in again, and the procession started off lightheartedly from the *ronde bos,* back to the fort in Table Bay. In front rode Jan van Riebeeck, dapper and elegant as always on his horse that tomorrow would be drawing heavy loads again.

The trumpeter was among the infantry, and Antjie Boom asked him please to blow the rust from his throat. Which he proceeded to do with good heart. In this changed, contented yet somewhat subdued mood they fell to singing, one by one. Past the golden-crowned corn field and for long stretches of the peaceful road homeward the men and women sang, gay songs and sad ones, also the one they all remembered best: the national anthem, the 'Wilhelmus van Nassauwe'.

CHRIS BARNARD

Bush

Translated from the Afrikaans by Sharon Meyering; revised by André P Brink.

There is a kind of stillness that consists of more than just the absence of sound; a stillness without movement; a stillness that is almost death itself. The air is still, the leaves and grass are still, the birds are unbelievably still. In the afternoon when the women leave the mango pips and disappear amongst the trees, that is when the stillness comes. It is the hour without cicada – the lifeless hour when one begins to suspect that even the sun has become stuck somewhere.

It is in an hour like this that Kirst comes.

The hollow footpaths of the bush bring him here, over a hundred rivers and just as many plains – each river, each plain, each night's hyenas closer to a godforsaken moment. He approaches over the rock ledge where the women dry the mango pips in the morning, over the bright and hard yard; I hear his footsteps over the stones, see him climbing the wooden stairs of my high stoep, into the shadows. Then he stands between the pot plants and I wait for him to cross the threshold.

His face shines, presumably from sweat. He looks at me where I sit at the table, and perhaps I think that he has grown old. But I recognise him despite this. I have already recognised his footsteps.

'Good day, Kirst,' I say.

Or perhaps we don't speak. Kirst says nothing either way. I hear him approaching and wait for him, as I have waited for him all these years. Yes, my heart thumps in my chest, and there is a warm feeling on my tongue; but that is all that has changed. I don't move. I do not try to escape. My eyes are fixed on the door and I wait for him. He appears – his face wet with sweat. That's right: his face shines with sweat. He says nothing and I say nothing.

It's dead simple.

Perhaps even the same revolver; a small black Beretta with a snub nose. He trains it on me and I take my pipe out of my mouth and put it down on the table.

Is he swaying slightly on his feet? Or is it I moving to and fro? Initially,

I can't decide. Only later do I realise what is wrong: it is my head; I am shaking my head. Maybe I am trying to say: 'No, Kirst, not after all these years!' Or maybe there is something inside me that merely wants to say how terribly old he's become.

But it's not I who eventually speaks; it's Kirst who says, 'It's you ...'

How well I remember you, Kirst! For almost an entire lifetime, day in and day out, I have been breaking down and building up your face, piece by piece: the broad forehead under windblown hair, brown eyes that probe everything, sharp cheekbones and a full, manly mouth and square chin. But now? What is this, Kirst? What is this wrinkled forehead, thin hair, hollow cheeks with stubble, this toothless raisin mouth? Only the skull is unmistakably you.

You cross the threshold and see me and say, 'It's you ...' as if you believed, until this very moment, that all your searching for me would turn up nothing.

If you are surprised to see me sitting here, Kirst, it is probably because I haven't stayed the same either: for almost a lifetime you searched for a young and inexperienced man, and now that you have caught up with him ...

It would be inappropriate to offer you something to drink. And I dare not ask about your wellbeing.

Talk about myself? What can I say? That I was expecting you? That I am glad you came?

There is, however, something we could speak much about. Loneliness. But then again your loneliness and mine were never the same. Mine was that of someone waiting for his punishment; yours, that of someone who had punishment to inflict. Self-pity and hate. But perhaps they are the same thing.

I think about it, every day. And of all the places in Africa where I noticed you on a street corner, or in a bar, alongside a quay, on a river boat, by a customs house, in a lodge. But every time I was disappointed that it was not really you.

On a godforsaken town square in Zanzibar I see a man with his shoulders. And it is him. After all these years it is him. And he turns and sees me and walks towards me. And I wait for him, wait for his hand to move to his pocket, wait for the small Beretta and the white knuckles. But the man with Kirst's shoulders walks past, bored, and doesn't see me.

In a sultry hotel room in Luanda, a room with cockroaches and cracks in the wall, someone comes slowly up the stairs. I recognise Kirst's footsteps. I wait. Know, at long last, now. But he passes by; his footfalls disappear down the passage.

Somewhere in the Karoo, on a cold station where I wait between the milk cans for the next train, he appears suddenly out of the signal room. He has a flag in his hand, but his flag and tattered uniform do not fool me. I recognise his nose and high forehead. He comes closer in the dusk, very slowly. And I wait. I know: if he stands beside me, the Beretta will appear under the flag and he will lift the barrel and a blue flame will burst out into the dusk. He stands near me, for more than a quarter of an hour; and the train comes and I climb in without him noticing me.

In front of the post office in Mbabane, between the dead fish at the market in Beira, suddenly on an afternoon, some distance behind me between the silver trees near Seinheuwel, on the open deck that night on Lake Victoria en route to Muhutwe, in Swakopmund, Coquilhatville, even in Ibadan the last summer before I came here.

And since I came here, I have been expecting him.

I stand among the banana trees and watch two bantams scratching in the dusty backyard under a small, withered lemon tree. The afternoon sun shivers against the white kitchen wall and the bougainvillea is a feverish purple dance against the steel-grey sky. And suddenly he stands in the footpath that leads up from the river, the sweat silvery in his eyebrows.

It is different from what I expected it to be.

All these years had made me resign myself to the idea of his ultimate coming. I thought I would remain dead still if I saw him; I wouldn't move, wouldn't run.

But the fear is suddenly in me and as terrible as the sun. He stands there, weary and dishevelled, much older than I expected.

His hand moves towards his pocket and I know it is so he can take out the Beretta, but my hand comes up to my face and I want to say: 'Wait, Kirst – wait first!' Yet I say nothing. My throat is bone dry and no sound escapes; nothing. It is he who speaks first; Kirst says, 'It's you …'

You probably already know for yourself: one's memory, when one gets older, loses its sharpness. You have discovered this? And nevertheless, I hesitate to ask – you might think it is a ploy to try and prove my innocence. Like a naïve child who kills a cat and then faces his mother, whistling, with angelic eyes when she comes to punish him.

No, Kirst. I ask for nothing. I might not even try to hide my fear. I must only look at you. And wait.

Yet: it would actually be easier, wouldn't it? If I could just remember?

Strange, and maybe a bit comical, that for some reason or other one starts running, and becomes compelled to keep running, focusing one's whole life on running, abandoning oneself completely and utterly to the chase – so totally that in the process one forgets the cause of it all.

That is not important. I know. What is important is that you came, at last you have finally caught up with me.

It's late afternoon and the reeds stand motionless in the lazy river. I kneel barefoot among the round stones, scoop up the tepid water with cupped hands, rinse the soap from my face and shoulders and chest. The foam dams up around my pale knees, comes free and disappears on either side of my calves. Drops of water cling between my eyelashes and in these drops the sun sets, a thorn tree squats lopsided on the riverbank, a reed stem pricks the green evening sky. And, suddenly, close to the sun, between the trees and reeds, he stands motionless looking at me.

I close my eyes. But his image remains. Through my red eyelids I see him standing, watching, his face expressionless, his arms slack against his body – only one hand slightly more alert than the other.

He looks at my naked body as if looking at a rock. And I suddenly remember what I look like. The chest muscles already limp, the shoulder bones much more prominent these days, the elbows sharper, the thighs whiter and skinnier, the veins on my hands bluer.

You could have spared me this, Kirst! This naked moment.

But even this, I fear, is of less importance now. And I struggle to stand up, step awkwardly between the round and dark stones. I stand erect before you in the water and my hands grope humiliated over my shapeless genitals.

God, was this really necessary? On top of everything *this* moment of complete defencelessness? Since your childhood you have been merciless, Kirst – very thorough and frighteningly precise.

So this is the moment, I take it.

Don't laugh, but all of a sudden I remember a strange finger on a map of Africa. How many different nights did I send it out on safari, bored, a small divining rod searching for water that suddenly stops triumphant over Angola or the Sudan and says: Kirst is here tonight.

And sometimes, less triumphant, more tired, mostly in the tepid and smothering heat of the summer, bent over an increasingly crumpled continent, the embittered prayer: I give up; I don't want to play any more.

In the white lamplight, the night an unspoken word outside, the night sweet about the ferns and bats, I suddenly know it is him at the window. And I look up and see his lonely figure, slightly unsure under his hat.

He comes out of the wet night. While I stand and wait in front of the window for the small gecko to come for his grain of sugar, the lightning flashes quickly, almost invisible behind the rain. But the fleeting moment is enough to recognise him: he stands watching the house, tired, in his dark raincoat.

Where the women dry their brown mango pips in the sun every day between the dark trees, the first light rosy against the bunches of frangipanis, he suddenly appears.

He doesn't know that I see him. Or perhaps he knows. But he stands a long time, looking. He is waiting.

And I watch him while he waits. I don't know if I am afraid. I only know that this is entirely different from what I imagined. Nothing in this moment is out of the ordinary. It is merely daybreak and he is standing in the yard.

Then, much later, he moves, I see his hand disappear into his trouser pocket. And it stays there. And in the backyard, half-heartedly, I hear the bantam crow. And he comes across the yard from the trees.

The morning smells of damp earth, of autumn grass, of plover eggs.

The morning smells of Africa, Kirst.

And I see you coming. I see you approaching slowly over the dry gravel. And the wooden stairs creak as you ascend, at your leisure, without haste, not at all afraid.

I don't look at your trouser pocket, although I want to. No, I look at your eyes; I search for your eyes – because, God, you've grown old, Kirst! Entirely too old.

Entirely too old.

And I say, without meaning to: 'Good day, Kirst.'

And he says, 'It's you …'

KAREL SCHOEMAN

Seed in a New Earth

Translated from the Afrikaans by Wallie Smuts.

It was in 1905 that my grandfather came to Bloemfontein with his wife and children – a Dutch teacher who had accepted a post here and so emigrated to the Orange River Colony. Dominee Postma met them at the station, and for a time they stayed at the parsonage.

My grandfather was soon wholly caught up in the work of the newly-founded school and in various activities of a language-and-politics nature, where he strove with characteristic Dutch energy and intransigence; but his wife stayed at home, and for her there was no escape from each day's reality. They already had two little girls, and soon after their arrival in Bloemfontein a third was born. They had little money, and she toiled alone without the help of servants in one rented house after another – from Blignault Street they moved to Grey Street, from Grey Street to Victoria Road, from Victoria Road to Charles Street, from Charles Street to St John Street, from St John Street to Cromwell Road and back again. That was her life; packing and unpacking, irons heating on the stove, bread being kneaded in the kneading pail; grime in the bath, dishwashing, darning, scrubbing the floors; food to be cooked, and clothes that had to be made, so that the children, when in bed at night, were lulled to sleep by the soothing whirr of her sewing machine.

The baby that came soon after their arrival did not live long, and she sat before the window, pregnant for the fourth time, and watched as her husband left in a hired cab, with the little coffin on his knees, away up the long, straight road, under the summer sun, past the last few scattered houses and bluegum trees to the cemetery in the veld.

When the burial was over he returned alone to the house leaving his child in the strange earth, the soil of the new land. Alone in the silence of the day, scorched by the sun, where a bird called somewhere in distant trees and the veld stretched bleakly away to the horizon, alone with no shadow before him on the dust of the road; and from the top of the little rise he saw again the town with its orange roofs and brick walls among the green pepper trees and karees, cypresses and pines, a tiny oasis in the vastness of the veld. He drove on down the slope, his child left behind in this earth: down to the long shadow of the bluegums, streets with carriages and horses, houses with open front doors, and children playing; over the market square and past the church back home.

It had always been a country town, nothing more, a simple place with long straight streets and rows of unpretentious houses sheltered from the sun by scattered trees. At Nagmaal – the Communion services – the farmers came and pitched camp with their wagons and tents, and market days brought a bustle to the square, but nothing else disturbed the tranquillity, only the wind soughing through the leaves, and a driver calling to his oxen somewhere down the street. And the eddying dust settled again.

The war came; the enemy's soldiery, travel-worn from their long advance through the summer, marched into Bloemfontein, and the English took over. The people of the land stayed on in their little 'church' dwellings, shaded by pepper trees; they came from the country districts in their horse-drawn carts, sun-bonneted women and bearded men. They passed the long days, and went to church on Sundays with Bible and hymn book; they thought of their lost ones, and in the evenings they gathered by lamp or candlelight, their rare utterances dropping into the great silence.

The silence enclosed them and swallowed up their last dismayed words. The land with its distant horizons and lofty sky, the land with its blockhouses and scattered ruins had passed into the power of strangers, and in this town a strange flag waved from the flagpoles and outlandish uniforms moved on the streets.

The rulers were foreigners who possessed the land, though it could never have a claim on them; they governed it, but never had any love for it. They had come to the colony as strangers, and as strangers they left it. Their stay was merely a temporary exile which could wring no concession from them, and their lives in this foreign clime consisted of a series of gestures and conventions that bore no relation to reality, but which was at the same time very gracious, so gracious that the years of the occupation were perhaps also the golden years of the town's history.

It remained a little town, nothing more, with peaceful streets and dogs and children playing; at dusk the cows were brought in from their grazing on the commonage, and each one took her own way home to be milked. The status of capital rested somewhat uneasily on this simple rural community, what with the presence of a Lieutenant-Governor and garrison, government offices, high court of justice and cathedral; but the people who came to sojourn here were little concerned with the harsher facts of their existence.

They have all long since left, or have died, but their memory has lingered like an aroma, and one still unexpectedly comes across faint reminders of their tenure. They dwelt in great brick houses with gables and turrets and wide stoeps; they lived in shaded rooms filled with furniture and ornaments. Behind the dim green of spreading creepers they gathered in the coolness round their tea-tables, under masses of wistaria and pergolas glowing with roses, under acacias where the bees buzzed in the cloying sweetness of the blooms. Scent of flowers and smell of dust in the heat of summer, with men in light suits and women trying to dispel the heat with their fans. The land sweltered in the sun, with shadows dark beneath the trees, and no motion in the leaves. In the distance Bantu women called to each other and then the sound was lost again in the silence; only the woman in the rocking chair moved gently to and fro as she looked out at the green of the garden and the blinding glare of the street beyond.

A vehicle would pass – buggy, spider, cab – with the beat of hoofs muffled in the dust, and then the street was empty again, empty and straight with its rows of houses, and rows of shops, and nothing at all moved until the wind breathed, making the flag before the city hall stir lazily. Dusty streets and brick houses and pepper trees and corrugated iron hoardings; a dog asleep in the shade, a shopkeeper standing in his doorway. Slowly the shadows lengthened, and the civil servants drank their whisky while, from the veranda of the Club, they watched the colour changes wrought by the late afternoon, the dust clouds bright gold in the last declining light. It became cooler, and the man in shirtsleeves, watering his garden, heard the drops from his watering can rustle over the banked flowers.

Periodicals were paged through, meals planned; tables were laid and innumerable bits of bric-a-brac dusted; servants polished stoeps and rubbed the harness bright. Invitations were sent out and accepted, newspapers unfolded, letters written. A woman stepped across the street under her parasol, the hem of her dress slightly raised, and the dust retained the narrow pointed impressions of her shoes. People gathered for races, gymkhanas, and parades, and when the orchestra played in the park they came to saunter over the lawns, and far under the trees, to the measure of the music; they went to the theatre, and dined with each other, little enclaves in the gentle intimacy of the lamplight, with a toast to the Queen at the end of the meal. They played cards, they listened to music. The nights were oppressive and dark and hot, with little night creatures that called in the silence, and the fragrance of roses lying heavy on the air. On the tables brightly polished crystal caught the light, glittering and translucent.

In the details of old photographs and the finely printed columns of the newspapers you can rediscover their world, their gestures and voices caught and fixed for all time – the bend of an arm, the sweep of a train;

the hand raised, the head turned – and from reports of weddings and receptions, the guest-lists, names and colours of dress materials, and all the incidental detail, one can recapture the texture of their lives. The carriages assembled, gentlemen helped the ladies alight for the social gatherings that brought variety to the long uneventful days ('the bride, who looked charming, was attired in purest white crepe de Chine'), and they paused to exchange greetings and bows, and chat in bright clear voices, the men in dark suits or morning coats, glossy top hat in hand, and the women brilliant as flowers. ('The bride's mother wore a pretty reseda green gown and white toque, trimmed with pink roses and reseda green velvet.') Everyone knew everyone else, and each one had his place in the hierarchy of this outpost: Lieutenant-Governor, clerics, justiciaries, the military, and the civil service officials – a tightly integrated band, a small garrison for foreign service ('the sergt-majors and others of the regiment formed up outside the porch of the cathedral and formed an arch with their swords, under which the happy bride and bridegroom repaired to their carriage'). No doubt or fear disturbed their self-assurance, and there were no threats to set the security of their little world aquiver. Bolstered by pride, prestige, wealth ('Mr and Mrs Fawkes, silver inkstand; Mr Sennett, card stand') they bowed and took their leave, returned in their equipages to the great, over-furnished houses ('Sir Andries and Lady Maasdorp, silver card case'), and carried on ('Mr and Mrs GA Hill, set of bon-bon dishes'), day after day, performing the ritual gestures, until the exile finally ended, and freedom returned. Then they departed, and their going held no pain or loss.

Just as they, my grandmother never gave her love to the land, and she too remained a stranger and an uitlander. She was Dutch like her husband: as a child she had come to Rotterdam with her parents, and lived there till she was thirty, near the cattle market where the pigs were dragged squealing by their tails from the carts, in the city where wagons and carriages clattered over the cobbles and the harbour was full of foreign ships. She had minded children and knitted stockings and scrubbed the doorsteps; from the water channels in the park they had gathered duckweed for their goldfish. She became a teacher, and had met my grandfather during a vacation, one summer in the green rusticity of Oosterbeek.

She had followed her fiancé to South Africa just before the war broke out, and they were married in Pretoria. One Sunday morning they had walked down Church Street, and seen the old president sitting on his stoep. They stayed on a farm for a while where my grandfather taught at the school, until the war broke out. He was taken away by the English as prisoner of war, and she, ill with malaria, had remained behind when everyone else fled. The farm buildings were burnt down, and for days the smoke pall hung in the air.

The war came to an end; children were born; they came to Bloemfontein and settled there. Life went on. The bread rose under the blanket with its lion design, white sheets on the line billowed in the wind; on Sundays they went to church. With the years came acquiescence, but nothing more.

This land does not ask to be loved, neither does it try to command love: it is just there, to be accepted or not, without any dependence on man, its starkness unrelieved by the chance beauty of mountain or forest. It is just there – the flat, monotonous land, vast under the sun, with its profound silence and its remote distances, far-away hills hazy in the heat, the wind in the long grass and the dry scent of the afternoon; thorn trees, a rare road, an arching heaven – what else can one say of it? An aloof, detached land that asks no love, but when love has once been given it is given irrevocably, and nothing else matters, nothing else worth loving remains.

Her love she never gave. From the line where she hung her washing, from the kitchen door where she paused with a dishcloth in her hand, she could see the veld stretching beyond the last bluegum trees with the clear horizon etched against the sky. She heard the bird calling in the distance and the wind that stirred the leaves; she saw the clouds gather sparkling white in the sky, and she turned her back on them to go inside. The land remained alien to her, and the people with their flat intonations and long silences were not her people.

Like the English colonials she remained a stranger and an uitlander, and who can blame her? For like them she had her memories: the high-stacked greyness of a city, misty mornings and the tenderness of the light, parks and trams and trains, and voices calling in another, a familiar language; a cool, damp atmosphere, and mud-trampled streets after the thaw set in; Spangen and Kralingen and the Bergsche Plassen, Delfshaven, Waalhaven and Katendrecht. She never succeeded, as her husband had done, in freeing herself of the world into which she had been born, and she never attempted to do so.

Yet, even though, cherishing all these memories, she remained a stranger, she was not like the soldiers and the officials. She never gave her heart to this land, but she did give her life, more than fifty years long; she gave her loneliness, her homesickness and longing for what had been, and which she had now yielded up for ever; and so this land, after all, became hers too, and not as it was with the English colonials.

Wounds heal with time, but the scars remain. As time passed the sharpness of her longing became dulled – her children married and grandchildren were born – but she retained her memories and the heartache lessened very slowly. She was a silent, withdrawn woman, with little weakness or self-pity, and she did not complain. As a child I often heard her speak of Holland, but the things she told were merely stories to me, and I never realised the actuality all these things held for her. So she bore them around within herself, dwelling solitarily in that past from which she stemmed.

Wounds heal and grief gradually passes, until even their memory is finally erased. In a later war Rotterdam was levelled from the air, street after street destroyed, and house after house razed to the ground, all the familiar landmarks blotted out. Oosterbeek was also ravaged by great fires, and the trees that had shaded and made green the days were all consumed. My grandmother died when she was well in her eighties, and her husband died a few days later. In Bloemfontein, too, old houses have been pulled down and old trees felled: what remains is forlorn, neither town nor city, with the earlier graciousness gone, and only an awkward attempt at modernity to replace it. The dust has not retained the track of the foot; the glass has slipped, fallen, and lies shattered on the ground. The pressed flower has not kept its sweetness, and old paper has become yellow and fragile. She is dead, and the silence has finally enfolded her.

I knew her as a child, but I did not know then how desperately lonely one can be in a strange land, how nostalgia for the things that have been part of you can grow to be a physical pain. Long, long after her death did I get some inkling of what her exile must have cost her, and what never-ceasing longing she must have endured in a strange land for fifty years; and then, in this single facet of her life, I realised how, in an accumulation of individual lives, a new country and people originate, a new nation is born. It is not easy for seed to germinate, to burst its sheath in the darkness of strange soil. Only in the second or third generation does the plant grow to maturity, the roots reaching deep and wide into that new earth.

NADINE GORDIMER

The Credibility Gap

'You go.'

'No, it'll be for you.'

The timid ring of the front doorbell or the two-syllable call of the telephone produced the same moment of obstinacy: everyone appeared to be going on with what he was doing. The young brother continued to hammer away somewhere. The elder, if it so happened that he was in the house, absolved himself because he now had his own flat with his own front door and telephone. A house guest – there was usually someone who had nowhere else to live – didn't feel it was his or her place to get up. The mother knew it wouldn't be for her. It was for the daughter, inevitably, since she was in one of the expanding periods of life when one moves through and with the zest and restlessness of the shoal. But often there were reasons why she did not want to respond without an intermediary: the complex social pattern meant that she was supposed to be out when she was in, or in when she was out.

You go. It'll be for you.

The schoolboy Rob took no notice, anyway. The cats were disturbed by anyone leaving a room or entering; they lifted back their heads from bodies relaxed to tiger-skin flatness before the fire, and opened their eyes. Pattie's casual, large-footed friends trod into flowered saucers scummed with disdained milk that stood about all over the place. Cats and saucers were the mother's – old-maidish possessions that could be allowed a woman who, if she had no husband by now, had among other things the contrary testimony of children grown and half-grown who were half-bother and -sister. Pattie never thought of her mother when she was alone with friends her own age, but sometimes when she and the friends and her mother were drinking beer and arguing in the living room at home she would have an impulse the converse of that of the parent to show off its child. 'Don't tease her about her cats. It's her passion for cats that got her out of solitary confinement when she was in jug. Honestly. She was supposed to be in solitary for leading a hunger strike among the political prisoners, but the chief wardress was as dotty about cats as she is, and they were such buddies discussing their dear little kitties, the old girl used to let her out secretly to sit in the prison yard. It's true.'

Yes, there once had been a ring at the door in the dark early hours of the morning that was for Mrs Doris Aucamp. Years ago, when the children really were still children, and there still were real political opposition movements in South Africa. The two elder children – Andrew and Pattie – at least, remembered something of that time; someone had moved into the house to take care of them, and they had been set up on the Johannesburg City Hall steps one Saturday among the families of other political prisoners, wearing placards round their necks: WE WANT OUR MUMMY BACK. Most of the friends drinking beer in the living-room and discussing the authoritarianism of the university system or the authenticity of the sense-experience known as getting stoned had heard about the massacre of Sharpeville – if from no other source, then from references to it that came up in overseas magazines; one of the boys, studying abroad, had even discovered that in New York there was a commemorative rally at Carnegie Hall on the anniversary of 'Sharpeville Day', held by South Africans in exile. It was with quite a momentary thrill of admiring curiosity that they realised that this woman – somebody's mother – had actually served a prison sentence for what she believed (of course, what they *all* believed) about the idiocy of the colour bar. It both added to and detracted from the aura of those among them who now and then were moved to defy minor-sounding laws against marching the streets or assembling for protest: so these 'activists' were not the discoverers that danger, in some times and places, is the only form of freedom? They had only dug up, afresh, to offend the docile snouts of the population, what the major punishments of those minor-sounding transgressions had forced people to bury, and forget where.

This woman wasn't bad, either, in spite of her age, not bad at all. There was at least one of the young men who wouldn't have minded indulging a kind of romantic lust in response to that mature sexuality, confidently lived with for a lifetime, vested in her blunt, nicotine-tanned hands as she stirred her tea and the turn towards the table of those rather big breasts, sloping away from each other a bit like an African woman's bubs – she was a short, broad woman with nice, nine-pin calves, too wide in the hip ever to wear trousers. Mrs Doris Aucamp caught the look and was smiling at him, not taking it up but not offended – kindly amused: of course, as well as having been a jailbird, she was also a writer. He hadn't read her; but it was a well-known name.

* * *

I'll go – it's for me.

There were times when Pattie leapt up because she had the instinct that some irreparable usurpation would take place if anyone other than herself were to open the door upon the face she expected, or respond with a voice other than hers to the summons of the telephone. A word of criticism of one of her friends roused a fierce solidarity. 'Oh Kip's not what you think at all. People get it all wrong. People just don't understand. He wouldn't trust anyone else. You have to be one of us.'

Her mother slapped down a cat who was trying to filch off a plate. 'Of course. Every set of friends has private dependencies that make it hang together. Why do I put up with Scoresby? Why do any of his pals?' The man she spoke of was a long-time friend, long-time alcoholic.

Rob was finely paring the wart on the inner side of his third finger, right hand. He looked up a moment, saw that man, who sometimes played chess with him, lying as he had once found him in a lumpy pool of pink vomit in the bathroom. He turned the blade towards his finger once more; everyone told him it was dangerous to cut warts, but he was getting rid of his by persistently slicing them away, right down to the healthy flesh, without squeamishness.

'It's not that so much. I mean, you think it's peculiar because I bring someone home and don't know his surname – even if we don't know each other personally, *we know* –'

'But you don't really think it's a matter of age? There're people under thirty you couldn't trust as far as I could throw this greedy, shameless cat – mmh?'

'No – I'm sorry – in some ways *you* just can't –'

Her mother nodded her head as if in sympathy for some disability. 'You know what Lévi-Strauss says? Something, something "...as man moves forward he takes with him all positions he's occupied in the past and all those he'll occupy in the future." Wait, I'll get it.' They heard her running upstairs; padding down more slowly, probably leafing through the book on the way. She stood behind her daughter, silently following the passage over the girl's shoulder. *As he moves forward within his environment, Man takes with him all the positions that he has occupied in the past, and all those that he will occupy in the future. He is everywhere at the same time, a crowd which, in the act of moving forward, yet recapitulates at every instant every step that it has ever taken in the past.*

The girl put the book down; the two of them looked into each other, but it became purely a moment of physical comprehension: Pattie saw that the skin of her mother's forehead would never have the shine of tautness again, the mother saw that little scars of adolescent turmoil had left their imperfections on the slightly sulky jawline that attracted men.

* * *

No – it's all right, I'll go. I'm expecting a friend.

Some of the girls feared themselves pregnant, one or two had had abortions, and there were even beginning to be a few contemporaries who got married and furnished flats. Pattie knew that if she became pregnant, her mother could deal with the situation; on the other hand, if she got married and bought furniture, well, that was all right, too.

'Isn't there anything else?'

Her mother was putting flea powder on the cats: Liz and Burton, Snorer, and the mother cat of all three, Puss. Snorer's name was really Schnorrer, dubbed for his greedy persistence at table by the Jewish professor who – the girl understood, looking back at things she hadn't known how to interpret then – had been her mother's lover for a time. Dolly, the black servant, had heard the name as Snorer; and so it had become that, just as the professor was now become a family friend, like Scoresby, only less troublesome.

'No. You meet them years later and they tell you their son is married, their daughter's engaged. All smiles, big surprise.'

'Except you. You count yourself outside.' The girl had trudged the summer through in a pair of Greek sandals whose soles had worn away completely beneath each big toe. She was examining with respect these alien, honest, workmanlike extremities of herself, thickened, ingrained with city dirt round the broken nails, assertive as the mechanic's black-ringed fingernails that can never be scrubbed to deny their toil. After a pause: 'People say that story you wrote was about me.'

'Which story?'

'The one about the donkey.'

'It wasn't about you, it was about me.'

'But I saved up for a donkey?'

'Never. It was something I told you about myself.'

* * *

You go.

No, you.

Rob did not know that Snorer was not the cat's name any more than he knew that Julius, the professor, had not always been an old family friend. He didn't answer the phone because he was not yet interested in girls, and his boy friends used the kitchen door, coming tramping in past Dolly without knocking. Dolly's man repaired bicycles on the pavement outside the local hardware shop, and she treated the boys like the potential good customers they were, sycophantically addressing them as 'My baasie', 'Master' Johnny or Dick, although her employer didn't allow her to corrupt the young people of the house in this way into thinking themselves little white lordlings. '"Master" my eye! Really, Dolly! You should be putting them across your knee and warming their behinds. Nothing's ever going to change for the blacks, here, until people like you understand that nobody's born "master", never mind white kids in short pants.' But Dolly was unresponsive, for another reason. She resented having been given, with equal forthrightness, an ultimatum about closing her backyard trade in beer.

When the children of the house were small the front door had opened often upon black faces. The children had sat on the knees and laughed at the jokes of black men and women who were their mother's friends and political associates. Pattie remembered some of them quite well; where was so-and-so now, she would sometimes remark; what happened to so-and-so? But all were in exile or prison. She had tentatively, through her own student set, a different sort of association. The political movements were dead, the university was closed to black students, but there were Africans, usually musicians, with whom was shared the free-for-all of jazz, the suspension from reality in the smoke of the weed – white hangers-on, black hangers-on, there: it depended whose world you decided it was. She even went once or twice on a jaunt to one of the black states over the border, and there met Africans who were not creatures of the night but students, like herself.

'If I fall for a black one, how would we manage?'

'You must leave the country.' Before the mother or anyone else could answer, Rob had spoken.

He put down the coloured supplement on vintage cars he was studying. His gaze was hidden under lowered lids, but his head was slightly inclined to the polarity of his mother as she sat, a cigarette comfortably between her stained first and third fingers, her square-jawed, sunburned face looking on with a turned-down neutral smile. They were waiting for her to speak, but she said nothing. At last she put out her hand and passed it again and again through the boy's hair, firmly, as the cats loved to be raked along the fur of their backs.

'There's a nice, God-fearing guardian of the white race growing up.' Andrew had dropped in to pick up his allowance; he addressed the room after his younger brother had left it.

Mrs Doris Aucamp remained serenely in her silence; as her Professor Julius had once remarked, she could turn bullets to water. She irritated her elder son by giving him the brief, head-tilted, warm glance, old childish balm for sibling fears of favoured dispensation granted the last-born.

'Sorry, no dice, my little brother doesn't think we should do it.' Pattie was amused. 'Poor kid.'

'A man once gave me up because I didn't know the boiling point of water.' But the elder son didn't accept his mother's diversion of subject; in his turn, did not appear to hear.

'Fahrenheit or centigrade?' A Peace Corps girl from Uganda, in the house for the time being, was eager to show herself to be on the family wavelength.

'Neither. I'm sure that was it. Couldn't get over it. Thought he'd found a real intellectual to appreciate him, and then discovers she doesn't even know a thing like that.'

'Black or white?' Pattie asked.

There was laughter. 'Oh he was white, *very* white.'

When the two of them were alone together, the daughter returned to the subject. She did not know, for sure, of anyone since Julius. 'When you were young? The man with the boiling water?'

'Oh no, only a few years ago.'

The girl was looking for a number in the telephone directory. She covered her silence by saying kindly, politely, 'What is the boiling point of water, anyway? I've forgotten.'

'Oh I found out quickly enough. Two-hundred-and-twelve Fahrenheit.' Mrs Doris Aucamp had the smoker's laugh that turns to coughing.

The number Pattie tried was busy. Resting on the receiver fingers wearing as many rings as a Renaissance pope, she said of her little brother, 'It's just that he wants God-to-keep-his-hand-over-us.'

'Of course.' The expression was a family one, derived from a grandmother who mistook superstition for piety.

'Poor little devil.' The girl spoke dreamily.

* * *

You go. Go on. It'll never be for me.

When their mother was out, no one – certainly not Dolly – would answer the bell for Pattie. One afternoon it was a student friend standing there, come to tell her one of their friends had been killed. He and some others had been climbing with the girl the day before on a Sunday picnic, and she had slipped and fallen before their eyes. They picked her up fifteen minutes later at the bottom of a waterfall, her neck broken.

Mrs Doris Aucamp was waylaid by Dolly as she got out of the car in the garage. She thought for a moment Dolly had been drinking again, but it was not drink that widened her nostrils with drama but the instinct of all servants to enter swiftly into those fearful emotions that they can share with employers, because there, down among death and disaster, there are no privileges or exemptions to be claimed by anyone.

'The friend with the big eyes. The one that always laugh – that Kathy. She's die. It's true.' A big shuddering sigh took the black woman by the throat.

In the doorway of the living room the mother stood before her daughter and the young man, two faces for which there was no expression to meet the fact of death. They merely looked ashamed. There were tins of beer and cigarettes about. Their eyes were upon her, waiting.

She must have a face for this, of course.

But she stood, with the cats winding themselves about her calves. She said, 'Oh *no*?' People said that in books they had all read or films they'd seen. Then she saw the untidy hair and rosy nose of her daughter, alive, and, hand over her open mouth a moment, emotion came for what hadn't happened just as if it had: it could have been this one, mine. There was no face to meet that at the door.

The three of them sat drinking beer, breaking the awkward silences by repeating small certainties left by the girl who had died. 'She was here for supper last week. Didn't she forget a raincoat?'

'It's behind the door in my room. I noticed it this morning. It smells of her –'

'She always looked just like that when she was asleep. Honestly, it was just the same. Limp. Soft.' The young man himself looked afraid; sleeping with her, making love to her, then, he had been holding death in his arms.

He was a witty young man whose instincts were always to puncture the hot air of a distrusted solemnity. As the talk drifted away from the dead girl, tugged back to her, away again, he dashed off one of his wry mimicries of someone, and they found themselves laughing a little, slightly drunk by now, anyway. There was a closeness between them, a complicity of generations.

It had grown dark. Mrs Doris Aucamp got up to pull the curtains and wandered off upstairs by way of the kitchen, telling Dolly there would be an extra mouth at dinner. And then she met her younger son; he was repairing Dolly's radio. 'I wish my darned sister would leave my things alone. I look all over the house for my small pliers, and where are they? Lying around in the mess in her room, of course.'

'Well, don't make a fuss now. You see, darling, Kathy –'

'I heard about it.'

'It isn't the time. She's upset.'

There were shiny patches on his thin, dirty fingers where the warts had been pared away. The patches were watermarked, like moiré, in a design of whorls unique to him out of all the millions of human beings in the world. He was carefully, exasperatedly scraping the insulation tape from wire. He lifted his face and the preoccupation fell away. He said, 'She wasn't crying at all. She and Davy were yapping in there, quite ordinary. And then when one of her girl friends phoned she started to make herself cry over the phone, she put it on.' His face was without malice, clear, open, waiting.

His mother said, 'I wanted to cry – for a moment.'

He asked, 'Did you believe in it?'

'What?'

He gave a little jerk to his shoulder. '*It* ... I mean, you didn't see that girl lying dead.'

'Davy did.' She searched his eyes to see if the explanation was one.

He said nothing.

She said, hesitantly, 'Davy says she was the same as when she was asleep. It didn't seem she was dead.'

He nodded his head: *you see* – in the manner of one who accepts that no one will have an explanation for him.

This time she did not put out her hand to touch him. She wandered back into the dark hall of the house, her bent head making a double chin; the followers of those African prophets who claimed bullets could be turned to water had, after all, fallen everywhere on battlefields, from the Cape to Madagascar.

PART THREE

1970-1990

HENNIE AUCAMP

The Coat without End

(For Percy and Clara Gersholowitz)

Translated from the Afrikaans by Ian Ferguson.

I must say at once, the source of my story is not *The Overcoat* although all stories about clothing have been, ever since Gogol wrote that one, automatically related to his masterly story. Some variations are, like Wolf Mankowitz's *The Bespoke Overcoat*, close family to Gogol's tale.

What makes my assurances suspect is that my story has a Jewish flavour with a pinch of Russian mysticism if you take into account Miriam's eventful youth in Russia. But truly, as I tell it to you so it happened, here in Cape Town and, to be specific, in Vredehoek where the wind always roars down.

Actually, my story really begins in Ireland.

Jacob Lipschitz of Cape Town went there to further his studies in medicine even though he was an established family man. In Ireland, note, where it can get terribly cold. He and his wife, Miriam, consulted each other, concluding that a custom-made tweed coat would be a good investment since they would have to survive three Irish winters.

Now to the appearance of the coat: it is a short coat, one could say, more of a jacket or, rather, a three-quarter coat. In any case, it is made of heavy herringbone tweed, fully lined with black satin. It has a collar that can be pulled up against the wind, deep pockets and a broad belt made of the same tweed. At that time it cost an arm and a leg to have that sort of coat tailored; today only the very rich can consider having such a coat custom made.

That coat saw its owner through three cruel Irish winters; heavy enough to keep out arctic winds. But for Cape Town it was, alas, too heavy.

Even in Vredehoek where the wind slices down from Devil's Peak was it seldom cold enough to wear the Irish tweed coat and Jacob stored it in a wardrobe in the spare room. Miriam, always provident, put soap in the cupboard and mothballs in the pockets of Jacob's Irish coat.

Miriam had a domestic called Maria Mbekushe: she was a quiet, dedicated worker who took in sewing for extra income. Until late into the night Maria would sit in her room at her sewing machine. At weekends she went to her husband who cared for a congregation somewhere on the Cape Flats. Occasionally her husband would visit her, a courteous, slightly stocky man who liked to discuss the Bible with Miriam since she was a formidable authority on the Old Testament.

It was Maria's husband, Alfred Mbekushe, who made Miriam think of the coat. Within a few weeks Alfred was to leave for the Transkei on parish business and, according to the radio reports, it was freezing in the Eastern Province as well as the surrounding areas. Miriam discussed it with Jacob who had no objections; if it was indeed as cold in the Transkei as the radio reported Alfred was a worthy beneficiary of the coat.

Now even later into the night the sewing machine sang, or whatever sound a sewing machine makes, since Maria had to work hastily to alter the coat in time for Alfred's departure. It had to be opened up and gussets inserted. For these she used material from the belt: Alfred could use an ordinary leather belt, a black one would go nicely with the herringbone.

On the day of his departure Alfred, wearing a neat felt hat and with an umbrella over his arm, came to show off the coat. At Maria's request, Jacob took a photograph of her with Alfred, and Miriam said, 'Now we also have a portrait of the coat as well for the family archives.'

That snapshot of Maria and Alfred led to many tears and sorrows for, on the way back from the Transkei, Alfred was murdered on the train. Possibly he was killed for his coat since his body was discovered without it. Maria resigned from domestic service and went out to continue her husband's work on the Cape Flats.

Meanwhile Jacob and Miriam's daughter, Sarah, reached a marriageable age. She was going out with a fellow student, Max, who was also from a good Jewish family but somewhat leftwing in his political beliefs. He accepted as little as possible from his parents and out of sympathy for the underprivileged he bought his clothes from street markets in the black residential areas. His trousers and jerseys, all, were second hand. He bought a tweed coat, one with a herringbone pattern.

When, one windy night, Max visited his future in-laws it was a good excuse to show off his great bargain. 'Oh,' he said, 'not that I cheated the seller, I gave him double what he asked for this coat.'

Miriam and Jacob looked as if they had seen a ghost. 'The coat!' Miriam shouted and Jacob cried out at the same time, 'My coat! You have my coat on!'

Jacob embraced his future son-in-law while he tried to define the smells in the coat; whether it smelled of him, or of Alfred or Max or of a dry-cleaners. The only smell that he could discover, and it could have been his imagination, was of smoke from a dung fire.

Max and Sarah's astonishment grew by the minute. Sarah knew nothing of the history of the coat that had been given to Alfred Mbekushe since she had been at boarding school when it happened and, in any case, she had long since forgotten about the coat.

Jacob and Miriam from years of living together thought like one person. They looked conspiratorially at each other, then Miriam said, 'Please take off the coat, we will explain in a minute.' She spread the coat across the dining-room table and she and Jacob bent low over it as if they were both myopic. They turned the coat over, turned it satin side out, then they turned it back and fingered it. No, thank the Lord, there were no knife cuts, no dried blood. The coat was still of a piece.

Then they told the story of the coat that had, since Ireland, experienced so much. Sarah listened open-mouthed and Max grew pale. 'No, no, no,' sighed the future son-in-law, 'how could I wear the coat now? It can only bring misfortune.'

'Especially now,' said sensible Miriam, 'especially now. Do you not see this is a coat without end? Chagall could have made a painting of it.' Miriam pointed to an etching on the wall.

'And Malamud could have written a big novel about it,' Jacob added.

Max found the mythologising of his street-market coat somewhat naïve, but to please his future in-laws he wore the coat to an intimate family festival. Miriam lit the candles and their flames were reflected in the copper pans that hung on the walls. Jacob carried in a cast-iron casserole of chicken pieces to the table and much later Miriam brought a glass dish of stewed quinces, red as cherries, to the table.

After the meal Max asked permission to take off his coat. His shirt was soaked through and Miriam loaned him one of Jacob's although it was rather too tight for him.

That was probably the last time that Max wore the tweed coat. Spring was early that year and it was a summery sort of spring.

A few months later, when they were married, Max and Sarah decided to give the coat away as soon as a worthy candidate presented himself. Their flat was far too cramped to keep unnecessary things and, in any event, the coat had become a sullen presence and a constant reproach. Providence, or a happy accident, brought – as it usually does – a solution. Sarah fell pregnant and Max was obliged to hire domestic help since Sarah had much trouble with her back and had to lie flat for long periods.

Ruby Fubesi was lively and cheerful by nature; she became Sarah's friend and companion, and Max could leave Sarah with confidence in Ruby's care.

When the first winter rains fell, Max fetched the Irish coat from the wardrobe where it pressed against Sarah's dresses and fur coat. He held it against himself asking Ruby selfconsciously, 'Can you at least use it?'

Ruby clasped her hands together as if in prayer. It was just the thing for her husband, Jonathan, for when he conducted church services.

Naturally I will have to alter the coat, thought Ruby, my husband is much thinner than Max. But yes, it wouldn't present any difficulties. I'll take the coat in, remove the gussets and turn them into a belt. Look, it already has loops.

But I will need to hurry up, Ruby anxiously concluded, for in less than a month, Jonathan would be leaving for the Transkei.

KEN BARRIS

The Questioning

Martin Bennet was a large, greasy poet of uncertain stability. He had a gentle mild face and an unsteady eye. It blinked at you, or twitched at the worst possible times. There was something independent about the left one. It was slightly smaller than the right, drooped, roved more restlessly than its neighbour. His irrational eye. In fact, it was dyslexic, being unable to order perceptual sequences correctly.

He wrote poems about mournful gnats, the defunct river mill of his childhood, and faded hydrangeas.

He was unemployable in other respects. He had a pathological fear of structures and was prone to serious depressions. Like Joyce, he disliked water, and the consequences were obvious. Not that he was overtly dirty; he was simply stale in appearance and smell, he had the impact of a mildewed cabbage on an unexpectant world.

He lived off a hedge of capital that his mother had left him. Over the last seven years, it had grown smaller. He was often desperately worried about where he would get more money when inflation made that lot completely worthless.

Despite the fact that he was thirty-seven years old, he lived in Rondebosch in a student boarding house occupied by youngsters suffering from pimples or excessive religion or no friends. It had avacado-green high-gloss enamel corridors with echoing wooden floors. Their portable TVs and Philips record players bounced tinny sounds along this space, making the claustrophobia worse.

Not that he was unhappy: when he was insomniac he could take out his pad of yellow paper, and his black fountain pen, and scribble lengthy rhyming odes. On Saturday nights he could walk along Rondebosch Main Road, around the Pig, or look into the Hard Rock and smell the steak fumes, or go round the corner and watch the water of the Liesbeeck Canal flow under the Belmont Road bridge. On Sunday mornings he could eat at the Wimpy Bar, where he liked to treat himself to a *Sunday Times*, a Bender Brunch, and a glass of Horlicks.

He was called to the phone one morning. It was a wistful winter morning, with the sun attempting to shine through a drizzle. When he was a child, that was called a monkey's wedding. He picked it up, and the line went dead. It happened again that morning, and twice more the next week.

He didn't know what to make of it, but the mystery upset him. He found himself confined to the toilet with diarrhoea. To make matters worse, he had no one to confide in. He had nothing to confide in anybody about. Then the incidents receded glibly into the past.

He began to feel that he was being followed. Once he imagined that the occupants of a large white Japanese car, which was idling along behind him, were scrutinising him. As soon as he looked squarely at it, it accelerated away with a smooth whine. The glass was polarised, so he couldn't see who was in it. While sitting in a restaurant having anchovy toast and tea, he thought he saw a man standing outside training a video camera on him. But that proved nothing.

He was quite put off his food. Although there were no repetitions of the telephone incident, he found it difficult to sleep. The net result was that he wrote more poetry than usual, under greater pressure. The poetry showed no improvement.

* * *

The security police came for him in the early hours of the morning. He heard the bell ringing, footsteps echoing down the passage – heavy footsteps, many people – then his door burst open and the light was snapped on. He shrieked and sat up in bed, with the covers up to his chin. He felt intensely foolish.

There were five men crowding his small bedroom, looking at him. Their expressions were serious and unreadable. They wore loud sports jackets and open-necked shirts.

'Martin Bennet,' pronounced one of them. 'You are Martin Bennet.'

'I am,' said Martin. His voice shook. 'Who are you?'

'Lieutenant Strimling, Security Branch.' He stepped forward and showed Martin a green plastic card. It had his name, rank and number, and identified him as a member of the South African Police. 'I have bad news for you. You are now under arrest, in terms of Section 29 of the Internal Security Act.' He leaned forward and showed Martin a form on a clipboard. It had a state letterhead, and was stamped and signed by a magistrate. Martin felt too sick and guilty to see, let alone read it.

'Get up, please,' said Lieutenant Strimling, 'and get dressed. It will be in your interests to do so as quickly as possible. We are going to search your room, and we must do so in your presence.'

Martin looked around. There was no way his presence could be avoided in his room. It was the only one he had, and it was virtually impossible to move in. He got out of bed, and shifted carefully past the nearest of the five policemen and walked to his cupboard. He looked at them. They stood there waiting for him. He took out the clothes he needed and put them on as quickly as possible. They watched him in silence. He could feel them watching his white, plump flesh. He was shivering.

The search did not take long. There was very little in his room to find. One of the policemen found a file of his poetry and showed it to him. 'What's this?' he asked.

'Poetry,' said Martin.

'Pro-ANC,' suggested the policeman.

Martin said nothing for a whole minute. Then: 'I don't know why you are doing this. Are you sure you have the right person? I'm not a political person at all. I know nothing about politics.'

The official holding his file of yellow pages shook it at him and grinned.

There was a small crowd of sleepy, puzzled, worried lodgers standing in the passage when they came out. Martin looked at them, trying desperately to make some kind of contact with the people with whom he lived, but his left eye went into its tic. He was horribly worried that they would think he was guilty. The Security Police only detain people who are involved in something. The onlookers blurred. He wanted to tell one of them something, leave a message, arrange for his rent. Lieutenant Strimling stopped, and gave him an opportunity. Then he realised there was no one to give a message to, and he felt too helpless about the rent to do anything about it. The four policemen hurried him on.

He was bundled into a white Ford with Lieutenant Strimling and two others. The remaining two climbed into another car, and they all sped off down Main Road in the direction of Muizenberg. 'Where are you taking me?' he asked. He could hear his tongue sticking against the roof of his mouth. He needed to brush his teeth.

They ignored him. They chatted to each other about people he didn't know. It was as if they were on their way to meet some friends, or to a movie.

They turned right into Lansdowne Road and took him to the Claremont Police Station. The cars squealed in through the side gate in First Avenue, and jerked to a halt. He was taken into a dimly lit room and told to wait. All the policemen disappeared. There were five dustbins in the room. He counted them. The floor was dirty anyway.

A young constable came in. He was stooped and had a hooked nose.

He was very ugly, and obviously stupid. Martin felt sorry for him. He had a clipboard in his hand with some forms on it, and there was a government-issue ballpoint pen tied to it with a string. He started to take down Martin's particulars. Martin had to help him with his spelling, and then gave up. The man was obviously dyslexic. He completed his form.

'I must just check this out with Staff,' he said. He disappeared. Martin waited in complete terror. He was sure that if a more senior officer came along, he could explain that it was a mistake, and then they would release him.

The constable came back. 'Staff says this are the wrong forms. I must fill in this other lot.' Martin wondered who Staff was. He thought Staff was some mysterious form of control. Like Weather. I must check with Weather, or with Meteorology. They filled the new forms in, and the constable disappeared.

Martin wanted to pass water badly.

A new person came back. He was very fat and had a gravel voice. He was holding the clipboard. There were new forms in it.

'Name?' he asked.

Martin wanted to cry. 'I've told him that,' he said.

'Told who?'

'I told this other man who was here.'

'Told him what?'

'I told him ...' Tears spurted into his eyes. He started again. 'I told him all that.'

The staff-sergeant looked uncomfortable. He didn't like to see men cry. 'He filled in the wrong forms,' he explained.

'I know that. He filled in another set.'

'Ja,' said the policeman. 'That's the problem. You see, he signed those. He's not supposed to fill in those other forms. I am.'

They filled in the new forms.

Martin was taken upstairs by the first policeman to have his fingerprints taken. But first he was taken into a washroom – where at last he had a chance to relieve himself – to wash his hands. 'You must dry them,' said the constable. Martin looked around at the empty towel rack, then under the basin. He couldn't see a towel. He looked around again, because he was sure he must be wrong. 'There are no towels,' he said.

'Dry your hands!' shouted the policeman.

Martin could feel the blood draining from his face. 'What with?'

The policeman looked round. 'Fuck it, man,' he said, 'just dry your hands on any fucking thing.' Martin wiped his hands on his pants.

They walked across the passage to the room where fingerprints were taken. 'Are your hands dry?' asked the corporal in charge. The corporal pressed each of his fingers and thumbs hard onto the appropriate blocks, and rolled them round so that the whole profile would show. They rolled off the paper stickily.

His first night in the cell was too distressing to bear. The only problem was that he had to bear it. Down the road was Checkers. Just up the road was Tonneson's Garage. It was so normal out there. He just had to raise his voice and shout, or reach out his hand, and normality would see and hear him. But there was no way that he could reach normality. There was no reason for its absence either. He was simply locked up.

He was in a single cell with its own toilet and washbasin. It was a very little toilet, the kind they have in nursery schools. Although the enamel was deeply stained, it was reasonably clean. There were no other people in his cell; there were a couple of drunks in the cell next door who spent the night moaning and vomiting. By the time morning announced itself and he could hear the traffic in Lansdowne Road, he was distraught.

The day passed like the next three: no one would answer his questions. He remained alone in his cell, although from the sounds and the people passing in the passage it was a busy police station filled with criminal or merely vagrant traffic. A breakfast of grey porridge in an aluminium bowl was slid under his door before it was light outside; he was given seven slices of bread at eleven, with a square of margarine, a square of jam, and a spoon with which to spread them. At half past three he was given supper: stywe pap, mashed potatoes, boiled cabbage, and a sprinkling of shredded chicken.

He couldn't believe how hungry he grew by midnight. On the third day he held back three slices of his lunchtime bread and waited till sunset. Then he nibbled one after the other, as slowly as he could, drinking mugs of water in between and walking around his cell until he judged it was time to start on the next slice. He finished the bread before it was completely dark.

He still had no idea what the police intended to do with him, or why he was there. No one found it necessary to inform him.

* * *

Martin Bennet was placed in the back of a yellow police van and driven to a huge police station in the centre of Cape Town that he didn't know. It was like a fort of naked red brick. He was taken into a cell that faced inwards into an open courtyard. The coir mattress on the steel bed stank, and there were obscene, lonely graffiti scratched on the enamel green walls. There were no washing or toilet facilities. Every few hours a warder came round and took him to the toilet. He was allowed out to shower once a day, and had to stand in a queue with the other prisoners. They terrified him.

The food was worse than at the Claremont police station. He became extremely depressed. In the afternoon of his fourth day in the new prison – possibly his fifth – a policeman came round and poked an orange through the bars at him, grinning in pleasure and gesturing invitingly. He approached, and the policeman thrust the orange through the bars. Martin took it. The act of kindness was too much for him. This time he did cry.

There was a high window in his cell. By standing on his cot and pulling himself up by the bars, he could catch a brief glimpse of Table Mountain. Then he would fall back again.

The nights were extremely cold, but he had been given enough blankets. It was almost like camping outside, because air moved freely through the bars, and he could see the cells opposite his across an outdoors space. In the stillness of the early hours, he could hear the sounds of many people dreaming or snoring, turning in their cells restlessly, the distant nightmarish clanking of gates. Occasionally a police van would come in or go out through the large central entrance. It was as if he had been swallowed by a gargantuan animal that moved with difficulty, and wheezed rather than breathed. Only something like the vital roar of a motor bike outside could break its lassitude.

The whole jail stank.

The day he was fetched for his first interrogation, it was pouring with rain, and the smells closed on him more heavily. Two warders came to fetch him from his cell. One was the benevolent policeman who had given him the orange. He didn't know the other one. He was taken upstairs to a dusty grey office and left to wait. There were two metal tables with telephones, and a filing cabinet. He noticed a dark stain on the floor and his bowels turned to jelly. He had trouble not disgracing himself.

Thick-limbed, absent-minded people wandered in and out of the office – it adjoined another one, which seemed to be more the centre of activity. He couldn't see what was in it, although he timidly craned his head towards the door.

He was getting tired of standing when an important-looking policeman or official of some kind came in. He was in his forties, and he had large, definite hands. Each feature was terribly definite: his lips and nose might have been carved crudely out of wood, his eyes were bulbous but clear. He looked Martin up and down.

Martin's intestines contracted. The official sighed, and pressed down his intercom button with his thumb. A crude male voice answered. Then a young uniformed policeman came in. 'Take him out and get him cleaned up. I can't speak to someone in such a distasteful condition.' The constable shook his head sadly at Martin. 'Didn't your mother teach you what to do?' he asked.

They left him alone until the next day. This time the one who had given him an orange came on his own. 'You mustn't worry so much,' he told Martin. 'Fuck it, man, they're not going to kill you.' Martin couldn't say anything in reply. His voice wasn't working, but he was determined he would stand up to anything they did to him. He was not going to degrade himself again.

At that point his left eye went into its spasm and started blurring. This almost gave him courage: it was the one condition he was used to. The trouble was that his right eye was astigmatic, and he had difficulty seeing an undistorted world at all.

He was taken to the same office. There was no waiting this time. There were three officers behind the desk, including the one who had frightened him so much.

The man lit a cigarette and smiled at Martin. 'I haven't introduced myself. I'm Captain van Wyk. Pieter van Wyk.'

Martin stared at him like a trapped rabbit.

'Look, Martin,' he said, 'we are reasonable people. We just want to talk to you, really. Just think of this as a friendly chat.'

Martin looked around at him in confusion. They waited for him to speak. 'Why am I here?' he asked.

The captain looked a little embarrassed. He even had to clear his throat. 'We were hoping you could tell us that,' he asked. 'You see, we don't seem to have a file on you.'

Martin stared at him. Van Wyk turned to the man next to him, who scraped back his chair, got up and left the room. He returned with a chair, placed it behind Martin, and disappeared.

'Ja,' said Captain van Wyk. He didn't seem to know what to say. He picked up a pencil and fiddled with it. 'You don't seem to be terribly involved in much. I mean, not much that we consider important. In the sense of subversive, that is. In fact, you don't seem to be involved in terribly much at all.'

Martin was still standing. Van Wyk gestured. 'Please take a seat,' he said. Martin sank into the chair. His heart was thudding so hard he thought it would fail, and the face across the table was blurring into a kind of stewy mist. He didn't dare look at the other face next to it.

'Jesus,' said Martin.

'We're only human,' said the captain. 'If you had to do our job, you could also make mistakes. Not that that proves anything,' he added warningly. 'Remember, we don't actually know that you're innocent.'

Martin could feel time sucking away at him, with suffocating brightness. He was shaking violently.

'Can I go?' he asked. 'I mean, is there any reason why I am still here?'

'Well, yes. We'd like to offer you a cup of tea. I'm sure it's on its way.'

It's a trap, he thought. They let you go and then they shoot you in the back. He looked around wildly. There was a terrible crash from the room next door. The policeman bringing the tea had tripped.

⋆ ⋆ ⋆

Martin celebrated his release by dining at a restaurant that he couldn't afford. He chose the Hard Rock Cafe in Rondebosch. There were large photographs on the wall of Marilyn Monroe, John Wayne, and other icons of Western culture. There was a dais at the far end, on which sat a pianist inaudibly playing songs like *Moon River* and *Tennessee Waltz*. The waitresses were all attractive women wearing white dresses that weren't quite virginal and hairstyles that weren't quite androgynous. He ordered a steak Rossini rare, understanding that that was how things should be done.

He sat on his own, bemused and lonely – drowning in the bright noise and conversation of others. Everyone seemed to have so much energy with which to celebrate their mouths, one way or another. All around him sat people wading through enormous platters piled with red juicy meat and steaming salted chips, or prime seafood and wondrous salads. Everyone was drinking wine, gesturing animatedly, telling jokes and roaring with laughter, or leaning forward and gazing intimately into each other's eyes.

When Martin's steak came, saliva spurted into his mouth. He scraped the rich red sauce off and cut into his meat. It was far bloodier than he thought it would be. In fact, blood leaked effortlessly from the pink flesh and collected in a shallow pool. He cut off a piece, put it into his mouth and chewed it slowly.

He couldn't swallow. It was an excellent piece of beef but something made it grow larger and more rubbery the more he chewed. He had to spit it into his serviette. Then he folded it out of sight, cleared his throat, and stood up. He tried to say something, but no one was interested in listening to him. Besides, even if they were, he had a very small voice.

He cleared his throat more loudly, but it didn't help at all. 'It's not normal,' he shouted out. No one heard him. Glancing wildly about to see the effects of this pronouncement, his eye fell on the pianist, who was still morosely doing his duty. There was a microphone standing nearby.

Martin started towards it. The conversations around him grew louder and louder as he waded through chairs and ankles towards his destination. One particularly vital gust of laughter from a large table almost extinguished him. But a strange singleness had taken hold of his movement. He tapped on the microphone. It was on. The pianist looked up at him, but carried on playing *Blueberry Hill*. 'It's not normal,' he shouted into the microphone. He recoiled at the volume of his own voice. 'All this,' he explained to the microphone. 'You think they only take the guilty, but it's not like that. Not only them!'

The voices were gradually dying down, and people were swivelling their faces towards him. The pianist gave up. The manageress was struggling through the crowded room towards the dais, a competent, attractive hostess in her thirties. Martin leaned forward again, speaking as quickly as he could. 'Where there's smoke there's fire – that's what they say, but it's not like that. Not only commies or whatever. They're controlling you, right now. Just because they're there. You think you're free!'

There were a few ripples of laughter. Someone pointed his finger at his head and whirled it round and round. By now the manageress had almost reached Martin. 'The rule of law, I mean,' he shouted lamely, realising that he hadn't mentioned what he was talking about. The manageress switched the microphone off. Martin stared at her.

Her face was a terrible mixture of emotions: outrage, bewilderment, amusement. Beneath the set of her make-up. All of them were pointed at Martin. 'Do you have a problem, sir?' she asked, very firmly. 'Can you please come down from there.'

'I'll go quietly,' he said. 'No fuss, no bother. I'm going.' He raised his hands in surrender and stepped down. Tears started streaming down his face, effortlessly. She couldn't look at him. He couldn't see. 'Would you mind leaving,' she asked. Around them the voices started rising again as people realised the show was over, although many had stopped eating to stare at Martin.

'I haven't paid for my meal yet.'

'Don't worry,' she said, competently and inarguably, 'it's on the house.'

She took his arm and hurried him on towards the entrance. She could feel his helplessness: she led him out.

* * *

It was cold outside the restaurant. Green and mauve neon lights robbed flesh of colour, and streams of headlights went by, blinding and indifferent to Martin's anguish. He turned around a few times, stared into the restaurant, sighed, shrugged his shoulders, stared up at the sky. The low clouds overhead reflected back the sodium vapour light of the city. He felt like a vast sac filled with clear fluid, close to tearing.

A brightly dressed couple passed Martin and turned into the Hard Rock. As they opened the door, warm air and laughter gusted out. Martin turned and walked wearily away. Perhaps he would go and stand on the Belmont Road bridge, and watch the shallow black water scurry under it in the Liesbeeck Canal.

AHMED ESSOP

Hajji Musa and the Hindu Fire-walker

'Allah has sent me to you, Bibi Fatima.'

'Allah, Hajji Musa?'

'I assure you, Allah, my good lady. Listen to me carefully. There is something wrong with you. Either you have a sickness or there is an evil spell cast over your home. Can you claim that there is nothing wrong in your home, that your family is perfectly healthy and happy?'

'Well, Hajji Musa, you know my little Amir has a nasty cough that even Dr Kamal cannot cure and Soraya seems to have lost her appetite.'

'My good woman, you believe me now when I say Allah has sent me to you?'

Bibi Fatima's husband, Jogee, entered the room. Hajji Musa took no notice of him and began to recite (in Arabic) an extract from the Qur'an. When he had done he shook hands with Jogee.

'Listen to me, Bibi Fatima and brother Jogee. Sickness is not part of our nature, neither is it the work of our good Allah. It is the work of that great evildoer Iblis, some people call him Satan. Well, I, by the grace of Allah' (he recited another extract from the Qur'an) 'have been given the power to heal the sick and destroy evil. That is my work in life, even if I get no reward.'

'But Hajji Musa, you must live.'

'Bibi Fatima, Allah looks after me and my family. Now bring me two glasses of water and a candle.'

She hurried to the kitchen and brought the articles.

'Now bring me the children.'

'Jogee, please go and find Amir in the yard while I look for Soraya.'

Husband and wife went out. Meanwhile Hajji Musa drew the curtains in the room, lit the candle and placed the two glasses of water on either side of the candle. He took incense out of his pocket, put it in an ashtray and lit it.

When husband and wife returned with the children they were awed. There was an atmosphere of strangeness, of mystery, in the room. Hajji

Musa looked solemn. He took the candle, held it about face level and said: 'Look, there is a halo around the flame.'

They looked and saw a faint halo.

He placed the candle on the table, took the glasses of water, held them above the flame and recited a verse from the Qur'an. When he had done he gave one glass to the boy and one to the girl.

'Drink, my children,' he said. They hesitated for a moment, but Bibi Fatima commanded them to drink the water.

'They will be well,' he said authoritatively. 'They can now go and play.'

He extinguished the candle, drew the curtains, and sat down on the settee. And he laughed, a full-throated, uproarious, felicitous laugh.

'Don't worry about the children. Allah has performed miracles on what are coughs and loss of appetites.' And he laughed again.

Bibi Fatima went to the kitchen to make tea and Jogee and I kept him company. She returned shortly with tea and cake.

'Jogee,' she said, 'I think Hajji Musa is greater than Dr Kamal. You remember last year Dr Kamal gave me medicines and ointments for my aching back and nothing came of it?'

'Hajji Musa is not an ordinary doctor.'

'What are doctors of today,' Hajji Musa said, biting into a large slice of cake, 'but chancers and frauds? What knowledge have they of religion and the spiritual mysteries?'

'Since when have you this power to heal, Hajji Musa?'

'Who can tell the ways of Allah, Bibi Fatima. Sometimes his gifts are given when we are born and sometimes when we are much older.'

'More tea?'

She filled the cup. He took another slice of cake.

'Last month I went to Durban and there was this woman, Jasuben, whom the doctors had declared insane. Even her own yogis and swamis had given her up. I took this woman in hand and today she is as sane as anyone else.'

'Hajji Musa, you know my back still gives me trouble. Dr Kamal's medicine gave me no relief. I have even stopped making roti and Joggi is very fond of roti.'

'You should let me examine your back some day,' the healer said, finishing his tea.

'Why not now?'

'Not today,' he answered protestingly. 'I have some business to attend to.'

'But Hajji Musa, it will only take a minute or two.'

'Well that's true, that's true.'

'Will you need the candle and water?'

'Yes.'

She hurriedly went to refill the glass with water.

'Please, Jogee and Ahmed, go into the kitchen for a while,' she said, returning.

We left the room, Jogee rather reluctantly. She shut the door. I sat down on a chair and looked at a magazine lying on the table. Jogee told me he was going to buy cigarettes and left. He was feeling nervous.

I was sitting close to the door and could hear Hajji Musa's voice and the rustle of clothing as he went on with the examination.

'I think it best if you lie down on the settee so that I can make a thorough examination ... Yes, that is better ... Is the pain here ...? Bibi Fatima, you know the pain often has its origin lower down in the lumbar region. Could you ease your ijar a little ...? The seat of the pain is often here ... Don't be afraid.'

'I can feel it getting better already, Hajji Musa.'

'That is good. You are responding very well.'

There was a silence for some time. When Jogee returned Hajji Musa was reciting a prayer in Arabic. Jogee puffed at his cigarette. When Bibi Fatima opened the door she was smiling and looked flushed.

'Your wife will be well in a few days,' Hajji Musa assured the anxious man. 'And you will be having your daily roti again. Now I must go.'

'Hajji Musa, but we must give you something for your trouble.'

'No nothing, Bibi Fatima. I forbid you.'

She was insistent. She told Jogee in pantomime (she showed him five fingers) how much money he should give. Jogee produced the money from his pocket, though inwardly protesting at his wife's willingness to pay a man who asked no fees. Bibi Fatima put the money into Hajji Musa's pocket.

* * *

In appearance Hajji Musa was a fat, pot-bellied, short, dark man, with glossy black wavy hair combed backwards with fastidious care. His face was always clean-shaven. For some reason he never shaved in the bathroom, and every morning one saw him in the yard, in vest and pyjama trousers, arranging (rather precariously) his mirror and shaving equipment on the window sill outside the kitchen and going through the ritual of cleaning his face with the precision of a surgeon. His great passion was talking and while shaving he would be conducting conversations with various people in the yard: with the hawker packing his fruit and vegetables in the cart; with the two wives of the motor mechanic Soni; with the servants coming to work.

Hajji Musa was a well-known man. At various times he had been a commercial traveller, insurance salesman, taxi driver, companion to dignitaries from India and Pakistan, Islamic missionary, teacher at a seminary, shopkeeper, matchmaker and hawker of ladies' underwear.

His career as a go-between in marriage transactions was a brief, inglorious one that almost ended his life. One night there was fierce knocking at his door. As soon as he opened it an angry voice exploded: 'You liar! You come and tell me of dat good-for-nutting Dendar boy, dat he good, dat he ejucated, dat he good prospect. My foot and boot he ejucated. He sleep most time wit bitches, he drink and beat my daughter. When you go Haj? You nutting but liar. You baster! You baster!' And suddenly two shots from a gun rang out in quick succession. The whole incident took place so quickly that no one had any time to look at the man as he ran through the yard and escaped. When people reached Hajji Musa's door they found him prostrate, breathing hard and wondering why he was still alive (the bullets had passed between his legs). His wife and eight children were in a state of shock. They were revived with sugared water.

Hajji Musa's life never followed an even course: on some days one saw him riding importantly in the chauffeur-driven Mercedes of some wealthy merchant in need of his services; on others, one saw him in the yard, pacing meditatively from one end to the other, reciting verses from the Qur'an. Sometimes he would visit a friend, tell an amusing anecdote, laugh, and suddenly ask: 'Can you give me a few rands till tomorrow?' The friend would give him the money without expecting anything of tomorrow, for it was well known that Hajji Musa, liberal with his own money, never bothered to return anyone else's.

Hajji Musa considered himself a specialist in the exorcism of evil jinn. He deprecated modern terms such as neurosis, schizophrenia, psychosis. 'What do doctors know about the power of satanic jinn? Only God can save people who are no longer themselves. I have proved this time and again. You don't believe me? Then come on Sunday night to my house and you will see.'

On Sunday night we were clustered around Hajji Musa in the yard. As his patient had not yet arrived, he regaled us with her history.

'She is sixteen. She is the daughter of Mia Mohammed the Market Street merchant. She married her cousin a few years ago. But things went wrong. Her mother-in-law disliked her. For months she has been carted from doctor to doctor, and from one psychiatrist to another, those fools. Tonight you will see me bring about a permanent cure.'

After a while a car drove into the yard, followed by two others. Several men – two of them tall, bearded brothers – emerged from the car, approached Hajji Musa and shook hands with him. They pointed to the second car.

'She is in that car, Hajji Musa.'

'Good, bring her into the house.' And he went inside.

There were several women in the second car. All alighted but one, who refused to come out. She shook her face and hands and cried, 'No! No! Don't take me in there, please! By Allah, I am a good girl.'

The two brothers and several women stood beside the opened doors of the car and coaxed the young lady to come out.

'Sister, come, we are only visiting.'

'No, no, they are going to hit me.'

'No one is going to hit you,' one of the women said, getting into the car and sitting beside her. 'They only want to see you.'

'They can see me in the car. I am so pretty.'

Everyone living in the yard was present to witness the spectacle, and several children had clambered onto the bonnet of the car and were shouting: 'There she is! There she is! She is mad! She is mad!'

'Come now, Jamilla, come. The people are laughing at you,' one of the brothers said sternly.

Hajji Musa now appeared wearing a black cloak emblazoned with sequin-studded crescent moons and stars, and inscribed with Cufic writing in white silk. His sandals were red and his trousers white. His turban was of green satin and it had a large round ruby (artificial) pinned to it above his forehead.

He proceeded towards the car, looked at Jamilla, and then said to the bearded brothers, 'I will take care of her.' He put his head into the interior of the car. Jamilla recoiled in terror. The lady next to her held her and said, 'Don't be frightened. Hajji Musa intends no harm.'

'Listen, sister, come into the house. I have been expecting you.'

'No! No! I want to go home.' Jamilla began to cry.

'I won't let anyone hurt you.'

Hajji Musa tried to grab her hand, but she pushed herself backwards against the woman next to her and screamed so loudly that for a moment the healer seemed to lose his nerve. He turned to the brothers.

'The evil jinn is in her. Whatever I do now, please forgive me.'

He put his foot into the interior of the car, gripped one arm of the terrified Jamilla and smacked her twice with vehemence.

'Come out, jinn! Come out, jinn!' he shouted and dragged her towards the door of the car. The woman beside Jamilla pushed her and punched her on the back.

'Please help,' Hajji Musa said, and the two brothers pulled the screaming Jamilla out of the car.

'Drive the jinn into the house!' And they punched and pushed Jamilla towards the house. She pleaded with several spectators for help and then in desperation clung to them. But they shook her off and one or two even took the liberty of punching her and pulling her hair.

Jamilla was pushed into the house and the door closed on her and several of the privileged who were permitted to witness the exorcism ceremony. As soon as she passed through a narrow passage and entered a room she quietened.

The room was brilliantly lit and a fire was burning in the grate. A red carpet stretched from wall to wall and on the window sill incense was burning in brass bowls. In front of the grate were two brass plates containing sun-dried red chillies.

We removed our shoes and sat down on the carpet. Jamilla was made to sit in front of the grate. She was awed and looked about at the room and the people. Several women seated themselves near her. Hajji Musa then began to recite the chapter 'The Jinn' from the Qur'an. We sat with bowed heads. When he had done he moved towards the grate. His wife came into the room with a steel tray and a pair of tongs. Hajji Musa took some burning pieces of coal and heaped them on the tray. Then he scattered the red chillies over the coals. Smoke rose from the tray and filled the room with an acrid, suffocating smell. He seated himself beside Jamilla and asked the two brothers to sit near her as well. He pressed Jamilla's head over the tray and at the same time recited a verse from the Qur'an in a loud voice. Jamilla choked, seemed to scream mutely and tried to lift her head, but Hajji Musa held her.

As the smell of burning chillies was unbearable, some of us went outside for a breath of fresh air. Aziz Khan said to us: 'That primitive ape is prostituting our religion with his hocus-pocus. He should be arrested for assault.'

We heard Jamilla screaming and we returned quickly to the room. We saw Hajji Musa and the two brothers beating her with their sandals and holding her face over the coals.

'Out Iblis! Out Jinn!' Hajji Musa shouted and belaboured her.

At last Jamilla fell into a swoon.

'Hold her, Ismail and Hafiz.' Hajji Musa sprinkled her face with water and read a prayer. Then he asked the two brothers to pick her up and take her into an adjoining room. They laid her on a bed.

'When she wakes up the jinn will be gone,' Hajji Musa predicted confidently.

We went outside for a while. Aziz Khan asked a few of us to go with him in his car to the police station. But on the way he surprised us by changing his mind.

'It's not our business,' he said, and drove back to the yard.

When we returned Jamilla had opened her eyes and was sobbing quietly.

'Anyone can ask Jamilla if she remembers what happened to her.'

Someone asked her and she shook her head.

'See,' said the victorious man, 'it was the evil jinn that was thrashed out of her body. He is gone!'

* * *

There had been the singing of hymns, chanting and the jingling of bells since the late afternoon, and as evening approached there was great excitement in the yard. Everyone knew of the great event that was to take place that evening: the Hindu fire-walker was going to give a demonstration.

'There is nothing wonderful about walking on fire,' Hajji Musa declared in a scornful tone. 'The Hindus think they are performing miracles. Bah! Miracles!' And he exploded in laughter. 'What miracles can their many gods perform, I ask you? Let them extract a jinn or heal the sick and then talk of miracles.'

'But can you walk on fire or only cook on fire?' Dolly asked sardonically. There was laughter and merriment.

'Both, my dear man, both. Anyone who cooks on fire can walk on fire.'

'If anyone can, let him try,' said the law student Soma. 'In law, words are not enough; evidence has to be produced.'

'Funny, you lawyers never get done with words. After gossiping for days you ask for a postponement.'

Everyone laughed boisterously.

'Hajji Musa,' Dolly tried again, 'can you walk on fire?'

'Are you joking, Dolly? When I can remove a jinn, what is walking on fire? Have you seen a jinn?'

'No.'

'See one and then talk. Evil jinn live in hell. What is walking on fire to holding one of hell's masters in your hands?'

'I say let him walk on fire and then talk of jinn,' said Raffia the dwarfish Hindu watchmaker, but he walked away fearing to confront Hajji Musa.

'That stupid Hindu thinks I waste my time in performing tricks. I am not a magician.'

A fire was now lit in the yard. Wood had been scattered over an area of about twenty feet by six feet. An attendant was shovelling coal and another using the rake to spread it evenly.

Meanwhile, in a room in the yard, the voices of the chanters were rising and the bells were beginning to jingle madly. Every now and then a deeper, more resonant chime would ring out, and a voice would lead the chanters to a higher pitch. In the midst of the chanters, facing a small altar on which were placed a tiny earthenware bowl containing a burning wick, a picture of the god Shiva surrounded by votive offerings of marigold flowers, rice and coconut, sat the fire-walker in a cross-legged posture.

The yard was crowded. Chairs were provided but these were soon occupied. The balconies were packed and several agile children climbed onto rooftops and seated themselves on the creaking zinc. A few dignitaries were also present.

The chanters emerged from the doorway. In their midst was the fire-walker, his eyes focused on the ground. He was like a man eroded of his own will, captured by the band of chanters. They walked towards the fire which was now glowing flames leaping here and there.

The chanters grouped themselves near the fire and went on with their singing and bell-ringing, shouting refrains energetically. Then, as though life had suddenly flowed into him, the fire-walker detached himself from the group and went towards the fire. It was a tense moment. The chanters were gripped by frenzy. The coal-bed glowed. He placed his right foot on the fire gently, tentatively, as though measuring its intensity, and then walked swiftly over from end to end. He was applauded. Two boys now offered him coconuts in trays. He selected two, and then walked over the inferno again, rather slowly this time, and as he walked he banged the coconuts against his head several times until they cracked and one saw the snowy insides. His movement now became more like a dance than a walk, as though his feet gloried in their triumph over the fire. The boys offered him more coconuts and he went on breaking them against his head.

While the fire-walker was demonstrating his salamander-like powers, an argument developed between Aziz Khan and Hajji Musa.

'He is not walking over the fire,' Hajji Musa said. 'Our eyes are being deceived.'

'Maybe your eyes are being deceived, but not mine,' Aziz answered.

'If you know anything about yogis then you will know how they can pass off the unreal for the real.'

'What do you mean by saying if I know anything about yogis?'

'He thinks he knows about everything under the sun,' Hajji Musa said jeeringly to a friend. He turned to Aziz.

'Have you been to India to see the fakirs and yogis?'

'No, and I don't intend to.'

'Well, I have been to India and know more than you do.'

'I have not been to India, but what I do know is that you are a fraud.'

'Fraud! Huh!'

'Charlatan! Humbug!'

'I say, Aziz!' With a swift movement Hajji Musa clutched Aziz Khan's wrist.

'You are just a big-talker and one day I shall shut your mouth for you.'

'Fraud! Crook! You are a disgrace to Islam. You with your chillies and jinn!'

'Sister …!' This remark Hajji Musa uttered in Gujarati.

'Why don't you walk over the fire? It's an unreal fire.' And Aziz laughed sardonically.

'Yes, let him walk,' said the watchmaker. 'Hajji Musa big-talker.'

'The fire is not as hot as any of your jinn, Hajji Musa,' Dolly said slyly, with an ironic chuckle.

'Dolly, anyone can walk on fire if he knows the trick.'

'I suppose you know,' Aziz said tauntingly.

'Of course I do.'

'Then why don't you walk over the fire?'

'Jinn are hotter!' Dolly exclaimed.

'Fraud! Hypocrite! Degraded infidel, you will never walk. I dare you!'

'I will show you, you fool. I will show you what I can do.'

'What can you show but your lying tongue, and beat up little girls!'

'You sister …! I will walk.'

While the argument had been raging, many people had gathered around them and ceased to look at the Hindu fire-walker. Now, when Hajji Musa accepted the challenge, he was applauded.

Hajji Musa removed his shoes and socks and rolled up his trousers. All eyes in the yard were now focused on him. Some shouted words of encouragement and others clapped their hands. Mr Darsot, though, tried to dissuade him.

'Hajji Musa, I don't think you should attempt walking on fire.'

But Dolly shouted in his raucous voice: 'Hajji Musa, show them what you are made of!'

Hajji Musa, determined and intrepid, went towards the fire. The Hindu fire-walker was now resting for a while, his body and clothes wet with sweat and juice from broken coconuts, and the chanters' voices were low. When Hajji Musa reached the fire he faltered. His body tensed with fear. Cautiously he lifted his right foot over the glowing mass. But any thought he might have had of retreat, of giving up Aziz Khan's challenge and declaring himself defeated, was dispelled by the applause he received.

Crying out in a voice that was an invocation to God to save him, he stepped on the inferno: 'Allah is great!'

* * *

What happened to Hajji Musa was spoken of long afterwards. Badly burnt, he was dragged out of the fire, drenched with water and smothered with rags, and taken to hospital.

We went to visit him. We expected to find a man humiliated, broken. We found him sitting up in bed, swathed in bandages, but as ebullient and resilient as always, with a bevy of young nurses eagerly attending to him.

'Boys, I must say fire-walking is not for me. Showmanship … that's for magicians and crowd-pleasers … those seeking cheap publicity.'

And he laughed in his usual way until the hospital corridors resounded.

NADINE GORDIMER

The Termitary

When you live in a small town far from the world you read about in municipal library books, the advent of repairmen in the house is a festival. Daily life is gaily broken open, improvisation takes over. The living room masquerades as a bedroom while the smell of paint in the bedroom makes it uninhabitable. The secret backs of confident objects (matchwood draped with cobwebs thickened by dust) are given away when furniture is piled to the centre of the room. Meals are picnics at which table manners are suspended because the first principle of deportment drummed into children by their mother – sitting down at table – is missing: there is nowhere to sit. People are excused eccentricities of dress because no one can find anything in its place.

A doctor is also a kind of repairman. When he is expected the sheets are changed and the dog chased off the patient's bed. If a child is sick, she doesn't have to go to school, she is on holiday, with presents into the bargain – a whole roll of comics tied with newsagent's string, and crayons or card games. The mother is alone in the house, except for the patient out of earshot in the sickroom; the other children are at school. Her husband is away at work. She takes off her apron, combs her hair and puts on a bit of lipstick to make herself decent for the doctor, setting ready a tea-tray for two in the quiet privacy of the deserted living room as for a secret morning visit from the lover she does not have. After she and the doctor, who smells intoxicating, coldly sweet because he has just come from the operating theatre, have stood together looking down at the patient and making jolly remarks, he is glad to accept a cup of tea in his busy morning round and their voices are a murmur and an occasional rise of laughter from behind the closed living-room door.

Plumber, painter, doctor; with their arrival something has happened where nothing ever happens; at home: a house with a bungalow face made of two bow-window eyes on either side of a front-door mouth, in a street in a gold-mining town of twenty-five thousand people in South Africa in the 1930s.

Once the upright Steinway piano stood alone on the few remaining boards of a room from which the floor had been ripped. I burst in to look at the time on the chiming clock that should have been standing on the mantelpiece and instead flew through the air, and found myself jolted down into a subterranean smell of an earth I'd never smelled before, the earth buried by our house. I was nine years old and the drop broke no bones; the shock excited me, the thought of that hollow, earth-breaking dark always beneath our Axminster thrilled me; the importance I gained in my mother's accounts of how I might so easily have injured myself added to the sense of occasion usual in the family when there were workmen in.

This time it was not the painters, Mr Strydom and his boys, over whom my mother raised a quarrel every few years. *I'm not like any other woman. I haven't got a husband like other women's. The state this house is in. You'd see the place fall to pieces before you'd lift a finger. Too mean to pay for a lick of paint, and then when you do you expect it to last ten years. I haven't got a home like other women.* Workmen were treated as the house guests we never had; my mother's friends were neighbours, my father had none, and she wouldn't give house-room to a spare bed, anyway, because she didn't want his relatives coming. Mr Strydom was served sweet strong tea to his taste many times a day, while my mother stood by to chat and I followed his skills with the brush, particularly fascinated when he was doing something he called, in his Afrikaner's English, 'pulling the line'. This was the free-hand deftness with which he could make a narrow black stripe dividing the lower half of our passage, painted dark against dirty fingerprints, from the cream upper half. *Yust a sec while I first pull the line, ay.*

Then he would drain his cup so completely that the tea leaves swirled up and stuck to the sides. This workmanlike thirst, for me, was a foreign custom, sign of the difference between being Afrikaans and English, as we were, just as I accepted that it must be in accordance with *their* custom that the black 'boys' drank their tea from jam tins in the yard. But Mr Strydom, like the doctor, like deaf dapper Mr Waite the electrician, who had drinking bouts because he had been through something called Ypres, and Mr Hartman who sang to himself in a sad soprano while he tuned the Steinway upright my mother had brought from her own mother's house, was a recurrent event. The state the house was in, this time, was one without precedent; the men who were in were not repairmen. They had been sent for to exterminate what we called white ants – termites who were eating our house away under our feet. A million jaws were devouring steadily night and day the timber that supported our unchanging routines: one day (if my mother hadn't done something about it you may be sure no one else would) that heavy Steinway in its real rosewood case would have crashed through the floorboards.

For years my mother had efficiently kicked apart the finely-granulated earth, forming cones perfect as the shape taken by sand that has trickled through an egg timer, that was piled in our garden by ordinary black ants. My father never did a hand's turn; she herself poured a tar-smelling disinfectant down the ant-holes and emptied into them kettles of boiling water that made the ground break out in a sweat of gleaming, struggling, pin-head creatures in paroxysm. Yet (it was another event) on certain summer evenings after rain we would rush out into the garden to be in the tropical snowfall of millions of transparent wings from what we called flying ants, who appeared from nowhere. We watched while frogs bold with greed hopped onto the veranda to fill their pouched throats with these apparently harmless insects, and our cat ate steadily but with more self-control, spitting out with a shake of her whiskers any fragment of wing she might have taken up by mistake. We did not know that when these creatures shed their four delicate dragon-fly wings (some seemed to struggle like people getting out of coats) and became drab terrestrials, and some idiotically lifted their hindquarters in the air as if they were reacting to injury, they were enacting a nuptial ceremony that, one summer night or another, had ended in one out of these millions being fertilised and making her way under our house to become queen of a whole colony generated and given birth to by herself. Somewhere under our house she was in an endless parturition that would go on until she was found and killed.

The men had been sent for to search out the queen. No evil-smelling poisons, no opening-up of the tunnels more skilfully constructed than the London Underground, the Paris Metro or the New York subway I'd read about, no fumigation such as might do for cockroaches or moles or wood-borer beetles, could eradicate termites. No matter how many thousands were killed by my mother, as, in the course of the excavations that tore up the floorboards of her house, the brittle passages made of grains of earth cemented by a secretion carried in the termites' own bodies were broken, and the inhabitants poured out in a pus of white moving droplets with yellow heads – no matter how many she cast into death agony with her Flit spray, the termitary would at once be repopulated so long as the queen remained, alive, hidden in that inner chamber where her subjects who were also her progeny had walled her in and guarded and tended her.

The three exterminators were one white and two black. All had the red earth of underground clinging to their clothes and skin and hair; their eyes were bloodshot; the nails of their hands, black or white, were outlined in red, their ears rimmed. The long hairs in the nostrils of the white man were coated with red as a bee's legs are yellow with pollen. These men themselves appeared to have been dug up, raw from that clinging earth entombed beneath buildings. Bloodied by their life-long medieval quest, they were ready to take it up once more: the search for a queen. They were said to be very good; my mother was sceptical as she was about the powers of water diviners with bent twigs or people who got the dead to spell out messages by moving a glass to letters of the alphabet. But what else could she do? My father left it all to her, she had the responsibility.

She didn't like the look of these men. They were so filthy with earth; hands like exposed roots reaching for the tea she brought. She served even the white man with a tin mug.

It was she who insisted they leave a few boards intact under the piano; she knew better than to trust them to move it without damage to the rosewood case. They didn't speak while children watched them at work. The only sound was the pick stopped by the density of the earth under our living room, and the gasp of the black man who wielded the pick, pulling it free and hurling it back into the earth again. Held off by silence, we children would not go away. We stolidly spent all our free time in witness. Yet in spite of our vigilance, when it happened, when they found her, at last – the queen – we were not there.

My mother was mixing a cake and we had been attracted away to her by that substance of her alchemy that was not the beaten eggs and butter and sugar that went into it; even the lightest stroke of a quick forefinger into the bowl conveyed a coating of fragrant creamy sweetness to the mouth which already had foreknowledge of its utter satisfaction through the scent of vanilla that came not only from the bowl, but from her clothes, her hair, her very skin. Suddenly my mother's dog lifted his twitching lip back over his long teeth and began to bounce towards and back away from the screen door as he did when any stranger approached her. We looked up; the three men had come to the back steps. The white gestured his ochre hand brusquely at one of the blacks, who tramped forward with a child's cardboard shoebox offered. The lid was on and there were rough air holes punched in it here and there, just as in the boxes where we had kept silkworms until my mother thought they smelled too musty and threw them away. The white man gestured again; he and my mother for a moment held their hands the same way, his covered with earth, hers with flour. The black man took off the lid.

And there she was, the queen. The smallest child swallowed as if about to retch and ran away to the far side of the kitchen. The rest of us crowded nearer, but my mother made us make way, she wasn't going to be fobbed off with anything but complete satisfaction for her husband's money. We all gazed at an obese, helpless white creature, five inches long, with the tiny, shiny-visored head of an ant at one end. The body was a sort of dropsical sac attached to this head; it had no legs that could be seen, neither could it propel itself by peristaltic action, like a slug or worm. The queen. The queen whose domain, we had seen for ourselves in the galleries and passages that had been uncovered beneath our house, was as big as ours.

The white man spoke. 'That's 'er, missus.'

'You're sure you've got the queen?'

'We got it. That's it.' He gave a professional snigger at ignorance.

Was she alive? – But again the silence of the red-eyed, red-earthed men kept us back; they wouldn't let us daringly put out a finger to touch that body that seemed blown up in sections, like certain party balloons, and that had at once the suggestion of tactile attraction and repugnance – if a finger were to be stroked testingly along that perhaps faintly downy body, sweet and creamy stuff might be expected to ooze from it. And in fact, when I found a book in the library called *The Soul of the White Ant,* by Eugène Marais, an Afrikaner like the white man who had found the queen's secret chamber, I read that the children-subjects at certain times draw nourishment from a queen's great body by stroking it so that she exudes her own rich maternal elixir.

'Ughh. Why's she so fat?' The smallest child had come close enough to force himself to look again.

'S'es full of ecks,' the white man said. 'They lays about a million ecks a day.'

'Is it dead?'

But the man only laughed, now that his job was done, and like the showman's helper at the conclusion of an act, the black man knew to clap the lid back on the shoebox. There was no way for us to tell; the queen cannot move, she is blind; whether she is underground, the tyrannical prisoner of her subjects who would not have been born and cannot live without her, or whether she is captured and borne away in a shoebox, she is helpless to evade the consequences of her power.

My mother paid the men out of her housekeeping allowance (but she would have to speak to our father about that) and they nailed back the living-room floorboards and went away, taking the cardboard box with them. My mother had heard that the whole thing was a hoax; these men went from house to house, made the terrible mess they'd left hers in, and produced the same queen time and again, carrying it around with them.

Yet the termites left our house. We never had to have those particular workmen in again. The Axminster carpet was laid once more, the furniture put back in its place, and I had to do the daily half-hour practice on the Steinway that I had been freed of for a week. I read in the book from the library that when the queen dies or is taken away all the termites leave their posts and desert the termitary; some find their way to other communities, thousands die. The termitary with its fungus-gardens for food, its tunnels for conveying water from as much as forty feet underground, its elaborate defence and communications system, is abandoned.

We lived on, above the ruin. The children grew up and left the town; coming back from the war after 1945 and later from visits to Europe and America and the Far East, it bored them to hear the same old stories, to be asked: 'D'you remember Mr Hartman who used to come in to tune the piano? He was asking after you the other day – poor thing, he's crippled with arthritis.' 'D'you remember old Strydom, "pulling the line" ... how you kids used to laugh, I was quite ashamed ...' 'D'you remember the time the white ant men were in, and you nearly broke your leg?' Were these events the sum of my mother's life? Why should I remember? I, who – shuddering to look back at those five rooms behind the bow-window eyes and the front-door mouth – have oceans, continents, snowed-in capitals, islands where turtles swim, cathedrals, theatres, palace gardens where people kiss and tramps drink wine – all these to remember. My father grew senile and she put him in a home for his last years. She stayed on, although she said she didn't want to; the house was a burden to her, she had carried the whole responsibility for him, for all of us, all her life. Now she is dead and although I suppose someone else lives in her house, the secret passages, the inner chamber in which she was our queen and our prisoner are sealed up, empty.

PJ HAASBROEK

Departure

Translated from the Afrikaans by Lynette Paterson.

The train was to depart at 22h00. You all arrived a little early with your families, your girls and a few friends, with your kitbags and rifles, and stood about on the platform, self-conscious because the train was not there and the wind was blowing so; uncomfortable in brown uniforms amidst the colourful, soft people who have come to see you off. Fortunately you are all spruce again, even those who have come out of the plastic bags. The authorities have at least arranged that properly.

'This will take some getting used to,' you hear Petrus Bosman's father say. 'We had so many plans.' You glance in his direction, because you remember what Petrus had said about his father's plans, and you see how his mother clutches the man's arm in both her hands. 'I'm going to miss him so,' she says. 'I can tell what Christmas is going to be like without him. Everyone will come for a swim and a braaivleis again. Carol-Anne will probably arrive early to help with the salads. Now I won't even be able to send him a little something any more,' and she begins to sob. 'We'll just have to vasbyt,' says his father.

You feel you could laugh. 'Vasbyt!' Easily said. Easy army talk. Like 'min dae'. No, certainly not that. 'Vasbyt', yes but not 'min dae'. You keep a casual eye on the other men, a little surprised at the civilised geniality, the playful bravado at how different your companions are amongst their families. It is clear that they want to caress their girls, that they are anxious to comfort and to keep sentimentality at bay, but every now and then they glance at the signal in the distance which has been an unwavering green for the past quarter of an hour.

Even though you are alone, you also wish that the train would come. The station is a no-man's-land, a place one comes to only to depart for somewhere else. It was not designed or built for people who wish to be together, but for separation. Domestic chats do not belong in these stark, rectangular, open spaces. The dirty concrete and tar, red brick and steel are unfriendly, intentionally unfriendly like the massive pillars and the cold gleam of the tracks in the dark under the electric light. The station is open so that the wind can blow in and snatch at people's clothing to separate them from each other. You tap your pipe against the side of the platform and watch the coals spill out in the dark and die. Why can't departure be just as easy?

You pick up your bag when you see the train light, a sudden star growing, brightening and blinding as it approaches. The pitch-black locomotive passes you with a gnashing of steel wheels on steel. For a moment you see red fire and the white, curious face of the engine driver in his window, and then come the third-class passenger cars. The pale yellow light is like thin oil washing over the crowded commuters. 'Are they actually going to send the blacks with them?' a man behind you enquires angrily.

You all walk down the length of the train in search of your compartments. The last two carriages are yours. You throw your kitbags onto the luggage racks and hang your rifles on the clothes hooks. Many get off the train again, but others remain in the passage, leaning out through the window to say goodbye. You sit in the compartment and gaze through the window at the deserted, windy platform on your side of the train, relieved not to have any part in the farewell. The train jerks, and you hear the wails of the people and comforting words of the soldiers. The station glides slowly by.

They were only shunting. Your carriages now stand alongside another platform, number 6, without a locomotive. The devil alone knows where in the dark night it has been moved to with the blacks' cars in tow. Fortunately all the people left before you were returned here, and you all are alone; there is not even a railway worker in sight.

Slowly, cautiously, the men begin to question one another. How it had happened, where, on what day and at what time, and are surprised at the degree of similarity, often the exact concurrence, but you keep quiet. Your story is none of their business. Your honour is your own.

In their conversations they return to the border camps surrounded by trenches, and machine-gun installations protected by sandbags, to the sand-tracks reaching in endless straight lines to the flat horizons, and the bush where all memories have become indistinct like the haze in the afternoon sky. Whatever may have happened before is no longer relevant. Only that which caused you all to end up on this train. Nothing else.

You have taken the hidden bottles of alcohol from your bags and drink large mugs of brandy and coke, cane spirits, vodka and beer with great gulps straight from the bottles. Each one has a story to tell, each one knows a joke, and there is much boisterous laughter and comradely backslapping. No longer accustomed to the raw, strong spirits, you are all soon drunk.

Men fall about, cursing. Some pick quarrels and fist fights break out.

Petrus laughingly holds a quarrelsome soldier by the wrists, but when he tries to butt Petrus with his head, Petrus flings him off. The soldier staggers into someone else, and begins to swipe wildly at the broad, dense face which confronts him. His fists strike bone, eye socket, nose and chin, but the sweaty, shiny skin shows no damage; no bruising, no blood, the eyes expressionless, uncomprehending. The soldier abruptly stops his blows, turns and walks out of the compartment, his anger quenched.

You can hear the noise of fighting in the passage and the other compartments too, but you ignore the hubbub. That is just your way of keeping to yourself, and here it is each to his own. You sit with your head in your hands, as you always do, and feel your companions' shoulders against you, their breath warm as blood. Their hands grab at you when they stumble but you do not look up. Nor do you answer their questions, trying only to concentrate on the hissing and heaving of the train, the rocking, rolling and upward rearing. The loud, shrill voices recede to a soft continuous sigh.

It occurs to you that the authorities have left you here with a purpose. Were you meant to get drunk and start brawling before the journey could begin? Were you meant to confront each other with the meaninglessness of your short lives and your deaths, or are they allowing you first to reconcile yourselves to the journey? You stand up, suddenly suspicious, and put your head out of the window.

There is a man crossing the platform. He is carrying a zinc basin and is elderly; he looks about fifty to you, with his thin hair and his bent-over, plodding walk. Judging by his khaki trousers, open-neck shirt and dirty, crumpled jacket, you presume that he is a labourer. He has either been misdirected or he has misunderstood, but this cannot be the train he intends to catch. He pays no attention to the lists of passengers' names, slogs unsuspectingly by to the door at the end of the carriage, and climbs in.

You feel you should warn him.

'Oom,' you say, 'you're on the wrong train.'

He looks blankly at you and lowers his little bathtub onto the floor of the passage. 'No,' he says, 'I'm going with you.'

'This is a troop train,' you say, afraid of alarming him. 'You are not a soldier, Oom.'

'I do not mind with whom I travel,' he says. 'This is my last journey. Don't spoil everything now. Where can I find a seat?'

You wanted to tell him that the train is full, but then it occurred to you to play a trick on the old man. He would not know that this train does not stop anywhere. He would have to make the entire journey.

'Let's put the tub in the toilet,' you say. Maybe he'll still realise his mistake.

'No, I'd rather keep it with me,' he says.

The tub is bulging, covered with a towel and tied with a string. You carry it ahead of him to your compartment.

The others are surprised. 'Jesus, Oom,' says one, 'where do you think you're going?'

'At least I know where I come from,' the old man says and sits down next to Petrus. 'And that's enough for me.'

You nod at the soldier. 'The Oom knows,' you say.

Someone else asks about the bathtub, and the old man begins to undo the string. No one stops him. He removes the towel. In the tub is a framed wedding picture, a sheaf of papers, a toolbox and a few articles of children's clothing neatly folded. He unpacks the contents onto his lap so that he can dig deeper. He uncovers a worn blue overall and a white tie. He hesitates. 'They said I must bring this all with me,' he says. 'It must show who I am. It's easy. Apprentice, carpenter, married, had two little girls. And I was church warden in my day.' His hands fold lovingly around the bundle of possessions. 'My whole life,' he says.

'That's more than we've had,' says Petrus. 'I've not even had a job.' He takes the overall from the basin and holds it up to his chest as though to measure it for size, but you are no longer watching him.

Right at the bottom of the bathtub are two dolls. A pink rubber doll like the ones children play with in the bath, and a grinning black golliwog with white eyes and checkered pants. Suddenly you remember, you see them, and the blood roars in your ears like an approaching storm. You feel your guts contracting beneath your chest, a miserable nausea rises thickly in your throat, and your body begins to convulse as it did on that day. You vaguely hear someone say: 'Look what we have here. A terrorist!' and someone else adds: 'And sharing a bath with the white baby.'

You see them standing around you in their tattered bush wear, see them dragging you from the hut where you were hiding. You hear them laughing as they shove you with their rifle butts. You had no idea what they were planning to do. The sun pierced your eyes and you found yourself at the split-pole fence, at the high, sharpened corner stake, and you felt their hands. They lifted you. You screamed, but no sound came from between your clenched teeth.

You lift your rifle from the hook and fix the bayonet.

The old man looks in amazement at the golliwog. 'It's just a doll,' he says.

The blade impales it and you lift it high, higher than the old man's snatching hands. Right up to the light where it hangs like a flopping dead bird against the sun on the point of the bayonet.

The old man shakes his head. 'We are on the point of departure,' he says. 'And you have still not made your peace.'

Then you realise that the old man knows where you are headed. Your destination is also his.

The black locomotive barks abruptly a few times into the wide mouth of the dark, and your journey begins.

BESSIE HEAD

The Wind and a Boy

Like all the village boys, Friedman had a long wind blowing for him, but perhaps the enchanted wind that blew for him filled the whole world with magic.

Until they became ordinary, dull grown men, who drank beer and made babies, the little village boys were a special set all on their own. They were kings whom no one ruled. They wandered where they willed from dawn to dusk and only condescended to come home at dusk because they were afraid of the horrible things in the dark that might pounce on them. Unlike the little girls who adored household chores and drawing water, it was only now and then that the boys showed themselves as useful attachments to any household. When the first hard rains of summer fell, small dark shapes, quite naked except for their loincloths, sped out of the village into the bush. They knew that the first downpour had drowned all the wild rabbits, moles and porcupines in their burrows in the earth. As they crouched down near the entrances to the burrows, they would see a small drowned nose of an animal peeping out; they knew it had struggled to emerge from its burrow, flooded by the sudden rush of storm water and as they pulled out the animal, they would say, pityingly: 'Birds have more sense than rabbits, moles and porcupines. They build their homes in trees.'

But it was hunting made easy, for no matter how hard a boy and his dog ran, a wild rabbit ran ten times faster; a porcupine hurled his poisonous quills into the body; and a mole stayed where he thought it was safe – deep under the ground. So it was with inordinate pride that the boys carried home armfuls of dead animals for their families to feast on for many days. Apart from that, the boys lived very much as they pleased, with the wind and their own games.

Now and then, the activities of a single family could captivate the imagination and hearts of all the people of their surroundings; for years and years, the combination of the boy, Friedman, and his grandmother, Sejosenye, made the people of Ga-Sefete-Molemo ward smile, laugh, then cry.

They smiled at his first two phases. Friedman came home as a small bundle from the hospital, a bundle his grandmother nursed carefully near her bosom and crooned to day and night with extravagant care and tenderness.

'She is like that,' people remarked, 'because he may be the last child she will ever nurse. Sejosenye is old now and will die one of these days; the child is a gift to keep her heart warm.'

Indeed, all Sejosenye's children were grown, married, and had left home. Of all her children, only her last-born daughter was unmarried and Friedman was the result of some casual mating she had indulged in, in a town a hundred miles away where she had a job as a typist. She wanted to return to her job almost immediately, so she handed the child over to her mother and that was that; she could afford to forget him as he had a real mother now. During all the time that Sejosenye haunted the hospital, awaiting her bundle, a friendly foreign doctor named Friedman took a fancy to her maternal, grandmotherly ways. He made a habit of walking out of his path to talk to her. She never forgot it and on receiving her bundle she called the baby Friedman.

They smiled at his second phase, a small dark shadow who toddled silently and gravely beside a very tall grandmother; wherever the grandmother went, there went Friedman. Most women found this phase of the restless, troublesome toddler tedious; they dumped the toddler onto one of their younger girls and were off to weddings and visits on their own.

'Why can't you leave your handbag at home sometimes, granny?' they said.

'Oh, he's no trouble,' Sejosenye would reply.

They began to laugh at his third phase. Almost overnight he turned into a tall spindly-legged, graceful gazelle with large, grave eyes. There was an odd, musical lilt to his speech and when he teased, or was up to mischief, he moved his head on his long thin neck from side to side like a cobra. It was he who became the king of kings of all the boys in his area; he could turn his hand to anything and made the best wire cars with their wheels of shoe-polish tins. All his movements were neat, compact, decisive, and for his age he was a boy who knew his own mind. They laughed at his knowingness and certainty on all things, for he was like the grandmother who had had a flaming youth all her own too. Sejosenye had scandalised the whole village in her days of good morals by leaving her own village ward to live with a married man in Ga-Sefete-Molemo ward. She had won him from his wife and married him and then lived down the scandal in the way only natural queens can. Even in old age, she was still impressive. She sailed through the village, head in the air, with a quiet, almost expressionless face. She had developed large buttocks as time went by and they announced their presence firmly in rhythm with her walk.

Another of Sejosenye's certainties was that she was a woman who could plough, but it was like a special gift. Each season, in drought or hail or sun, she removed herself to her lands. She not only ploughed but nursed and brooded over her crops. She was there all the time till the corn ripened and the birds had to be chased off the land, till harvesting and threshing were done; so that even in drought years with their scanty rain, she came home with some crops. She was the envy of all the women of the surroundings.

'Sejosenye always eats fine things in her house,' they said. 'She ploughs and then sits down for many months and enjoys the fruits of her labour.'

The women also envied her beautiful grandson. There was something special there, so that even when Friedman moved into his bad phase, they forgave him crimes other boys received a sound thrashing for. The small boys were terrible thieves who harassed people by stealing their food and money. It was all a part of the games they played but one which people did not like. Of them all, Friedman was the worst thief, so that his name was mentioned more and more in any thieving that had been uncovered.

'But Friedman showed us how to open the window with a knife and string,' the sobbing, lashed boys would protest.

'Friedman isn't as bad as you,' the parents would reply, irrationally. They were hypnotised by a beautiful creature. The boy Friedman, who had become a real nuisance by then, also walked around as though he were special. He couldn't possibly be a thief and he added an aloof, offended, disdainful expression to his pretty face. He wasn't just an ordinary sort of boy in Ga-Sefete-Molemo ward. He was …

It happened, quite accidentally, that his grandmother told him all those stories about the hunters, warriors, and emissaries of old. She was normally a quiet, absent-minded woman, given to dreaming by herself but she liked to sing the boy a little song now and then as they sat by the outdoor fire. A lot of them were church songs and rather sad; they more or less passed as her bedtime prayer at night – she was one of the old church-goers. Now and then she added a quaint little song to her repertoire and as the night-time, fire-light flames flickered between them, she never failed to note that this particular song was always well received by the boy. A little light would awaken in his eyes and he would bend forward and listen attentively.

'Welcome, Robinson Crusoe, welcome,' she would sing, in clear, sweet tones. 'How could you stay, so long away, Robinson how could you do so?'

When she was very young, Sejosenye had attended the mission school of the village for about a year; made a slight acquaintance with the ABC and one, two, three, four, five, and the little song about Robinson Crusoe. But girls didn't need an education in those days when ploughing and marriage made up their whole world. Yet Robinson Crusoe lived on as a gay and out-of-context memory of her schooldays.

One evening the boy leaned forward and asked: 'Is that a special praise-poem song for Robinson Crusoe, grandmother?'

'Oh yes,' she replied, smiling.

'What great things did he do?' the boy asked, pointedly.

'They say he was a hunter who went by Gweta side and killed an elephant all by himself,' she said, making up a story on the spot. 'Oh! In those days, no man could kill an elephant by himself. All the regiments had to join together and each man had to thrust his sword into the side of the elephant before it died. Well, Robinson Crusoe was gone many days and people wondered about him: "Perhaps he has been eaten by a lion," they said. "Robinson likes to be a solitary person and do foolish things. We won't ever go out into the bush by ourselves because we know it is dangerous." Well, one day, Robinson suddenly appeared in their midst and people could see that he had a great thing on his mind. They all gathered around him. He said: "I have killed an elephant for all the people." The people were surprised: "Robinson!" they said. "It is impossible! How did you do it? The very thought of an elephant approaching the village makes us shiver!" And Robinson said: "Ah, people, I saw a terrible sight! I was standing at the feet of the elephant. I was just a small ant. I could not see the world any more. Elephant was above me until his very head touched the sky and his ears spread out like great wings. He was angry but I only looked into one eye which was turning round and round in anger. What to do now? I thought it better to put that eye out. I raised my spear and threw it at the angry eye. People! It went right inside. Elephant said not a word and he fell to one side. Come, I will show you what I have done." Then the women cried in joy: "Loo-loo-loo!" They ran to fetch their containers as some wanted the meat of the elephant; some wanted the fat. The men made their knives sharp. They would make shoes and many things from the skin and bones. There was something for all the people in the great work Robinson Crusoe did.'

All this while, as he listened to the story, the boy's eyes had glowed softly. At the end of it, he drew in a long breath.

'Grandmother,' he whispered, adroitly stepping into the role of Robinson Crusoe, the great hunter. 'One day, I'm going to be like that. I'm going to be a hunter like Robinson Crusoe and bring meat to all the people.' He paused for breath and then added tensely: 'And what other great thing did Robinson Crusoe do?'

'Tsaa!' she said, clicking her tongue in exhaustion, 'Am I then going away that I must tell *all* the stories at once?'

Although his image of Robinson Crusoe, the great hunter, was never to grow beyond his everyday boyish activities of pushing wire cars, hunting in the fields for wild rabbits, climbing trees to pull down old birds' nests and yelling out in alarm to find that a small snake now occupied the abandoned abode, or racing against the wind with the spoils of his latest theft, the stories awakened a great tenderness in him. If Robinson Crusoe was not churning up the dust in deadly hand-to-hand combat with an enemy, he was crossing swollen rivers and wild jungles as the great messenger and ambassador of the chief – all his activities were touchingly in aid of or in defence of the people. One day Friedman expressed this awakened compassion for life in a strange way. After a particularly violent storm, people found their huts invaded by many small mice and they were hard-pressed to rid themselves of these pests. Sejosenye ordered Friedman to kill the mice.

'But grandmother,' he protested, 'they have come to us for shelter. They lost all their homes in the storm. It's better that I put then in a box and carry them out into the fields again once the rains are over.'

She had laughed in surprise at this and spread the story around among her women friends, who smiled tenderly, then said to their own offspring: 'Friedman isn't as bad as you.'

Life and its responsibilities began to weigh down heavily on Friedman as he approached his fourteenth year. Less time was spent in boyish activities. He grew more and more devoted to his grandmother and concerned to assist her in every way. He wanted a bicycle so that he might run up and down to the shops for her, deliver messages, or do any other chore she might have in mind. His mother, who worked in a town far away, sent him the money to purchase the bicycle. The gift brought the story of his life abruptly to a close.

Towards the beginning of the rainy season, he accompanied his grandmother to her lands which were some twenty miles outside the village. They sowed seed together after the hired tractor had turned up the land but the boy's main chore was to keep the household pot filled with meat. Sometimes they ate birds Friedman had trapped, sometimes they ate fried tortoise meat or wild rabbit; but there was always something as the bush abounded with animal life. Sejosenye only had to take a bag of mealie meal, packets of sugar, tea and powdered milk as provisions for their stay at the lands; meat was never a problem. Midway through the ploughing season, she began to run out of sugar, tea and milk.

'Friedman,' she said that evening, 'I shall wake you early tomorrow morning. You will have to take the bicycle into the village and purchase some more sugar, tea and milk.'

He was up at dawn with the birds, a solitary figure cycling on a pathway through the empty bush. By nine, he had reached the village and first made his way to Ga-Sefete-Molemo ward and the yard of a friend of his grandmother, who gave him a cup of tea and a plate of porridge. Then he put one foot on the bicycle and turned to smile at the woman with his beautiful gazelle eyes. His smile was to linger vividly before her for many days as a short while later, hard pounding feet came running into her yard to report that Friedman was dead.

He pushed the bicycle through the winding, sandy pathway of the village ward, reached the high embankment of the main road, peddled vigorously up it and out of the corner of his eye, saw a small green truck speeding towards him. In the devil-may-care fashion of all the small boys, he cycled right into its path, turned his head and smiled appealingly at the driver. The truck caught him on the front bumper, squashed the bicycle and dragged the boy along at a crazy speed for another hundred yards, dropped him and careered on another twenty yards before coming to a halt. The boy's pretty face was a smear all along the road and he only had a torso left.

People of Ga-Sefete-Molemo ward never forgot the last coherent words Sejosenye spoke to the police. A number of them climbed into the police truck and accompanied it to her lands. They saw her walk slowly and enquiringly towards the truck, they heard the matter-of-fact voice of the policeman announce the death, then they heard Sejosenye say piteously: 'Can't you return those words back?'

She turned away from them, either to collect her wits or the few possessions she had brought with her. Her feet and buttocks quivered anxiously as she stumbled towards her hut. Then her feet tripped her up and she fell to the ground like a stunned log.

The people of Ga-Sefete-Molemo ward buried the boy Friedman but none of them would go near the hospital where Sejosenye lay. The stories, brought to them by way of the nurses were too terrible for words. They said the old woman sang and laughed and talked to herself all the time. So they merely asked each other: 'Have you been to see Mma-Sejosenye?' 'I'm afraid I cannot. It would kill my heart.' Two weeks later, they buried her.

As was village habit, the incident was discussed thoroughly from all sides till it was understood. In this timeless, sleepy village, the goats stood and suckled their young ones on the main road or lay down and took their afternoon naps there. The motorists either stopped for them or gave way. But it appeared that the driver of the truck had neither brakes on his car nor a driving licence. He belonged to the new, rich, civil-servant class whose salaries had become fantastically high since independence. They had to have cars in keeping with their new status; they had to have any car, as long as it was a car; they were in such a hurry about everything that they couldn't be bothered to take driving lessons. And thus progress, development, and preoccupation with status and living standards first announced themselves to the village. It looked like being an ugly story with many decapitated bodies on the main road.

CHRISTOPHER HOPE

The Fall of the British Empire

Having been introduced to the boys by the headmaster, Mr Sessi stands silent for a moment with a look both bright and pleasant on his face. He is the first Sierra Leonian we have seen, certainly the first to whom we can put a name, and we gaze back with interest. To the students slouched in their uncomfortable chairs, Mr Sessi is familiar only by the colour of his skin, the prevalence of which, in all its shades, is deplored across the Midlands even if seldom seen in such blackness, a special item of interest in Mr Sessi's case. So many people have said to me: 'We used to have very good relations with the coloured people but, of late, we've been feeling rather overwhelmed.' On such occasions, I never know what to answer, so I nod and look away, which is often taken as an expression of sympathy. Since I am known as a South African, I don't suppose it could be taken any other way.

To the boys who comprise his audience, Mr Sessi could not be more remote in his origins, in the cast of his mind and the exoticism of his perspiration, had he come from the dark side of the moon. These boys are fourteen years old, the Easter School-Leavers the staff call them; to the school they are known as the dum-dums. Their clothes are carefully chosen to show that they regard themselves as pretty tough, showing a lot of denim, carefully faded and raggy in the right places, and heavy boots, studded at heel and toe. In the matter of his foreignness, I have the advantage over them because Mr Sessi comes from black Africa which is geographically close to South Africa, and geography is my subject. That is to say, I'm paid to teach it. In actual fact, I spend lesson times fending off diversionary questions about Zulu chiefs and witchdoctors, but no matter.

Sierra Leone, named by the Portuguese (England's oldest ally), was firstly famous for its slaves, and secondly for its role as a settlement for destitute Negroes, native chiefs having ceded the peninsula to Britain in 1787 for this purpose – features of his country which Mr Sessi is too obliging to mention. Patently he is not a slave, although his great-grandfather may well have been. Mr Sessi is from the Mende tribe, in the south of the country, and this tribe, now that the Creole influence is finally broken for ever, is growing in prestige and breeding fine administrators. Perhaps he will be one of them. You can be sure that they think so at the University, and at the Embassy, which he mentions so happily, so often. No doubt the government of Sierra Leone think the money that they're paying out on Mr Sessi's education at Birmingham University, where he is probably reading sociology or social anthropology, well spent. In South Africa, Mr Sessi would be called a clever kaffir, and he would probably be doing much the same thing that he is doing in England; reading sociology or anthropology at one of the new tribal universities.

'I'm not going to talk to you for very long,' Mr Sessi explains kindly, 'and when I finish we will take a look at a film of my country, Sierra Leone, which I have had sent to the school from my embassy in London. I'd be glad if you would keep any questions that you may have until then.' He smiles charmingly. 'Your headmaster tells me that at these sessions, usually after the film show, you break up into groups to originate the questions you wish to put to me. I'm sure that some of them will be real stinkers! I only hope that I can oblige you with the answers when the time comes.'

His audience, though no less stony-eyed, leans forward, shoulders hunched; their sign that they are prepared to suspend judgement on Mr Sessi, in the face of such pleasantries. They have no hope that his lecture will interest them – but it just might be diverting.

Mr Sessi turns and faces the portable cinema screen that has been erected on a table at the head of the class, contemplating it with a cock of his head, this way and that, then he turns back to the waiting audience: 'Perhaps someone has a piece of chalk?' he asks diffidently, with an upward shift of the eyebrows, a flick of the head, including in his enquiry the boys and teachers who stand beside and behind them.

The Deputy Head, flustered by the request, hurries from the hall. He has no sooner disappeared through the big double doors in search of a box of chalk than a boy stands up in the first row and produces from his blazer pocket a piece of chalk which he offers to Mr Sessi who beams his thanks. A murmur, of approbation I think it is, rises from his classmates who doubtless approve of this brutally swift response; natural dramatists, they appreciate any device that safeguards the smooth development of the action. Although it is impossible, it seems that Mr Sessi has mistaken the cinema screen for a blackboard.

He stands gazing at it, chalk in hand. His back is turned for a few seconds only before he faces us again. His smile continues but he makes no secret of his perplexity. His chalk hand, the right, is thrown out behind him, gesturing, as it were, towards the white screen. The murmur grows louder amongst the rows of intent boys. I won't swear to this, but it seems as if Mr Sessi is about to lose his air of good-humoured, honest confusion, and become rather quizzical. He is certainly sensitive to the unmarked silvery white screen at his back and the silent boys before him. He scrutinises the piece of chalk he holds: 'Please,' he says rather diffidently, as if he were sparing us embarrassment, 'do you write on a white board with white chalk?'

The class groans and snuffles to itself. All this, their frantic wrigglings clearly say, is too much to be borne. 'We've gorra right 'un here, all right.' It's one thing for the stupid black bugger to take a cinema screen for a blackboard, but to go so far as to offer to write on it with a piece of chalk, in good faith, is simply too good to be true. The class casts around desperately, looking for the Head, wanting to gauge his reaction to their reaction to these extraordinary goings-on. It would be unreasonable for him, their contorted expressions say, to expect from them the usual decorum he demands during these lectures. It is enough to have to stop themselves from laughing out loud.

Fighting his face muscles into a disarming, apologetic, unembarrassed smile, but reddening to the roots of his hair, the Head shuffles his slack-kneed way down the aisle and lifts up the heavy linen flap of a large Phillips map of Africa, obviously an old one, still patched in Imperial pink, which is displayed beside the cinema screen, to reveal beneath it a portable blackboard pegged on a tripod. The Deputy Head returns and hands a fistful of chalk to Mr Sessi.

'In the University,' says Mr Sessi, graciously accepting the chalks and the discovery of an orthodox blackboard with an unwavering smile and not the slightest hint of irony, 'we usually write with coloured chalks on a white board.'

We are unprepared for the novelty of this suggestion and it gives us that faintly uncomfortable feeling we have when we catch someone out in a clumsy evasion and yet feel at the same time that to point it out to him would be more embarrassing still. So we flush, as the Head is doing, and look the other way. Yet it is a little tiresome to observe how blandly Mr Sessi ignores our scruples. I put this down to an iron nerve. God knows what the boys think of it. Probably that Mr Sessi is making a swift but silly effort to slip out of a tricky situation, choosing to make up this unlikely explanation rather than risk our scorn by admitting that he has never been face to face with a blackboard in his life. Who knows, perhaps he has never seen the inside of Birmingham University either. Certainly he has a very thick skin if he thinks he can brazen it out like this.

At the same time I can't help wondering whether any of the boys envy Mr Sessi his black face at this moment. Surely, in one or two minds, there is the thought that the guilty blush, which to their irritation they know may spread across a face with treacherous suddenness regardless of innocence, does not show on a black face. With sidelong glances I see them searching his face for the tell-tale flush. It is a waste of time, unless you know what you are looking for. Of course, black faces do blush, as any South African will tell you, and it is becoming plain to me that Mr Sessi doesn't share our embarrassment.

Some weeks later, when Mr Sessi's visit was barely remembered, I was to discover in a trade magazine an advertisement for a piece of classroom equipment described as a magnetic white marker board, the 'Twinlock Saxo Wyte Bord'. Writing and drawing are accomplished with coloured marker pens. The 'Wyte Bord' has an additional advantage; it can double as a cinema screen, so the advertisement claimed, and it is often used in the universities.

At the time of Mr Sessi's lecture on Sierra Leone, I will admit that I was more interested in Worcestershire than in Africa. I was living and working there, so it was the part of England most open to study. Some people associate Worcestershire with countryside, with the Vale of Evesham, with apple orchards, cherries and whatnot. As a geographer I find this curious. Worcestershire, the closer one gets to Birmingham, seems to be far more factory than farm to the visitor from a less industrially developed, emptier, larger country. An area of 716 square miles with a population of some 700 000, Worcestershire melds in the north into the indistinguishability of Birmingham's environs. Villages, dispossessed by characteristic housing estates of their surrounding countryside, seem to run one into another, village into suburb, into town, into city: unsettled places floating aimlessly around and about the blast furnaces of Birmingham. This displacing instils a feeling of edginess in the inhabitants, most now drawn from the farms into the manufacturing industries, or those industries that service the manufacturing industries.

This is Worcestershire for me, perhaps for Mr Sessi too. But for both of us, this is also Africa. Simply by being here, we affect the geography of the place, we Africanise it a little. Only for a moment perhaps, but that is as long as anything lasts. This has been proved to me, as it will be to Mr Sessi, and as painfully. We are strangers to this place, quickly recognised by the natives as fearsome Captain Cooks. Since we are apparently peaceful, and come bearing gifts of novelties and wonders, they are prepared to wait before deciding what to do with us. Yet they are wary nonetheless, and hostile, in a dull, taciturn way. Men may very well be islands, as the geographer suspects, as Captain Cook learnt to his dreadful cost. And where is this more likely to prove true than on this most insular of islands?

But Mr Sessi of the Mende tribe of Sierra Leone, now of Birmingham and the University, sooner than later to be of the Civil Service, earnest and willing ambassador to the English Secondary Schools, incipient administrator, smiles on the sons of men who brush shoulders with too many of his colour in a working day to bear it without protesting: 'I'm no racialist, mind, but there's too many of them coloureds around these parts now.'

He speaks plainly and very slowly, determined to be understood. Whether he does this from long experience in a hundred school halls built to the Department of Education's uniplan, I couldn't say. His bland, unreasonable composure offers no clue. The chances are that he has never faced an audience like this: boys of fourteen, who failed to get into grammar school and failed thereby to qualify for any jobs but those only slightly better than black immigrants take on nowadays.

Then again, perhaps I romanticise, and all he feels up there on the rostrum is uncertainty in his new role of lecturer, and in the faces of boys who have inherited sevenfold their fathers' frustrations and fears, he sees nothing but young white students eager for a glimpse of how the other half of the world lives; and perhaps, too, his smile is really benign and falls on each equally. It is not possible for a South African to know.

'Sierra Leone is not a very big country. Now, when I say big, I don't know what picture comes into your heads. Perhaps it will help to give you an idea of the size of Sierra Leone if I tell you that my country is not much more than half the size of England. Who knows the size of England?'

No one answers. It is unlikely that many of the class even hear the question. Resistant to language, they are still undergoing a process of adjustment to the strange presence of the speaker. It is not simply that Mr Sessi is so shiningly black and speaks a queer sort of English in a peculiar accent. No, the extraordinary thing about Mr Sessi is that he somehow manages to suggest that he is a person of some importance – to somebody. Despite his not very firm control of the language, he has an air of assurance. He doesn't speak with a Birmingham accent. It is unlikely that he comes from Bradford. He is in the country, the Head has reassured them in comforting tones before the lecture, to study. He is not an immigrant, then, and he does not speak like a coloured. They are puzzled.

Who can blame them? I know something of their incomprehension. In South Africa we would call Mr Sessi an educated kaffir. He speaks English like every blackface parody from Cape Town to Baton Rouge. He is Uncle Tom, Malcolm X and Shaka, King of the Zulus, rolled up into one. And yet - he is *real.*

'Sierra Leone, you might be interested to know, has an area of 27 925 square miles. But I think that I will leave you the problem of working out from that figure how big England is by comparison,' Mr Sessi says, and his smile does not falter. 'I'm sure that you will discover that my country is a small country, relatively, but then, with only two and a half million of us, we do not face the problem of over-population.'

I see the Head smiling sheepishly and he looks almost longingly at the speaker, trying to communicate his extreme sadness at the thoroughly unsuitable mode of address which Mr Sessi has chosen to adopt. To ask specific questions of these boys on any subject other than football is so novel that it might actually have succeeded in diverting the now increasingly restless class. But to expect answers from them looks like madness.

'Our climate is rather different to yours. I wonder if one of you can tell me what kind of climate you have here in Britain?'

The silence which follows this question pains me, as it will pain all geographers. More so one who has talked for weeks to these same boys in cunningly colloquial fashion, in no way resembling a geography lesson, of the vagaries of the English weather. It is specially galling to a South African to observe such ignorance in the face of black assurance, made worse because the boys are exchanging contemptuous and knowing smiles between themselves, confidently imputing the ignorance of procedure to Mr Sessi.

Yet he waits good-naturedly for an answer, and astonishingly, it comes:

'Rainy?' someone enquires tentatively.

I control an impulse to laugh. Luckily I succeed, because the boys do not laugh. In fact, from the anxious looks on their faces it appears that they are actually considering the answer, hoping that it will somehow do as a gesture of their good faith and Mr Sessi will now stop asking questions.

But Mr Sessi is unaffected. He simply replies, 'No, no – temperate, I would say.'

Merely by extracting an answer, Mr Sessi has scored, and it rankles. To prolong my chagrin, I go over in my mind all that I know of Sierra Leone, the last of the English monarchical possessions in Africa. It is no longer a country which holds significance for Britain and thus for the world at large. The industrious slavers who worked their monopolies so successfully are dead, gone and forgotten. When slaving was found to be no longer viable as an industry, those patriarchs, that is to say, their Imperial bookkeepers, allowed the trade to be written off and did not object when the Imperial abolitionists turned it to their credit. Sierra Leone, with its apt capital of Freetown, became the settling place of freed slaves from America, Europe and the surrounding colonies in Africa. They put their freedom to the test by cohabiting with the white settlers of Sierra Leone. The Creoles, born of this union, learned the craft of government from their British masters. When the British began to leave, it was the Creoles who took over the job of administering the indigenous tribes, from Freetown with its excellent harbour, once a Second-Class Imperial Coaling Station. Now the Creoles are in decline. It is Mr Sessi of the Mende tribe who is being groomed for the business of administration. For the tribes of Sierra Leone are a little fractious, and need proper government.

'You must understand that I come from what is known as a developing country, in the Third World. Please realise that as you in Britain have had your industrial revolution, we are just beginning now to have ours. We are learning to stand on our own two feet. And if Sierra Leone is to progress and to take her rightful place among the free nations, people in faraway countries must get out of their minds the notion that we are a small, uninteresting country offering no more than a good harbour and exportable crops of kernels, nuts and palm oil.'

Mr Sessi's longest speech: I find myself nodding in agreement or sympathy, I'm not sure which. It is plain that Mr Sessi is sentimentally attached to his former colonial masters. He pays them the compliment of studying at one of their newer universities, aping their manners and dress, and continually comparing with just the right amount of patriotic pride and fervour his homeland with the Old Country. By the standards of diplomacy, he is inarticulate, but then he is young, and will soon improve out of all recognition. This lecture to this speechless class in a secondary modern school in semi-rural Worcestershire is good practice for a man who will one day have charge of an area the size of this county and who will have to deal there with tribes no less sullen, inarticulate and suspicious than the young men he now faces.

Does it occur to him, I ask myself, that the British have no one left to administer but themselves, nowhere left to direct their energies? Mr Sessi from post-Imperial black Africa stands lecturing this bored, uncomprehending audience of resentful, truculent and occasionally dangerous young men who chafe at school discipline – so like colonial paternalism – on the complexities of familial and tribal structures, and the difficulties of administering mutually antagonistic tribes in a huge country.

'In Sierra Leone we have only two seasons in the year. Can one of you tell me how many seasons you have here in Britain? You have four, right? Who knows what they are called? No one? Well, for a start there is spring – now, which are the others? Summer, that's right, well done, and …? Come on, now. What about autumn? Right! And the last one …'

Obviously the spell which Mr Sessi's performance before the cinema screen cast upon the audience has worn off. No one answers him. But he is undeterred.

'You see, where you in Britain have four seasons a year, we in Sierra Leone have only two - the rainy season and the dry season. Now, is there anyone here who knew that? Hands up!' He delivers the injunction like an actor in a gangster film.

Obviously the Head finds the breathy silence that follows this remark more than he can bear. He stands. 'It's very unlikely that we could accustom ourselves to the extreme climate which you experience in Sierra Leone. Luckily your people are bred to withstand it.'

I have the feeling that he means this as a compliment, and a salutary reflection for the boys to ponder on in case they feel too cocky about their own toughness. He considers strength of character to be the best of virtues.

Mr Sessi says nothing, but waits politely for the Head to finish talking. The Head continues: 'We don't always realise, enjoying as we do a temperate climate, what rigours of weather must be faced by people living in the wilder parts of the globe. How harsh the conditions must be for a white man unused to great heat, dust or tropical rainstorms. The very worst that we in Britain have to worry about is a cold winter.'

He has given up the meagre pretence of including Mr Sessi in his remarks and is now talking directly to the boys. He is talking with that tone of voice, cock of his head, hunch of his shoulders, very pose of a none too bright but nonetheless articulate, properly English, uncle, which he affects on occasions when his students are baffled by something outside their range of experience. He manages to soothe without subjecting them to the stress of having to digest new information, while at the same time appearing to be teaching them something. To those who know him, his demeanour also suggests a rebuke to the speaker for his handling of the lecture and manages to imply that by smoothing over the unsightly gulf yawning between Mr Sessi and his audience he has earned our gratitude. The effect of his intervention is to reassure the boys that all is well, despite this black man's strange behaviour; that England, in the guise of this northern corner of Worcestershire near Birmingham, still stands. Mr Sessi has only made a temporary incursion upon this stable place. Soon he will be gone and by tomorrow or the next day, the Head's tone promises them, they will have forgotten all about him. But in the meantime, it is surely not too much to ask that they put up with his strange manners. He will be quick to step in and iron out any misunderstandings, they can feel sure of that. Besides, his look says, we must know, just as he does, that the black man is not really odd, but only appears so to us.

The Head's demeanour leaves none of this unsaid. The class is calm again, for a while. While he speaks, we all, boys and teachers, gaze at the floor, sneaking glances at him. When he finishes, we can look Mr Sessi in the eye again. No one in the hall has listened to what he has said, except perhaps Mr Sessi, but the fact that he has spoken brings comfort.

I am uneasily aware how my identity as a white South African, were it known to Mr Sessi, will alter his conception of his audience. As it is, I felt uneasy when the Head talked of the difficulties white settlers have with lousy weather. Remarks like this often have the boys in assembly turning round to gawp at me. They do so whenever anything is mentioned which is associated in their minds with the other side of the world, however oblique the reference, whether to missionaries, David Livingstone, the Dark Continent, Zulu chiefs or witchdoctors. When their attention is too pointedly drawn to their own country, it has much the same effect. Goggling heads on craning necks stare at me as if my foreignness reassures them that universes other than their own really do exist, for I stand as living proof of them. Perhaps they are grateful for this because it means that they do not have to take on trust everything they see on television.

Mr Sessi shows no resentment at the Head's interruption. He seems anxious to get on with his lecture. But I notice that he has stopped smiling. I am beginning to feel something for Mr Sessi. His English is no more than makeshift, his assurance is irritating, his knowledge of the geography of his own country is limited. But in this depressing school hall, he is someone with whom I feel a kinship. I would like to reach out and touch him. However, he might not like that. Certainly such behaviour would be novel and unwelcome. I am the geography master. I might seem eccentric because I am from Africa and the boys confuse my foreignness with eccentricity, and in their unplumbable ignorance are moved to play superstitious, rather giggly aborigines to my Captain Cook. My trinkets are welcome diversions in the monotony of their prison island. But if I dared to express my sense of closeness with Mr Sessi, I'd immediately be damned as a lunatic. I am expected to show myself in every important respect to be British. So too, of course, is Mr Sessi.

At times like this I am always grateful for my training which has taught me to stick to the facts. I am most at home with geographical facts. The Republic of South Africa lies at the southern tip of the African continent. It was once a refreshment station of the Dutch East India Company; later the gold mine of the British Empire. In an area some five times that of Great Britain there are 21 448 169 people of varying colours of skin – not only black and white, but the varying intermediate colours of Bushmen, Hottentots, Chinese, Japanese, Malays and Englishmen.

These are the facts. I verify them in my books. I am sure of them. I have many more at my fingertips.

Mr Sessi is still talking, but more incoherently now. If only his sense of geography were better and he knew where he was. He is explaining the role of the chief in the tribes of Sierra Leone, quite oblivious to the fact that he has lost his audience. He talks to us as equals; working on the assumption, no doubt encouraged at his university, and his embassy for that matter, that in academic matters at least skin colour plays no part. It's not going to help him with these boys. They are pragmatists. They admit only the evidence of their senses. They accept only those illusions that entertain them.

But the good-humoured interrogation does not stop, or even wind down. Mr Sessi is deaf to the widespread, almost frantic fidgeting of the boys and the soft shrieks of the rubber-tipped chair legs on the floorboards. But we hear it.

The Head intervenes again. He senses that the boys are on the point of mutiny. He is on his feet and talking before anyone is aware of it. We turn interestedly to see him newly risen from his chair, right foot flung forward giving the impression of leaning into a stride while standing still, his right hand raised with two fingers erect in a gesture recalling papal benediction, or absolution, his face pink and earnest beneath its cap of silver-grey hair.

'I think perhaps we could have the film now,' he is saying, 'and after that we will divide the class up into their groups for a question-and-answer session.'

Mr Sessi stops in mid-sentence as the Head's voice reaches him. 'Oh, yes …' he says, 'but of course, the film, of course.' He casts around desperately behind him, fluttering his eyelashes at the blackboard, then at the cinema screen.

'Would you care to sit here, perhaps?' The Head indicates a seat beside him. Mr Sessi makes his way down the aisle between the rows of boys, smiling and nodding from side to side. The Head signals to the boy operating the projector, and gives me a meaningful glance. I walk to the back of the hall and switch off the lights. A greenish twilight settles on the hall. Things darken to a blur.

The film is barely on the screen before we realise that it is not what we had hoped. However hard we may have longed for the kindness of darkness to allow us to relax into the pleasant distractions of faraway Sierra Leone, after the assaults of the indefatigable Mr Sessi, there is to be no rest for us in the flickering images on the screen. This is not what we expected: the public relations creation of colourful native life, the import of industrial plant and motor cars, the export of palm oil, nuts and kernels for which the country is famed, together with unusual views of derricks and cranes in Freetown harbour, and ships with recognisable Union Jacks on their funnels being loaded with the country's fruits by singing stevedores, and everywhere the smiling black faces of happy Sierra Leonians. Instead I am staring at the broad back of a white man sitting across a table from an earnest, bespectacled black man. Both are talking at once. It seems that we are being exposed to another interrogation. The sound track is muddy and very noisy. Yet it approximates to the sound of human voices in conversation, and instinctively I try to make out what is being said. The black man is doing most of the talking. His lips move rapidly, he shifts in his chair, giving the other's questions serious consideration before replying lengthily. The film is in black and white and the print is grainy. After five long minutes of this I am suddenly certain that the scene will not alter while the projector continues to run. The boys slump miserably in the darkness. Rubber chair legs begin their cries again. Blurred white faces turn to the back of the hall where the Head and Mr Sessi sit side by side in the darkness. I can see him conferring with Mr Sessi who is nodding a great deal. The Head whispers to the projectionist and the conversationalists fade from the screen. I walk to the back of the hall and switch on the light. Everyone blinks furiously, rubbing their eyes, hiding their embarrassment so painfully renewed. The Head is on his feet again, his head bobbing about the way a hen's does, vigilant for any sign of trouble. Mr Sessi remains seated. His head hangs low. The Head calls for silence.

'We're going to stop the film there. Hmm, yes, we have to end it, I'm afraid. Mr Sessi tells me that there appears to have been a misunderstanding. Got the film at the last moment, you see, and didn't have time to check it. Took it for granted, hmm, that the people at his embassy in London knew what they were doing. As you'll have noticed, seems somebody has slipped up. This was, hmm, a political film, dealing with the trade union movement in Sierra Leone and, er, its relationship with the International Labour Organisation. Not really your cup of tea, ha, as Mr Sessi himself was quick to point out. I'm sorry, of course, you'll have no glimpse of Sierra Leone after the valuable insights of Mr Sessi's lecture. But these things happen.'

Mr Sessi rises slowly to his feet. Giving the Head a little bow he walks up to the head of the class and takes up a position in front of the cinema screen, with his hands behind his back. Clearly he is unhappy. He has a hangdog look to him now. He clears his throat. He appears to be having trouble with his eyes, passing his hand across them – when he speaks, his voice is soft: 'In view of what has happened, for which I cannot apologise too much, I think you can dispense with your usual discussion groups. In the time remaining, I will simply invite questions from the floor.' There is no response. For a moment he stands silently, with his head drooping almost to his breast; then he straightens and it looks as if he has regained some of his old cheerfulness. At any rate, he faces all of us unflinchingly.

'All right,' he says, 'fire away.'

MAUD MONTANYANE

Two Minutes

Tosh and I were an odd pair; she was tall and thin, and I was short and plump. People called us the big and small twins, or B & S for short. In very many ways we were different, and yet there was something strong that bound us together. We stood out like sore thumbs from the rest of the girls, who were adventurous and full of pranks. They were wild, while Tosh and I tried to lead a life as pure as possible.

It is twenty years since I last saw Tosh, and I feel guilty that I have not been back to see her. I am sure she is plagued by the same guilt. We made a vow many years ago, and we promised to keep it whatever happened. We crossed each other's hearts and spat on the ground as we promised.

'Strue's God, my friend, if I ever do it I will come back and tell you.' There was only one 'it' that little girls in a convent school could promise not to get themselves involved in. According to Sister Marietta, the matron of the convent, boys came second after witches and ghosts as the deadliest poison for little girls. It could take less than two minutes for a boy to ruin a girl's entire life, she said.

The Little Flower Girls' Hostel formed part of a huge mission station founded by Catholic missionaries at the turn of the century. Most of them were of European origin, but over the years the mission, set in the village of Asazi in Natal, had become a fully fledged community, producing its own breed of African nuns and priests from the surrounding villages.

Sister Marietta was a mouse-like creature of German origin. Armed with a Bible and a strict Catholic upbringing, she was determined to save the whole African continent from death and destruction. Her biggest challenge while at The Little Flower was to keep the girls away from the evil clutches of men. Old Marie, as the girls referred to her, made it her business to slot in her anti-male propaganda whenever she could. Her best performances were a day or two before we broke up for the school holidays. She seemed to think that a good dose of lecturing would protect us from the menacing world outside.

She marvelled at the story of a boy who once cast a spell on a girl by simply looking at her. The girl, she said, had trusted her own worldly strength instead of asking for protection from the Virgin Mary. The boy had looked at the girl, the story went, and without him saying a word the girl had felt weak. So weak was she that, of her own accord, without the boy even propositioning her, she asked him to 'please kiss me and carry me to the bush'.

'I need not tell you what happened in the bush,' the nun would conclude.

As a rule, anyone who was caught eyeing the boys, whether in church, in class, or in the street, was punished severely. Ten bad marks in Sister Marietta's black book was the highest number one could get at a go, and they indicated the seriousness of the crime. As a result, trying to avoid boys and not being seen with them in a lonely place became our biggest challenge at The Little Flower.

'They will take you and use you, leaving you an empty shell,' Sister Marietta would say, indicating with her hand how a girl would be tossed away as something useless. So ominous was the prospect of being thrown away as a useless shell that Tosh and I would spend long nights discussing ways and means to avoid being subjected to that kind of treatment. Although we did not admire Sister Marietta personally, the idea of being sinless and celibate appealed to us a great deal. Often our night sessions would end with us saying the rosary together, asking for forgiveness for sins we had never committed.

Anastasia, Tasi to her friends, was the most popular girl at The Little Flower. While the rest of the girls loved and admired her, Tosh and I despised her. She dressed in the best fashion clothes, and had all the answers to life's problems. A dark person by nature, Tasi relied on skin lightening cream to make her skin look lighter. So light was her face at one stage that her ebony hands looked borrowed next to it. Somehow her ears never got lighter, no matter how much cream she used on them. They stuck out like little appendages above her oval face. Tosh and I laughed about her ears behind her back. We did not dare do so in her presence. Tasi's tongue was much too scathing.

'I wonder how Old Marie can be so knowledgeable about matters of the flesh when she has never been involved in them,' Tasi would say mockingly. 'She must be displacing her own fears and using us to fight her own inward physical desire. Celibacy … what nonsense. Old Marie must be jealous of our freedom. After all, *we* never sent her to tie herself to a life devoid of male pleasure.'

Tasi had quite a following, and her bed, which was at the corner of the hundred-bed dormitory, became the girls' rendezvous. This was where all subjects ranging from politics to sex were discussed. Tasi owned a small transistor radio, and often her gang would convene at her bed to listen to the Hit Parade. This had to happen behind Sister Marietta's back because to her, love and rock 'n roll constituted mortal sins. Often the music-listening session would end in a row, with the participants arguing about the lyrics of a song, or which song had been number one on the Hit Parade the previous week.

It was at the rendezvous that the anti-missionary politics were discussed. As far as Tasi was concerned, the missionaries, and that included Sister Marietta, had left Europe because of frustration, hunger and poverty. 'Under the guise of Christianity, they came to save us. Save us from what? When they themselves are guilty of racism and bigotry?' Tasi would ask, pointing at the stone building in which the black nuns were housed.

The Little Flower was not immune from the country's racial laws, which decreed that blacks and whites live separately. The white missionaries were clearly a privileged class. They lived in a glass building at the top of the hill, while their black counterparts were housed in a stone-and-brick building at the bottom of the hill. It looked more like a cave than a hut and, because of the density of the trees around it, it was cold and dark in winter.

Politics was a sacred subject at The Little Flower, and Tasi was the only one who openly challenged the racism of the convent. 'If they were like Jesus, they would be defying the laws of the country,' Tasi would say angrily. When Tasi questioned the school principal at assembly one day, we feared that she would be expelled from school. She was not. Instead she was fobbed off with an 'it was not the policy of the church to get involved in politics' statement, and asked never to bring up the subject again. That did not deter Tasi. She continued to question and attack what she termed inexcusable behaviour from the people of God.

It was at the rendezvous that a perfect plan for smuggling letters was hatched. As a rule, letters sent in and out of the convent were read and censored by Sister Marietta. Incoming parcels were opened too, and every little gift considered to be too fancy for life in a convent school was kept, and not given to the owner until we broke up for the school holidays.

Love-story books were banned from the library, and any pages with kissing couples, or people holding hands were either cut out or blocked with paper. The same applied to movies. Scenes which were remotely sexual were edited out of the movie. We were allowed to watch *The Sound of Music* in my matric class. The movie was so butchered that when I saw it again a couple of years later, it looked completely new.

The smuggling of letters to and from the boys' side took place during morning mass. As the heads bowed down in silent prayer after holy communion, letters would be thrown across the aisle dividing the boys' from the girls' pews. The little pieces of paper, which for some reason were called schemes, would fly like missiles right above the nuns' heads.

One day a scheme which was thrown from the girls' to the boys' side landed right in the lap of Sister Marietta. Her face lit up with glee as she pocketed the letter, waiting for the perfect moment to pounce on the culprit. By the time she did, the school was buzzing with the news of the person who had been found with a scheme. Most of us were not sure who it was, but we were sympathetic because we knew what this would mean.

I had always suspected Sister Marietta to have a mean streak, but never thought her capable of doing what she did with Thoko's letter. Of course Thoko's boyfriend denied any association between them, so she had to face the music alone.

Not only was the letter read to the whole school, it was sent home to her parents, with a letter instructing them to arrive at the school to reprimand Thoko 'or else she will be asked to pack her things and go'.

I could not understand how a private thing such as a letter could be read to the whole school. That convinced me that Sister Marietta was downright malicious, doing that kind of thing to a nice girl like Thoko. Though remote, the thought of becoming a nun had often crossed my mind. What made me hesitate, however, was my mother's deep and sincere wish that I become a nurse. She would have been disappointed if I had gone the way of celibacy. Old Marie made the decision for me. Her reaction to Thoko's letter dashed my wish of ever becoming a nun. I was disgusted.

Tasi teased Thoko for having allowed herself to be caught with the letter. To her it was a big joke, and her friends laughed heartily when she described how foolish Thoko had been.

'There are only two rules,' Tasi said jokingly, 'it is either you keep away from trouble, or get involved, but be smart enough not to get caught.'

Tasi always boasted about how she and her boyfriend Michael smooched right under the nose of the Virgin Mary. She was referring to the statue of Mary on the lawn outside the school's courtyard. For those who had guts like Tasi, the grotto was a perfect lovers' nook.

More than once I heard Tasi tell the story of how she and Michael had climbed into one of the church towers. 'We stood there kissing to the chime of the bells next to us, while the priests heard confessions in the church below. Old Marie herself was playing the organ!' Tasi boasted. 'We did not get caught. What fool has any business to be caught?'

The stigma of being a boy's love followed Thoko until she left The Little Flower. She was banned from going to the movies on Fridays, and all the newcomers were warned that she was a bad influence. With the interesting parts censored out of all movies, Thoko didn't miss much, but it was the boring evenings that drove her nuts.

Thoko's every mistake became a big issue. She was ostracised by the rest of the girls who feared reprisals from Old Marie. As punishment for an offence Thoko was made to clean the local graveyard. It was not so much the hard work which caused grave-cleaning to be regarded as the most severe form of punishment. According to African culture graves are sacred ground where children are not allowed unless they are there to bury a very close relative such as a brother, a sister, or a parent. When Old Marie sent Thoko to dig round the graves for the second time, Tasi suggested we send a delegation to her to protest, and to make it clear what our tradition was regarding being in the cemetery.

'It is a bad omen, and shows no regard for our culture,' Tasi had protested. Although the delegation was given a hearing, their arguments were dismissed as primitive and unChristian, and Thoko was sent to clean up the graves a third and a fourth time. Such punishment was meted out to various other people, but Tasi vowed she would rather pack her bags and leave The Little Flower than dig round the graves. As if to avoid a confrontation, Old Marie never gave her the grave-digging punishment, robbing the girls of a chance to witness a showdown.

Once Sister Marietta embarrassed Thoko by pulling out the hem of her dress, saying that her dress was too short. As a rule, dresses had to be an inch above the knee. Thoko's must have been slightly more than an inch. The poor girl had to walk around with a funny dress the whole day because Sister would not let her change into another. It was her way of punishing her for, according to her mind, trying to be attractive to the opposite sex. But trying to make Thoko unattractive was an impossible task. Besides her God-given beauty, Thoko had natural style which made her look good with or without a torn hem. She looked elegant even in her gymslip, and Sister Marietta hated her for that. So intense was her hatred that she was forever looking for a reason for her to be expelled from school. 'You will dig the graves for a week, or pack your things and leave The Little Flower,' became the nun's familiar cry whenever Thoko did something wrong.

Tosh and I were both eighteen when we left The Little Flower. As we hugged and said goodbye, we renewed the vow we had made so many times before. If we ever slept with a boy, we would write or telephone to say we had finally fallen. I do not know exactly what motivated Tosh to make that vow. But for me, it was Thoko's experience that pushed me and forced me to make that decision. If a love letter could elicit so much hatred and anger, I thought to myself, then surely boys must be a real threat to girls. I sincerely believed that there would be no place for me in the world if I ever fell into the trap which every man around had set to catch me. As Old Marie said, 'The world will spit at you.'

Twenty years have passed since I last saw Tosh. I did not try to find her after my first encounter with a man. I did not feel the urge to write to her that I had finally fallen. To my mind, it had not happened. I remember the incident very clearly. It was on the couch in my mother's own lounge, not even in the bush as Sister Marietta had warned. Because he was Catholic like me, I trusted Sipho more than I would have trusted an ordinary boy. Somehow, I thought he knew the same rules that I knew.

He pleaded with me and told me it would not take long. He fondled my breasts and kissed me all over. I still cannot say whether the feeling was pleasurable. It was as though a cold and a warm shiver went through my body at the same time. I heard two voices, that of Sipho in one ear pleading with me that 'it won't be long', and Sister Marietta in another, warning 'it will take two minutes'. I saw myself being discarded like an empty shell and the whole world spitting at me.

Suddenly I fought like a little monster to push Sipho away. It was too late. I heard him take one deep breath and the act was over. It was exactly two minutes. I pulled myself together and walked out of the door, leaving Sipho sitting on the couch. When I walked away from him, I also walked away from the fact that he had made love to me. As far as I was concerned the incident had not happened. How could I admit that I had been used?

I have had a lot of sexual encounters since that day on my mother's couch. I am married now with two children; still I have not made love to a man. Sister Marietta never told me that there would come a time when being in a lonely place with a boy would be a right and a safe thing to do. So every private moment I have spent with a man has been wrong, and something I have to be ashamed of. Even as I go to bed with my husband every night, Sister Marietta's voice rings in my mind. 'He will take you and use you and throw you away like an empty shell.' When she drummed those words into my innocent mind, she tied a knot that I am unable to undo.

How can I give myself on a platter to a person – a man – who will con me and leave me spent and useless? As I pull myself away from each sexual act, I feel used and unclean. A sense of guilt and emptiness comes over me. Often I have felt the urge to go back to The Little Flower, lock myself into a confessional with my priest, and say, 'Father, I have sinned. I have slept with a boy.'

I have not gone back to Tosh to tell her that I have broken the vow we made so many years ago. I have slept with none of the men I have made love to, none of the men I have met over the past twenty years. Maybe one day I will be able to untangle the knot in my heart and mind. I will be able to say to a man, 'Let us eat together from the sexual pot, let us share the pleasure equally.' I will not write to Tosh. No, not until I reach equality with my men. Tosh has not written either. Could it be that she is plagued by the same anguish, or is she still pure?

PT MTUZE

The Way to Madam

Translated from isiXhosa by N Saule.

The year was 1933. There was a severe drought throughout the country. Farmers had sleepless nights because their cattle and sheep were dying like flies. The state of the economy had caused prices to skyrocket and South Africa, once regarded as the land of milk and honey, was in the grip of a severe depression, with all its misery.

Most farmers had sold their farms and gone in search of jobs in town, at road construction companies or with the railways, leaving their farm labourers to fend for themselves. As a result the labourers were found wandering all over the country, although they avoided the towns as they feared the corruption of these places.

There was, however, one particular farmer who refused to leave his farm. He was Rooi Willem Poggenpoel, a man known for his strict discipline. He was notorious and even the police would not take chances with him. He was a man of few words but was quick to jump heavily on anyone who opposed him.

Poggenpoel was short and stout. His character was accurately described by the nickname Madangatye (one who spits fire) given to him by his workers, who did not stay long in his employment. At four o'clock each morning he would ring a bell to start the day's work. Any latecomer would be punished, then paid off, and would have to leave the farm by eleven o'clock that very morning. If any worker took the matter to court, Madangatye would lay counter-charges of lost property and the case would simply end.

Among the labourers who worked for him, there was only one who stayed with him for more than ten years. This was Jackson, who had started working for his master at a very young age, had grown up on the farm, and never married.

He was not liked by the other workers because they believed that he was an informer. They believed that was the reason he had stayed for so long. Jackson, on the other hand, knew that it was because he was a hard worker. He felt those who accused him were just jealous.

'Once your employer shows some favour towards you, the others will always accuse you of something. That is a well-known fact, especially amongst the Xhosas,' Jackson used to murmur angrily.

Only once did a black worker show no fear of Madangatye. That was Ngxamfinya, a very muscular Mpondo man who had strong arms and a broad chest. After an argument, he laid Madangatye on the ground with one hand and told him he did not want to hurt him, but was only teaching him a lesson. Madangatye did not argue but paid him his wages and told him to leave the farm lest the other workers should learn from him not to respect white people. The Mpondo man took his time in leaving, while Poggenpoel, obviously shaken, took no chances and kept his distance.

After that Madangatye tried to convince his workers that he was not really a cruel man, but soon he simply went back to his old cruel ways.

One day Madangatye called Jackson to him, the only servant who never gave him any problems. He was not afraid to say that if all the Xhosa people were like Jackson, this whole world would be a wonderful place to live in. Jackson used to appreciate being called 'good kaffir'. To him there was absolutely nothing wrong with that, because it showed that he was unlike the other 'kaffirs'.

'Jackson, I am very grateful for all you have done for this place all these years. I say again that you are the best of all the people I have ever employed, including the ones I now have on this farm. Maybe it is because your grandmother was a coloured person.' This beginning to the conversation obviously pleased Jackson.

'Therefore I have decided to make you an offer,' Madangatye continued. 'Ask for anything your heart desires and I will give it to you. Don't be worried, just say what you want. I am doing this in appreciation of your support, especially during this time of drought. You have always been on my side. If you had left me, like those fools Ngxamfinya and the others who left, I would have been made a laughing stock. They wanted to see my farm perish just like that of Baas Koos Lategan. Baas Koos Lategan is not a cruel person, isn't that so, Jackson?' he asked with a grin on his face. Jackson made little noises of compliance, and rubbing his hands he said, 'I agree with you, Baas Rooi.'

'What I do not want is a loafer on my farm,' said Madangatye, and again insisted that Jackson should ask for anything he wanted.

Jackson did not know what to say. There were many things on his mind. He would love a car, but he could not drive, and he once saw a man killed because he could not drive. Then something else he badly wanted came to mind: a wife – a white girl who would help him get his own farm.

He brightened, and again asked if he could really request anything. Madangatye once again assured him that he could have anything he wanted. Madangatye had a grown daughter who was attending school, and during her holidays she had taught Jackson how to write.

'Say something, Jackson. What would you like me to do for you?' insisted the white man, becoming impatient at Jackson's delay.

'Baas, I am not sure whether my request will be acceptable. I want to ask you to give me your little daughter Emmarentia to be my wife,' said Jackson, surprised at how the white man's face instantly reddened. He had hardly finished speaking before he found himself lying flat on the ground with his master on top of him.

'You ungrateful servant! What a disgraceful thing to say! You have shown your true self today. I have always suspected that you wanted to be the master on this farm,' said Madangatye, shaking him like a cat playing with a mouse. He was so tightly gripped that he could only move his legs.

The other workers, now aware that the friendly conversation had turned violent, looked on, amused at the spectacle. Some incited the boss by saying, 'He's got what he deserves!' There were a few who sympathised with Jackson but could do nothing to save the situation.

Rooi's next move shocked all of them. He shouted: 'Throw him into the oven! I am going to watch from the top of that hill. If he escapes, I'll fix him!' The servants went for Jackson without giving him a chance. In the meantime, the white man went to fetch his rifle. It was the rifle with which he hunted game. Then he walked slowly to the hilltop.

Jackson pleaded in vain. He was tied very securely. The white woman, Madangatye's wife, could not bear to see such punishment. She cried hysterically and fainted.

This gave the servants an opportunity to save Jackson. They grabbed a dog and threw it into the oven instead of the man. They told Jackson to run away as fast as he could. The smoke from the oven rose slowly into the sky and convinced the servants that they had got the better of Madangatye who was lying watching from the hill.

After many years the event became a legend. In time, Madangatye's daughter died and so did her mother, while Madangatye remained a lonely old man on the farm.

One day Madangatye heard a knock on the door. To his surprise it was Jackson. He had a broad smile on his face as he entered.

'Jackson, didn't you die a long time ago? Where have you been?' asked the astonished old man.

'I am from heaven, Baas. I am very happy there, together with Madam. Little daughter Emmarentia is also very happy. Madam has sent me to ask if you could make her a special dinner. You must prepare the dinner yourself …' said Jackson, very politely as usual.

'Jackson, how did you come back?' asked the master again. 'I thought you were dead.'

'Baas, that does not matter, forget it. It's a very long story. All you have to do is to carry out Madam's wish so that I can go back,' Jackson answered.

'Jackson, how can you take food to my wife when you are so untrustworthy? You are just not the right person. Just tell me how I can get there. Which is the right way to Madam? I'll go there myself. I won't mind not coming back. After all, I haven't long to live anyway,' said the master, looking very sad.

Madangatye continued begging to be told how he could be reunited with his wife, and eventually Jackson decided to show him.

He looked at him with great sympathy and said, 'Well, Baas, come with me. The way to heaven is very easy, if you are honest and sincere. The way to heaven is through the oven.'

NJABULO S NDEBELE

Death of a Son

At last we got the body. Wednesday. Just enough time for a Saturday funeral. We were exhausted. Empty. The funeral still ahead of us. We had to find the strength to grieve. There had been no time for grief, really. Only much bewilderment and confusion. Now grief. For isn't grief the awareness of loss?

That is why when we finally got the body, Buntu said: 'Do you realise our son is dead?' I realised. Our awareness of the death of our first and only child had been displaced completely by the effort to get his body. Even the horrible events that caused the death: we did not think of them, as such. Instead, the numbing drift of things took over our minds: the pleas, letters to be written, telephone calls to be made, telegrams to be dispatched, lawyers to consult, 'influential' people to 'get in touch with', undertakers to be contacted, so much walking and driving. That is what suddenly mattered: the irksome details that blur the goal (no matter how terrible it is), each detail becoming a door which, once unlocked, revealed yet another door. Without being aware of it, we were distracted by the smell of the skunk and not by what the skunk had done.

We realised something too, Buntu and I, that during the two-week effort to get our son's body, we had drifted apart. For the first time in our marriage, our presence to each other had become a matter of habit. He was there. He'll be there. And I'll be there. But when Buntu said: 'Do you realise our son is dead?' he uttered a thought that suddenly brought us together again. It was as if the return of the body of our son were also our coming together. For it was only at that moment that we really began to grieve; as if our lungs had suddenly begun to take in air, when just before we were beginning to suffocate. Something with meaning began to emerge.

We realised. We realised that something else had been happening to us, adding to the terrible events. Yes, we had drifted apart. Yet, our estrangement, just at that moment when we should have been together, seemed disturbingly comforting to me. I was comforted in a manner I did not quite understand.

The problem was that I had known all along that we would have to buy the body anyway. I had known all along. Things would end that way. And when things turned out that way, Buntu could not look me in the eye. For he had said: 'Over my dead body! Over my dead body!' as soon as we knew we would be required to pay the police or the government for the release of the body of our child.

'Over my dead body! Over my dead body!' Buntu kept on saying.

Finally, we bought the body. We have the receipt. The police insisted we take it. That way, they would be 'protected'. It's the law, they said.

I suppose we could have got the body earlier. At first I was confused, for one is supposed to take comfort in the heroism of one's man. Yet, inwardly, I could draw no comfort from his outburst. It seemed hasty. What sense was there to it when all I wanted was the body of my child? What would happen if, as events unfolded, it became clear that Buntu would not give up his life? What would happen? What would happen to him? To me?

For the greater part of two weeks, all of Buntu's efforts, together with friends, relatives, lawyers and the newspapers, were to secure the release of the child's body without the humiliation of having to pay for it. A 'fundamental principle'.

Why was it difficult for me to see the wisdom of the principle? The worst thing, I suppose, was worrying about what the police may have been doing to the body of my child. How they may have been busy prying it open 'to determine the cause of death'.

Would I want to look at the body when we finally got it? To see further mutilations in addition to the 'cause of death'? What kind of mother would not want to look at the body of her child? people will ask. Some will say: 'It's grief. She is too grief-stricken.'

'But still ... ,' they will say. And the elderly among them may say: 'Young people are strange.'

But how can they know? It was not that I would not want to see the body of my child, but that I was too afraid to confront the horrors of my own imagination. I was haunted by the thought of how useless it had been to have created something. What had been the point of it all? This body filling up with a child. The child steadily growing into something that could be seen and felt. Moving, as it always did, at that time of day when I was all alone at home waiting for it. What had been the point of it all?

How can they know that the mutilation to determine 'the cause of death' ripped my own body. Can they think of a womb feeling hunted? Disgorged?

And the milk that I still carried. What about it? What had been the point of it all?

Even Buntu did not seem to sense that that principle, the 'fundamental principle', was something too intangible for me at that moment, something that I desperately wanted should assume the form of my child's body. He still seemed far from ever knowing.

I remember one Saturday morning early in our courtship, as Buntu and I walked hand-in-hand through town, window-shopping. We cannot even be said to have been window-shopping, for we were aware of very little that was not ourselves. Everything in those windows was merely an excuse for words to pass between us.

We came across three girls sitting on the pavement, sharing a packet of fish and chips after they had just bought it from a nearby Portuguese cafe. Buntu said: 'I want fish and chips too.' I said: 'So seeing is desire.' I said: 'My man is greedy!' We laughed. I still remember how he tightened his grip on my hand. The strength of it!

Just then, two white boys coming in the opposite direction suddenly rushed at the girls, and, without warning, one of them kicked the packet of fish and chips out of the hands of the girl who was holding it. The second boy kicked away the rest of what remained in the packet. The girl stood up, shaking her hand as if to throw off the pain in it. Then she pressed it under her armpit as if to squeeze the pain out of it. Meanwhile, the two boys went on their way laughing. The fish and chips lay scattered on the pavement and on the street like stranded boats on a river that had gone dry.

'Just let them do that to you!' said Buntu, tightening once more his grip on my hand as we passed on like sheep that had seen many of their own in the flock picked out for slaughter. We would note the event and wait for our turn. I remember I looked at Buntu, and saw his face was somewhat glum. There seemed no connection between that face and the words of reassurance just uttered. For a while, we went on quietly. It was then that I noticed his grip had grown somewhat limp. Somewhat reluctant. Having lost its self-assurance, it seemed to have been holding on because it had to, not because of a confident sense of possession.

It was not to be long before his words were tested. How could fate work this way, giving to words meanings and intentions they did not carry when they were uttered? I saw that day how the language of love could so easily be trampled underfoot, or scattered like fish and chips on the pavement, and left stranded and abandoned like boats in a river that suddenly went dry. Never again was love to be confirmed with words. The world around us was too hostile for vows of love. At any moment, the vows could be subjected to the stress of proof. And love died. For words of love need not be tested.

On that day, Buntu and I began our silence. We talked and laughed, of course, but we stopped short of words that would demand proof of action. Buntu knew. He knew the vulnerability of words. And so he sought to obliterate words with acts that seemed to promise redemption.

On that day, as we continued with our walk in town, that Saturday morning, coming up towards us from the opposite direction, was a burly Boer walking with his wife and two children. They approached Buntu and me with an ominously determined advance. Buntu attempted to pull me out of the way, but I never had a chance. The Boer shoved me out of the way, as if clearing a path for his family. I remember, I almost crashed into a nearby fashion display window. I remember, I glanced at the family walking away, the mother and the father each dragging a child. It was for one of those children that I had been cleared away. I remember, also, that as my tears came out, blurring the Boer family and everything else, I saw and felt deeply what was inside of me: a desire to be avenged.

But nothing happened. All I heard was Buntu say: 'The dog!' At that very moment, I felt my own hurt vanish like a wisp of smoke. And as my hurt vanished, it was replaced, instead, by a tormenting desire to sacrifice myself for Buntu. Was it something about the powerlessness of the curse and the desperation with which it had been made? The filling of stunned silence with an utterance? Surely it ate into him, revealing how incapable he was of meeting the call of his words.

And so it was that that afternoon, back in the township, left to ourselves at Buntu's home, I gave in to him for the first time. Or should I say I offered myself to him? Perhaps from some vague sense of wanting to heal something in him? Anyway, we were never to talk about that event. Never. We buried it alive deep inside of me that afternoon. Would it ever be exhumed? All I vaguely felt and knew was that I had the keys to the vault. That was three years ago, a year before we married.

The cause of death? One evening I returned home from work, particularly tired after I had been covering more shootings by the police on the East Rand. Then I had hurried back to the office in Johannesburg to piece together on my typewriter the violent scenes of the day, and then to file my report to meet the deadline. It was late when I returned home, and when I got there I found a crowd of people in the yard. They were those who could not get inside. I panicked. What had happened? I did not ask those who were outside, being desperate to get into the house. They gave way easily when they recognised me.

Then I heard my mother's voice. Her cry rose well above the noise. It turned into a scream when she saw me. 'What is it, mother?' I asked, embracing her out of a vaguely despairing sense of terror. But she pushed me away with an hysterical violence that astounded me.

'What misery have I brought you, my child?' she cried. At that point, many women in the room began to cry too. Soon, there was much wailing in the room, and then all over the house. The sound of it! The anguish! Understanding, yet eager for knowledge, I became desperate. I had to hold onto something. The desire to embrace my mother no longer had anything to do with comforting her; for whatever she had done, whatever its magnitude, had become inconsequential. I needed to embrace her for all the anguish that tied everyone in the house into a knot. I wanted to be part of that knot, yet I wanted to know what had brought it about.

Eventually, we found each other, my mother and I, and clasped each other tightly. When I finally released her, I looked around at the neighbours and suddenly had a vision of how that anguish had to be turned into a simmering kind of indignation. The kind of indignation that had to be kept at bay only because there was a higher purpose at that moment: the sharing of concern.

Slowly and with a calmness that surprised me, I began to gather the details of what had happened. Instinctively, I seemed to have been gathering notes for a news report.

It happened during the day, when the soldiers and the police who had been patrolling the township in their Casspirs began to shoot in the streets at random. Need I describe what I did not see? How did the child come to die just at that moment when the police and the soldiers began to shoot at random, at any house, at any moving thing? That was how one of our windows was shattered by a bullet. And that was when my mother, who looked after her grandchild when we were away at work, panicked. She picked up the child and ran to the neighbours. It was only when she entered the neighbour's house that she noticed the wetness of the blanket that covered the child she held to her chest as she ran for the sanctuary of neighbours. She had looked at her unaccountably bloody hand, then she noted the still bundle in her arms, and began at that moment to blame herself for the death of her grandchild ...

Later, the police, on yet another round of shooting, found people gathered at our house. They stormed in, saw what had happened. At first, they dragged my mother out, threatening to take her away unless she agreed not to say what had happened. But then they returned and, instead, took the body of the child away. By what freak of logic did they hope that by this act their carnage would never be discovered?

That evening, I looked at Buntu closely. He appeared suddenly to have grown older. We stood alone in an embrace in our bedroom. I noticed, when I kissed his face, how his once lean face had grown suddenly puffy.

At that moment, I felt the familiar impulse come upon me once more, the impulse I always felt when I sensed that Buntu was in some kind of danger, the impulse to yield something of myself to him. He wore the look of someone struggling to gain control of something. Yet, it was clear he was far from controlling anything. I knew that look. Had seen it many times. It came at those times when I sensed that he faced a wave that was infinitely stronger than he, that it would certainly sweep him away, but that he had to seem to be struggling. I pressed myself tightly to him as if to vanish into him; as if only the two of us could stand up to the wave.

'Don't worry,' he said. 'Don't worry. I'll do everything in my power to right this wrong. Everything. Even if it means suing the police!' We went silent.

I knew that silence. But I knew something else at that moment: that I had to find a way of disengaging myself from the embrace.

Suing the police? I listened to Buntu outlining his plans. 'Legal counsel. That's what we need,' he said. 'I know some people in Pretoria,' he said. As he spoke, I felt the warmth of intimacy between us cooling. When he finished, it was cold. I disengaged from his embrace slowly, yet purposefully. Why had Buntu spoken?

Later, he was to speak again, when all his plans had failed to work: 'Over my dead body! Over my dead body!'

He sealed my lips. I would wait for him to feel and yield one day to all the realities of misfortune.

Ours was a home, it could be said. It seemed a perfect life for a young couple: I, a reporter; Buntu, a personnel officer at an American factory manufacturing farming implements. He had travelled to the United States and returned with a mind fired with dreams. We dreamed together. Much time we spent, Buntu and I, trying to make a perfect home. The occasions are numerous on which we paged through *Femina, Fair Lady, Cosmopolitan, Home & Garden, Car,* as if somehow we were going to surround our lives with the glossiness in the magazines. Indeed, much of our time was spent window-shopping through the magazines. This time, it was different from the window-shopping we did that Saturday when we courted. This time our minds were consumed by the things we saw and dreamed of owning: the furniture, the fridge, TV, video cassette recorders, washing machines, even a vacuum cleaner and every other imaginable thing that would ensure a comfortable modern life.

Especially when I was pregnant. What is it that Buntu did not buy, then? And when the boy was born, Buntu changed the car. A family, he would say, must travel comfortably.

The boy became the centre of Buntu's life. Even before he was born, Buntu had already started making inquiries at white private schools. That was where he would send his son, the bearer of his name.

Dreams! It is amazing how the horrible findings of my newspaper reports often vanished before the glossy magazines of our dreams, how I easily forgot that the glossy images were concocted out of the keys of typewriters, made by writers whose business was to sell dreams at the very moment that death pervaded the land. So powerful are words and pictures that even their makers often believe in them.

Buntu's ordeal was long. So it seemed. He would get up early every morning to follow up the previous day's leads regarding the body of our son. I wanted to go with him, but each time I prepared to go he would shake his head.

'It's my task,' he would say. But every evening he returned, empty-handed, while with each day that passed and we did not know where the body of my child was, I grew restive and hostile in a manner that gave me much pain. Yet Buntu always felt compelled to give a report on each day's events. I never asked for it. I suppose it was his way of dealing with my silence.

One day he would say: 'The lawyers have issued a court order that the body be produced. The writ of *habeas corpus.*'

On another day he would say: 'We have petitioned the Minister of Justice.'

On yet another he would say: 'I was supposed to meet the Chief Security Officer. Waited the whole day. At the end of the day they said I would see him tomorrow if he was not going to be too busy. They are stalling.'

Then he would say: 'The newspapers, especially yours, are raising a hue and cry. The government is bound to be embarrassed. It's a matter of time.'

And so it went on. Every morning he got up and left. Sometimes alone, sometimes with friends. He always left to bear the failure alone.

How much did I care about lawyers, petitions and Chief Security Officers? A lot. The problem was that whenever Buntu spoke about his efforts, I heard only his words. I felt in him the disguised hesitancy of someone who wanted reassurance without asking for it. I saw someone who got up every morning and left not to look for results, but to search for something he could only have found with me.

And each time he returned, I gave my speech to my eyes. And he answered without my having parted my lips. As a result, I sensed, for the first time in my life, a terrible power in me that could make him do anything. And he would never ever be able to deal with that power as long as he did not silence my eyes and call for my voice.

And so, he had to prove himself. And while he left each morning, I learned to be brutally silent. Could he prove himself without me? Could he? Then I got to know, those days, what I'd always wanted from him. I got to know why I have always drawn him into me whenever I sensed his vulnerability.

I wanted him to be free to fear. Wasn't there greater strength that way? Had he ever lived with his own feelings? And the stress of life in this land: didn't it call out for men to be heroes? And should they live up to it even though the details of the war to be fought may often be blurred? They should.

Yet it is precisely for that reason that I often found Buntu's thoughts lacking in strength. They lacked the experience of strife that could only come from a humbling acceptance of fear and then, only then, the need to fight it.

Me? In a way, I have always been free to fear. The prerogative of being a girl. It was always expected of me to scream when a spider crawled across the ceiling. It was known I would jump onto a chair whenever a mouse blundered into the room.

Then, once more, the Casspirs came. A few days before we got the body back, I was at home with my mother when we heard the great roar of truck engines. There was much running and shouting in the streets. I saw them, as I've always seen them on my assignments: the Casspirs. On five occasions they ran down our street at great speed, hurling tear-gas canisters at random. On the fourth occasion, they got our house. The canister shattered another window and filled the house with the terrible pungent choking smoke that I had got to know so well. We ran out of the house gasping for fresh air.

So, this was how my child was killed? Could they have been the same soldiers? Now hardened to their tasks? Or were they new ones being hardened to their tasks? Did they drive away laughing? Clearing paths for their families? What paths?

And was this our home? It couldn't be. It had to be a little bird's nest waiting to be plundered by a predator bird. There seemed no sense to the wedding pictures on the walls, the graduation pictures, birthday pictures, pictures of relatives, and paintings of lush landscapes. There seemed no sense anymore to what seemed recognisably human in our house. It took only a random swoop to obliterate personal worth, to blot out any value there may have been to the past. In desperation, we began to live only for the moment. I do feel hunted.

It was on the night of the tear gas that Buntu came home, saw what had happened; and broke down in tears. They had long been in the coming ...

My own tears welled out too. How much did we have to cry to refloat stranded boats? I was sure they would float again.

A few nights later, on the night of the funeral, exhausted, I lay on my bed, listening to the last of the mourners leaving. Slowly, I became conscious of returning to the world. Something came back after it seemed not to have been there for ages. It came as a surprise, as a reminder that we will always live around what will happen. The sun will rise and set, and the ants will do their endless work, until one day the clouds turn grey and rain falls, and even in the township, the ants will fly out into the sky. Come what may.

My moon came, in a heavy surge of blood. And, after such a long time, I remembered the thing Buntu and I had buried in me. I felt it as if it had just entered. I felt it again as it floated away on the surge. I would be ready for another month. Ready as always, each and every month, for new beginnings.

And Buntu? I'll be with him, now. Always. Without our knowing, all the trying events had prepared for us new beginnings. Shall we not prevail?

MARGUERITE POLAND

The Wood-ash Stars*

Once, long ago, a small band of San (also called Bushman) hunters lived near a water hole far off in the desert wastes. There, each family built its fire and its low shelter of branches and grass.

Early in the day the men would prepare their delicate small arrows, poisoning the shafts, and go off hunting. While they were gone the women and young girls would take their digging-sticks, tie their karosses around them and walk out together to look for tsama melons, mongongo nuts, tsin beans, and all the other roots and fruits they gathered for their food.

When they returned in the afternoon to cook what they had gathered, the children and young girls would play games, using a hard round tsama melon as a ball. Then they would sing and stamp as they threw the melon to each other.

They could sing many different songs as they played: the song of the grey loerie bird that calls *'kuri mama, kuri mama'*, and the song of the wasp and the slow puffadder. But Xama, who was young and whose hair was decorated with loops of ostrich-eggshell beads, would sing her own lament: that she, of all the young girls, wore an old and ragged kaross. What she wanted most was a kaross that was sleek and new, made of soft gemsbok skin. Her old one had holes in it through which the small, cold fingers of the wind crept. Wearing it, she felt as shaggy as a brown hyena.

As she sang she hoped that Gau was listening. If Gau could kill an eland or a gemsbok or a hartebeest with his small poisoned arrows, and make her a kaross, she would surely be the most contented girl in camp.

Gau heard her songs as she stood in the line with the others, tossing the tsama melon back and forth. And though it was the driest time of the year and the herds of buck were scattered so widely across the plains that they were hard to find, he gathered up his bow and arrows and his hunting-bag and went to his brothers and companions asking if they would go with him to hunt.

But this they refused to do, for the hottest winds of summer were blowing that day. The sky was grey with dust. Where, they asked, would Gau find a gemsbok in all that waste, when only the desert scorpions and lizards would be out? So Gau set off alone.

'Where is Gau?' asked the girls.

'Gau has gone to hunt a gemsbok to make a fine kaross for Xama.'

'Ah, ah, ah, ah, ah!' cried Xama, her hands fluttering to her face. 'At such a time!' She looked at the fierce midday sun, afraid of what she'd sung.

All day Gau hunted, finding nothing. Night came. The moon rose up above the hills. He stared at it, thinking that its face was round and light and shining as the face of Xama. Then he took his firesticks from his bag, made a small fire, and lay down to sleep.

The next day he travelled on and, at last, he found the prints of many hooves. A herd of gemsbok had passed that way some time before. He followed, trotting now – trotting as a jackal does, intent upon a trail.

At midday, when the sun is fiercest and highest in the sky, he found some gemsbok resting in the shade of thorn trees. Gau laid down his quiver and his bag, stuck a number of arrows in his belt and crept forward, moving slowly towards the herd.

The buck watched him, stamping their hooves every now and then. Closer and closer crept Gau. Then he drew back his bowstring, tight in the notch of the arrow, and fired. And though he knew his arrow had found its mark somewhere in the herd, the buck all turned and stampeded away through the bush.

Back at the encampment Xama waited.

'Xama, come and play the melon game with us,' cried the others.

She shook her head and sat to one side. A day passed. A night. Another day. Already the crickets were singing loudly in the shadows and still Gau had not returned. Xama wept for having sung the song of the old kaross that had sent Gau out into the desert all alone to hunt.

Out on the plains, the hunter Gau followed the tracks of the wounded gemsbok for many, many hours. Then he saw – far over the Aha hills – the vultures gathering in the sky. He set out, jogging fast, his arrows rattling in the quiver. When at last he saw the big buck lying dead in the sand, he squatted by it and stroked its smooth skin. He thought of Xama's joy and how she would clap her hands and sing a song of praise. Then he would bray the hide so Xama could fold it softly round her. And she would smile.

Gau could not carry the dead gemsbok away by himself and so he skinned it and cut the meat into strips. These he placed in the skin, which he tied to his carrying-stick. When the sun rose the next morning he set out for home.

But in the time that he'd been gone, the winds had blown up and down the plains smoothing away his tracks in the sand. Gau was young and he could not read the signs of the bush as well as the older hunters. So on he went uncertainly – this way, that way. But no matter which direction he took he saw no sign of his passing – no tree, no stone, no bush that was familiar. The sun came up. The sun went down. It rose again and Gau the hunter, whose thirst was as sharp as the sting of a scorpion in his throat, knew he was lost.

All day he walked. Then towards evening he found a small water hole. He drank and drank until he could drink no more. But when he picked up his carrying-stick with the gemsbok skin tied to it, and turned away, he knew that not very far behind, something followed silently. Something followed … followed on his tracks.

If he walked, so the bush behind him moved a little in his wake. If he stopped to listen, so he knew that something listened too, as if the wind had held its breath. Gau went faster, keeping just ahead of the footfalls in the sand. When night came there was no moon, but from the bush nearby a pair of eyes gleamed in the dark.

Hastily Gau hung his hunting-bag in a thicket, took his firesticks, dragged together twigs and grass and brush and made a flame. Suddenly, into the clearing stepped a huge hyena. It was bigger than any Gau had seen before. It put back its head and howled. Then it stood and watched Gau, whuffling to itself. It shuffled nearer, nose quivering to catch the scent of gemshok meat. Gau dragged the meat-filled skin closer and stretched out his hand for his bow and quiver. He would drive the hyena away with an arrow.

Then Gau saw, with alarm, that he had left his hunting-bag slung in a bush. He could see it hanging there – out of reach – at the other side of the fire. He shouted at the hyena. But it only stared at him and growled deep in its throat, backing off a little. And as it did, it caught the scent of Gau's hunting-bag. It jumped up on its hindlegs and pulled at the bag with its strong teeth.

It fell with a clatter. The hyena licked at the prints of Gau's meat-smeared fingers on the strap. It scratched at it with a paw and then looked once more towards the gemsbok skin over which Gau sat huddled. It approached, its long shadow creeping towards him in the firelight.

Xama sat outside her mother's shelter and listened to the calls of the night birds. No moon rose. The stars were dim. The wind was fierce and cold. Far off she heard – again and again – the whooping of a lone hyena. Somewhere in the darkness of the plains was Gau the hunter, who had gone to shoot a gemsbok so that he could make a soft, warm, grey kaross for her.

Gau poked the fire and made it blaze. He was afraid. Never had he seen a beast so bold and powerful and unafraid of man. He shifted round the fire, keeping it between the hyena and himself. His arms and legs ached with tiredness but he dared not close his eyes and sleep.

The embers of Xama's cooking-fire glowed softly, for it was late.

'It is the darkness,' she cried. 'There is no light for Gau to guide him home. Oh foolish Gau for going out alone! Oh foolish Xama for wishing for a fine kaross!'

In despair Xama plunged her hands among the coals of the fire. She flung the embers high – as high as she could reach. Again she thrust her fingers in the fire and tossed the fine red ash up into the night.

'Light the way for Gau the hunter!' she cried.

She held her small, burnt hands before her face and wept. The tears stung her eyes and slid painfully between her blistered fingers, cooling them. Then she stared in disbelief as the embers of the cooking-fire she'd thrown in her despair were driven forward by the wind. They glowed in the darkness, stretching out into the desert sky.

The hyena crept closer. Gau peered into the dark, looking for a tree into which he might climb with the gemsbok skin. But there was none. The hyena licked its jowls and Gau, not knowing what else to do, threw it a piece of meat – and another, and another, until his store was almost finished. Still the hyena, growing bolder all the time, came nearer.

Desperately Gau threw the last strip of meat. As he did, the sky flared as embers do when blown suddenly to send sparks scattering. Then, across the sky there blazed a strange soft light. Thousands of little stars burned like wood-ash strewn in the sky. The path of stars arched low – from the far horizon to just above where Gau stood.

The hyena howled and whooped. It cowered low on the sand and stared at the sky, cringing, its lip drawn up above its yellow teeth. Shaking its shaggy head from side to side, it backed away and slunk into the gloom, moaning to itself

'It is a sign for me!' cried Gau. He leapt up and took his hunter's bag, bow, quiver and carrying-stick and ran, unafraid, following the pathway in the sky.

Xama nursed her burnt and blistered hands. She sang sadly to herself and gazed every now and then at the wood-ash stars she had made. Only in the dawn, when she heard the loud cries of the people, did she leave her brooding and turn and run to where they stood together, pointing excitedly.

There, walking down across the plain, swaggering as if he'd been no further than the waterhole, came Gau. And tied to his carrying-stick hung a gemsbok skin, soft and mauve and grey as a rainy summer sky.

So it was that Gau, the youngest hunter in the band, shot his first big buck and made a warm kaross for Xama, the keeper of his heart.

And so it is – the old ones say – that the thousands of little stars that form the Milky Way are really a handful of wood-ash glowing in the dark. For once a young San girl named Xama threw the embers of her fire into the sky to light the way for Gau the hunter, lost out in the desert wastes in the darkness of the night.

*See the San tale 'The Girl who Made Stars' [ed.]

JAYAPRAGA REDDY

The Spirit of Two Worlds

The old woman pounded the spices in a wooden mortar. She sat on a grass mat in the sartorial position adopted by generations of women before her. It was cool under the mango tree and the gentle susurration of the breeze among the leaves was like the voice of God murmuring His comfort. Out there it was quiet and she could think her thoughts in peace as she prepared the mangoes for pickling. But today her thoughts were not very pleasant. They were troubled and she was forced to acknowledge the disturbing fact that there was rebellion in her household. Ever since Veeran, her youngest son, had married, there was dissension in her home. He hadn't heeded her advice and had obstinately followed his own desires. So now he reaped the consequences. But a shadow hung over her normally peaceful household. Nothing pleased her new daughter-in-law. Nothing was good enough for her. She complained that the semi-detached house in the Indian township was too cramped and that there was not much diversion in the district. Her discontent and aloofness did not invite intimacy and she remained isolated. She kept to herself, joining the family only when necessary. The other daughters-in-law were tolerant at first but now there was an open resentment. It was time, they maintained, that she took interest in the family and did her share of the housework. She couldn't deny the truth of it. Sharda was headstrong and wilful. By bringing in her new ideas and an alien lifestyle, she had upset the smooth running of her home. In her days, oh in her days, none of this would have been permitted, she lamented inwardly.

Radha, her eldest daughter-in-law, came out to her. 'You like some tea, Ma?' she asked, speaking in Tamil.

The old woman nodded and as she watched her go again, she thought how good and obedient a daughter-in-law she had been. She always wore a sari and her hair was still long and worn in a simple plait. No task was too much for her. Not when it came to doing things for her.

Radha returned with the tea that frothed like beer in an enamel mug. Just the way she liked it, she thought sipping it slowly. The hot, fragrant brew dispelled some of her depression. She wished Radha would go away and leave her to her thoughts. But Radha lingered.

'There is trouble,' Radha informed her. 'Now she wants to go to work. He said she cannot go to work. She was very angry.'

The old woman sighed but refrained from comment. She did not ask how she came by such knowledge. In the rather cramped living conditions of the council house, nothing was very private. Quarrels became public and one's tears, unless one cried quietly, were heard by all. Radha went on, giving her all the details, but the old woman stopped her with a gruelling gesture. She rose and went indoors.

Veeran stood at the window looking out vacantly. Sundays were usually so peaceful, the old woman thought as she studied him. Sundays were meant for outings, attending weddings and functions and visits to relatives. Now Sundays were torn by strife and tension.

'What is wrong, my son?' she asked quietly.

He did not turn around. She sensed his humiliation and hurt.

'She wants to … work,' he said reluctantly.

'Then let her work, my son,' she said.

He turned and regarded her with disbelief.

'You … want her … to work!' he exclaimed.

She shook her head sadly. 'No, I don't want her to work. But if that is what she wants and if it will make her happy, then let her work.'

He turned away, his jaw setting in a grim, obstinate line.

'She doesn't have to work,' he pointed out.

'All women are not the same,' she reminded him.

'She says she is dying of boredom,' he told her.

Boredom. She left him then and went back to sit under the tree where she reflected upon this new and alien plague which afflicted the young. Her mind went back over the years searching for something that remotely resembled this malady, but there was nothing. There had been hardships, countless sacrifices which had been made willingly, much pain and heartbreak and some rare and memorable moments of joy and happiness, but never boredom. She had married at thirteen, a child bride in an arranged marriage. In those days one did not question these things, merely complied with one's parents' wishes and submitted silently to whatever was arranged. She had nine children, six of whom had survived. An early marriage was followed by early widowhood and at forty she found herself alone at the helm. She hired a stall in the Indian market and managed to keep the family together. Over the years her struggle eased a little when her children were educated and settled in comfortable jobs. Soon she was able to give up the stall and retire, and so come to a quiet port.

But there were so many lessons in one's life that one could not pass on to the young.

Sharda went to work as a hairdresser in an elegant new salon in Durban. The old woman wondered whether her new-found financial independence brought her any happiness. She bought a whole lot of new clothes, all modern and fashionable. Her short hair was styled often and in different ways. There were murmurs of jealousy and resentment among the other daughters-in-law. Even Radha fell prey to this.

'What does she work for? Only her clothes and her perfumes! While we stay at home like slaves, she lives like a queen!' Radha observed acidly.

But that was only the beginning. Having got her way once, Sharda demanded other things. Her heart heavy with grief, the old woman looked on while Veeran weakly surrendered to her whims. Sharda learned to drive and demanded a car of her own. Bus journeys were long and tedious, she maintained. With a car of her own, she could get home earlier and have more time. More time for what? the old woman wondered. He was as malleable as clay in her hands. It was not right. No woman ought to have that much power over any man.

The car was small and sleek. The day she brought it home, the other daughters-in-law stood at their windows and watched her furtively. She drove with an enviable ease, and they could sense her irrepressible excitement as she sprang out of the car. But her pleasure was short-lived.

At supper that night the family sat around the table in a grim silence, united in their resentment and disapproval. For once, Sharda was not immune to their feelings. At first she ate in quiet defiance. A small knot of anger began to form at the pit of her stomach. It was unfair! What had she done that was wrong? Was it her fault if she could not fit in with their narrow conformity? Surely not! She rose abruptly and left the room. The silence around the table intensified. The old woman watched her go with a heavy heart.

In the weeks that followed, the old woman tried to hold her disintegrating family together. But the task was too much for her. There were lessons in this for her too. She was discovering that her matriarchal authority had its limits and had to give way to a way of life that was rapidly becoming the norm. The things her generation had cherished and valued were being replaced by an alien culture which sacrificed love and caring on the altar of Mammon and whose devotees foolishly pursued the things of the flesh. The old woman took her troubles to her gods in prayer. But there were no answers. Her heart heavy with grief, she saw the rift between her and Sharda widen and was powerless to halt the inevitable. And the inevitable came one afternoon when Veeran announced that he was moving out on his own. The old woman received the news in chill silence. Her initial reaction was one of grief and then anger. Anger because he was allowing it to happen. He didn't want it to happen but he was giving in to his wife once too often. She studied him for a long moment, undeceived by his outward composure. He did not meet her eyes directly for he feared the betrayal of his true emotions.

'Are you sure you want to do this, my son?' she asked quietly.

It took him a long while to answer, and when he did it was with an effort.

'It ... is ... for the best.'

Surely he did not believe that! She rose and left the room and he did not see the naked pain in her eyes.

She sat in her room for a long while, her hands resting in her lap, numb with pain. He had been her youngest son and her best loved. Perhaps that had been a mistake. Sons were not yours to hold. They were arrows to be released into the world.

The old woman read the surprise in her daughter-in-law's eyes. For the first time they were confronting each other directly. For a long moment their glance met and held. It was the younger woman who looked away first. The old woman recalled the day Veeran told her of his wedding plans. He had met her at a party, he said. She was very pretty and so full of fun. She hadn't objected to his choice but had merely advised him to wait. But he hadn't waited. Alas, the young wanted everything quickly and easily.

'So you are splitting my home,' the old woman commented.

The younger woman's glance wavered. Then she straightened and her glance sturdied.

'No, that's not true. All I want is to live on my own. Is that wrong?' said Sharda.

The old woman did not reply for a long moment. 'Have you slipped so far from our teachings that you've forgotten a son's first duty is to his mother?' she reminded grimly.

Sharda looked up and met the old woman's eyes. There was none of the old defiance or antagonism. But in the wordless silence the old woman studied her for a long while. There was strength in silence. She would not give her the satisfaction of having the last word. 'You came to this house in peace, so leave in peace. You are leaving this house on your free will. All I ask is that you look after my son. You have my blessing and I hope you will be happy. If this is your wish, then let it be. But know this, you too will have children. And you too will need them in your old age. I hope when you do, they will be there.'

Sharp words sprang to Sharda's mind then. She wanted to remind the old woman that her son's duty was now to his wife. That times had changed. That she had tried to fit in with her family but had failed. But something within her checked her. Something of her mother's teachings came to her mind. She looked away. The old woman's words touched a chord in her mind and, dimly, she recalled something about respect for the elderly and submission to one's husband. Did these things really matter in these times? Perhaps they did. Who was she to question these things? Her world, her generation had all the questions but no answers.

Sharda and Veeran moved into a flat in Durban. Occasionally they came to visit the family. With time, the old woman came to accept the change. Some of the hurt was gone. But although she treated Sharda with the fairest consideration, she could not easily forgive her. Pride would not allow her to acknowledge defeat. There were some things she would not give in to. Like visiting Sharda. On special occasions, Sharda would try to get her to visit her, but the old woman always declined. When pressed for reasons, she maintained a tight-lipped silence. She was determined that nothing would make her yield to that. On one occasion, Sharda left in tears, chagrined by the old woman's obstinacy. The old woman watched her go and savoured the lone power of triumph. Let that be a lesson to them, she thought. She was not putty in their hands, to be moulded according to their will. Age did not mean easy capitulation to the whims of the young. She would not bend to their will! The winds of change were blowing down all the old pillars, but there were some things she would not easily give in to. There were times when the thought came to her mind unbidden, that perhaps she ought to bow to change gracefully, while time and strength were on her side. But she harboured the thought only fleetingly. The old, unyielding core of obstinacy would come to the fore, she would be strengthened in her resolve to remain adamant.

One morning Veeran came to see her. She wondered why he should call so early. She sensed his excitement and knew it meant good news.

'Ma, Sharda has a son,' he announced. 'You must come and see him.'

She received the news with mixed feelings. Her grandson. A new life, a new beginning. This was a moment for rejoicing, for thanksgiving. For a long moment, she struggled with herself, longing for the release of surrender. Her spirit was tired and she was strongly tempted to call a truce. Wordlessly, she followed Veeran to the car.

Later, as she held the child in her arms, she recalled another birth in the distant past, when she cradled her last born who looked so very much like this child. She looked at Veeran and smiled.

'He's a beautiful child and he looks just like you did,' she said.

'Sharda will have to give up work now,' he pointed out.

The old woman turned to Sharda. When their eyes met, there was a new gentleness, a new peace in the old woman's eyes.

'No, she doesn't have to. I will look after the child,' she stated serenely.

She put the child down and rose. The spirit of two worlds had emerged in a new beginning.

PETER WILHELM

Jazz
(In memoriam KM)

I had left school and was in my first year at university; eighteen years old, scrabbling around the campus with my bag of books and short-sightedness. Jane was in my English class and we sat near each other. She was very beautiful, a target for the predatory men who stalked women there in those times, in all times. But she held aloof, being an intellectual and, for those times, a radical.

Joseph Conrad, DH Lawrence, Henry James: prompted by mid-century critics and moralists such as FR Leavis, we read their famous books and wrote clever papers on them. I struggled, for my background was impoverished; not simply in the cash valuation you could put on it, though that was scant enough: but in the very aridity of the mental climate. I moved in the remotest suburbs of thought; in the remotest suburbs west of the city. Far away I saw the lights, and was drawn like a moth.

I cannot easily describe Jane. Her hair was blond, she was tanned and 'athletic' (my mother's curious euphemism for big-breasted). Etc. The fact of beauty was there, like a cat in the house: but then I could match that by being handsome in a parodic fashion, and I played all the sports. She would not have been drawn to me through a reciprocation of prettiness. Had that been on, other men would have put her in their pockets with their meaty hands: after all, just ahead is the man who is better than you in every respect.

But because I had a carnal wish for learning, Jane came my way.

We dated regularly. We went to art movies. Now in those days sex had not yet reached our shores, so to speak. One took oneself to extremes of passion in parked cars or bedrooms when parents were out for the night: but the essential was infrequently consummated. Rebuttal was somewhat more in force then than now, but with no certainty of outcome: we drifted in grey sexual nothingness, always afraid. At the end of a fruitful and natural consummation could come a burgeoning foetus. And after that marriage, abortion, God knew what. Alien territory. So one did not transgress easily, and there was an understanding implicit in the gropings that in the end we would go home in sexual agony.

I had worked part-time to buy an electric guitar, and I was a member of a band that played on Friday or Saturday nights at various student parties. We barely got by, musically and financially. There were four of us: lead guitar (myself), electric bass, drums, and a perpetually stoned proto-hippie who played all kinds of instruments very well – piano, saxophone, flute. We had no real musical 'voice'.

We played to order, like robots. There was no improvisation, no complexity, no jazz unless a few rehearsed riffs in the midst of a twelve-bar-blues number can be accounted such.

I had no ambitions musically; I played to earn money to keep up payments on my crotchety old Ford, so essential to getting around, and for spare change to buy Jane hamburgers after we had seen Ingmar Bergman's latest contribution to cosmic pessimism. Jane generally accompanied me to the various dances at which I played, but was mostly bored. 'Why don't you ever play *real* music?' she would ask. She meant jazz.

'It's not that kind of band,' I would reply, hotly on the defence. 'I can play jazz if I want to.' Jazz was the fashion.

She came from a very rich background; her parents had a castle in Houghton, with uniformed servants, a bar, everything. She did not merely have her own room; it had an adjacent study. Her father was the head of an important liberal organisation, and needed a study to concoct his ringing denunciations of apartheid; so, in a kind of dreamy intellectual deliverance, he had provided his sons and daughter with studies. They would need them. Everybody needed them, right?

'Prove to me you can play jazz,' Jane said once. 'Bring your guitar to my house and see if you can play along with Parker or Mingus.' She had all the records. 'See if you play like Coltrane, or only imitate Cliff Richard and The Shadows!' A later generation might have said 'The Pet Shop Boys'.

Damn right I was going to try. So I practised at home, sending my fretful fingers over the frets, learning apparently spontaneous sequences of notes. I went over them, and over them again. Mother threw fits. 'Switch that thing off or I'll break it over your head! You'll have me in the bladdy lunatic asylum if you go on.'

'I make money out of it,' I would reply. 'I pay for my textbooks by playing the guitar.'

'No you don't. Your father pays for your textbooks by repping in the northern Transvaal, leaving me alone here to listen to your crap. You just play to show off to your rich little girlfriend.'

So it went on.

I went to Jane's house and played along with Parker and Mingus, their rich organic sounds coming out of vast hi-fi speakers that cost more than

I could make out of my playing in a year. I played along, not very well, but surprisingly well enough to please Jane. Jazz, she explained to me (after all this was the Sixties), was the authentic music of the 'Negro'. It was, therefore, a bold statement about life from men who lived on the raw edge of danger and prejudice.

By implication, even listening to jazz showed not merely one's solidarity with an oppressed people, but was in itself a quasi-revolutionary act. Your heart was in the right area.

However. Jazz – as codified in those giant piles of records she had in racks and on shelves – was an imported subversion; the players were Americans. I put a hard point to Jane: isn't all this a posture? In what way did it relate to the life content of South African blacks, 'our' blacks?

'It's the same thing. They use music in the same way. Look at Dollar Brand and Adam Moletsi.'

Adam Moletsi was invited from time to time to play on campus. The attentive white liberals would listen to him producing tortured notes from his saxophone, veritable cries of anguish and pride on which they would comment favourably.

After I had played along with Jane's records, we lay together on the bed and kissed. I took matters further.

'No, no.'

'Yes, yes.'

'No, stop.'

'I'll do anything for you. I want to make love to you.'

'You'd never respect me afterwards.'

'Of course I'd respect you afterwards. I'd respect you even more.'

'No.'

I sat upright, hurt and almost angry. 'You talk so much about freedom and all: why can't you be free with me?'

She shook her head. 'I'm not like that. I don't want to be used and thrown away.' Poor Jane: in a decade or so she would find the strong female voices she heard distantly in our future. But when she did, it was too late. 'I'm not that kind of girl,' she murmured sadly.

'Well perhaps you should become that kind of girl. You're nothing but a …' But there I stopped short of using a term very familiar in my background, though alien to hers.

'A what?' she snorted, also sitting up. 'Just what am I? Go ahead and say what you were going to say.'

'A hypocrite,' I mumbled slackly, for that was the most acceptable alternative that occurred to me right then.

She laughed. 'So I'm supposed to go to bed with you because I believe in freedom for the African people? That's the most nonsensical argument I've ever heard.'

'Well,' I said, producing like a magic rabbit an idea, a threat, a strategy. 'Would you go to bed with me if I stood up on stage with Adam Moletsi and played jazz just as well as he can?'

The proposition had coalesced out of the variant threads of our conversation, our relation of bodies, our sense of each other's dimensions of soul.

And: 'Yes,' she said.

It happened that Adam Moletsi was coming to the campus within the next week. He would bring his usual backing band with him and would give a mid-afternoon concert in a medium-sized hall. Several hundred students could be expected to attend; the University Jazz Society (to which Jane and I belonged) would charge admission to non-members; and Adam and his band would be given the money that was taken in. It was an easy arrangement.

I went to the president of the Jazz Society and told him I wanted to play with Adam.

'No, you can't do that,' he said firmly. 'People will be paying to hear Adam, not you. Besides, it would be ridiculous if you, a white, went up and tried to compete with an assured black jazzman.' The president spoke snottily; I had offended some sense of racial propriety.

'Well,' I said, 'I'm going to ask Adam if I can play with him. It's his scene; he can decide.'

'I still say no,' said the president; but he was unsure now. 'Perhaps if Adam says yes it'll be OK. But I don't want trouble.'

'Piss off.'

'Piss off yourself, you arrogant twerp.'

Let me speak about myself briefly, as I then was. I was just a young white boy from a succession of poor suburbs. Blacks were not, so to speak, visible to me. I had been brought up in the proprieties and rectitudes of a normal lower-middle-class family for that time and place – except that an entire section, a nation one might say, had been rendered invisible to me. My parents spoke easily of 'boys', and I seldom met black people who were not servants – not of that amorphous gestation of 'garden boys' and 'kitchen girls' who scurried around and beneath the skirts of white society, cleaning up and being humble. My view of the real world was therefore unbalanced.

Jazz players, for people like Jane, myself, and indeed the president of the Jazz Society, represented far more than a musical ambience: they stood for their people, a symbol in the liberal's mind. Yet, after all, they were simply men and women; they struggled under an additional yoke when the liberals made their play of them, as if they were cards in a bridge game.

No wonder Adam Moletsi drank. He had to stand up there in the face of those white youths and play at being a nigger – for them. Who of us saw him otherwise?

I made my preparations for the afternoon of the concert. Because I, a white, was going to stand up with those said representatives of blackdom, I would take upon myself a quantum of blackness. I knew that (and knew it was why Jane would go to bed with me because of it: in muted rebellion, she really wanted to sleep with a black man). However, because I realised my physical limits when it came to playing the guitar, and knew I would be up front with professionals, I prepared myself psychologically for the encounter: I boosted my pride, lest there be cataclysm.

The hall filled. Adam and his band arrived. He was drunk. He waved to the girls and waggled his hips. There was some laughter in the hall.

Adam. A tall, cadaverous man, his liver mostly gone but giving to his light skin a yellow tinge. His blackness was inside him, not folded over his bones.

I went up. 'I want to play with you.' I pointed to a corner where I had in advance stacked my guitar and amplifier: a mean red Fender and a fine wood and metal amplifier with a great speaker attached.

Adam laughed, swaying over me. 'Hey man, you want to play with us?' He had an adopted American accent, like many black men of his generation. He was perhaps forty-five. An old soul, as they said.

The whole band laughed. The president of the Jazz Society, blushing like a rose, came up and whispered to Adam. I saw Jane sitting in the audience. Then Adam turned to me and said, 'Sure, you can join in on some numbers. Get set up.'

The band went straight into 'Bloomdido', the Bird and Diz number that is scatty and great. Adam played a solo and then turned to me to bring me in. I felt total exposure. 'Bloomdido' was far out of my range. Absurdly, I shook my head and Adam let the drummer go for thirty-two bars, an impressive explosion that diverted attention away from my initial, devastating failure. I sensed Adam's concern not to embarrass me and was swayed by curious emotions. Not merely gratitude, but not least wonder.

The next number was a straightforward twelve-bar-blues: three chords, up and down. A child could do well. Adam, I was certain, had set this up for me and I played a perfect solo when my turn came, being really fancy and overriding notes so that it sounded like Chet Atkins had come in, but funky, good. You could feel it was good. I was applauded.

So it went. Adam now knew what I could do, so he did not ask me in on numbers beyond my scope. At one point he took a nip of brandy out of his coat pocket, sipped, and offered it to me. I took it, proud in front of all those envious white dudes.

The concert came to an end and the students filed out. I was left standing with Adam and the band, the president, and Jane, who came up and took my arm like Miss Universe. That was the proudest moment of my youth. I felt on fire. Perhaps the brandy helped, but I was at ease with Adam, and the thought of sex with Jane – assured now, on the line – lent me an enormous physical assurance.

'You were very good,' said Jane. She smiled.

The president of the Jazz Society paid the band out and the men split, except Adam who sat back in one of the chairs, just like a student, and thoughtfully drank his brandy. His saxophone was in a case on the bench before him.

Finally, there was just Adam, myself and Jane. We talked desultorily, unsure of each other. Then Adam said: 'Hey, man: you got a car?'

'Sure.'

'Let's go for a ride. Us three.'

This was Life. I was tense and excited. So was Jane. 'Us three.'

So we went driving, packed into my Ford with conversation and brandy. Adam told us a lot about himself, how he lived close to the edge but had good high-class gangster friends who helped him out. He actually sat there, reclining in the back seat and told us stuff like that, nodding off from time to time. He directed me, and soon I found that we were on our way to Alexandra township. A black area: I felt trepidation.

But we were not soon into the township when Adam sat up alertly and told me to park.

'You stay here,' he instructed Jane. Then he took my arm and we walked out together in those bitter streets, frozen in the early winter, to a shop where a Chinese man sat and watched.

We bought from him dagga, the weed, *boom*: that which I had always associated with precipitation into blackness, the revenge of the black man on the white whose consciousness cannot bear alteration.

A secret about drugs: any hell they give is better than the hell of the white man for the black.

We drove out of Alex, through mute, manicured, varnished suburbs, all order and the law incarnate, drove 'us three' with our cargo of hallucination and communication and blazing withheld sex. We smoked the stuff and laughed like crazy as the world twisted and warped, and we twisted and warped and flickered into bizarre, meaningless awareness: that point where just one more toke will be too much, or will reveal all.

The Allness waiting there in the next joint, like reality about to serve a summons.

We drove to the top of the Melville Koppies, looking down on the suburbs and the city itself: far from any cop, smoking, smoking, pushing out smoke from our lungs as if we were on fire.

And what did we talk about? God knows.

But I came to clarity when Adam said: 'Listen man, give up playing. You're no good. This afternoon, that was just playing games.'

'But I was … fluent … I was OK, wasn't I?'

Jane looked intently at us two.

'You were OK, but you don't understand it. You don't understand jazz. You don't understand the pain, the suffering, the longing, the rocking, the rolling …' Adam was almost gibbering. He was very stoned. But, of course, I understood him all too well.

'I tried,' I said defensively.

'Sure. But that's not good enough. You'll never get there man: just face it, and you'll be happier.'

'What was wrong with my playing?'

'It was the wrong colour, man, that was all.'

'I don't …'

'It was the wrong colour! It's not your music and you can't play it and you never will play it. Even if you put out sounds just like Charlie Parker, just the same, there will still be a difference. It's not your music.'

Then he turned to Jane: 'But you're my woman, you're my music.'

'No she's not,' I shouted. 'Take your hands off her.'

We all pummelled each other; it was a farce. At last Adam gave up and simply laughed. 'OK, white boy, she's your woman. Just take me to the station and drop me off. She's all yours.' Then, abruptly, he leaned over to me and kissed me; I could actually feel the essence of love there, a tolerance and an anguish; I smelt him.

I kissed him back.

I gave up my guitar. Jane gave me up. Adam died of cirrhosis of the liver. Jane married and had a child who drowned in her swimming pool, so she committed suicide.

The difference between youth and all that comes afterwards is a simple one, a stage or an event that puts matters into perspective. Real people really die. Real people have real limits.

Jazz is something I have on my record player.

PART FOUR

1990-

ABRAHAM H DE VRIES

Ruins

Translated from the Afrikaans by Ina Rousseau.

It started with the letter. She wrote:

The school about which you often spoke is still there, high up against the Karoo koppie, but it's just a skeleton, virtually a ruin, the window panes are shattered, some of the window frames have been removed, the door frames are long gone, the roof tiles clatter in the wind.It's a cold northwesterly wind this time of the year, that makes one imagine that one hears the school bell, the shuffling of feet, the voices of the children drifting from the direction of the playground. But the ring at the top of the netball pole has been rusted off and now the pole itself has been removed and used as firewood.

Regular prayer meetings were held in this school, serving all the farms. But there wasn't a soul who knew the first two lines of any hymn or psalm. The lead singer was old Jan Bekkies and his friend, old Piet Skapie, was his very real help. Jan had a deep, husky voice which sounded wobbly, like a branch dragged over corrugated iron; when he set in the tune it felt as though it echoed in one's stomach. Piet's voice, on the other hand, sang in tune, but it was high pitched, almost a whistle, and when he really wanted to impress (for instance, when the dominee was present), the notes broke up like a musical morse code. Jan would set in the tune of *On a Hill Far Away* at too low a pitch, then Piet would drag it out with the line about the old rugged cross, and the other prayer-goers only joined in singing about the emblem of suffering and shame.

Now, prayer meetings on the farms took place in the evening. And this is where the devil himself regularly filled his lungs and joined in the singing. The school had no electricity, there were lamps and candles in the windows, on the table and on the little bookshelf at the back of the classroom. Only the two lead singers had their own candles.

Need I say more? To sing a note, one needs to breathe, but breath extinguishes candles easily.

At every prayer meeting. The candle in the candlestick would appear between the eyes and the hymnal, the flickering light would reflect brightly in the old reading glasses and on the unsteady white page of the book, then the first note sounded, then there was darkness. That is why no one attending those prayer meetings knew the first two verses of any psalm or hymn.

In previous years quite a few of the farmers were in the habit of milking their cows to the rhythm of *The Storm May Roar without Me* or *Praise the Lord O my Soul*, sung softly. I'm sure they still do it at present, the world doesn't change all that fast. Or one could hear the women kneading loaves of bread. 'Jesus loves me that I know' – the notes drawn out lengthily in a whiny manner. But on returning from the prayer meetings, they didn't sing the words, they only la ... la ... la ... laaaed amongst the cows and over the bread flour.

What makes one remember this kind of triviality more vividly than the sermons? Laughter is – to quote Balzac from memory – a privilege granted to man alone because he has sufficient causes for tears within his reach.

What saddens us so are the dilapidated homesteads in the district. The substantial farmers have bought the land of the lesser ones and on every small farm there used to be a homestead too, as you know. Some of them have been restored, four of them, next to the road as one drives to town; they are now inhabited by professional people who prefer not to live in town, I know of a teacher and an attorney's clerk, that's the type of person. But many of the homesteads have been abandoned to the mercy of the elements and you know what happens: at first a large rust spot appears on the corrugated iron roof, the outlet-pipe between the roof and the tank disappears; where the water runs down the wall, the plaster peels off piecemeal. The termites eat tunnels and holes into the walls, until they crumble and collapse.

A few of the homesteads are maintained by the owners at as little cost as possible. Coloured families of farm labourers have been permitted to go and live there. In fact, two, I can't think of any more now. And I say permitted but that's not quite what happened. Some farmers are quite glad to have people whom they know well living there and more would presumably grab the chance, but some of the houses are haunted, they say. Where this or that family used to live, an old man in a nightshirt with a candle in one hand and a rifle or sjambok in the other walks from room to room. Just their way of saying: we know those families and none of us ever ventured beyond the kitchen. Many bad and ugly things happened there. Let go, let go, let the past be over and done with. Let those houses crumble and fall to dust.

Ghosts past and present still abound here.

So it was. Don't let nostalgia erase from our memory that which those who were separated from us by law remember. I won't name the man in this story, out of shame because he could have so many names. Let's just say that he lived on Sias's farm against the koppie behind the irrigation canal. When his wife was still alive it was a pleasant-looking, neat house overlooking Sias's dam and the finches settling on the willow branches at nightfall.

They always used to say that when his parents were still alive (they also lived there), he already had a foul temper. People blamed his father for not scolding him sufficiently for this. I don't attach overmuch importance to the guilt of the fathers, he got mixed up with the wrong bunch of friends in the school of agriculture, that's where he already hit the coloured servant in the dining hall so hard with his fist that the poor bloke had to go to hospital. The principal suspended him for two months. Only two months and he had already had a warning. No, I never knew his wife, but I attended her funeral because it was during the school holidays and I was at home. He walked beside her coffin, cursing, when they passed me (I was standing underneath the pepper tree) he was cursing her for doing this to him. A week before that he had arrived from town early one afternoon, something he very seldom did – and a scarf which she used to tie around her hair-knot was floating on the dam. He couldn't find her anywhere.

After that he turned the devils in him loose on his labourers. Two or three times he was sentenced for assault (every time with a money fine). Norry Willemse who worked for him at the time was the first labourer who hit back and spent almost a year in gaol for that. Yes, I am talking about the same Willemse about whom you are probably thinking now.

Then a strange thing happened. The police were there with him on the farm, they had gone there to warn him after a fight with Norrie. But it wasn't necessary and he told them so. He stopped drinking and in what was left of that year a complete change came over him. That is the way people told the story, they say he even attended a prayer meeting one Wednesday. Things were getting better for him.

And at the same time things became worse. The story of the locks I heard from De Necker, who used to work at the Co-op. He told me that man had him guessing, because every week, every blessed week, he walked in there to buy a different kind of lock. Until De Necker's curiosity got the better of him one day and he enquired about it point blank; that's how he came to know. Because the old man no longer drank at that time, he was lying awake at night, and as a result of that wakefulness, I suppose, his conscience started to niggle him. He developed a terrible fear of burglars. De Necker told me there were locks inside and around that house, on the gates, on the screen doors, the windows, whatever could be locked, he closed with a lock. Even the tap of the water tank.

It must have gone on like this for the best part of a year, because Willemse was sentenced in February, the sentence was reduced because of good behaviour, he walked out of prison at the beginning of October. On the very evening that Willemse was released the man who was responsible for his unjust imprisonment once more locked his house from front to back, every outside door, all the windows, all the inside doors. The next morning the police wanted to call in a locksmith from Mossel Bay, they didn't know how to gain entry, because he had the keys with him, they found the keys under the bed.

The old man was lying on the bed, a corpse, he had been strangled. But the windows showed no sign of a break-in, on the contrary, the pane was lying outside in smithereens. Someone must have tried to get out. It didn't take the police long to arrest Willlemse again. He admitted that he had been waiting in a concealed corner of the bedroom until the man for whom he had felt such hatred had both of them locked up in the room.

What can one do about the ruins? It was only here that we heard the expression for the first time; the people say that an old house mourns when uninhabited. It is as though the house is aware of the fact that there is no longer anybody to accommodate, nobody to be sheltered against the onslaught of wind and weather. As though the hollow sounds of the wind in the rooms and the passages become unbearable. Then the tears start streaming down the gutters.

But I don't want to create the impression that everything just collapses into a state of rack and ruin, even around the old dwellings new farmlands developed. The vineyards are trellissed high because a harvesting machine brings the harvest in more rapidly than hands. They foresee a time in the future when manual labour will become even scarcer. By means of filter irrigation the farmers can now plant vineyards halfway up some of the koppies where previously only elephant's food and Karoo shrubs had grown. This landscape has changed more dramatically in the past few years than in the previous decades.

... But it was also different, oh yes, it was different.

As one drives into town from your farm, just about where the tarred road starts, you'll find on the left side of the road, beside the river, an earlier flat-roofed house which was provided with a stoep and broekie lace and still later a pitched roof of Sandveld thatch. Neels, the owner, was a respected and wealthy man for those days, he didn't buy on credit and he didn't undertake extensions on his farm for which he couldn't pay in cash. His wife, Isa, supported him in everything. But Isa was not very well – one could notice that in her appearance, she was pale and in her eyes she had that strange softness of people who had made their peace with the worst that could happen to them. They were gregarious, Neels and Isa. On Sunday afternoons, parked underneath the pepper trees, there were always cars of townsfolk, of neighbours, of guests from as far as Riversdale and Worcester. On the chairs in the sitting room and on the backs of the benches the antimacassars were spotlessly clean and for coffee or tea drips there was a little round serviette in every saucer. Every Friday Isa baked melkterte and raisin tarts and a few loaves.

In the late afternoon after the cars had all left, Neels would say to Ouma Janie, who worked for them: Janie, come, I will take you home, then I will come and help missus Isa with the dishes, come on, let's go, we can start again tomorrow. And usually Ouma would then reply, the kitchen is my pride, meneer Neels, it is an unknown night we are entering, please wait for me a little longer.

But that afternoon even before Neels had taken Ouma Janie home, he had noticed that Isa was not herself. She had been so quiet while the guests were there. Janie had said: Meneer, I'm sleeping in the outside room tonight, some of my laundry still needs ironing, and also in case meneer and missus need me. And Neels did not stop her.

Neels and Isa went to bed early, when everything in the farmyard was quiet, the cows back in the little field, the milk foaming warm in the big tank where the big lorry of the cheese factory was to come and slurp it up in the morning, the chickens asleep on the lowest branches of the fig tree, the mountain behind the house dark and far away and peaceful.

Towards the small hours of the morning he woke up and reached over to light the candle. But in the light of the moon shining through the slits in the blinds from the side of the fig tree, he saw that Isa was lying still, very still beside him, the one hand on her breast, the other on his arm. That must be the reason why he woke up, he thought.

Her hand was cold. He listened but there was no breathing, no heart beating any longer. Neels then lit the candle, took his Bible and started reading. Then he went to her side of the bed, knelt down and said a prayer for her immortal soul, for the empty place in his home and for everybody on the farm who would miss her so much. After his words dried up, he remained on his knees for a while, then he said amen. And even before he'd finished talking to his God, he resumed in his heart the conversation with her of so many years.

The next morning when Ouma Janie knocked on the door to bring the coffee, he said to her: 'Come in. But, Janie, bring from now on only one cup, please.'

That is also how it was.

Tinus has survived the dark times following in the wake of his dismissal. He no longer at night in his sleep grinds his teeth. And he no longer talks about it. Foreign affairs and the missions in which he served, The Hague, Washington, Oslo, served one purpose only: we came to stay here as though we were sent here, it's also the game which we used to play with each other when we were still on the move from country to country. We'll stay here till we're called back. Let's not get too involved with local matters. Remember it's temporary.

I can hear you laughing. All right, laugh. It's now getting to be more than five years and even I now admit, there is no longer any 'home' to which we want to return, we have been generally adopted. I can cook tripe already, I know how to prepare jam from pieces of *kambro*, we belong to the open tennis club and Tinus has been chosen as a director of the KWS.

Last night Jan (Le Grange; Jan van Zijlsdamme, as he is called) came to visit and was talking about the ever-topical good old days (as though we had experienced them, I suppose it is these folks' way of saying: it feels as though you have been living here all along), Jan said he had thought about you the whole day, I must write to you and ask what could be done about the old buildings and the new problems. Of the latter I haven't written. Things will improve, we do believe that. The Little Karoo gave us back our future.

I started answering you yesterday. Some deterioration we can never stop, I wrote. Dilapidated old farmsteads are ugly, they are not worthy of those who lived in them and of their histories. I said, they gave shelter to ways of life, and I have added, you should take note of the plural, the spirit of the time sometimes wants to make one believe that there was only one kind of relationship in all the houses: that of master and slave. Those also occurred – let us not deny anything. I wanted to add that we dare not ever forget what happened to all of us, no matter how tragic, how repulsive, how silly, we know by now how our stories outlive our judgements.

But then the telephone rang, it was Izak and he told me about the cruel and senseless murders of Hannes and Anna Marais of Bobbejaankrans, a farm twelve miles away from you. Why did I think farm murders are committed elsewhere, in Gauteng, in the Free State, but never in the Little Karoo, never involving people whom I know? (The policeman who was murdered in Lindley last week was a friend of Hannes, we met him on their farm and Anna told me on the telephone just last week how brave his wife was.)

Further than that I didn't write, you'll understand. I walked around in the back garden because I wanted to let at least part of the night pass before telling my family.

Towards the early hours before going to bed I reread your letter. And then more clearly than ever I realised it is not any earlier time we long for, it is not with the crumbling ruins of the past that we know not what to begin.

I long for now, for a present, for the village and the people about whom you write, the vineyards, the lucerne fields, the houses, the Karoo koppies, irrigation, neighbours who talk about the weather and about the country and about problems and about where in the Swartberg mountain the most beautiful *Protea Aristatas* grow this year.

I yearn for all our dreams and for all our illusions of being at home.

NADINE GORDIMER

Once upon a Time

Someone has written to ask me to contribute to an anthology of stories for children. I reply that I don't write children's stories; and he writes back that at a recent congress/book fair/seminar a certain novelist said every writer ought to write at least one story for children. I think of sending a postcard saying I don't accept that I 'ought' to write anything.

And then last night I woke up – or rather was wakened without knowing what had roused me.

A voice in the echo chamber of the subconscious?

A sound.

A creaking of the kind made by the weight carried by one foot after another along a wooden floor. I listened. I felt the apertures of my ears distend with concentration.

Again: the creaking. I was waiting for it; waiting to hear if it indicated that feet were moving from room to room, coming up the passage – to my door. I have no burglar bars, no gun under the pillow, but I have the same fears as people who do take these precautions, and my windowpanes are thin as rime, could shatter like a wineglass. A woman was murdered (how do they put it) in broad daylight in a house two blocks away, last year, and the fierce dogs who guarded an old widower and his collection of antique clocks were strangled before he was knifed by a casual labourer he had dismissed without pay.

I was staring at the door, making it out in my mind rather than seeing it, in the dark. I lay quite still – a victim already – but the arrhythmia of my heart was fleeing, knocking this way and that against its body-cage. How finely tuned the senses are, just out of rest, sleep! I could never listen intently as that in the distractions of the day; I was reading every faintest sound, identifying and classifying its possible threat.

But I learned that I was to be neither threatened nor spared. There was no human weight pressing on the boards, the creaking was a buckling, an epicentre of stress, I was in it. The house that surrounds me while I sleep is built on undermined ground; far beneath my bed, the floor, the house's foundations, the stopes and passages of gold mines have hollowed the rock, and when some face trembles, detaches and falls, three thousand feet below, the whole house shifts slightly, bringing uneasy strain to the balance and counterbalance of brick, cement, wood and glass that hold it as a structure around me. The misbeats of my heart tailed off like the last muffled flourishes on one of the wooden xylophones made by the Chopi and Tsonga migrant miners who might have been down there, under me in the earth at that moment. The stope where the fall was could have been disused, dripping water from its ruptured veins; or men might now be interred there in the most profound of tombs.

I couldn't find a position in which my mind would let go of my body – release me to sleep again. So I began to tell myself a story; a bedtime story.

⋆ ⋆ ⋆

In a house, in a suburb, in a city, there were a man and his wife who loved each other very much and were living happily ever after. They had a little boy, and they loved him very much. They had a cat and a dog that the little boy loved very much. They had a car and a caravan trailer for holidays, and a swimming pool that was fenced so that the little boy and his playmates would not fall in and drown. They had a housemaid who was absolutely trustworthy and an itinerant gardener who was highly recommended by the neighbours. For when they began to live happily ever after they were warned, by that wise old witch, the husband's mother, not to take on anyone off the street. They were inscribed in a medical benefit society, their pet dog was licensed, they were insured against fire, flood damage and theft, and subscribed to the local Neighbourhood Watch, which supplied them with a plaque for their gates lettered YOU HAVE BEEN WARNED over the silhouette of a would-be intruder. He was masked; it could not be said if he was black or white, and therefore proved the property owner was no racist.

It was not possible to insure the house, the swimming pool or the car against riot damage. There were riots, but these were outside the city, where people of another colour were quartered. These people were not allowed into the suburb except as reliable housemaids and gardeners, so there was nothing to fear, the husband told the wife. Yet she was afraid that some day such people might come up the street and tear off the plaque YOU HAVE BEEN WARNED and open the gates and stream in ... Nonsense, my dear, said the husband, there are police and soldiers and tear gas and guns to keep them away. But to please her – for he loved her very much and buses were being burned, cars stoned, and schoolchildren shot by the police in those quarters out of sight and hearing of the suburb – he had electronically-controlled gates fitted. Anyone who pulled off the sign YOU HAVE BEEN WARNED and tried to open the gates would have to announce his intentions by pressing a button and speaking into a receiver relayed to the house. The little boy was fascinated by the device and used it as a walkie-talkie in cops-and-robbers play with his small friends.

The riots were suppressed, but there were many burglaries in the suburb and somebody's trusted housemaid was tied up and shut in a cupboard by thieves while she was in charge of her employers' house. The trusted housemaid of the man and wife and little boy was so upset by this misfortune befalling a friend left, as she herself often was, with responsibility for the possessions of the man and his wife and the little boy that she implored her employers to have burglar bars attached to the doors and windows of the house, and an alarm system installed. The wife said, She is right, let us take heed of her advice. So from every window and door in the house where they were living happily ever after they now saw the trees and sky through bars, and when the little boy's pet cat tried to climb in by the fanlight to keep him company in his little bed at night, as it customarily had done, it set off the alarm keening through the house.

The alarm was often answered – it seemed – by other burglar alarms, in other houses, that had been triggered by pet cats or nibbling mice. The alarms called to one another across the gardens in shrills and bleats and wails that everyone soon became accustomed to, so that the din roused the inhabitants of the suburb no more than the croak of frogs and musical grating of cicadas' legs. Under cover of the electronic harpies' discourse intruders sawed the iron bars and broke into homes, taking away hi-fi equipment, television sets, cassette players, cameras and radios, jewellery and clothing, and sometimes were hungry enough to devour everything in the refrigerator or paused audaciously to drink the whisky in the cabinets or patio bars. Insurance companies paid no compensation for single malt, a loss made keener by the property owner's knowledge that the thieves wouldn't even have been able to appreciate what it was they were drinking.

Then the time came when many of the people who were not trusted housemaids and gardeners hung about the suburb because they were unemployed. Some importuned for a job: weeding or painting a roof; anything, *baas*, madam. But the man and his wife remembered the warning about taking on anyone off the street. Some drank liquor and fouled the street with discarded bottles. Some begged, waiting for the man or his wife to drive the car out of the electronically-operated gates. They sat about with their feet in the gutters, under the jacaranda trees that made a green tunnel of the street – for it was a beautiful suburb, spoilt only by their presence – and sometimes they fell asleep lying right before the gates in the midday sun. The wife could never see anyone go hungry. She sen. trusted housemaid out with bread and tea, but the trusted housemaid saı these were loafers and tsotsis, who would come and tie her up and shut her in a cupboard. The husband said, She's right. Take heed of her advice. You only encourage them with your bread and tea. They are looking for their chance ... And he brought the little boy's tricycle from the garden into the house every night, because if the house was surely secure, once locked and with the alarm set, someone might still be able to climb over the wall or the electronically-closed gates into the garden.

You are right, said the wife, then the wall should be higher. And the wise old witch, the husband's mother, paid for the extra bricks as her Christmas present to her son and his wife – the little boy got a Space Man outfit and a book of fairy tales.

But every week there were more reports of intrusion: in broad daylight and the dead of night, in the early hours of the morning, and even in the lovely summer twilight – a certain family was at dinner while the bedrooms were being ransacked upstairs. The man and his wife, talking of the latest armed robbery in the suburb, were distracted by the sight of the little boy's pet cat effortlessly arriving over the seven-foot wall, descending first with a rapid bracing of extended forepaws down on the sheer vertical surface, and then a graceful launch, landing with swishing tail within the property. The whitewashed wall was marked with the cat's comings and goings; and on the street side of the wall there were larger red-earth smudges that could have been made by the kind of broken running shoes, seen on the feet of unemployed loiterers, that had no innocent destination.

When the man and wife and little boy took the pet dog for its walk round the neighbourhood streets they no longer paused to admire this show of roses or that perfect lawn; these were hidden behind an array of different varieties of security fences, walls and devices. The man, wife, little boy and dog passed a remarkable choice: there was the low-cost option of pieces of broken glass embedded in cement along the top of walls, there were iron grilles ending in lance-points, there were attempts at reconciling the aesthetics of prison architecture with the Spanish Villa style (spikes painted pink) and with the plaster urns of neoclassical façades (twelve-inch pikes finned like zigzags of lightning and painted pure white). Some walls had a small board affixed, giving the name and telephone number of the firm responsible for the installation of the devices. While the little boy and the pet dog raced ahead, the husband and wife found themselves comparing the possible effectiveness of each style against its appearance; and after several weeks when they paused before this barricade or that without needing to speak, both came out with the conclusion that the ... ɪrth considering. It was the ugliest but the most honest in ... f the pure concentration-camp style, no frills, all evident ... the length of walls, it consisted of a continuous coil of stiff ... etal serrated into jagged blades, so that there would be no ... ɪng over it and no way through its tunnel without getting entangl... its fangs. There would be no way out, only a struggle getting bloodier and bloodier, a deeper and sharper hooking and tearing of flesh. The wife shuddered to look at it. You're right, said the husband, anyone would think twice … And they took heed of the advice on a small board fixed to the wall: Consult DRAGON'S TEETH The People For Total Security.

Next day a gang of workmen came and stretched the razor-bladed coils all round the walls of the house where the husband and wife and little boy and pet dog and cat were living happily ever after. The sunlight flashed and slashed off the serrations, the cornice of razor thorns encircled the home, shining. The husband said, Never mind. It will weather. The wife said, You're wrong. They guarantee it's rust-proof. And she waited until the little boy had run off to play before she said, I hope the cat will take heed … The husband said, Don't worry, my dear, cats always look before they leap. And it was true that from that day on the cat slept in the little boy's bed and kept to the garden, never risking a try at breaching security.

One evening, the mother read the little boy to sleep with a fairy story from the book the wise old witch had given him at Christmas. Next day he pretended to be the prince who braves the terrible thicket of thorns to enter the palace and kiss the Sleeping Beauty back to life: he dragged a ladder to the wall, the shining coiled tunnel was just wide enough for his little body to creep in, and with the first fixing of its razor-teeth in his knees and hands and head he screamed and struggled deeper into its tangle. The trusted housemaid and the itinerant gardener, whose 'day' it was, came running, the first to see and to scream with him, and the itinerant gardener tore his hands trying to get at the little boy. Then the man and his wife burst wildly into the garden and for some reason (the cat, probably) the alarm set up wailing against the screams while the bleeding mass of the little boy was hacked out of the security coil with saws, wire-cutters, choppers, and they carried it – the man, the wife, the hysterical trusted housemaid and the weeping gardener – into the house.

STEPHEN GRAY

The Building-site

A lot has changed in my life since the builders arrived, especially as regards Dan. At the beginning of the year I paid no attention, but by Easter their activities on the building-site next door had so intruded into my routine that I'm not surprised we became acquainted.

Omar, my new neighbour, had acquired the modest mining cottage with such difficulty against the Group Areas Act and was converting it into – let's call it – a Muslim pleasure-palace. He was using the unregistered labour of Husein, the foreman who packed all eight of them in on his pick-up from the East Rand. This all takes place in my inner city suburb of Johannesburg, which is integrating faster than the government can do anything about it. During the time I have known Dan I've also become the last white householder within these four blocks.

Husein was to build at Omar's instructions a common wall between our properties to be in line with his general fortifications. To this I had to contribute on a fifty-fifty basis – about eighty per cent of the cost, as it turns out. I wasn't used to their methods of dealing. Husein had me lined up for a sucker, and conned me as well into having a security gate built alongside the wall in his own time, on Sundays which were not a holiday for him. He laid the bricks himself to make a bit extra. Dan brought them round on a wheelbarrow. Dan was the show-off type who enjoyed negotiating planks and trenches and muck-heaps of torn-down creeper. He'd jerk up his wrists and pile out the stolen goods.

Husein gave me no choice, really, about tightening up on security. I felt threatened because his ragged labourers were so poorly paid on the Friday, when the building-site whore and her pimp had been around and cleaned them out by the Saturday they were broke again. The petty robberies began on Sundays: washing from the line, the iron in the laundry at the back, spades and secateurs and, once when I was having a bath with the back door open, they tiptoed into the kitchen and filched the clock. I stood on the veranda, dripping, watching my kitchen clock go down the road to be pawned at the dagga-dealers. With the corrugated-iron fence down and no wall up yet, the security gate seemed pointless, but Husein persuaded me I must think of the future; crime was always on the increase. I knew that once his gang moved on the thefts would abate. They slept eight in the one room at the back of Omar's, four yards from my office – each with their patch marked out on the concrete floor and a skimpy blanket ... and me all alone in my seven-room mansion, guarding my privacy and possessions.

Husein was outrageous in his small talk. While his capacious wife sat in her smock in the truck hooting for him, he'd tell me of the luscious mistress he'd found in neighbouring Fordsburg: 'A man's got to have some sex life, you know; hell, I'm not over the top yet.' He looked forward to talking dirty with me, patting a few more bricks into cement.

He had me sorted out for what I was, so worked around to his early experiences. These took place in prison in the Cape, before his conversion and reform. During a long term he rose from ripped-apart catamite to gang-boss himself – see his tattoos – protecting his favourite slaves. For ever in his mind homosexuality meant the degradation of prison. Some grew so used to it and unable to adapt to the outside world they'd do anything stupid to be sentenced again – insult a policeman, shit on the mayor's doorstep – just to be back inside with their buddies. 'And some of them got big cocks, hey – *so* big. They not moffies, hey, they really men. But that's all they know, you understand.'

What was he behind bars for? Husein, who was now making my house impregnable, was in for armed robbery with assault.

'Dan, maak gou,' he'd complain, and Dan would trundle off for another load of larceny.

I more or less said that if ever Husein wished to come around for a service (his expression) – no charge – he was welcome, but he really preferred dressing up in his embroidered robes, skullcap on his curly locks, and squandering a fortune in the Fordsburg harem.

One day taking advantage of the quiet (Husein was also building a mosque out his way, so there were weeks without action – but that only protracted the ordeal), I was contemplating what to get on with in my office at the back. I suppose I was aware of a dull chopping sound and that they'd left Dan behind to guard their side of the property. In fact, when I opened my lounge curtains I'd seen the big-shouldered form of Dan and ignored looking at him, as we all agreed to ignore one another despite the enforced proximity. I knew perfectly well they knew every detail of my daily existence, as I knew theirs. With a whipping and twisting and thundering smash, the apricot tree in Omar's yard came down in my direction, the uppermost branches scraping onto my roof. This I could not ignore –

it was yet another day wiped off my schedule, without any prior consultation or my consent. I was furious actually, as it was one of the oldest trees in the suburb; it produced enough fruit to fill thousands of jars of that poor African staple – apricot jam – that had always gone to waste and now was weighing down my retreat in its fruity death-throes.

I could not be angry with Dan; Omar was to blame. Nevertheless, I had to go out and help clear the branches off my property, if only to hurry the sad process. Dan had few verbal skills, but he did have the buzz saw, so without any preplanning he sawed off the branches with an excruciating noise and smell of petrol while I dragged them over to Omar's dump. He had dismembered the venerable trunk before I was finished, so we jointly hauled for a while in the blazing sun. Then I gave him a rake to tidy up my garden and went inside.

When I heard he was done, I went out with two glasses of Coke, and we sat on the rockery, sweating and exhausted, and drank them. He didn't look me in the eye and I studied him obliquely. About all we said was, 'Cooldrink,' 'Koeldrank, ja …' 'Ja.' Country-boy, spoke only Afrikaans. Then in the evening he guarded Omar's, playing the local black music station on the radio.

Omar and Husein fell out, which inevitably had implications for my half of the wall – still with only the foundations laid, although all the rendering and extensions Omar wanted on the walls of his house had been done. They went at each other fanatically; money grievances, I suppose, not religious ones, for they were brothers in faith. Husein shouted for his men to lay down tools; Omar that they must continue or no pay (instant hammering). The two of them whaled into one another, grabbing up demolition hammers and taking positions in the street. Logically I was the one positioned to intervene. I wanted the whole business not to stretch over another six months. I stepped reluctantly forth to where all my new neighbours were keyed up, egging them on. They had both lost their tempers – were dangerous, hammers smashing at the glazed tiles and panes of glass. I moved forward, arms held out to separate them. As I jumped towards the breach, I felt hands clutching my belt behind. Dan advised against this intervention and had stopped me. I glanced at his really worried face, and got out of there in disgust. Saved from a broken skull by Dan! He knew I had miscalculated, would only have lost out yet again. It took a lot of guts to get a white man to change his course.

They settled their disagreement only with Husein expelled from Omar's domain and Omar taking over the men personally (since it was all illegal anyway), and good progress was made. Husein crept in at night to work on his subcontract with me for the gate, but only because I had not yet paid him for that part. When I did, he absconded, leaving the gate insecure and incompletely attached. He took the cash and tore off in his truck, which he'd had to hide blocks away. Later I learned from Dan he had gone without giving them their pay for over a month.

Now Friday was the only day I could count on for some peace because Omar was more rigorous and decreed prayer day. So off he went to pray and the rest smoked grass, and I could actually do some work. From my clean-living, occasional domestic servant I found out how bad things were if I went out on a Friday. She did her job with all the windows tightly closed against the fumes and the doors locked for fear that she would be gang-raped by the men on their highs next door. So I stayed home whenever I possibly could, now to protect my maid. The wall, when they finally got it up to ten feet, was no reassurance; they may have built it well, but not well enough to stop themselves climbing over.

On a Friday when I came back from an unavoidable meeting with an editor, I found Dan in my yard, doing his washing and in long conversation with my maid, who explained Omar had cut the water off for them. I said 'Good afternoon,' leaving them to it, knowing she knew best. She had sons of her own whom she kept strictly in Christian marching order. But there in my yard was the incredibly well-built young labourer with admirable shoulders and biceps and the skinny legs of undernourishment wearing an old towel of mine, while his rags dried on the line. Evidently he did not smoke grass, but he had a cigarette and flicked ash into the pots. I knew enough of my maid's interests to understand that in emphatic and school-sounding Xhosa they were discussing their favourite passages of the Bible. They belonged to similar sects. All this was a great relief.

One freezing winter night with a wind howling straight over the veld from the Antarctic and, if you weren't used to it, the tin roof clanking would drive your hair on end, I was trying to finish up when the front doorbell went. I thought to ignore it, but this was obviously an emergency. I was afraid to respond, frankly. But I opened the door and turned on the dim light, and nearly puked at what I saw. A black shape had been stabbed all over, blood pouring like oil down his face and it was squelching out of his boots, leaving ghastly footprints. I'm afraid I said he should go next door to the building-site where they would know how to help him. My fear accounts for my lack of charity.

In due course the bell went again and obviously next door they had elected Dan to soften me up, because they knew I was sweet on Dan. I had misjudged everything: the walking wounded *was* from there in the first place; he had gone to the last café open where they wouldn't let him use the phone – the ambulance would not come for any inarticulate black request, anyway. He had been stabbed ten blocks away by their old dagga-dealers for deserting them for closer and cheaper ones, and now Dan had come to me as a last resort. The victim was one of *them*; in fact, he was the very monster who had whipped my clock!

In the rush of desperation Dan and I were communicating perfectly. I told him to wash the man down and keep him warm; I would phone.

I phoned and the ambulance said they would come and – I'll give them that – they didn't ask if I was white or black, as in the old days. They were next door with sirens going within twenty minutes. Feeling bad about my initial hesitation, I swathed myself in gowns and scarves, and waited in the howling gale with Dan and the towering bloody wreck. He was in pain past communication. I coaxed him to sit out of the wind, as Dan did on one side of the rubble and I did on the other. Such an automaton was he that he built himself a stool out of bricks first, then squatted on it.

When the ambulance made its spectacular arrival, he could let go, and passed out in the drive. All stretcher-bearers are ready for that kind of thing. The commotion brought out the other neighbours. From the few houses of my once tranquil all-white suburb came no less than eighty-nine illegals, wrenched out of sleep in their bedspreads. When the ambulance went round the block they all streamed up to the traffic light to get one last glimpse of the vehicle flying through. He was back at work on the Monday with many stitches.

With the Berlin wall up between us I had little further sight of Dan. Occasionally if I got my car out of an evening, he'd be sitting on the pile on the sidewalk, smoking. And the regular prostitute would be on Omar's veranda, suckling her baby as if she owned the place, waiting for her man to fetch her. God knows what really went on in the back of Omar's place; I no longer wished to know. Eight months had gone by and *still* they were not finished. I'd nod or wink at Dan, and he'd give me a smile, and I'd carry on with my life. Somehow in the back of my mind was the thought that if I left my house empty while he was there, things would be all right.

Then I'd regale my white friends with the Frankenstein episode and how the snitching had become so commonplace I even put out old clothes so that they'd take them in preference to anything else. The finer points of the social mix I was experiencing were not really discussable in bourgeois South Africa, so we settled for decrying the inconveniences of neighbouring building-sites.

Omar came to having his corrugated-iron roof pulled out by the roots. The crashing of tin sheets and rotten roof timbers now really became unbearable. What use was it to explain yet again that as a writer I work at home and need my sanctuary? I had arranged the previous week with

Omar that I would be away for their re-roofing, but no, they could never make any convenient accommodation. Try corrugated-iron for a din with African enthusiasm for demolition, all a few feet from your writerly calm. With wax in my ears and a towel round my head, I tried to get my so many words a day done, the chair quivering each time a piece of architectonic plate was smashed free. I was turning into a shuddering wreck.

All of a sudden, the destruction halfway, the shift ended. To soothe myself I went out into my walled garden, to tidy up the new debris and maybe encourage a plant or two with the hose. The soil was warming with spring. I pulled out some runners of grass and clipped at the hydrangea, which was going to bud beautifully. I knew I was being studied at my old-womanish tasks, inexplicably finicky. Dan on the rooftree, up in the clouds in his rags, surveying the neighbourhood.

I gazed at him, shaking with relief from the quiet. I said: 'Do you want a beer?'

He said edgily, no … no way, he didn't drink beer.

Wine, a glass of?

He didn't drink.

Coffee?

He drank coffee.

I said later on he could come round if he wanted for coffee, but he must have misunderstood for within seconds the doorbell was going.

I made him coffee with lots of milk and lots of sugar.

We settled at opposite ends of the kitchen table. He was hunched in terror, never having shared a social occasion with a white before. Where he came from if he ordered and paid for coffee at a white establishment, a plastic throwaway cup came out and the hatch slammed down. I emptied six biscuits on a plate and shoved it across to him. When I eventually thought to have one myself, the whole lot had gone. No pay again; he was actually starving.

I offered him a cigarette, but he declined, although I knew he smoked and the sight of me exhaling must have made him desperate. So on an impulse I grabbed a plastic bag and opened the fridge. I emptied into the bag the half-eaten steak and other delectables I was saving for myself, and handed it to him. He took it respectfully. As I wished to continue gardening while the quiet endured, I showed him out. At the front door the TV very obviously came into view and, before I closed the door on him, I said he was welcome to watch it in the evenings if he had nothing better to do. I went back to my budding plants and he to eat his spoils across the wall.

That evening when I had the news on he came to watch with me. He perched on a corner of the bed as if he didn't mean to dirty anything. I tried to gauge how much he took in, because language was a great problem between us. Gorbachev swooping into Malta and Bush braving the swell for a summit important to us all, even to backwater South Africa, I thought might be proving inexplicable to Dan. Anyway, I showed him how to use the remote control and once it had got to the soccer which he loved, went off to have a bath. I was no longer interested, so he could choose what he liked.

Once I'd bathed and, instead of getting into night garb, re-dressed in honour of my guest, I saw he had lost interest in the box and smoked out the end of his pack. I offered him a cigarette and this time he took it. His monosyllables of deference were giving way to more confident sentences of ordinary chat. My pink, waterlogged hands closed over his damaged workman's ones to shield the flame.

After a thoughtful smoke he clearly wasn't ready to go, and had fixed up a way of explaining his absence next door. So I dared to ask the usual give-away question – wouldn't *he* now like to have a bath? He would, so I stacked up all the bath oils and towels I could find and turned on the gushing hot and left him to it. All that prevented me from going any further (rubbing his back, insisting he try on new clothes for old, etc.) was the thought of some unforeseeable reaction at the building-site. If he returned there in new garb, sweet-smelling, they would know. Their revenge would be against him, not me. Besides, I was not sure I was ready to admit an illiterate black worker into my life just then, no matter how great the temptation. The gap was too great, or so I thought.

But Dan thought differently. When he was not at work next door he never had anything better to do than take a bath and watch TV with me. These were his special privileges in the neighbourhood. Omar's gang were finishing up and the place was transformed: inlaid brick yard with not a piece of greenery to make a mess, sunken walk-in bath, venetian blinds, wrought-iron burglar bars, Italian tiles. But it was still not too late for Dan to get a screwdriver through him out of sheer jealousy for being someone's pet. I could hear complaints over their pot of stewing chicken gizzards that someone among them was getting the whole mixed grill with the moffie white boss next door.

It also occurred to me that they might have set me up with Dan. I'd come back one night to find everything of value in the house, that he had marked, gone. This was a mean thought on my part, but since Omar was never likely to pay them any more than Husein had, and they had all run up debts at hire-purchase stores on what anywhere else in the world would be considered workmen's basic essentials, provided by the employer (overalls, tools, footwear), and they had now stripped my outside of everything movable, what else could I think?

I was going out one evening to post off an article at the quickest box in the city and I had forgotten Dan was in the bathroom, performing his toilette. The thought did occur: can I leave him alone inside? I mumbled that I would be back soon and left him to it. I posted the article and did a few things I had to do at a late-night bookshop, and returned. The TV was going, but Dan was not before it. Instead, he was before the mirror in the bathroom – door now open – studying the spectacle of himself – stark naked – wiping his skin to a gloss with Vaseline. Obviously I could trust him with all my valuables, and probably with everything else, including my life.

There was a dull strip on his back his fingers had not rubbed over, so I obliged, working the jelly in until he looked polished, agleam. Let me inspect him; I pronounced him stunningly, dazzlingly skin-preserved from scalp to toe. That we both obviously had erections by then, which he could do little to hide, was probably the decisive factor.

I asked Dan what he was going to do once the house next door was finished and he said he didn't wish to continue with Omar-Husein, as they either didn't pay or not enough. I muttered something about I'd need someone to finish the security gate. Then I lavished his shining body in what clothes I had left for him to try on – we were much the same height. When the TV reached its end, the sort of fiddling, stroking, childish glee with which we had gone about this (his incredible narcissism and my only too eager puckering and adjusting) came to an end as well. We reluctantly agreed he'd better return to the site – for now – in his wretched rags with their built-in reek of grime, decay and sweat. For now, because we were both determined to sit this one through.

One evening Dan did not come and I was working to beat an old deadline, anyway. The crazy thought that I'd better pull in more cheques drove me on, now that the racket next door permitted, to afford Dan a new wardrobe, to prepare for a spending spree … But an unbelievably violent uproar over there interrupted. Clearly it was reckoning-up time, as the next morning Husein would collect them at the corner, not daring to come any closer to Omar (or to me, for that matter). Their building-site whore was the cause of it, she who'd been hired out to all of them for far more than sexual favours - darning their shredded socks and treating their sores and nursing them through bouts of hangover and dagga-depression. To drive her out they threatened her baby – even that, the baby who had learned to walk holding their knees, now that it was reckoning time. She shoved the baby onto her pimp and ordered them both out while she screamingly handled this matter of eight dishonest, exploitative black brutes.

She had to disunify them, pick on a vulnerable target – Dan. She had to stir up their resentments.

'Who done *your* washing for you?' she launched into him.

'It was not you, sisi,' he pleaded, 'for the others, yes.'

'*Where* you have your finger fixed when it was sore?'

'It was not you, sisi, who fix it.' He could not say it was the white man next door who plastered it over.

'Where you get *clean* when you only got *shit*?'

'Please, sisi, I was cleaning my T-shirt all by myself.'

'And where you got your stomach full when you never get pay?'

'No, sisi, no …'

'Where you get money when no one else has? Hey? From the moffie over there!'

'Hai, sisi,' from Dan.

Judging by the rumpus, the tactic didn't work. She could only stride into their circle and shove the contents of their three-legged pot out on the ground. That was her last protest, apart from stomping out and slamming Omar's front door.

Now their final meal together was ruined and Dan was to blame. One of them cracked him a shot, I think the sewn-up oaf, and from over the wall I heard Dan yelp. I was all for getting the ladder and climbing over to extricate him. But Dan had already shown me what little power I had to regulate the affairs of the building-site. I could not stand the thought of his delicate body becoming as smashed and dented as theirs – the scars they bore, the terrible damage they had brought only on themselves; the way they had let themselves be brutalised.

I went into my office. I put my hands over my ears and clenched my eyes and was too deeply shocked even to think if it was that wrong to offer him a glimpse of an alternative way of life. They had no one else to take their frustrations out on other than moffies, those men.

Early the next morning they all stomped out with their toolbags and enamel mugs and scraggy blankets. Back to work on somebody else's mosque on the East Rand. I was not sorry, after close to eleven months, to see the very last of them. Omar came round with his wife, warmly inviting me over to dine – any night, every night, six o'clock – that's when they always eat, curry and special stuff I would like; always they catered for at least six people, in case anyone dropped around, they would always be honoured to have a neighbour; oh and sorry, said Omar, for all the noise.

Just for a while, I replied, I had a lot of work to catch up on and wanted to be left in peace. The very thought of their hospitality and its human cost physically repulsed me. What I really wanted was Dan – nothing else would compensate for what they'd caused: a year of my life lost. And of course Dan had been gone for over a week.

And then a fortnight. I had done nothing to stop him being beaten to a pulp.

'Why don't you come over for dinner?' said Omar, his hairy elbows over the wall, as I was mowing the lawn.

'It's just because I've got a lot of backlog to cope with,' I said.

'You don't like Indian neighbours, that's what it is,' he said.

'I don't like Husein – look how he left that gate. Next thing the wind'll blow it out into the street,' I said.

'That Husein,' he replied. 'He's a real bastard crook. Imagine how my house'd be if I let him carry on like that! Just get yourself a boy, man – he'll fix it up if you supervise him properly.'

I switched on the mower so that I didn't have to hear more neighbourly advice.

I was mowing the lawn down to the toppling gate a month later and there, on the other side of it, behind the bars, was Dan. He had his mug and blanket with him. I could see from the way his eyebrow drooped the physical wounds were not yet healed.

'Come in, come in,' I hauled the gate open. 'How are you, where have you been?'

He was very afraid I would turn him away. He stepped in and put his possessions on the cut grass.

'See, it needs bricks up to here, and a firm socket – and lots of broken glass on top and plaster.'

Dan nodded. He was able to do all that.

'Go inside and put the kettle on, please. I just want to finish off. Honestly, now with summer rains it grows so fast …'

When I had done and put the mower away, Dan had two mugs of coffee made in the kitchen. He had placed them so that we would sit opposite each other, not far apart.

I washed my hands and poured out the obligatory biscuits. He took one and I took one.

We sat facing each other. He looked so emaciated.

'Can I getta job?' he said.

'Yes,' I said.

LIZ GUNNER

Cattle Passsing

Aunt Alex, this is for you. It's the story you never told. It's the story your father told me once – half told me – in a tossed-aside sentence that took on a life of its own and wouldn't die down, so that in the sunlight of another afternoon, when I asked to hear it again, he denied its existence, trying to pretend it had never been born. You can't do that to stories.

Look, reader, whoever you are, I'm leading you on, don't expect too much from this. It's about something that never happened – that's the story. But you know, maybe the most important things in the world are the things that never happened? Don't get impatient and turn away; this won't take long. You see, it is this deep, nagging question – 'Why?' I ask myself, 'why all those years after the story and its half-telling, so many, many years after the little event, why disown it? Why disown a non-event?'

'Tell me about the droughts? The really bad ones. Tell me how people coped?' I was sitting close to him, on the cane chairs, stone floor beneath us and the sky ahead. He was chewing his pipe, puffing at it with short spurts and stabs, corroding his one remaining lung, holding the bowl in one powerful, sunburnt hand.

oh hands! They tell you so much, think of Dürer's Praying Hands, knotted supplicant fingers, the hands of the Queen of England in the new portrait, mottled, blunt, ugly, the hands of an old woman, tired, capable hands, then the hands in the taxi – the art man, so quiet, self-effacing, holding all his power inwards, keeping it all to himself, and then I saw his hands, square, large, lying still and watchful, carrying the ancestral memory of coal, wood and iron, at ease with the clamped distant vowels of Sheffield sliding on London polish. The taxi emptying us out on the cobbles at cruel King's Cross. 'Here,' said I, wanderer and dreamer, 'I'll pay, here's my share.'

So I remember his hand on the pipe and the hawk's gaze fixed on the northwest horizon, the land rising to the thick fringe of pines he had planted and the hills girdling the eye to the north and the east. 'Please, tell me about droughts, the real droughts?' He seemed to unfold his mind, peeling back the pages like the notebooks he kept to record, meticulously, the rainfall – usually twenty-nine inches a year – the bags of wheat from each land, the sacks of maize, the milk, the rations, the pay, the loans, the prices, the comings and the goings, the hail. The notebooks were large with dark-blue mottled marble covers and he filled them with his sloping cramped writing – year after year, day upon day. They stayed piled unobtrusively in the cool shade of his office.

'The real droughts? These,' he says, 'are not real droughts. This is just very, very dry.' And yet we sit sometimes day after day, looking at the sky. He peers into the distance and claims to see a cloud, 'the size of a man's hand'. He spends a lot of time sitting, watching, he stays quite still, he is almost a tree, a shape in air that remains. We watch 'the man's hand', we watch it drift imperceptibly in the blue. It wisps out a little. We sigh. We drink tea, our feet on stone. We look again – the hand is a string of beads on the far horizon. It will not rain today.

When he does speak, it seems after so long that I have almost forgotten the question. 'Yes, there have been droughts, terrible ones, not like this one. There was the drought of 1931 and then there were the two others, 1924, and 1907. 1924 – that was the time the cattle moved. The whole country quivered under the sun that year, like whiplashes, a punishment. Children died, the old died, cattle, sheep. People were desperate to live, to keep what stock they could, and you know how very much cattle mean to the native. So they moved whole herds – took them across the whole country, or that's what it seemed like to us as we sat here and they came through, passing along the top there, near the pines, which were still growing then and not as tall as you see them now.' He points, jabs his hand ahead and I notice, remember, that his third finger is missing, and he's never told me how that happened and I've never asked.

'Huge herds of cattle came this way, a few men with them, sometimes just young boys but they loved their cattle, you could see that and they knew how to handle them and they grieved for them and wanted to save them. Oh yes, you could see that. They had heard there was food left down in the Natal grasslands so they came this way, close to the mountains, coming up from the south. Word must have gone round that I had water that was holding out in the north dam so they would come and ask if the herds could drink.

'We would sit here, where you and I are sitting now, just the same place, and from a distance they would look like vast herds of game, tawny colours, black, some the colours of mud. You've never seen drought animals drink? The dry muzzles, the long, groaning slurps, kneeling, butting and then they raise the head, the muzzles are damp and soft, the muddy water drips down, the dewlaps quiver. And their eyes, huge, soft brown eyes, holding all the pain. Sometimes I would go down and look at the cattle, thin with their haunches like planks, their sharp bones, and at times they would come up to the house to thank me and we'd talk. After all, we were all cattle men.

'One of them – I heard the women talking – they said he was a chief. He was quite a tall man and very – how can I put it – very well spoken, courteous like one of those old-style English gentlemen only of course he wasn't talking English. He thanked me for helping them and I asked the maids to give them some mealie meal, just to give them food for the road. He took it gravely and said and I remember these were his exact words because somehow they surprised me. He said, "Father of Kindness we thank you, God has blessed you with beautiful daughters. It is as it should be."

'The next morning, the cattle were still there spilling over into the pines. It was still early but very hot even then. I saw two figures coming back towards us from the cattle. I wondered what delayed them, they had so far to go and no promise of anything when they arrived. We exchanged greetings and then I waited. When the man they said was a chief spoke again it was slowly and carefully, "I would like to ask for your daughter, to be my wife. Your beautiful daughter with hair like golden rope. I would not ask her to come now. These are terrible times. I will send my people back for her with cattle and gifts when times are better and when God ..." – he used the word "Modimo", you know, their word for God – "when God blesses us again. You should not worry. We will look after her well. She will be a – " I stopped him. I look at his hand, his arm hangs loosely at his side like a broken branch. He is clasping nothing.

'"My friend. You ask the impossible. You anger me. I let your cattle drink, I give you food for your long journey and you ask for my daughter! Do not anger me. Go! My daughter is not for you." And then, I remember, this man they said was a chief stepped back as if he had seen a snake on the path in front of him and they turned and went. I didn't look at his face but when they walked away, they walked slowly, talking softly and the one who was with him laughed. The laugh I remember very well.

'When I told her – perhaps it was a mistake, but I did – she was quite silent. It is true she was very beautiful then. Her thick hair in its braids, the pale skin and her quick and gentle movements and blue eyes.

'The next morning early they were gone. They must have moved before dawn, travelling before the heat of the day, heading east towards the mountain passes and Natal.'

He did tell me. It is not a dream of the apartheid imagination. The story shocked me and of course fascinated me. I remembered the song of 'The raggle taggle gypsies' – 'She's off with the raggle taggle gypsies oh!' and I wondered if, if ... if she had gone? If she had run away, if she had really loved him? What would have become of her? How would it have been? How would they have spoken? And would he have spat her out like a plumstone and taken other wives? Concubines? Kept her as the senior wife? Honoured? Lonely? And if she came back? And if she were happy?

She. Her. You. Of the hair like golden rope seen like that only through words and the portrait in the dining room. You married and led an exemplary life, you worshipped in our small, white church. Your husband was handsome and sturdy, he laughed a lot and he kept you well. You were happy and you bore him beautiful children, your garden was a jewel and your pantry was always full. You had tall grace, but a cutting edge. People loved you, but not too much.

'Tell me again,' I ask him, 'the story about the drought, and the chief who wanted to marry Aunt Alex?'

He puts down his pipe.

MAUREEN ISAACSON

I Could Have Loved Gold

Dad talked about gold all the time. Gold standard and shares and world markets and creating work for the masses. The intonation of his voice acted as a soporific on mother and her already pale countenance and air of absence further dissolved. My little brother Jonathan would dip his middle finger into the butter and my aunt would yawn. But sometimes she'd say something and the two would hiss like prize bantams in a sparring match.

Into the spotless order of our Houghton mansion, Aunt Sal would bring the smoke and jazz of the streets of Sophiatown. It was in her walk and in her talk and in her eyes. She vibrated with the sax of Kippie Moeketsi and the huskiness of Dolly Rathebe and all the musos she heard there. As soon as Dad got going, she'd lose that bluesy cool; she'd talk and move fast, like a train chasing its own steam.

'Do you know what happens in the gold mines? About the hostels where there's no place for loving and precious little money to show for it when the miners do get back to their families?'

Dad would swell up with argument and a watery silence would envelop mother. It seemed that this dissension was irrelevant in the face of having an Anglo magnate husband who swathed her in nine carat this and twenty-two that.

She wore it burnished in her ears and round her neck, her wrists and waist and in her teeth. Her eyes were dull with it, with easy living and the loneliness of Dad being away so often.

Aunt Sal adored Jonathan and me. Whenever one of us felt sad she'd say that nothing stays the same and she'd sit with us until it went over. She'd tell us stories; it was only through her that we ever got to hear of cottages in woods and baskets to be taken to grandmothers and people like Rapunzel letting down their hair. She told her own version; with syncopated rhythm and high drama.

Dad believed in facts. When he did tell us stories they would invariably be about gold.

'The Incas of Peru,' he said, 'believed that the tears of the Sun fell in golden drops. They wore huge golden circles in their ears, just like the wooden ones the Nguni natives wear in South Africa.

'If you're going to tell kids something, make sure it's useful,' he said. He told us tales of ancient Roman gold mines. He talked about gold leaf death masks, thin as gossamer, used by the early Greeks and said that gold was civilised; it was something to believe in. It had changed his life. 'I didn't make it big through fairy stories. Nor jazz for that matter,' he said.

Aunt Sal laughed at the way my parents listened to the sounds of Elvis Presley and the Everly Brothers, when there was all that going on just around the corner. My parents weren't interested in what was going on round the corner, and told friends that Aunt Sal had a basic problem that made it necessary for her to go into the world of the 'Natives'.

She brought us Glen Miller records and blues and *marabi*, the sounds of the shebeens, and we'd dance until we dropped. It gave mother a headache, she would say, then she'd go and lie down.

Once I heard Aunt Sal say to mother, 'You weren't like this before, Sarah.'

'Well now I am,' mother said.

I was at primary school at the time, and my experience of the world was limited to our Houghton mansion, our many servants and mother's golden unhappiness. She remained passive and inert, it was as if she'd been alchemised into some mystical substance, and was no longer with us. She looked into mirrors for a long time and I wondered what she was thinking; if she was thinking. She was always around, but I missed her.

We waited for Aunt Sal's jazz; she brought us records of Miriam Makeba, the Harlem Swingsters and Zig Zag Zakes. 'I bring you the Bantu Men's Social Centre special,' she'd say. Then she'd roll up her red trousers and she'd ramba and samba and talk about the way people lived in the townships.

'Eight people live in a house the size of this kitchen, minus the breakfast nook, no kidding.'

I couldn't really see how they did it. It all seemed so strange to me, like some foreign country somewhere.

I spent hours playing with mother's jewellery and holding it up to the sun to see what Dad meant when he talked about the purity of gold, the essence of it. I studied the gold plates and vases he brought back from his travels and encased in glass, the gold-bound books, and thought about being as good as gold and silence being golden. I would have loved gold if it wasn't for Aunt Sal.

When I think about the mansion now, maid-polished and ordered, it echoes with a drab silence. Into the odourless shine, Aunt Sal sped; alive with the fumes and stains and conversation of nights in shebeens. Crazy with tales of dark side-streets where gangs of men with American clothes and accents flicked knives and tongues. Talking about the way these guys would ruin concerts and break up cosy evenings in shebeens.

'Aren't you scared?' I asked.

Then the corners of her mouth lifted slightly and turned, and the green of her eyes deepened and she took a draw of her cigarette. She said nothing, but I often saw that expression again.

It was the expression she got when she talked about music and about a friend of hers called Albie. Although I never met him I knew exactly how he walked, hand in one pocket, cigarette dangling; hat cocked, because Aunt Sal would show us. Albie played piano and sang in one of the shebeens where Aunt Sal had her heart torn apart by the blues of Snowy Radebe and the late-night throb and *bebababerop* she came home singing. It was where she drank the home-brewed spirit *skokiaan*, a bout of which Aunt Sal said could knock your head right across the nation.

'Hardly suburbanite stuff,' she said.

My parents' friends were other mining magnates and their wives, and sometimes Jonathan and I would be allowed to join them for dinner. It was the only time mother would come alive. On such occasions Joseph, who cleaned the floors and served at table, would wear a white jacket with a diagonal sash, red as a wound.

The wives would ask us how we were enjoying school and if we liked our teachers and what our friends' names were, then they'd talk to each other about clothes and hair and Italian gold collars with streams of half-point diamonds and say things in very hushed tones. The men would talk loudly and clearly about gold exports and foreign exchange and balance of payments and South Africa's economic role in the world.

Mother said that our cook, Sanna, was a genius at whatever she turned her hand. She cooked Fish Soup Basquaise and Lamb Charlotte to perfection. Mother loved to surprise the guests with treats like black truffles in Italian rice, fresh foie gras or watermelon in glazed wine. Imported white wines were a favourite; their chill glistened from generous crystal glasses.

One such evening, just as mother was saying, 'Children, don't you two think you should be getting to bed now?' Aunt Sal burst in.

'No thanks, I've eaten,' she said. 'How do you do? How do you do?' she greeted everyone, and kissed Jonathan and me. The wives touched their half-moon gold earrings and chunky bracelets and stared at Aunt Sal.

Suddenly, without warning, she shouted, 'Yaabo! Yaabo!' Everybody stopped talking and father said, 'C'mon Sal, not now.'

Then she smiled and said, 'That's what the small boys shout when the police come near the home-brewed beer in the townships.'

'Sal ...' said Dad.

'They keep it in tins underground and cover them with sand and wet sacks – it's illegal to brew beer because of the liquor prohibition for blacks, you know. When the police come they pierce the tins and everyone runs away before they can be arrested.'

'Have some wine, Sal,' Dad said.

'Thanks. Very nice, what vintage?'

'Forty-nine.' Dad looked relieved and everyone relaxed and started talking again. Jonathan pinched me and giggled.

'Mm, very nice wine,' Aunt Sal said again. 'Nothing like *Tswala*.'

'*Tswala*?' asked a magnate's wife.

'Yes, *Tswala*. It's the stuff they give black mineworkers. A kind of non-alcoholic beer, rich in vitamin B.'

Mother wiped the corners of her mouth with her serviette. Father breathed audibly. Then that steam-train speed got hold of Aunt Sal and there was no stopping her.

'*Tswala*, loudspeakers, heat and unbearable noise – that's what you get when you work on the mines.'

One of the magnates said: 'Do you know what you're talking about? To what do you think the country owes its wealth? Has it ever occurred to you that the industry provides work for people? The Natives love the mines. They even call Johannesburg "Egoli", which means "City of Gold". South Africans have a damn lot to thank the people who discovered gold and the mining corporations for.'

'Egoli safoot!' said Aunt Sal. 'A city built on cheap mineworker-sweat, what do you know about their lives?'

'The mines provide employment.' He was rigid.

'Okay, so what about the danger they work with, poison fumes, fires, accidents, rockbursts, and all the people that get killed?'

'Safety measures ...' started the magnate. He was red-cheeked and everyone seemed to have forgotten their food.

'Don't tell me about safety and about us having the deepest mines and not being able to compare with the rest of the world, I know that argument. I'm talking about people's lives!' Aunt Sal's voice quavered.

'Well so are we. We're providing people with an opportunity to eat, people who would otherwise starve.' The magnate was redder.

'What do you know? Have you been there? Have you ever heard of faction fights? Have you ever seen the way they fight amongst themselves? Everyone knows they'd kill each other if we didn't put a stop to it!'

Aunt Sal said nothing. Mother called Joseph to clear the plates and bring in the chestnuts and poached pears.

'It's way past your bedtime, you two,' she said to Jonathan and me. So we left the table and hid in the passage to see if anything more would happen. It didn't.

My parents didn't refer to that evening again and neither did Aunt Sal, but Jonathan and I went over and over the way the red-cheeked magnate who'd shouted at Aunt Sal had never known that there was a piece of lamb lodged in his beard all the while. And how his wife, the one who asked us how school was, had cut up three tomatoes into a million tiny pieces throughout the conversation.

After that Dad and Aunt Sal didn't talk to each other for a while. She visited when he was away. The ice thawed slowly and things returned to normal for a while.

One day she came in, eyes heavy as clay. She wouldn't say what was the matter but I knew it had something to do with Albie.

'Has he gone away?' I asked her.

'Don't talk about it,' she said.

'The shebeens and the bioscopes and the dancehalls were empty,' she said. 'The jazz don't sound and the blues make me cold inside instead of warm and I want to be at home, waiting, in my little tower, to let down my hair.'

But as she believed that things never stay the same, she smoked and drank into shebeeny nights, waiting, becoming thin and ashen, a shadow of her silent older sister.

Time edged along slowly. Aunt Sal's misery encircled her, etching a darkness around her eyes. It weighed down the air. She smoked fifty cigarettes a day, and another twenty at night. She coughed all the time.

Then she decided to go and live in London. She promised to send for us when we were old enough. She left us in the mansion with a distant father who stored gold rings and earrings and promises in a safe for my coming of age.

He left us, finally, with a weight as heavy as a gold bar, and the price we had to pay for his contribution to world economy. He left us with a mother whose sheen was fast fading. She said less than ever, now that Aunt Sal had gone.

ASHRAF JAMAL

The Beggar-guest

She is a research psychologist. It is the phrase she uses during dinner conversations. The phrase implies, she hopes, that she does fieldwork; that she is in the field. She pictures herself there, in a field; a handkerchief tied to her head, seated on a foldout campstool, notepad in hand, Tabard on her legs and shoulders. Intrepid, she thinks. The illusion satisfies her, but only briefly. Why not home work? After all, it is there, in homes not in the fields, where the stories unfold. She uses a dictaphone. The notepad she uses for those compelling moments which, she believes, are the clues to the rest of the story. The conversation, more a pointed series of questions and answers, is invariably arduous to unravel. The children, young girls and boys, are not gifted speakers. Then again, neither is she. She has never been one to beat her breast. Over dinner she is usually the silent one. The mistake of others is that they believe that her silence implies she is a good listener. She is not.

She believes she has no gift. At no point does she dress up this lack as a kind of modesty. A drudge, she thinks, though those about the table who claim to be her friends protest. She supposes that they have a vested interest in making her more interesting than she is. She resolves, then, never to reveal what she thinks herself to be. The resolve is destined to fail her. No one cares for silence that means nothing. A *research psychologist* then. A *fieldworker.* She must satisfy. All the more so about a dinner table where illusion is more piquant than either wine or food.

A writer is there at the table, a recent arriviste on the campus. Bombastic, she thinks. However she cares enough for what he says. To value him she must disinter the words, fold them one by one, neaten the sense, remove them from the foul cavity that no wine will clean away. It is he who forces her to account for herself. Does he too disinter the words? Does he inwardly ask what a research psychologist might be? Does he dwell upon the unfortunate phrase – fieldwork – and say to himself: A white woman in a field, what is she doing there? Who could possibly tell her the truth? Before a woman like her – pale, fish-eyed – who could possibly reveal anything of value?

The writer's eyes are glazed, the mandible chugs. Food and wine disappear in equal measure. She cannot disavow his relish. His gluttony chastens her. While the others about the table demurely peck, he reveals the hunger that gnaws in all of them. Is it his words that ruin the general appetite? Is it because when he speaks he plunges the heart, draws the heart's conscience up so that it lodges there in the mouth? She watches her guests dab their lips with napkins. They are readying themselves. They expect – each and every one of them – that they will be forced to answer for themselves. It is because of the writer that they peck. Food intercedes. Food stops the heart's expression. It is the taste of conscience that lodges in each and every mouth. The writer has provoked unease. That is why she values his words.

It is to her he turns. She is waiting. He is speaking of *Disgrace,* a book she well knows and does not care for. The author of the book is his passion. She cannot understand why. When told one day in the corridor of the Social Sciences Building that the author of *Disgrace* has been short-listed for the Nobel Prize, she does not say that were he to receive the coveted award it would mean that the very earth on which we stand has been condemned. Now the writer at the table – who has received no award, no short-listing either – talks of disgrace. We are all disgraced, he says. Each and every one of us, he insists. He is given to declamation, hyperbole. He leaves it up to the rest to disinter, neaten, edit. It is a job, she imagines, which he believes to be the province of gifted men and every woman. She marvels at his complacency. She watches her guests as they pat their mouths.

En route to work in another city – he insists that it does not in fact matter where the incident takes place – he drives past a man exercising himself upon the body of a woman. She is struck by the relish with which he yields the telling phrase – *exercising himself upon*. She does not know that the phrase belongs to the author so highly prized by the Nobel committee.

Returning to Cape Town on a Monday morning, cars hurtling through fraught space, I looked to the Block River on my right, then, shifting to the left, my gaze mounting upward along a raised embankment of uncut green, I saw a man clothed from the waist up, his arse hollowed at the sides, taut, the legs sinuous, the trousers like a discarded sweet-wrapper about his legs. He was copulating; with whom was unclear. The man may have been exercising his strength upon a ghost, so insubstantial the figure seemed. Cars hurtled past, no one stopped. Did no one see what I saw? My fellow occupant certainly did not. I thought sex; she thought rape. Since then I've thought of how many cars passed before the man ejaculated. The man … bald, white, powerful, brazen. What I couldn't imagine was the woman, a ghost, fully clothed, prone, but for a flailing hand, brown.

SA Wildlife. I know the statistics. I read the paper. Rape is a fact I can imagine, simulate, arraign within my interactive cortex. Otherwise, the brutal integrity of rape escapes me.

There was a deliberateness to the bald man; a thoroughness. Shocking though it may sound there was in that one-sided act an impressiveness, a fearlessness, a wild rigour. Is there a difference to watching human beings copulate than, say, dogs? To me, at that moment, there was none. The flannel ghost was not exempt. She had too little shape to muster concern. And he? He was monstrous, fearless, driven, a figure from a Genet novel, in chains, yet free. As for her? There was no reprieve. And so it is in South Africa today. I struggle to be outraged, but my heart fails me; my mouth, aghast, merely sighs.

He proceeds to draw a link between this occurrence which, she is sure, he has reprised before to similar effect, with the novel *Disgrace*. It is a work intimately aware of the unnatural order of life in South Africa, he says. The novel does not dignify or apologise for the existence of the ugly. Disgrace simply is. It is our inheritance, our character, the state of our minds, the sum of our actions. Pleasurable. Revolting. Banal.

Here the writer stops. Throughout he has gazed at her, no one else. Nothing in the conversation has led to the writer's monologue. She suspects he never follows, always leads. A pity. While she acknowledges his ability to hold an audience she believes he would benefit greatly if his ear were not so general, his mouth too. His claims are too large, the illustration does not suffice. Because no one has anything to add, she neither, he casually proceeds. Would that he would listen. Would that he would stop. He shovels food, drinks.

The book deals with rape, the transfer of power, anarchy, the coupling of youth and age, death, the question of whether or not we own our selves, our bodies. It pivots on a charge of sexual harassment and, later, a gang rape. Sex is the seam, an act unlovely, loveless. Of the blurred moment between fucking and rape we read:

'Not rape, not quite that, but undesired nevertheless, undesired to the core. As though she had decided to go slack, die within herself for the duration, like a rabbit when the jaws of the fox close on its neck. So that everything done to her might be done, as it were, far away.'

His memory appears unimpaired. He well knows the power of quotation. No one eats or drinks. It is the writer they consume. Do they imagine themselves in the *salon* of a nineteenth-century novel? Is he the beggar-guest, she the host? And they, the others, who are they? Children, she thinks.

The dinner is proving a success. It is he who makes it so; he with his bile so eloquently wrapped. They will have something to talk about. No doubt she will increase in their estimation. What do they care that she utterly disagrees? What do they care that she sees hope where he, the writer, sees none? Are they such children, without guile, so easily won over by fluency that they cannot see that fluency will not do? Fluency has no place here. No words will contain this earth. No drunken sot. No glutton.

She sees that now their appetites have grown large too. They no longer peck and dab their mouths. He has restored a zest, an urgency, to the proceedings. The roast lamb is picked clean. When they are done with eating and drinking there is nothing left, nothing to do but nod before their effusive appreciation of the spread. One thing is certain, this is the first time she does not have to freeze the leftovers. There is nothing for the dog. The marrow is sucked dry. Not a single sprout is left in the salad bowl. The bareness of the table horrifies her though she feigns satisfaction. Better dissembled gratitude than such effusive pleasure. Better a stunted repartee about nothing than this twittering of birds, this laughter louder than she has ever heard. Obscene. All of this, obscene. Somewhere, in the midst of her disgust, she finds a lingering sympathy for the author of *Disgrace.*

The cigarettes run out. Those who smoke pat their breast pockets, riffle through their overcoats. The writer lights a butt-end. Those who do not smoke do the same and laugh. A plastic sachet containing dagga appears. This too is consumed. The guests, children all, quit the table. In groups they leave the room. The writer remains before her. His dull eyes see everything. He is thin. What does he do with the food he devours? What is he doing here, before her? A mistake, she knows, inviting him. A misplaced sympathy on her part. She searches for the reason she invited him. She realises it is he who invited himself. A chance remark in the common room. He overhears, draws himself into the fold. She mistakes his inclusion of himself as a sign of vulnerability. There is nothing vulnerable about him at all, though he knows all too well how to affect vulnerability. He is a Namibian, taut, jaundiced. Born in the desert he has regaled many about a dinner table in Oxford, Paris, Accra. He is a visiting lecturer in the School of Psychology. If she deems him a writer it is because this is what matters most to him. He publishes the occasional story, he has a novel in the pipeline. He has little patience for drudges such as her. Why, then, does he stay? Why won't he join the party by the pool? Does he wonder why she remains? Does he imagine her as a kind of prey, something else to devour now that the table is bare? She cannot decipher his eyes. A lion's eyes. Gold. There is nothing attractive about him. Nothing attractive about her either. Does this qualify them as mates? Is she one of an unfortunate couple with her bulbous eyes, her heavy hips, her breasts heavy too?

He thanks her for the dinner and heads for the pool. There, at least, he will have an audience. When he leaves – a seraph, an exclamation mark – she is appeased. She realises that more than the words she has disinterred, she values the simplicity of these final moments because, yes, they are final. She does not care for inference. She does not care for dull all-seeing eyes. She wants no man in her bed, no man in her heart. What then does she want? Peace, she thinks. But when there is none? What then? What does she want? She certainly wants this dinner over and done with. But what of the ricochet? What of the phone calls that will surely follow? Who is he? How do you know him? What is he doing here? Provincial questions; questions which, no doubt, will grow into gossip. She is single after all. She is the subject – the victim – of kindness. If she can disinter him from his words, then why not the rest? Is she not done with him, with the lot of them? She concludes that she is. She will have no more dinner parties. She will remove herself from the clutches of children. She wonders, for the last time, why she even allowed herself this disgrace.

Some time passes before she finally shuts the door. She adjusts the latch, draws the curtains. She moves from room to room securing each and every cavity. She has no desire to feed the dog. In her study, which opens onto her bedroom, she triggers the alarm. Alone at last. Shut off, shut up, she returns to her desk. She has drunk little. Her mind is clear. A glass of apple juice in hand, she switches on the desk lamp. She is annotating a series of interviews with young boys and girls. She refuses to think of them as teenagers. She does not believe in this awkward and damning middle sphere. After the dinner she wonders if there is such a thing as an adult. Children, she utters, we are all children. She a drudge amongst children.

She reads the handwritten gloss to an interview with an eighteen-year-old girl from Emzamweni. She is not pleased with the notes neatly inscribed in the margins. *Barrier: experience. Barrier: trust. Solution: keep quiet.* The notes refer to an isolation she feels. She has enough detachment to know that her isolation is not the girl's. What then are the barriers she separates with a colon then counterpoints with experience, trust, silence? What would he, the writer, think?

She pictures his dull knowing eyes; eyes, she thinks now, that know too little. Could he feel the plight of a girl from Emzamweni? Does she? What she knows – the little that she knows – is that no dinner-table talk of *Disgrace* would ever move her. How speak of disgrace to someone who knows all too well the meaning? She sees the girl before her. The knees scuffed and bruised. The hands gently folded on a skirt of plaid. Behind her – before her? – a dead mother, dead father, dead stepmother too. In her arms a three-year-old stepsister soon to be dead too. What would he, the writer, make of this? How would he explain the ignominy the girl feels? Outcast. A girl made of death because they, the ones who judge, make her so. In every transcribed interview she reads there is this silence. No one talks of the death that stalks them. Enfolds them. Death, she sees now, is a girl with arms enfolded on a skirt of plaid. She is not dying, the girl. For now she is exempt. It is the little one in her arms, the one the girl cannot save, that wounds. What would he, the writer, make of this? Is this our inheritance, this our character?

Better to have screamed and said enough! Enough of your generalisation! Better to have torn the food from his mouth, broken each and every wine bottle and said: Enough of your pleasure! Enough of your writer's callous fluency. And you, the children who listen and gorge, what of you? What do you know of disgrace? What do you care? And she? What does she make of the barriers that separate lives from hope? How does she vault the chasm that draws all into silence? What is the good of fieldwork? What is the good of listening when the disgraced die by the second; die because no one will heed, no one break the silence? No one, not even the writer, breaks the silence. No eloquence will fill the emptiness of a girl's hands. Without reprieve she sees the baby that no one but the girl will care for. And she with all her rooms, her dog, her salary, what will she do? Perhaps she needs the writer's eloquence. Perhaps she needs his complacency. What is left?

Before her desk, where the glass of apple juice topples, she weeps. She has grown tired with confusion. Grown tired with hope. She wishes she were never born. She cannot change the world. She can only listen. And what good is listening? For years she has believed that listening was enough. She has seated herself before the wounded, recorded their stories. And then? What then? Does she need a writer's skill to make something of their words? If she were capable of doing so – which she is not – what then? What is the good of words?

LEKOTSE'S TESTIMONY AT THE TRC

[retold by Antjie Krog]

The Sheep-herder's Tale

Krog: The next morning on my way to town I take a detour through the countryside. As far as the eye can reach there is rooigras. I stop. I once wrote: 'I adore *Themeda Triandra* the way other people adore God.' I want to lie down. I want to embrace. I want to sing the shiny silk stems upwards. I want to ride the rust-brown seeds, the rustling frost-white growth around ankles. Grass, red grass bareback against the flanks. This is my landscape. The marrow of my bones. The plains. The sweeping veld. The honey-blonde sandstone stone. This I love. This is what I'm made of. And so I remain in the unexplainable wondrous ambuscade of grass and light, cloud and warm stone. As I stand half-immersed in the grass crackling with grasshoppers and sand, the voices from the town hall come drifting on the first winds blowing from the Malutis – the voices, all the voices of the land. The land belongs to the voices of those who live in it. My own bleak voice among them. The Free State landscape lies at the feet at last of the stones of saffron and amber, angel hair and barbs, dew and hay and hurt.

* * *

Lekotse: My family was affected since that day. The woman who has testified before me is a picture of my wife. She cannot walk. She goes for treatment. I also go for treatment at Botshabelo Hospital. I took my *last* tablet this morning. Now my life was affected since that day. It was at night …

[Testimony in seSotho; interpreted by Lebohang Matibela]

Ilan Lax: I want to know about your children first.

Lekotse: I have ten children, two have passed away … now – on the day of this assault I was with three children at home and the grandchildren – five in number and they go to school – some of my grandchildren belong to my son who is mentally disturbed. The last-born has a pair of twins. Their father is also mentally disturbed …

Lax: Just try not to speak directly into the microphones … they are very sensitive and will pick up your voice very nicely. Which of these children are still living with you and your wife?

Lekotse: I am staying with Thomas Lekotse, my son, he is now the breadwinner and he is also taking care of the one that I just said is mentally disturbed.

Lax: Can you tell us about the incident that happened. Was it in May 1993?

Lekotse: Maybe you're right – you know my problem is, I was a shepherd. I cannot write and I forget all these days, but I still … Can I repeat what I said earlier on about the harassment? Now listen very carefully, because I'm telling you the story now.

On that day it was at night, a person arrived and he knocked. When I answered, the door just opened and I said, 'Who's knocking so terribly?' He answered, he said: 'Police.' And I said, 'What police are knocking on my door this way?' He forced his way through with many policemen. The door was already down. Three policemen were black and the rest were white and they referred to us as kaffirs. Many of them were white. They were together with big dogs – two in number. They said every door of the house should be opened. They pulled clothes from the wardrobes. I said, 'When a jackal gets into the sheep it does not do this – please unpack neatly and pack them back neatly.' They did not provide an answer. They pushed us outside. I felt on my shoulder: *kaboem!* I asked them, 'What do you want?' but they never provided an answer. They pushed us outside.

It was terribly cold on that day. The children were woken up. I said to them, 'Will you provide me with the money to take these children to the doctor?' They did not answer. I said to them, 'Please, the policemen are not supposed to behave this way.' I said, 'When a policeman goes to a farm he stops first at the farmer's house. If the farmer doesn't allow them entry they leave. Now where do you get the permission from to come into my house and break the doors – is this the way you conduct your affairs?' When I looked thoroughly the door was not just kicked, it was even broken down with their gun butts. Even to this day the doors are still broken. My children took pity on me this year, they bought a new door and a new frame and we had to get another person to come and fix the door.

At sunrise life began to be easier. They wanted to cut open the wardrobes that were locked. And I said to them, 'How dare you cut open these doors?' I said to my children, 'Prepare tea, prepare coffee for these people, they are hungry.' I asked them, 'Can I offer you beer, can I offer you drink, can I offer you boerewors? Are you hungry?' I said, 'These people are hungry. I have to provide them with food.' I said to them, 'You are not policemen, you are just boers.' One of them pushed me outside – that is where I fell on my shoulder and hurt myself. I was not supposed to speak that way, I admit but because I was hurt and disturbed that day I spoke wrong words. I said, 'I know you policemen are thieves. You want to take us all outside so that you can implicate us. I know. You're going to leave behind diamonds and dagga and you're going to drop them behind and implicate us.' I said, 'You bloody policemen.' That's what I said on that day, because I was hurt.

(audience laughs)

Lax: Please …

Lekotse: I ended up saying to them: 'Look here, my whole family is standing outside. It's cold. I want you to kill all of us now. I'll be very glad if you kill us all. They were … you know, it's a pity I don't have a stepladder. I will take you to my home to investigate …' I asked the policemen, 'What do you want?' They did not provide an answer. I told them: 'I don't have diamonds. I don't have dagga. What do you want?' No answer was given. I said to them, 'You want to leave after breaking my doors? When are you going to come back and fix them?' They said, 'APLA will fix them up.' I asked them: 'What is APLA?' No answer was given. I don't even know what APLA is, I am expecting APLA even today to come and fix my door.

Now it was just about sunrise. My son Thomas said, 'No, go and search in my garage.' They said, 'Where is the garage?' He said, 'Wait, I have to get a key.' And he said, 'You must be very careful – don't scratch my car.' They went into the garage with their dogs – these were fierce-looking dogs. After searching the garage, he said, 'You are not yet finished. I've got another place where you can search. I have a four-roomed house. Go and search. I also have a supermarket. Go and search it too because you don't seem to get what you want.' And they left with him. Now at sunrise they were still at home. They arrested him for the whole month … There were three kaffirs just like myself, the rest were white. They had many vans. The vans were lining the whole road …

Lax: Was your son Thomas connected to APLA or the PAC?

Lekotse: Yes sir.

Lax: Was he charged with anything?

Lekotse: I do not know whether they attended a court case. You know – an uneducated person is just down. You cannot follow anything. Just like the whites referred to us as dull donkeys. I do not know many things.

Lax: He would have told you if he went to court, wouldn't he?

Lekotse: Can I give you an answer on that?

(long pause)

I taught these children, but because I provided them with education, the whites used to say we have short hair and our brains and minds are just as short. Now these children do not tell us anything. They just go on their own, you just see things happening – they don't provide you with any information.

(audience laughs)

Lax: You indicate that you injured your shoulder. Did you sustain any other injuries?

Lekotse: I was not injured anywhere else – since that day that the jackals came into my house to bite us, I cannot even carry a spade to do gardening. Otherwise I'm not sick, it's just the usual sickness of old age.

Lax: In your statement you mentioned you were injured in your ribs? I'm just helping you to remember.

Lekotse: Are you not aware that the shoulder is related to the *ribs*, sir?

Lax: Did you or your son ever make a case against the police?

Lekotse: We never took any initiative to report this matter to the police, because how can you report policemen to policemen? They were going to attack us. That is why I said to them, 'Kill us all so that there is no trouble thereafter. It is much better to die – all of us.' It was even going to be easy for the government to bury us – they were going to bury us in just one grave. It could have been much better. If one of these policemen is around here, I'll be happy if one of them comes to the stage and kills me immediately …

⋆ ⋆ ⋆

Krog: During the lunch break I walk over to the Co-op with my tape recorder and approach a farmer getting out of his four-wheel drive. 'Sir, how do you feel about the Truth Commission's visit to Ladybrand?' He stops in his tracks. He looks me up and down, while his lip curls in disgust. 'The SABC and the Truth Commission. *Fôkôf!*' he explodes with such venom that passers-by look in our direction. '*Fôkôf! Fôkôf!*' he screams as he storms into the Co-op. I find myself on the pavement, my blood thick with humiliation. *God,* has nothing – nothing! – changed?

SINDIWE MAGONA

The Sacrificial Lamb

Before Siziwe was fully awake, the receiver – cold, hard and decidedly unfriendly – jabbed at the not-fully-awake flesh in the hollow between her shoulder, the pillow, and her ear. She did not remember how it had got there. There was a vague memory of the phone ringing; but even as she had struggled to hold it, sleep had left her in frustrating confusion with a tantalising overlap between reality and dream. But, of course, the phone must have rung, otherwise why had she picked up the receiver? And now, to the remote peep-peep announcing an overseas call she mumbled, 'Hello?' – relief washing through her. It was not the police, calling about her daughter, Fezi. She glanced at the bedside clock-radio thinking, *where, on earth, is that child?* Just then, a voice came through the line.

'Hello? Is that you, Sisi?'

'Yes, it's me. Who is this?' She no longer recognised the voices, her nieces sounded so grown to her whether on the phone or in their infrequent letters. No doubt, Siziwe was sure, distance and nostalgia accelerated and augmented the changes she perceived: with them ... with her.

'Is everything all right?' she asked; a new anxiousness replacing the earlier worry. What if her mother were ill? What would she do then? Go home? Or sweat it out here till ...? What would be the point of going then? But even as she argued with herself in her mind, she knew: of course, she would go.

'Sisi, it's me, Nozipho. Everything is fine; after a manner of speaking, that is. What else can we say?'

'What has happened? Is Ma okay?'

'Mama is okay. She says can you call her back?' And before she could say yea or nay, there was a clang and the line went dead.

She leapt out of bed and went to make herself a cup of coffee. Might as well make myself comfortable, she thought. Calling Gala was never a simple operation. The call had to go via the telephone exchange ... and the Gala Telephone Exchange was slack and inept, and often the lines were down.

The coffee burned her throat the way she liked it. Her mind went back to that long-ago day, the day she had not known would be her last for her to see her father. One would have thought there was a way of feeling, of sensing, of somehow presaging such an event; a kind of body seismograph, reading her the foreshadowing symptoms. But no, despite her great love for him, she had looked at her father, talked to him and then walked away from him with a casual goodbye. Next thing she knew, the sturdy tree that had given her shade from scorching sun and shelter from the storms of life had fallen.

On the second attempt, much to her amazement, she got through.

'Hello, Sisi? It's still me, Nozipho. There's something I forgot to tell you.'

'Yes, Zips? What is it?' She tried not to think of the money she was paying, listening to idle chatter. Sheer waste.

'I have written you a letter and given it to Bhuti Wallace. He is coming there and we gave him your address and telephone number. Please, Sisi, do respond positively to my request. Do not disappoint me, you know I have no one else I can depend on.'

'What is it?'

'No, I can't say it now. Wait till you get the letter.'

'That bad, is it?'

'No, it's not!' A burst of thrilling laughter fractured her speech. 'Sisi, I must get off this phone.' Siziwe knew what was coming. She could hear her mother grumbling in the background. 'Ma is giving me her wicked look. You know her. Bye, Sis'.'

'Bye!' Had she heard? wondered Siziwe for her 'bye' collided with her mother's 'Hello, Siziwe!' as belaboured breathing replaced Nozipho's breezy prattle on the line.

'Hello, Ma! Are you all right?'

'Siziwe, my child, the Lord keeps on minding us. But the devil is also busy, derailing us every which way we turn.'

'What is the matter?' And she had the presence of mind to stop short of adding the 'now' burning the tip of her tongue. But the irritation seared her brain. Can they never call just to see how I am doing? Is each telephone call always only going to be about some catastrophe?

'MaTolo is in hospital.' There was a slight pause, no doubt her mother waiting to hear her reaction to this piece of news. But Siziwe waited too … Whatever she said would end up upsetting her mother; she did not seem ever to come up with anything kind to say about her eldest brother; a complete wash-out of a man.

'Our kind neighbour, Majola, took him to Gunguluza Hospital in his car.'

'What is the matter with him?' This time she was forced to say something since her mother had gone silent on her.

'We really don't know what happened to him. Saturday, early evening, some people come and told us that he was lying, face down, at the corner of NY 1 and NY 3. When we got there, we couldn't even recognise him. Half his face had caved in, probably hit with a brick – what they call the Wonder Loaf here. He was completely covered in blood that had already caked. As yet, no witnesses have come forward to say who did what to him.'

'But what about him? What does he say happened?'

'He can't even say one word, my child. All he does is groan. He does not even recognise those who have been to see him. I, myself, have not been to see him; could not bring myself to go … no, I just couldn't go and see him looking like that … like a corpse.'

'I am sorry, Ma. I'm really sorry.' And, to her surprise, she realised that she meant what she said. Of course, she was only sorry for the worry MaTolo's troubles always caused her mother. Her sisters and brothers were slowly killing the poor woman; ageing her and wearing her down fast with all the troubles they visited on her: drunken brawls, job loss caused by bad work habits, unemployment due to lack of qualifications, and a host of other causes besides. The same problems that plagued everybody else in the black townships … why did she allow these things to disarrange her? Why would her family be any different from all the others?

Once more, her father's words of farewell led her to a decision. Often had she wondered whether they were a blessing or a curse. '*Mna, kuphela eyam intlungu yeyenyama*. My pain is only that of the flesh.' Thus had he thanked her … or, perhaps ordered is more like it … for those words had forever after directed her actions … especially towards her mother.

Even so far away, in this strange land, among people whose ways were stranger still, she still heard those words. *While other men in this ward cry, not because* of *physical pain but because they do not know what their children will eat that very day or a man's family is being thrown out of the house because they owe rent money, I am at peace because you, my daughter, see to the needs of the family.*

'So, we thought we should ask for some help from you, my child.' Her mother's voice broke into Siziwe's reflections. 'I know we are forever bothering you with all these stupid problems these children are always getting themselves into. But, what else can we do? Who else can we turn to?'

There was a moment's awkward silence. The unspoken words … *'Now that your father is no longer here'* … heavy between them.

Had her father, in thanking her for giving the family financial support, in fact appointed her his surrogate?

'You must help us, my child.'

'Of course, Ma.' She was embarrassed. 'What did you think I should do?' Of course, that too was just formality. She knew exactly why they had called her ... why they always and invariably called her: Money.

'Whatever little money you can send us, will help. We have to go to the hospital to see him. What would people think and how would he feel? We can't abandon him there all on his own ... and at a time like this.'

The next morning, a Monday, she got up half an hour earlier than she usually did. She liked to start her workday punctually and purposefully; more so Mondays. She was dressed and getting ready to leave when a groggy voice asked her, 'Want a cup of coffee, Mother, dearest?' Siziwe did not trust herself to say a word in reply. But the look she gave Fezi was more eloquent than anything she could have come up with.

By nine, she had made the transfer from Chemical Bank to her mother's account with Volkskas Bank in Elliot, the nearest town to Cala that boasted such facilities as banks. Over a cup of coffee, she thought about Fezi. *Hope she makes it to class.* When the girl had eventually found her way home the previous night, Siziwe had no idea. Mama's call had come well after two; nearer three than two in fact. And after the call she had gone to see whether Fezi was in her room. Not getting a reply to her knock, she'd gently pushed the door open. And the serene bed so incensed her, blind tears rolled down her cheeks before she even knew she was crying. How many times had she told the girl, 'All I ask is that when you are busy having fun, I should not be lying awake in bed, wondering if the next telephone call will be the police, telling me you've been shot or strangled; raped, robbed or pushed in front of a moving train.'

But her daughter behaved as though the mother were a big fusspot. As if these horrendous things were not happening, every day, in the city where they made their home. As if they were something Siziwe just conjured up to frighten herself and use to chain her daughter to the house. But then, that is the privilege of the young, the singular lack of fear of death; completely believing in their own immortality.

After work, she stopped for Happy Hour at The Ritz, a cosy little restaurant patronised by the foreigners because of its international cuisine. She was meeting Nomsa, a fellow South African who had lived in New York for almost thirty years. As usual, before long their talk was about home, the country, its people and, more particularly, their families.

'Hey, Siziwe, do you want to hear the latest about my crazy family?' When she nodded her head, knowing full well that whether she wanted to hear Nomsa's news or not, hear it she would, Nomsa told her, 'My sister is unbelievable! Do you remember her?' There was a pause but not for long. Nomsa answered herself, 'I've told you so much about her, you must. This is a woman, over forty, who dropped out of university. She is so bright, she had a first-class matric pass, passed the first two years in college with flying colours, but then, despite our advice, despite our protestations, decided she wanted to get married.

'Well, of course, that didn't last. Two children. No profession. Too proud of "My University Education" to do any job unless it is not beneath madam's status.

'Doesn't she call me, collect? Do you know how many times I have told her not to do that? Unless, of course, it is absolutely necessary: a death or grave illness, something of that nature.

'But no, each time she goes on a binge, she remembers she has this rich sister in America and calls me, but I have to pay for those calls. She is not that drunk she forgets that an overseas telephone call costs a lot of money.'

'I also had a call from home yesterday … or, early this morning, I should say.' Siziwe interrupted, still smarting from the hole the morning's withdrawal had made in her savings.

'Ah, but your family, listen to me, your family is reasonable. Mine? Mine, is something else, believe me!'

Siziwe started to tell her about her mother's call, Then, somehow, Fezi's staying out the whole night, '… for she must have come in well after four – came in and took centre stage.

'I miss having my family help me with the children. You know, at home, this wouldn't be just my problem alone. Her uncles, my brothers, would help. So would Mama. She would talk to her, show her how to behave herself.'

'Yes, that's true,' replied Nomsa. 'Our extended family is truly a blessing. One is never alone, whatever travails one is facing.'

Siziwe nodded her head, thinking of her mother and the strength she drew from her, just knowing she was there. Whatever would she do if anything happened to her mother? She told Nomsa, 'You know something? Often, when I'm troubled, I will pick up the phone and call Mama. But, when I hear her voice, realise how far she is, I ask myself: Why should I bother her with my little troubles? She would only worry. And the Lord knows, she needs that like she needs a second head on her shoulders. And, do you know what? Just hearing her voice; just knowing she is there, I already feel better.'

'Remember what you said, some time ago?' Nomsa was looking at her expectantly.

'No. What?' Which of the numerous things she had said to Nomsa over the years was the other referring to? Well, Nomsa would just have to remind her. Siziwe waited, eyebrows raised in question.

'You said, "Those of us who are supposed to have 'made it' are the ones whom, for whatever reason, the ancestors have chosen as sacrificial lambs for the family!"'

'Oh that? Sure,' said Siziwe, 'but this is slaughter! And when will I save for old age? Things are changing and I would be a big fool if I expected my children to look after me when I am retired.'

'Very true, my friend. But, as you yourself have said, we are helped to be successful, so that the family may endure. How else would so many of us have survived apartheid ... were it not for those who, despite overwhelming odds, "made it" to where they could support us?'

JOHN MATSHIKIZA

With the Lid Off

Of Renaissance and Rhino Stew

So what is the 'African renaissance', and where is it going? Cut to a new and kitsch clip joint called Caesar's Palace, Gauteng, perched just off the unfashionable side of Johannesburg International airport's runway number two (no relation) and close to the historically derided suburb of Benoni.

Why Caesar's Palace? I have no idea. But while the underprivileged of all conceivable races were hunched over blackjack tables and throwing their pensions into slot machines in the horrendously tasteless casino down below, in a conference room on the upper floor the minds of the African nation were gathered.

The Department of Arts, Culture, Science and Technology had invited a select few hundred of us to deliberate on the meaning of that very idea of an 'African renaissance', and come up with some ideas about how to put it into practice.

It was one of those gatherings where everyone showed up, dressed for a party, and then sat there looking at one another, wondering who was going to break the ice and tell us what was what. We all understood the question, but, from the urbane and charming Minister Ben Ngubane down, none of us knew the answers.

Fortunately there were some experts on board who took it upon themselves to give us some clues. Foremost among these, of course, was that celebrated 'Renaissance Man', Thami Mazwai.

Mazwai has many well-known opinions about how to make the 'African renaissance' happen, and is not afraid to regurgitate them, time and time again, in public. One of his recurring themes is that, in order to give Africa its pride back, everything in Africa should be Africanised, renamed and given its proper African place.

'We are still worshipping our former masters in everything we do,' he said, referring to the fact that we tend to dress, eat and think like the people who colonised us.

Notwithstanding the fact that he himself had driven to this most unAfrican of venues in an extremely unAfrican automobile, and was now standing before us in a shamefully unAfrican suit and tie, and addressing us in one of those oppressive ex-colonial languages we are all in the habit of using at functions like these (although he did point out that he should not be expected to get every nuance of this offensive and difficult language right – 'you can take me out of the Transkei, but you can't take the Transkei out of me!') he seemed to have a point.

Following his reasoning as he meandered through his theme proved to be a little difficult, though. He was indignant about the fact that you couldn't get African food on African airlines, including our own remarkably African national carrier.

'Why can't I eat *sadza* (pap) on Air Zimbabwe?' he asked. He didn't stop to ask himself how one would keep that notoriously difficult-to-handle staple fresh, hot and tasty at 30 000 feet, or how those dainty air hostesses would manage to stir the mealie meal to the right consistency in those huge cannibal-sized iron pots within the confines of the tiny airborne cabooses that the foreign devils have bequeathed us. Airline food, it seems to me, is about minimalist practicality, rather than national identity. But I'm no expert.

Food was definitely on Mazwai's mind, even when he expounded on environmental issues. 'No edict from Pretoria will make people feel inclined to protect the African rhino when they are hungry,' he said, referring subtly to the inherent contradiction between true Africans and the various bunny-hugging liberals with whom they are forced to share the continent.

Then, mysteriously, he corrected his reference to the 'African rhino' to the 'black rhino', to demonstrate his mastery of ecological themes. He did not pause to explain why true Africans preferred to eat the black rhino rather than the white rhino. It was one of many intriguing perceptions that were left unchallenged as the debate drifted onwards.

We were fortunate that at least three notable professors were on hand to bring some focus to the debate. Professor Lawrence Schlemmer reminded us that identifying what our true cultural reference points were was essential. The problem we face is that the political leaders who could guide us towards those references have generally withdrawn into a new kind of technocratic laager, where they become increasingly remote from the constituencies they should be representing.

Professor Herbert Vilakazi urged us to look at global models to identify our path. Africa, he said, had tottered into the early stages of an industrial revolution before meeting that essential precondition: an agricultural revolution.

And Professor Kwesi Prah gave a rousing intervention in which he pointed out that the key thing was language – not the simplistic idea that all African languages should be elevated to the same footing, but the more sophisticated idea that there is greater commonality than difference among many African languages, and that therefore unifying elements should be distilled to make up communication tools that could transcend our false colonial boundaries, mental and physical. Liberating the capacity of ordinary Africans to express themselves and communicate with each other was the only way forward towards the desired revolution.

Between the confused bluster and the elevated eloquence, there was consensus that the 'African renaissance' was not pie-in-the-sky (or *sadza*-in-the-sky, for that matter) but an inspiring and potentially liberating concept for Africa's long-awaited upliftment – spiritual, technological, cultural, political and otherwise. As Africans, we have a terrific talent for talking. Whether or not we have an equal talent for doing still remains to be seen.

[11 February 2000]

The Purple Man in my Bantustan

I met a purple man on the hills above the sea on the Transkei coast over Christmas. Now what does this mean?

Well, it was Christmas (whatever that means). And these were the hills of the Transkei – some of the most beautiful we have in this undiscovered country. And it was the Wild Coast sea that was breaking over this haunting part of our shores.

And I say it was the Transkei because that piece of our country remains a remote and seemingly forgotten 'homeland' within our complex territorial space, in spite of all the changes that we have lived through. Just look at the roads, and the way the people continue to live, to see what I mean.

The Transkei seems to have defied the elimination of boundaries established by a previous order and remained the same – treacherously narrow roads slicing through rolling hills whose green slopes give way to endless scars of soil erosion, the legacy of desperation and overpopulation. Cows, sheep, dogs, donkeys and mules roaming across the roads with mute abandon, blissfully unadapted to the perils of the mechanised age.

So it was in a remote part of this beautiful, stunted wilderness that I came across the purple man.

It became evident to me that the man himself was not purple. His face was purple. The man had been born with a birthmark that had covered the whole of his head with a purple cowl.

It could have happened to any of us. But if he had been born into a black family, of course, the birthmark would not have showed up in such a vivid shade of purple. To all other intents and purposes, therefore, in spite of the remarkable purple mask that covered his face, he was a white man.

Well, I was coming up the hill to look at the house the purple man had been staying in with his family over the Christmas holidays, with a vague view to buying it – well, you know, black people like you and me don't tend to own holiday homes on a timeshare basis, or any other basis, for that matter, anywhere in this country despite years of talking about liberation and reclaiming our grandparents' heritage. So I was taking up a local (white) man's challenge to consider this possibility.

So, anyway, here was this purple man standing in his faded blue shorts and naked yellow torso on the crest of the hill in the green Transkei, yelling at his whitish-yellow children outside a brown wooden house with an incredible view over the ocean, which I did not necessarily intend to buy. The purple man was somewhat taken aback when I hove into view.

That was the thing. The thing was, the purple man refused to see me. He could see the white man who was climbing up the hill with me, and who was bringing me to see the brown wooden house, with serious interest in having me buy the place.

But the purple man refused to acknowledge my presence (potentially the man with the interesting money) and would only acknowledge that he was seeing the white man at my side, to whom he was prepared to offer a civil and exclusive greeting in these wildly beautiful surroundings.

Now, we have all sorts of problems in this country and most of the time we would prefer to ignore them, considering how far we have already come. But when a purple man who is really a white man has a reality problem with a black man in what was formerly a black Bantustan, we have to stand back and look at what kind of situation we are actually sitting on.

But I have another question: do I blame the purple man and his people for hogging the country on their own behalf, or do I blame myself and the rest of the black bourgeoisie for failing to turn the country (and indeed the century) back over to the black people who still live here but have no stake in it?

Let's look at it again.

I met a purple man on the top of a hill overlooking some of the most dramatic land and seascapes in the country. We had nothing in common. We Christmassed with our separate families in our own separate worlds, in the same native space. We pretended that we couldn't give a damn about each other.

He couldn't chase me away, as he might have done in the old days, and

I couldn't chase him away, much as I might have wanted to in these new times. We were locked together in an unresolved space.

But that nagging question arises once again: to whom does this space belong?

We have easy solutions. Land and property are going begging out there. White people are building and buying into the hinterland like there's no tomorrow, quietly extending the frontiers of the laager.

The black bourgeoisie, on the other hand, prefers to ignore our rural splendours and spend their Christmas holidays on crowded beaches in Cape Town, along with the rest of affluent Johannesburg. Something has to be done if we are to turn our political transformation into something more meaningful. It is not enough just to take your cow with you when you move from Zondi to Bryanston and think you are making a powerful Africanist statement when you decide to slaughter in a white suburb. And it is not enough to drive around in a luxury four-by-four (one you know you cannot possibly afford) with a bumper sticker that says 'Thanx God I'm a Blackman, amen'.

So next time you meet a purple man with an unreconstructed white brain in an unexpected place, remind yourself of this: taking back the country demands engagement of a higher order. Nobody's going to offer you those spectacular timeshares, or anything else, on a plate. The country is being painted overseas as a spectacular land of opportunity. And spectacular it certainly is; when you get out there and look at it.

Now we have to be prepared to go out and get it, before the whole thing gets taken away again under our noses.

I rest my case.

[17 January 2003]

ROSEMARY H MOEKETSI

Guilty as Charged

I took the witness stand that morning. I was more confident than I had been on Monday. I knew that the white man in black robes, sitting in a commodious chair behind a long desk on an elevated platform, was the magistrate. I knew that he came into the courtroom when everybody else was already there. I knew that everybody had to rise when he entered and left the courtroom. I knew that he addressed the court seated, while everybody else had to stand when they talked to the court. I remembered, also, that he had said very little on that Monday. He had been writing most of the time.

MmaNtlhane had dropped me off earlier because her husband preferred her to be helpful at home, rather than waste time listening to lies in court. Morongwe could not accompany me; she had to take Mama to the Chris Hani hospital for her check-up. Thabiso could not stay away from work and forfeit a day's wages. I was a big girl. I was strong. I would manage just fine.

* * *

'Do you swear that the evidence you will give this court will be the truth, nothing but the truth? Raise your right hand and say: "So help me God."'

The court interpreter explained to me in seSotho that I had to respond to the defence lawyer's questions truthfully. He could have saved his energy because I had been taught the virtues of honesty from childhood.

'Why did you go to the police only three days later?' Mr van Vuuren asked suspiciously.

I had picked up his name on Monday, when the magistrate had repeatedly requested him to allow the court interpreter to complete what he was saying.

'I did not go to the police three days later. I went immediately. I was lucky to find MmaNtlhane home, and she took me there as soon as she heard what had happened to me.'

I was composed. I was no longer scared of this man because I knew that his intentions were to confuse and confound me, to trick me into saying things I might not be able to retract.

'But according to the statement you gave the police on 12 May, you were assaulted on the 9th,' he said contemptuously.

★ ★ ★

My father was a humorous person, and I have missed him ever since that treacherous train accident that bereft us of him. He used to say that it was a waste of time to respond to people who made unfounded statements; he would rather allow them to make fools of themselves.

'Is it not true?'

'I was assaulted two Wednesdays ago, sir, when the bus drivers were on strike, and MmaNtlhane took me to the police the same morning.' The court interpreter conveyed my message accurately, in such impeccable English that I suspected it had been specially polished for that occasion. Mr van Vuuren tried to interrupt him by demanding that I answer 'Yes' or 'No', but the interpreter ignored him and continued until he had completed his say. Thus the two engaged in simultaneous talk, like opponents vying for power.

'Please stop interrupting the court interpreter, Mr van Vuuren. I want to hear everything he has to say,' said the magistrate calmly.

He then turned to the court interpreter and requested: 'Could you repeat the witness' evidence?'

I could sense a tinge of victory in the court interpreter's voice as he repeated my answer emphatically, though quietly.

'Why did MmaNtlhane accompany you?' asked the lawyer.

How did he expect me to know? These lawyers spend years at school only to come out and ask stupid questions. Or is this the so-called art of advocacy?

My thoughts were rudely interrupted by Mr van Vuuren's reminder that he had asked me a question and was, therefore, expecting an answer. I looked at the court interpreter with uncertainty and said innocently, 'I have never really asked her.'

This must have enraged the lawyer because he suddenly changed his line of questioning, and bombarded me with a real barrage of short, direct missiles that gave me very little time to breathe. 'What were you doing in Mr Bongani's car?'

'He gave me a lift.'

'Where to?'

'To school, sir.'

'At a quarter to nine?' he asked in feigned and exaggerated disbelief.

'In fact, it was a quarter past nine, sir,' I said, putting stress on 'past'. After all, we had gone over this on Monday.

'What time does school begin?'

He was deliberate in asking this question. I could hear some uneasy shuffling in the audience behind me, and this gave me the confidence that someone was holding thumbs for me. 'School begins at ten to eight, sir.'

'And, at a quarter past nine you were still in the streets?' Instead of thinking that the defence attorney was casting aspersions on me, I could hear my late father laugh at people who make fools of themselves by making unfounded assertions.

'I was at the bus stop, sir, with about seven other children who attend the same school.' He abruptly changed the topic: 'What car did Mr Bongani drive?'

'A white van.'

'What model?'

'I don't know, but it was a very small one, sir. He normally drives it.'

'Did you say you were with seven other schoolchildren?' He made a precipitous return to information already provided, and the magistrate did not take kindly to this.

'Mr van Vuuren ...' The magistrate tried to reprimand him, but I had already answered with:

'Yes, sir, that number, roughly.'

'And you got into Mr Bongani's car?' He emphasised the word 'you'. I was not sure whether this was a question. He repeated his question with 'car' lengthened and raised very high. Was he trying to tell the magistrate that I was not responding properly to crucial questions? Did he think that I would deny getting into Mr Bongani's van?

Mr Bongani had called me by my name: 'Mpule, come let me take you to school, my child, you are going to be late. *Azikhwelwa namhlanje*.'

Indeed, no one could board a bus on that Wednesday because the drivers had disputes to resolve with their employers.

Mr Bongani usually visits Ntate Ntlhane. They often sit under the peach tree next to the fence between our house and Ntate Ntlhane's, and drink a beer or two. On several occasions MmaNtlhane has sent me to MaZola's shebeen to buy them their beer, and the men would often give me the small change to spend at school. Mr Bongani has often said that he liked me very much because I hurried with the beer and brought it still ice-cold to them.

'Yes I did.' Was I not expected to seize the opportunity of ultimately arriving at school?

'Yes I did, sir,' I repeated, emphatically.

'What about your friends?'

What friends? What about them?

'What about the other seven children? Why did they not hitch along with you?'

'I don't know, sir.'

I was already used to these questions that expected me to know exactly what was in other people's minds. On the other hand, the magistrate seemed to be running out of patience with Mr van Vuuren's line of questioning. The court interpreter leaned closer to me as though to protect me from anything sinister. I was brave. I was not scared of Mr van Vuuren and his incisive questions. I had already undergone the worst a child of my age could ever imagine.

'Did you tell this court that you alighted from the car and went into Mr Bongani's house?'

'Yes, sir, I did.'

'So you were no longer interested in going to school. Isn't that so?'

'Mr Bongani had left his driver's licence on his dining-room table, sir, and could not drive without it.'

That is what Mr Bongani had said when he turned left into Mokwena Street and stopped at his house. He had asked me to jump out quickly and get the licence from the dining-room table. The front door was not locked, so I just opened it and walked into a room that had no table. This could, therefore, not be the dining room. I went through to the next room and saw a big wooden table with about six chairs around it. This could be the dining room, I thought, but there was nothing that resembled a driver's licence on the neat and shining table. I wondered whether I had to go deeper into the house.

'Is it not there, Mpule?' Mr Bongani, who was already at the door between the first room and the dining room, frightened me because I thought he had remained in the car.

'It must be in the pocket of the trousers I had on yesterday,' he had said, walking through to where those pants apparently were. 'You will also grow old one day and forget where you put your things,' he had continued from somewhere in the house where I could not see him. 'Just look where I put it; even MaBongani would not have found it. Come and see where it is.'

I had obliged.

'Did you follow Mr Bongani to his bedroom?' Mr van Vuuren asked this question with such contempt that I am sure he thought I would be intimidated and humiliated.

'But I did not follow Mr Bongani to his bedroom; I just went to see where he said he had found his driver's licence,' I answered, with an obstinacy that was not characteristic of me.

'Did you, or did you not follow Mr Bongani to his bedroom?' Mr van Vuuren was generous. He gave me two options, and I boldly took the first.

'Now, when you got there, you admired Mr Bongani's luxurious furniture.'

This was, of course, a statement that assumed that I was susceptible to suggestion. How could I admire Mr Bongani's furniture? My mother also has her double bed, a dressing table, chest of drawers and built-in cupboards to hang her clothes in. What was there to admire in Mr Bongani's bedroom? 'You'll grow up and marry one day and have a bed as big and beautiful as this one. MaBongani likes to sleep on a big bed,' Mr Bongani had said, and emphasised that there was nothing wrong with that.

'And you threw yourself on Mr Bongani's bed.' Mr van Vuuren uttered these words slowly and deliberately, looking me squarely in the eyes. He made me so angry I could have skinned him alive with my fingernails.

'I did not ... throw ... my ...' I tried to resist, but choked on my tears.

* * *

Mr Bongani had pushed me onto the bed, muttering that I should try it and enjoy the pleasures that MaBongani experienced every night. That was completely unexpected. I had resisted. I had fought and kicked and scratched and screamed. He was stronger and heavier, but I was determined to fight him.

I had grabbed something weighty from somewhere and hit him very hard on his forehead. He had stumbled a bit and loosened his grip on me. Our eyes met. Mr Bongani had changed: his eyes were blood red, his hands were trembling, the front of his pants bulged strangely. He was raving mad and made groaning sounds I could not comprehend. I was scared. I crouched. I whined long and loud. Mr Bongani was not moved by my plaintive cry. I hid my face in my hands and whimpered like an exhausted baby left in the cold. I missed my father. He would have had the strength to match Mr Bongani's. I was only twelve.

My mother had warned us against strangers. But Mr Bongani was no stranger. He was Ntate Ntlhane's friend. They had sent me many a time to buy them this or that. He had greeted and chatted with my mother. He had remembered the days when my father was not too busy to join them with Ntate Ntlhane under the peach tree. Mr Bongani was not a stranger.

* * *

'I did not throw myself onto Mr Bongani's bed. He pushed me,' I gave Mr van Vuuren an exhausted response.

'And you took your clothes off?' Mr van Vuuren continued, as though he had not heard my answer. All the while I was thinking that one normally takes one's clothes off before one 'throws' oneself on the bed.

'I did not, sir. Mr Bongani ripped them off. He tore them to many, many pieces,' I reported accurately.

⋆ ⋆ ⋆

Mr Bongani had behaved like a wild animal. He had groaned and sweated and scared me and I had hid my face in my hands. I was cold and shivering. He had picked me up and thrown me on the bed, and I had crouched and tried to hide behind my hands. I had sobbed and sobbed and sobbed, and he hurt me like I had never been hurt before.

I must have passed out because, all of a sudden, I came to find myself in a small, dark room. Through the cracks in the door I saw that I was in an outside toilet. I opened the door slightly. I was in tatters – inside and out. I was weak and could hardly stand. I was aching all over. I was filthy and smelly, but not dazed. I knew exactly what had happened to me. Mr Bongani had raped me. He had violated me.

I stood up, opened the door and walked out. I found my bearings. This was Moleboheng's home. My home was eight houses away. I walked home, slowly, but determined to get there. Ndlela's dog barked, and I knew this was not a dream. I suddenly remembered that there was nobody at my home, and I therefore went to MmaNtlhane. Luckily, she was there.

I told her. I was not sobbing anymore. I told her everything. She looked at me sadly, put her warm hand on my shoulder, and said: 'Come, my child. Let us go and report this pig to the police.'

⋆ ⋆ ⋆

For the first time I looked around in the courtroom. I saw Mistress Vilakazi; she smiled and I smiled back. I saw Moleboheng and Thato, Morongwe's friends, and knew I was not alone. Then I saw Mr Bongani, and, indeed, he looked like a pig, plodding in a messy pigsty.

'I did not throw myself onto Mr Bongani's bed, sir, neither did I take off my clothes. Mr Bongani ripped them off, sir; he tore them to pieces. He raped me, sir. He violated me, sir.'

I uttered these words softly but boldly, pointing at Mr Bongani. I was not afraid of him. I was not afraid of Mr van Vuuren. They did not scare me. I hated Mr Bongani, and I despised Mr van Vuuren. I respected the court interpreter and I knew he was proud of me.

I looked at the magistrate, and he looked away.

I learned later that my case ought to have been heard privately.

SHEILA ROBERTS

Carlotta's Vinyl Skin

My friend David, a successful lawyer who helped me with my immigration papers for this country, is unhappy in a niggled, half-tortured sort of way because of the unimpressive salary I earn as an English professor. Once a month, regularly, he will phone me to beg me to write a lurid romantic novel that might get on the best-seller list and enable me to buy the house and car he thinks I owe it to myself to own. I have told him over and over again that I *cannot* write such a novel – I would become immobilised with ennui and self-disgust at my very typewriter. I would waste my time trying, and simply be inserting my hands and head into a stock-like writer's block.

'Sheila, can't you just prostitute yourself for once?' he pleads. 'Just once. Then you could keep writing the egghead stuff no one wants to read in comfort, at least.'

Sometimes a little inner voice joins its harangue with his. *If* I have endurance and energy (which perhaps I don't have and am therefore lacking the essentials of a full human being) I could indeed write a money-bringing book, the voice insists. Think up a simple plot, set it in a foreign country during a time of turmoil. Be prepared to write six hundred pages. Create a beautiful heroine who falls in love with a rebel/renegade/revolutionary/freedom fighter/innocent fugitive from justice/political activist/disinherited son later to be re-inherited/wildcat unionist/or even a handsome Dracula-like fellow, eyes heavy-lidded, soul possessed. Or she could be in search of a lost father. Contrive to have the lovers separated and then bring them together in a grand finale. They are both, or all three, hot-blooded. Here's your chance, Sheila, to portray the sex act from the woman's point of view. You could do a service to womankind while making money.

Weaving, weaving, I stick a sheet of paper in the typewriter. A foreign country? The only country I know well, whose landscape forms part of my own mental baggage, is South Africa. My setting will have to be South African – it's foreign enough to most Americans and it's their money I'm after. I couldn't presume to write about America: I know too little about American turmoil and even less about the various historic sites. I have no doubt that I could recreate in words the look of the Cape coast, the Karoo, the Bushveld, the Highveld, the Natal highlands, the Drakensberg. In fact, if I invented a country, calling it something like Sylvanvakia or Prinsenmania or Eendt-sur-Mer, I would only end up describing either the Cape coast, the Karoo, the Bushveld, the Highveld, the Natal highlands, or the Drakensberg. Geography is destiny.

Turmoil? If I want this book to sell, I have to keep all racial discrimination or conflict out of it, except for a bit of jungle-enshrouded sex to the beat of tom-toms, but that could come into the sub-plot. So I could go along with the myth of the 'white man's' war and set my story in South Africa on the eve of Anglo-Boer hostilities. My heroine will be a peaches-and-cream English girl who comes out with her wealthy father to visit the mines and falls in love with ... an Afrikaner? No, no. A descendant of the 1820 Settlers? A South African English Gentleman and a Rebel. How about that?

I visualise delicate Victorian blouses, thick blonde hair done up in a chignon, large hats, many petticoats, soft white hands, large blue eyes, a vulnerable but brave mouth. Oh no, I am regurgitating memories of Bo Derek starring in *Tarzan the Ape Man*. Why does schlock always stick? I must start afresh. I *must* start afresh. The image of one of my best-looking writing students comes to mind. She has slightly curly, untidy brown hair, a thin face, and slanting catlike eyes. She usually wears long peasant skirts or calf-length tight trousers in Hot Pink or Luminous Blue, and soft suede boots with a foldover at the ankle, such as medieval pages must have worn, three earrings in one ear and none in the other, oversized T-shirts or fifties blouses. I try dressing her in a Victorian outfit. She looks okay although her shoulders are a bit broad and she stands rather sardonically and firmly on the ground surveying the desolation of a burnt-down Free State farm. Allie, get those boots off, and for God's sake, wilt a little!

Get her off that farm. I'll send her in a donkey cart with her wealthy but dying father into the interior. They are on their way to Kimberley. But the father dies on the road and she is left a pile of money. I love bumping off fathers in my stories; like other egghead writers, I am haunted by Oedipus, Electra and Jocasta.

So there she is alone, on her way to Kimberley. She will have to have picked up some passengers, though. Poor girl. Look, I'm sorry, but I have to think about these things: how will she wash properly on the road? Wonderful complexions don't stay that way without cleansing. How will she be able to urinate and move her bowels out in the bush with all those skirts on? Just bundle them up? But won't they still get splashed and stained? How much toilet paper does her party have? Did they *have* toilet paper in those days? Did they have toothbrushes? When was the first toothbrush marketed, hey you Popular Culturists? What if she gets her period? Of *course* she'll get her period, unless she's anorexic. But an anorexic girl won't be able to handle the boisterous sex scenes in the book. And what about mosquitoes? I mean, have you *ever* spent a night out of doors in the summer without netting and that new insecticide you rub on hands, face and feet, or whatever parts of the body are exposed? The perspiration! The food going bad!

Let me tell you, I know from experience that when my skin breaks out, I lose all sense of the romantic occasion. I don't feel like going to bed with some guy whose skin is fine and who'll want to leave the light on while we make love. I don't like making love when I'm sweaty or dirty. I don't fancy sweaty or dirty men. Also, I find it excruciating to be 'confined' with a man in bed, or even in a car, when I'm suffering from flatulence. Yes, contrary to masculine belief, women *do* fart. Over the centuries we've worked hard to establish the conviction of our continence. But out in the bush the pretence would have to go. I simply cannot muster up enthusiasm for Romance as I regard Carlotta, my beautiful heroine, waddling like a duck as she squats, searching for a place to hold steady where the tough grass won't prick her bare butt.

In my imagination my student Allie walks into my office. Today she is sporting an old stained braided coat of the kind major-domos of hotels wear, a limp miniskirt and army boots. I know that she (like many other students these days) buys her clothes from a popular second-hand clothing store that sometimes stocks astonishing antique garments, things people have stolen out of their grandparents' attics, or defunct theatre companies have hawked. Allie has on bottle-green tights and a little head-hugging hat from the twenties.

'Why do you want to write that trash?' she asks me.

'To make money.'

'Then you've got to stop thinking about physical discomfort. Your heroine has to have skin of vinyl, teeth of white stainless steel (if that is possible), her polyfibrous hair does not grow damp and scraggly, and her crystalline eyes have the three or four necessary expressions, depending on the light, for your purposes: joy, indignation, love, and sorrow. She doesn't have periods, or perspiration, or pee, or poo!'

'I can't write about a vinyl *dummy*,' I say, my own eyes flashing indignantly.

'What is the least you can write about?'

'Well, to begin with, I need to see real people in my mind's eye, a woman like you, for instance. Say, what does your boyfriend do?' Deep down in me a little hope is born that she will say he is completing training as an officer in the Air Force Academy. A shadowy Richard Gere starts forming. *Would* such a gorgeous thing date Allie the Punk in her tights and boots?

'My boyfriend has a degree in Agriculture, but because of the recession he can't find a job in his field, no pun, so he's working as a male nurse at Hannah Hospital. Oh boy, you wouldn't believe the kinds of things he's learned to do! Give people enemas, stick catheters into them, give them shots in the bee-hind, and hold pans for them when they want to throw up. But it's done him good, especially seeing old people naked and having to wash the shit off them and all that. He's much more sympathetic toward people these days. He never criticises women for their bodies the way most guys do.'

'What does he look like?' I ask, a bit disconsolately, pulling the paper out of the machine.

'He's no Mister Universe. He's okay. He's going to have to go on a bit of a diet because of the tummy he's getting. Twenty-five's too young to get a tummy. Not that I mind. He's got a sweet face, but his skin is very pale. He can't suntan at all: he just goes red, mostly his nose, and he was never good at sports at school because of his flat feet. Would you listen to this: no one realised that he was flat-footed until he was about fourteen? He got out of the swimming pool at school and by chance the coach noticed his wet footprint. As flat as a fish.'

'What will he do? Keep looking for a job in his "field" or settle for nursing?'

'Naa ... he's decided to go on to grad school next year. He may as well. He's saved enough to put himself through, and he still wants to get into some branch of agricultural science, maybe at a higher level.'

'And you?'

'I'll keep on with my studio art. Though I wouldn't mind farming. I've always wanted to farm. That's why Percy and I get on so well.' She settles herself on the corner of my desk, running one hand over a pile of books. I see that each fingernail is painted a different colour. She looks at me confidentially. 'You know, Percy my boyfriend had a terrible time as a kid. His mom used to dominate him totally. Even when he was in high school she'd clean his room and go through all his things. She'd even examine the underclothes he'd thrown in the wash. He had no privacy whatsoever. And the one time he came home a little drunk, both his parents created such a scene, even though he was already twenty-one, that now he simply can't, *he can't* drink in front of them. Now his dad offers him beers and beers and beers, but he can't accept them. I've had a lot of trouble getting him to loosen up with me, you know. Do you know he stayed a virgin until he was twenty-four?'

'Allie, you don't have to tell me all this stuff.'

'I know you'll keep it to yourself.'

'Of course.'

'I had to teach him a lot,' she says coolly, getting off the desk and clumping to the door, her boots heavy against the floorboards. 'I hope you can write your Romance and make some big bucks,' she adds, but without much interest. She wiggles her painted nails at me and leaves. I put the paper back into the typewriter.

My story begins to take form. Percy, my male protagonist (I dare not call him a hero, which is not to say he isn't heroic), will be a civilian helper in the military hospital at Bloemfontein where more British soldiers are dying of diarrhoea than are being killed by the Boers. But I won't go into details that will nauseate the reader; I might draw a Daumieresque picture of grey skeletal bodies with sombre young faces in overcrowded wards. But Percy is a short, shy, pink-faced fellow with not too noticeably flat feet and a deep desire to be a farmer. He has never known a woman (in the biblical sense) until he meets Petronella, a farm girl who has had to take on many of the chores at 'Bloustroom' because the men are away fighting in the Transvaal. She wears army boots and hitches up her skirts for ease of movement by means of an old cartridge belt. She ties her hair up in pony tails with string, which causes her cotton sunbonnet to sit oddly on her head. The neighbours think she is eccentric if not mad (The Mad Woman of Africa – cliché alert!) and no young man comes riding up to 'Bloustroom' to court her when the farmer-fighters are on leave. But Percy doesn't notice anything out of the ordinary about Petronella. Besides, he is lonely. His widowed mother, who wielded inflexible control over his life, has herself passed on to the Fathers as a result of a stray shell crashing through Percy's suburban bedroom just as she was about to riffle through the things her son stores in his tin trunk. (Am I killing Mothers off too now?)

Petronella has great trouble with stomach wind, mostly because of the high-starch diet forced on all the population, but Percy is unaware of her sneaky farts – because of his job, his hair and clothes are infused with excremental and medicinal smells. One afternoon in the barn, she shows him how to make love (*this* will be my main sexual scene, putting male readers straight about female arousal once and for all), whereafter he becomes insatiably attracted to her. He nearly gets shot by the British at one point because they suspect that he is consorting with the enemy, but Petronella is not the enemy, nor do any of the enemy come near her. But Percy goes to gaol (SAD scene), and the British burn Petronella's farm (TRAGIC scene, Petronella's unusual silhouette seen against the brilliant orange and blues of the fire). But after the war Percy marries Petronella and takes up farming with her – her father and brother died in prison camps set up by the British for Boer prisoners in the West Indies. This information is conveyed to Petronella in a letter written by General de Wet, a letter which she frames.

My telephone rings. 'Sheila, honey …' (it is David, my lawyer-friend), 'I've just been reading in the Free Press about a housewife in Troy, Michigan, I mean *Troy*, Michigan! And she's making plenty of money writing these novels to a formula. Apparently her publishers supply her with an outline which she merely fleshes out. Now you could do that!'

The strong picture I have of Petronella and Percy clearing away the debris of the burnt-down farmhouse begins to dissipate. Behind them I see beautiful Carlotta, her blonde hair wisping the sides of her lovely vinyl skin, her lacy petticoats caught up against the breeze in one small hand, her lips pursed redly in anticipation. She waves. At a handsome horseman? No, at me. I am surprised. I see that she wants me to bring her to life, rescue her from that vinyl skin, allow her to experience hot tearful afternoons of toothache, days when she can't get a comb through her sweating hair, the bloated feeling of food moving through her digestive system, messy periods at the wrong time, just when she wanted to wear a white gown to the officers' dinner, and she wants me to give her the good sense to guide her lover's hand and penis so that they move in ways she wants, instead of having to submit to one of those writhing, grunting, quick, harsh sex acts always inflicted on Romantic heroines. I hesitate. I do pity her. Mmm … Carlotta could be Petronella's cousin from overseas. Percy introduces her to Captain Coninghame, the Chief Surgeon. Carlotta uses part of her fortune to rebuild Petronella's farm.

'Look, David, I don't think I want some publisher's outline. I can think up my own outline,' I say.

'Don't tell me I've persuaded you to *do* it?'

'I am thinking about … the project … very seriously.'

'I mean, if someone in Troy, Michigan, can do it, so can you.'

'Ja, ja, I'm thinking about it,' I say, beckoning to Carlotta.

RIANA SCHEEPERS

Book*

Translated from the Afrikaans by Sharon Meyering.

It was in the third year of the lecturer's academic career when it happened. She discovered in herself something unmentionably evil and malicious; a suspicion because of another person, a pool of anger, an emotion so new and overwhelming that she couldn't name it. She – who for three years had remained unaffected in the midst of rioting, student uprisings and striking, bad marks and toyi-toyiing in the lecture theatres; she who unemotionally rejected impertinent students' sexual advances and mercilessly refused the bribes of the desperate; she who had real compassion for the work-fatigued students who bunked evening classes, pregnant students who stayed away for months and on their return demanded that their lost classes be given to them – was enraged with unreasonable anger over a seemingly insignificant incident.

It happened when she saw a student who had just left her office throw her prescribed book in the bin, and guilelessly walk away.

The lecturer saw it by chance. She remembered that she still had to make arrangements for a tutorial and, seconds after the student left her office, walked out after her. And that was when she saw it happen.

Without hesitation, the student tossed the hardcover book in between papers, banana peels, crushed cold-drink cans and cigarette butts. And she walked on, without looking back, as if she had just rid herself of something of absolutely no importance.

The lecturer stood, looking in stunned silence, unwilling to believe what she had just seen. She could feel her colour drain. And then she became angry. With flames that crept up her throat and spread across her face, she wanted to run after the student and grab her by the arm, by her hair, by her clothes and wrench her to a standstill: How dare you! she

*Reference is to Adam Small's play, *Kanna hy kô hystoe* (1965) [Kanna's coming home], which in an achronological succession of scenes sets the hardships of a Cape coloured family against the ambivalent return of one of their own, Kanna, who having studied abroad (in Canada) is less than able to adjudge his commitment to the desperation at home over and above his sense of safety at the distance of a foreign (first-world) country. [ed.]

wanted to shout across campus. That was a book that I spent an entire morning looking for, that I paid for, that I gave to you, that you threw away as if it was rubbish! Why?

She leaned back against the wall where she stood and watched as the student disappeared into the crowd on campus. Then she walked slowly towards the blue bin clamped to a pole. The book lay with its flyleaf pages spread and open, facing the bottom of the bin. She picked it up, shook the pages loose as if there were sand or crumbs in them, and walked back to her office. It was her consultation hour, she was supposed to be available, but she locked her office door and wearily went to sit at her desk. In front of her lay the book. A drama for which the author should have received the Hertzog Prize, years ago already.

With her hands tightly clasped in her lap she let her head drop forward until it rested on top of the book. She stayed like that for a long time.

'Dear Lord,' whispered the lecturer in the silence of her empty office, 'I am not the right person for this kind of work. How can I possibly teach that girl again? How can I mark her answer papers, give her the marks she needs to pass the course? After she throws a book away, moments after I gave it to her as a gift?'

The lecturer, who walked through the lecture hall, stopping at each row to hand out a number of papers, had survived her first two years at the university. With the experience that comes with time, her self-confidence increased, she felt more at home and more involved with the university and her students. It is the new year's prescribed book list that she is handing out to the students. She knows in advance that they will soon complain about all kinds of things, that they can't get hold of the books on the list, that they are too expensive, that the books in the library are damaged. But she also knows in advance that they are poor, and stingy, that they would rather buy clothes and jewellery than books for a course that will only last a year. If they can't find it second hand, then the book won't be bought. Or it will be illegally photocopied. But for the lecturer it is serious, she insists that all students have their own books. As compensation she allows her students to use their books during the exams, as long as there are not notes written in them. She knows it is usually enough encouragement to buy the books.

It is just as she expected. One of the first students who knocked on her door during her consultation hour was Duduzile Nkulu.

'Yes, Ms Nkulu?'

The girl looked at her seriously. 'I can't get the books.'

'Which books?'

The girl named a few titles of the books she had to acquire. The lecturer, who that morning had dropped into the second-hand bookshop on campus, could hardly believe what she heard. 'Are you sure, Ms Nkulu? This morning I saw that there are second-hand books available of all the titles you are looking for!'

The girl looked at her without an excuse, sure of her case. 'There are no books.'

Without meaning to, the lecturer looked at the girl's clothes, her shoes, at the bag over her shoulder in which she carried her books. She saw they were clothes and accessories bought in a factory shop.

Everything new, but not expensive or durable. In a few months they will be past their prime and within a year they will be threadbare. Duduzile was not a student with a lot of money.

'Do you want to buy your books new, Ms Nkulu?' she asked.

'Yes,' answered the student.

'I will find out from the manager of the bookshop if the complete stock of books has come in yet,' she promised. 'Normally it takes a bit of time before everything is available. Luckily you don't need all the books right away. OK?'

'Yes,' said the student.

Once she had left, the lecturer looked at the student's information card. Something about the student's reserved, almost unfriendly attitude pricked her interest. Barely eighteen, and from KwaZulu-Natal. Her school results weren't too impressive, but satisfactory. She was studying on a bursary. The name of the town she comes from was completely unknown to the lecturer. Later she would see it was a hamlet on a map.

It was, in fact, as the student said. The books that she named were not available. The manager let her know that they were still waiting for stock. But as the semester progressed, the lecturer noticed that Ms Nkulu bought all her books. New. She was a thorough student, she soon discovered. In class she would never express her own opinion, but she never missed a lecture and her assignments were promptly handed in. At the beginning of the year she just-just scraped through her tests, but with time her marks improved considerably. Ms Nkulu became *the* achiever of the class without much effort.

When the module for the drama course started, Ms Nkulu sat without a book in front of her for the first time.

'Don't you have the book?' the lecturer asked her in class.

The student looked at her with big eyes that gave nothing away, remaining silent.

The lecturer went on with the reading, but right after the class she stopped in at the bookshop.

‘*Kanna* by Adam Small, is it available?’ she asked the assistant.

‘No, sorry, it’s completely out of stock. And it doesn’t look like the publisher will make a reprint soon.’

The lecturer walked the length of the campus to the second-hand bookshop. As always there was a hum and throng of students in the place where the books are displayed in reasonable disarray. A smell of old books, some mouldy and ruined, rose out of the area. As she suspected, there wasn’t a single copy of the book left. Those that were available had been snapped up long ago. The only copy in the library was also already out, and there was a waiting list of students who had reserved the book.

At the next lecture the lecturer asked to see Ms Nkulu after class. They walked together to her office.

‘I’m going to Cape Town this weekend,’ she told the student standing uncomfortably near the door, her bookbag tightly folded in her arms. ‘Shall I see if I can get hold of a second-hand copy of *Kanna* for you?’

‘I don’t have money,’ said the student. She said it without emotion, but her eyes glowed with a strange shine.

‘Come, we’ll see if I can get it first, then we can talk about the price.’

The student nodded her head, turned and left.

The lecturer’s search for the book took her to all the bookshops in Long Street. She spent the whole morning nosing through old, dusty bookshelves in old dusty shops. She discovered a bibliophile first edition of Eugène Marais’ poetry collection, a small book, bound in leather for sale at R300; she found Johannes Meintjes’s journals, Petronella van Heerden’s autobiography – loved, familiar books from her childhood – but couldn’t find Small’s drama anywhere. At eleven o’clock she drank coffee in a chic restaurant that was once the most famous antiquarian bookshop in the Cape. A shop with an owner who was so attached to his half-a-million books, that he couldn’t find it in his heart to sell them. ‘Not for sale!’ he shouted, maliciously, on more than one occasion as someone took a rare and expensive edition off the shelf and carried it to the counter. Or he made the prices so excessively expensive that no one could afford to buy them. Eventually the bookshop came tumbling down around him; he couldn’t afford the rent anymore. The books were sold per kilo and in the last weeks of the sale, they were taken in truckloads to be pulped. Shortly before closing time the lecturer rode to the last second-hand bookshop she knew of, a charity organisation that received books as donations. It was in this suffocating space, a shop crammed with books, magazines, maps and people, that she found it. For R10. She bought it immediately, relieved that her search was finally successful.

At home the lecturer carefully erased all the hasty pencil scratchings on the pages and covered the book neatly with plastic. It was practically a new book, she realised, one that was well looked after by its previous owner. She would give it to Duduzile Nkulu as a present, decided the lecturer; she had already decided before she went to all the trouble. Monday, right after class, she would call the girl and give her the book. She bought all her books; this one would be a gift.

She put the book in her briefcase, with strange excitement and pleasure at the prospect of giving a gift to someone who needed it.

* * *

The woman emigrating to Canada packs her suitcases with meagre earthly possessions. There is not much that will go with her. Not much has remained to take with her after the raid on her house.

If she could, she wouldn't take a single thing with her out of South Africa, thought the woman while she wrapped a pair of walking boots in newspaper, and if she could, she would prefer to leave without a single reminder. She would especially like to erase the last three months of her life, she thinks exhausted. Involuntarily she touches the injury above her eyebrow, a raised scar that is still painful to touch. I will carry this with me, knew the woman, luggage for a lifetime.

Like the frightening image of the nightmare night that made her finally decide to go for good. Go.

What about my books? thinks the woman. Where will I hear Afrikaans again?

Undecided she stands in front of her bookshelf, caressing the spines of the titles in thought.

Five books, she decides, only five.

Her choice is easier than she thought. Poetry, two collections for times when the language must be more than just words; a dictionary; a book with children's rhymes for the day when she perhaps, who knows … Her hands glide across the alphabet. They come to a standstill at *Die Uur van die Engel*. 'Karel Schoeman,' she says softly, 'I need to see an angel, you come too …' She takes the book out, places it on top of the others. Her hands pause at the gap in the bookshelf, by Adam Small. Her heart aches inside her. How can a person visualise the Afrikaans language without *Kanna hy kô hystoe*?

She flaps the book open. 'Kanna, I am going away,' she whispers in the empty house, 'and I am not coming back.' Her eyes follow the lines on the open page. Little Kytie. The woman sits on the floor.

She remains like this for a long time, reliving the trauma of her night of terror three months ago, hers and Kytie's.

'Kytie, little Kytie,' she whispers, the open book pressed against her chest, 'you couldn't get away, but I can. I'm going to speak a new language, I'm going to start over … and I can't take you with me to remind me of all this pain …'

The following day the woman drove to the shop of a charity organisation in Claremont with four wine boxes full of books. She unceremoniously handed them all over at the counter.

'What kinda books are these?' asked the assistant.

'Afrikaans literature,' she answered over her shoulder, already on her way out.

* * *

The school child in the small zinc building at Nqutu sits tightly packed between the forty-five other children in the class. They sit on planks that are supported by drums filled with sand at the ends and in the middle. There are no desks. If they must write, their books are pressed against their laps, the blunt pencil is sent skew over their uneven knobbly knees. But at the moment the children aren't writing, they sit with big eyes and watch the teacher in front of the class. He is busy hitting a child with a thin willow cane. The blows rain down at regular intervals on the child's shoulders and back. A naughty child, a stupid child that is worthless in class, will never get anything in his head, after a few years of school still can't write or read. The child wails, tries to block with his thin arms, but the blows strike him regardless on unprotected parts of his squirming body.

The children sit dead still, knowing that no word or sound may come out of their mouths now.

Eventually the teacher has beaten his anger out.

'Bring your books here, all of them!' he commands the moaning child who still stands with his arms over his head, as if he expects more blows.

The child sits on his haunches, takes the three books under the plank to the teacher. Two writing books and a textbook with dog-eared pages.

'Now go home,' commands the teacher, 'and don't come back! There isn't place here for a child without a brain!'

The child flees the classroom. Those who sat next to him on the plank spread out a bit wider, filling the extra space.

The teacher still isn't finished. He holds the three books up for all the other children to see.

'If someone thinks that he can have these books I want to warn you: read the books of an idiot and his stupid soul will transfer into you!'

The school child closes her eyes for a moment. She knows the books cost more than R10. Money her parents don't have.

In front of their eyes he begins to tear out pages. First the exercise books with the uneven pencil writing, then the textbook. The dog-eared pages flutter to the ground, collecting at his feet.

* * *

The lecturer lifts her weary head. It feels as if her head is filled with voices, as if the voices of Kanna and his people – voices that speak of judgement and injustice and a futile return – become part of her thoughts. She has a headache.

I am also a Kanna, she thinks. I can't help these people. And I can't teach with this anger in me; I will fail Duduzile Nkulu immediately if I have to mark anything of hers again. Let me forget that I ever searched for and bought this book!

She picks up the book and drops it in the waste-paper basket under her desk. She pauses for a moment, then bends and removes it again. She stands up, walks out of her office, down the passage to outside. She walks the few steps to the blue bin clamped to the pole – a bin full of papers, banana peels, crushed cool-drink cans, cigarette butts – and lets it fall.

MARLENE VAN NIEKERK

Labour

Translated from the Afrikaans by Michiel Heyns.

My sister who knows about gardening is standing with her hands on her hips surveying the wilderness surrounding my new house, 'a nifty little piece of property', according to my father.

She clearly finds nothing nifty about it. Inside the house itself she has already thrown up her normally all-capable hands in despair.

'Look,' she says, 'your single greatest problem here is going to be labour. It's expensive and it's complicated. That is to say if you can find it. Because on Saturdays they're drunk, and during the week you can't leave them here on their own, they'll rob you blind. Whatever you do, don't get people off the street, get a gardening service. And for inside you get a cleaning service. Avoid private employment, it's looking for trouble.'

'Yes,' says my brother, 'Cape coloureds, you can't trust them. One day they're all sweetness and light and the next day they switch just like that.' He swivels his hand in the air like an oar to show how they switch.

'You know I was building at my place and then out of the blue one day eight of them pinned me against the wall, in broad daylight. Because their contractor didn't pay them out of the money he got from me. And he just shrugs, the scumbag. So you'd better beware of contractors as well. It's a no-win situation with labour in this country.'

I discuss my plans for home and garden with my parents.

'Just be careful about who you employ, my child,' says my father.

'And keep the doors locked at all times,' says my mother. 'Remember, you're a woman alone.'

Woman alone rummages in her not yet unpacked crates and boxes looking for the warning sign that protected her for ten years against thieves, murderers and rapists. She sticks it in a prominent place against the sitting-room window, with the message to the outside. 'This property is protected by snakes.'

Under the English, the text is rendered also in some or other African language, she doesn't know which one. She grimaces at her own complicity in the ethnographic slandering of the lower orders: that's how they spit, that's how they mourn, that's how scared they are of frogs and snakes.

Well, at least she can say she doesn't own a firearm. And she'll never acquire one either. She can't kill. She can only bluff with pictures of flat-head cobras.

In her mother tongue there is no end to the snake. He goes on his belly in the dust. From him are descended all the laws and commandments of labour. In the sweat of your brow you shall toil all the days of your life.

She used to do all her own gardening. But now she is forty-six. She has tennis elbow and a bad back. And she can no longer give it everything she's got. She is dependent on labour. But she's not scared.

She'll be cautious and correct. Firm and friendly, with distance. She'll make firm arrangements about time, about money, about the use of the toilet. She'll give good food and regular refreshments, a bonus for commendable work. She won't let herself be caught with clever talk, loafing or cheeky behaviour. With her work is work, period.

'Look,' says the estate agent who sold me my house, 'you're welcome to use my gardener. I have first call on him on Saturdays, he knows that, but if you arrange it with me, you can have him. Or otherwise during the week. He's very reliable, and experienced, has been working in florists' gardens for years. And main thing, he's dry. But you're not allowed to pay him more than R45 a day, and he may not work more than three days a week and you may not fetch him from the farm. On Koelenhof station. It's sensitive, you see. He lives and does odd jobs on the farm, and then he gets a disability on top of that, because of his back so-called, and he may not earn too much, else he'll lose it. And then the farm owner's wife is my best friend, she does the flowers for all my clients, so I really don't want any trouble.'

The agent smiles sweetly. She told me once that they are the only agency in town that opens every morning with scripture and prayer. And it works, she assures me, they make a profit.

Because it's the first time, I collect Piet from the farm. The farm has a whitewashed gateway and flags and an estate logo. Cheep cheep cheep, go the sprinklers as far as the eye can see over the vineyards. Next to the gateway another entrance leads to the labourers' cottages. Piet is waiting for me at his garden gate. We shake hands.

'Piet, how is your back?' I ask, 'I don't want you to damage it any further.'

Piet laughs. 'No what, madam,' he says, 'if I stand with my legs nice and apart and I warm it up slowly then it lasts well. It's just when he gets cold, then things get bothersome around here.' He puts his hand on his coccyx.

'That's your sacrum,' I say, 'I have it too, but I'm not taking chances any more. Are you up to digging ditches, Piet? I have to install irrigation.'

Piet gets into the car before replying. 'Depends,' he says.

'On what?'

'Depends on what the madam is going to pay me.' Piet looks at me with an unabashedly calculating smile.

'Well,' I say, and put my cards on the table. I tell him the agent's whole story. Around me I can feel the labour situation congealing.

His reaction is direct. 'That's a bloody stingy woman, that one, madam knows. She'll tell you anything just not to spend money.'

Piet has a scar next to his mouth and tattoos on his arms. 'Friends are few,' I read aloud. 'Where did you get that?' I ask.

'In jail,' he says, 'but I'm on the straight and narrow now. Twelve years since I've had a drop over my lips.'

'Yes,' I say, 'so I've been told.'

Piet laughs. The negotiations are in full swing, that we both know. I push the Volkswagen hard in order to stay ahead.

'Fasten your safety belt, Piet,' I say, 'you never can tell.'

'Nice little car the madam drives,' Piet grins, 'madam doesn't perhaps want to sell it to me?'

At home we reach an agreement. R80 from nine to five. Because it's not routine work, because it's basic installation.

'It's the whole infrastructure,' I hear myself say, 'ditches, holes, carting around wheelbarrowsful of soil, sawing off branches, digging out rocks, it's hard work and hard work must be rewarded accordingly. But it stays between the two of us, not so, Piet? I don't want trouble. And the madam agent has first call on your Saturdays, you understand? It's thanks to her that you're here in the first place, okay?'

'That's fine, madam,' he says. 'We do that.'

He looks at the snake warning in the window. 'Hmmm,' he says, 'clever that, does it work?'

'What do you want for lunch, Piet?' I ask at one o'clock.

He leans on his spade, his whole face one great wrinkle of enjoyment, I don't even want to guess at all the possible reasons.

'Fancy, madam will probably think it's funny, but I don't really eat meat, I'm actually a salad man. Especially in the afternoon, it keeps me nice and light and lively, madam follows?'

Madam follows quite well and she goes off to make, with a dedication that she doesn't understand herself, a delicate and well-dressed little salad, and arranges it on the garden table with a bottle of balsamic vinegar and a bottle of olive oil and a big jug of fruit juice with ice.

All of the first day and the days following Piet works without a break. She sees no sign of a bothersome back. He's quick and he's accurate and he gives excellent advice on all sorts of matters. He gets the compost heap going in a few days and he prunes back the fig tree to manageable proportions. Every evening she gives him a Voltaren tablet from her own supply to drink after his supper for his back that will be cold and aching by then. And his eight new ten-rand notes and more food and fruit to eat at home. They enjoy each other, the woman and the labourer. He is a genuine gardener, she discovers, with a well-developed aesthetic sense. She is touched by the fact that he brings her cuttings and roses from his own garden.

'For a bit of colour,' he says, 'it's still so bare there in the madam's garden, but we'll get there, just give us a break.'

Piet works three days a week and also every other Saturday. And he rubs his hands over the alluring salads she concocts for him. He tells her that the agent is working overtime over weekends and is not at home to issue orders and doesn't need him for the time being. She finds it unnecessary to check these details with the agent.

One fine day she phones.

'I must have a serious talk to you about Piet,' she says. 'You're paying him too much. He now wants R10 an hour from me as well. And he says he's working for your sister in Paarl as well on some Saturdays, also for R10 an hour. So what is this? I thought we had an understanding? And for the rest I hear you go and fetch him from the farm every day. The other workers are grumbling, they know he gets an allowance and they won't think twice about reporting him. You don't understand, there's a lot of jealousy amongst these people. You're obviously not clued up on the situation here in the Boland. And furthermore, I know he likes lettuce, but now he's asking me where's the cheese and the olives and the dark brown vinegar. You're setting a dangerous precedent here. You don't know what it can unleash. You have to play according to the rules here, or you get taken for a ride, more often than not by the workers themselves. They have no loyalty and no respect. Just remember that in future.'

The setter of precedents is left with her head in her hands. She has a sudden backache. She takes a pill and decides not to say anything, to stop the train there and then. How could the man go and do such a thing? He's never worked for her sister in Paarl, and the olives, well olives in salad are a vanity and an acquired taste, she herself was surprised that they weren't left in the bowl. It was meant as a gesture, a kind of joke really, one that she thought he could appreciate because he's certainly not backward. It was a salad in quotation marks, one might say. In exchange for the cuttings, for the expert gardening advice, for the steaming compost heap, for the roses. You can't pay for things like that, can you? He did them from the goodness of his heart, she felt, and they asked for some kind of recompense. A thought rises to surface in her head, but she can't altogether get hold of it. Perhaps the roses were also in quotation marks – triple, quadruple ones.

She decides to leave them both just there without any explanations, the labourer and the estate agent, because she did murmur something about tea and cake, a literary afternoon. Scripture reading with client relations, she thinks now. The angels are posted with burning brands at the gates of her garden, she thinks. And it's high summer, perhaps in any case too hot to try and get the garden going now. She decides to concentrate on the interior for the time being. She phones a cleaning service.

'Hello, Northwest Breeze here,' says a long-suffering woman's voice.

'I'll bring my girls right over to you, I've taught them myself and I supervise them myself, every moment of the day. You never know with these people, we clean where you can never reach yourself: windows, cellars, gutters, garages. And we're used to everything, you'll never believe what my two eyes have seen in my day, you wouldn't say it's white people, sometimes I get quite ashamed before the girls and, you know, they notice everything, every single thing. How many people in your household, if I may enquire, Mrs ...?'

'I live on my own,' I say, 'I don't have a lot of stuff.'

'Oh, I beg your pardon, miss, then, in that case, it's R90 for the first time and R80 if it's regular.'

Within the hour they're there, piling rowdily out of a light-blue Cortina. There they are on her front stoep, with their vacuum cleaners and brooms and crates full of cloths and brushes.

'This is Gladys and Sophie and Dolla and Florence, all my little breezes together,' says Mrs Uys. 'Where they've blown it's clean as a whistle. What do you say, Dolla, you're my mainstay, not so? Come on, don't you greet the madam? Come, nicely now, "Good afternoon, Miss!"'

Dolla fixes her stare on the ground with a fuck-you expression on her face. 'Nnmiss-h' she mumbles under her breath.

'Mainstay, noway!' says Sophie, and sends a rich wad of phlegm arching over her shoulder splat on the garden path.

'Keep that trap of yours shut,' mumbles Dolla, 'and watch where you spit.'

'Hey, good hea-vens, what kind of ugly talk is this in front of the miss?' says Mrs Uys. 'You'll make her send us away before we've even started!'

The women stink of sweat and old cigarettes. Their clothes are in tatters underneath the pink dustcoats they're wearing. I see swollen eyes, a lip bruised blue and black. To a woman they are sullen and jibbing. One complains of a headache. Mrs Uys distributes Panados. 'For everybody, while we're about it,' she says and winks at me.

Another one displays a bloody cut on her finger, sustained at the previous house. The madam takes out the Band Aid. She casts glances at me implying comprehension, confidential, conspiratorial.

'Just like children they are,' she talks at me in a low voice. 'This is just their way of showing off in front of new people, it's just shyness, it will be all over just now.'

I pretend not to hear. I don't want to hear. How can she say such things in front of them?

'So where are the snakes?' Gladys asks me, with a face that says, 'Right on, ignore her, the old cunt.'

'What snakes?' I ask.

'Them!' Sophie jabs a quick index finger at the warning.

Mrs Uys is wide awake, it seems. She winks advice at me. I follow it without quite knowing why. I'm ashamed of my doubleness of heart, but my tongue is even more forked.

'Oh,' I say, 'them. Locked up in the study. You needn't clean in there.' Nobody is going in there, I've decided in advance. Better not cast my chaos of scribblings and scraps to the winds. Just in case I locked my handbag with cell phone and wallet in there as well. What the eye does not see, as my mother would say, the heart cannot desire.

You can't even trust the idioms, I think, removing Jackson Hlongwane's three-footed angel from Gladys's hurricane-like progress through my sitting room.

'Rainbow Warrior' the vacuum machines are called. The women poke the black trunks fiercely into every corner and behind every bed and wardrobe. When they see me watching, they mockingly mimic an exaggerated fear of snakes. When the vacuum cleaners now and again cease their noise I hear them name the things in my house. From the various rooms the voices sound.

'Second bedroom,' I hear.

And, from my bedroom, giggling, 'Co'look, the miss has a queensize. Cloud Nine, I say.' I hear my new mattress being whacked with the flat of a hand. The old one is stored in the garage. But to which of the four does one give it? Solomon himself couldn't solve this one.

'Eight-seater,' says one from the dining room. I smell Woodoc.

'Wall to wall,' shrieks another one.

'Chest freezer.' That's Dolla in the kitchen. I hear her slam the lid with gusto. Why would she have opened it? I wonder. And then again, why not? It wasn't locked.

Then, suddenly, from the bathroom, from the toilet, a harmony in two voices, as if they'd rehearsed it: 'Light the lights, close the doors, we're staying home tonight.'

We're of the same generation, I think. Beyond that I don't want to think too much about the implications of the song. They have me taped, that's all I know, my whole story is as clear as daylight to them.

It's half-time. I spread thick slices of bread with the syrup and peanut butter I acquired with a view to Piet's coming. I make big mugs of tea with lots of sugar.

'What do they eat?' Sophie asks with a mouth full of bread and a bold stare.

'What does who eat?'

'The snakes!' they yell in unison. They bend double in glee, heads to one side, buttocks in the air. They screech with open mouths full of bread.

'Oh,' I say, 'white mice, tame ones, from the pet shop.'

'Mouse, mouse, pudding and pie!' They grab at each other's crotches.

'Shame on you, behave yourselves!' the madam scolds. She looks apologetically at me. I ignore her. I improvise with a straight face and an ironic tone. Perhaps in this way I can find favour in their eyes. I shall make my lies visible. Then I will be safe.

'How many?' asks Gladys.

'Two. Michael and Raphael. They're brothers.'

'How big?'

I measure out four long paces on the Novilon in the kitchen.

'Hot stuff!' I hear behind my back.

'How thick?'

'Like that,' I say, and show with my two hands.

'Lord, have mercy!' they scream. 'So thick!' They use their hands. They stroke the snakes.

'He's coming, he's coming!'

'He's going to spit!'

'Every two weeks,' I say, 'I let them loose in the garden at the back so that they can catch squirrels. They have a bit more meat to them than the mice. And they wriggle. The snakes like that, a bit of resistance, otherwise they get depressed.'

'Yow,' says Dolla, 'what's the miss saying?'

'The miss is saying everything,' I say, 'fucking everything.'

Nobody takes any notice of my confession. It looks as if nobody has even heard it.

They yell with laughter, wriggle their bodies out of the back door onto the stoep. The wriggle borders on a ribald dance step. The power of the humiliated, I think.

'Do they bite people as well?' asks one, all sham innocence.

'Yes,' I say, 'of course, otherwise what's the point? Here, this is where they bite, here, on the heel, right there.' I crook my fingers around my heel to demonstrate snake fangs. I don't care any more, I have abandoned myself to insinuation, to try to save myself, to my fate, to embrace it.

I give them a bag of figs from my own tree to take along, counting the fruit carefully so that nobody should have more than her share.

'You're getting very spoiled here, aren't you?' says the Breeze. 'Have you all said thank you nicely?'

'Thank you, miss!' they shout in a little mocking chorus over their shoulders. With a deft foot one rubs the spit on the garden path into an unrecognisable blotch.

The work provider winks at me when she takes her cheque. I see how intently the women follow the cheque's progress into her handbag.

'Where in god's name do you find these people?' I ask her softly behind their backs.

'I collect them from the squatter camp, just the other side of Kuils River. And let me tell you something today, Miss, they're only too grateful, believe you me, only too glad and grateful, that somebody wants to come and collect them for work. They have strings of children, all of them, but the fathers you'll never clap eyes on.'

Sincerely, meaningfully, matter-of-factly, she smiles. A businesswoman with a heart. I shut the door quickly. It's just too many expressions on a single face. It's a mixture that could cause a revolution in Kuils River. Why doesn't it happen? I think. Why not?

Suddenly a brilliantly bloodthirsty fantasy blossoms in my mind. A quick grip, strong hands throttling and wrenching, blood against the windscreen of the Cortina, handbag eviscerated, Rainbow Warriors gone with the wind scouring the shacks, no word breathed about it. I think of Pirate Jenny in Nina Simone's version.

Winter comes. The branches and rocks that Piet piled up in front of the house must be carted away. I want to keep it anonymous. I phone the municipality.

'We no longer do that, lady, we contract out,' says a stolid man at the other end.

'Too many contractors,' I say. 'Don't you know a private person who can do it for me quickly?' 'Painlessly,' I want to add, but I don't. The mouth is too secret not to feel pain.

'There's a woman in Vryburger Street,' he says. 'She's cheap. She has her own truck. Take down the number.'

And so I get to phone Beauty du Toit.

Somebody with a clumsy tongue answers the phone. Can Beauty be drunk? I wonder, and for a moment consider putting down the receiver. That would be too much. After the picture-of-piety Breeze, the inebriated Beauty.

'Is that Beauty?'

'No this is Beauty's mother speaking. Beauty is not here at the moment. Can I perhaps take a message for Beauty?'

The sentences take a long time coming. Not only because the tongue is heavy. The voice dips and flounders with subservience, perhaps from a stroke, from strickenness. Poor whites in Vryburger Street. My curiosity carries the day. I want to see Beauty. I leave a message. Beauty must please come, here is the address. She must come and cart away my rubbish, it's a mess in front of my house, has been for months now. My neighbours look down their noses. This is a tidy neighbourhood.

A few hours later she turns up, corpulently brave and lightly moustached, with a heart of gold. She drives a rickety truck with a rickety trailer. In the back of the truck are three old men with puffy eyes. Baggy pants, liquor breaths. God help us.

Slowly, as if they are afraid their arms will break, they load my branches. They grope carefully like chameleons amongst the thorns. For a long time they ponder the heavy rocks. What would be their considerations? I wonder.

'I'm urgently looking for people to work in my garden,' I say. I sound to myself as if I am pleading. It sounds like a confession. 'I want to prepare it for spring, you see.' That sounds totally inappropriate. You can no longer say even the most ordinary things with a clear conscience in this country. It's almost as if you can only quote. I had a garden in Africa. I wanted a garden in Africa. We used to have a garden in Africa. Roses, foxgloves, snowdrops, blue forget-me-nots. Richman poorman beggarman thief. 'I'm looking for reliable labour,' I say.

'I have that,' says Beauty, 'but not these, these you have to watch all the time or nothing happens, as you can see for yourself. Is your husband around?'

She speaks loudly. They can hear everything. What in god's name must they think of it? I also speak loudly.

'No, he's not here at the moment,' I say. 'He gets home from work quite late in the evenings.'

'Never mind,' she says, 'I don't even have one any more. That's why I have to make a go of it on my own. I have my mother as well, you understand. But what's the use of complaining? And there are many who are even worse off. That's what I tell myself all the time. You have to count your blessings. Do you want to come along to the dumps? Then you can see all the places I get to.'

Friendly. Gullible. Unsuspecting. Am I the only one with agendas? I go along on the spur of the moment. Perhaps there will be old bricks that I can use as a border for my flowerbeds. In the front of the truck is a little boy with a grater of a voice and sores around his mouth.

'My grandson,' says Beauty. 'I get to look after him as well, never a dull moment.' Beauty slaps the outside of the truck with the flat of her hand. 'Hold on!' she shouts backwards to the chameleons.

'The other day one fell off, broke his leg. You won't believe me, the trouble I have with the people, and you see what they look like, just about broken with hardship. But perhaps it's all for the best. With me they earn enough to stay alive and I don't have to be scared of them. People often ask me, "Now Beauty, aren't you scared to be on the road day after day with this class of people?" But I believe the Lord has me in his keeping. And it's not as if I'm just going to lie down and give in. They've never tried anything with me. Or with my mother. But I'm a bit worried about her because they come and ask her for bread when I'm out during the day, and you know she can't say no.'

I look back. The old men like bundles of rags amongst the branches. Only the rough hands and the dull gleam of eye slits betray the presence of bodies.

'Do you hear that?' asks Beauty as we turn into the worn-out dirt road of the dump.

'I don't hear anything,' I say. 'What should I listen for?'

She points with her head towards a bunker-like concrete structure half-hidden in the reeds and Port Jackson trees. 'The dog pound,' she says, 'now there's something that keeps me awake at night. For a fortnight they bark away there in the kennels and if they still haven't found homes then, they get put down, too terrible, I tell you, I drive past here every day and then I hear it and then sometimes I can't stand it anymore and then I go and fetch another one. Dear little things, terribly neglected but just a few days' love and mealie meal then they're cock of the walk again. Then people even want to buy them from me. I find it hard to part from them.'

We drive along picturesque heaps of refuse. Everywhere there are black men and women in ragged clothes chipping away at bricks to clean them. Beauty greets a tanned white man stripping old TV sets. His black T-shirt is dusty and patched with sweat.

'I'm just going to dump the branches a bit further up,' says Beauty. 'It gets a bit grungy further along. Why don't you wait here so long with Gerrie, I won't be long.'

Suddenly I'm standing in the dust under a poisonously hot sun. It's about ten degrees too hot for the time of year. Around us hovers a stench that varies its nature from moment to moment, smelling of fish, of meat, of peels still fermenting, of a more general older smell of the already rotten almost returned to dust, the sweet rich smell of first-world compost.

It's an upside-down world, I think, as Gerrie extends his hand to me and shakes mine firmly. Here, for some or other reason, I am formally welcomed by an upside-down Hephaistos. Not a smithy of the underworld but a gatherer in a throw-away zone. He looks tough and strong. It's just his voice that is wheedling.

'I do it for my son, you see, madam, and it was plain luck that I got the tender. This town's municipality is too broke to work their own dumps. So now I get this little lot that you see here to work for half-shares. They take home some of what they clear and I keep enough to help my son.'

I look where he points. Some distance away I see a man loading old crates onto the back of a truck. 'Yes, that's him, just get a look at that pair of shoulders! You see, madam, he's a champion wrestler just like me in my day. But to get into the Olympic Games he has to go and wrestle his qualifying rounds in a tournament in Tunisia and so now I'm helping him get together the money for it. He works for the police and you know they get paid peanuts.'

The man is tying the crates to the truck with ropes. I see his muscles bulge. One, two big steps and he's on top of the crates. With the tremendous levers of his thighs he tramples a few underfoot to make space for more. The chunks of plastic crack and splinter under his feet. He looks huge against the sky. Behind him rise the blue blue mountains of the Boland. I look at his firm buttocks, the athletic dents in his hips, as he works. He's wearing old tracksuit pants with holes in them and a bedraggled T-shirt. The prime condition of the body in the old clothes looks comical. Like a circus or a Beckett play. But his face is too unambiguous for any play.

'So how much do you make out of this?' I ask.

'About R500 if we pack it well, they weight it at the other end.' He is friendly and helpful and answers my questions without a trace of suspicion or cynicism, as befits an Olympic hero.

'I manage to get together about three loads a week, I have to dig it out of the rubbish, it takes time and then I work shifts at the station and weekends I bounce a bit.'

'Bounce?'

'Yes, at the coloured clubs where things get rough. But I don't take nonsense. If there's trouble I bounce whole bunches of them. With the women you have to be a bit more careful, but often it's they who start it all. My orders are not to say a word and I bounce only on command.'

'And how much do you get for that?'

'I manage to clear about two fifty a night and at the clubs where the gangs go a bit extra danger pay.'

I hear a hooting. It's Beauty come to collect me.

'Shame,' she says, 'the poor guy, his wife dropped him three months ago because he was never at home. But all he wanted to do was work so that they could get ahead in the world. And all she wanted to do was sit at home with folded hands, lady at large waiting for her prince on a white horse to come home. She didn't even want to cook the pasta and steak he had to eat for his wrestling. She just wanted the limelight if he won. His dream is to open a school of wrestling in town. Proper wrestling, you know, not freestyle, he insists on that point. He lives for his wrestling, that young man.'

The next day I go to fetch the labourers that Beauty has organised for me.

'Jan and Simon from the night shelter,' she introduces me to the two on the pavement of Vryburger Street. 'You'd be surprised at what good people you find in the shelter. Many come from the farms where the farmers can't pay them under the new laws any more. So they know about work and they'll do anything now, won't they, because you can't fill your stomach with laws, not so, you two?'

The tone is friendly and patronising and directed half at them and half at me. Jan and Simon nod in feigned meekness. I feel Jan searching my face for signs of an understanding. Beauty clearly has the power of the mediator here. Without her presence, today would have been only another empty hungry day. I can see them assessing me. Will I overrule the mediator? Is there a possibility of more permanent work here and more money? What will the language sound like in which they summarise me? In which they discuss me?

I look at them. Jan is light of colour, with curly hair. He looks like me. He feels like family in a way. There is something mocking in his glance, but it's no longer sharp. It's misted over with equanimity and interest. Simon is dark and quiet. He says nothing, but he's thinking something, I can see that.

'But the madam drives half-and-half fast with the little beetle!' says Jan.

'So you're from Caledon?' I ask, pleased to find something concrete to interrupt my directionless reflections.

'Hey, how does the madam know that?' His voice is all affectation, he mimics the tone in which his betters make insincere small talk. The power of the mimes, I think.

'Because you say "half-and-half fast". It's an expression of the region. I grew up there.'

'I see,' he says as we draw up in front of the house, 'and now the madam lives here all alone or are the madam's people here as well?'

I see him register the size of the house.

'My people live around here,' I say, and then add, because I feel that more details are expected and because I feel it is time for bluffing, 'but my friend is coming tonight, he works late, and he has to feed the snakes.'

I point at the sign. Jan ignores the information with a light snort. I shouldn't try to bluff him, I realise. He doesn't find it funny. And he clearly is not satisfied yet. And why should he be? Aren't we from the same area, and haven't I confided our affinity to him? Half-and-half-quick, half-and-half clever.

'Husband or friend?' he asks in a meaningful way.

Simon looks up quickly and then down again.

I pretend not to hear, explain the work, show where the tools are stored and go inside, bolt the door, draw the sitting-room curtains.

Husband or friend, I think, what business is it of his? I feel mildly upset. I phone my lover.

'Mrs Robinson,' I say, 'why don't you come and visit me today at some point, the people working in the garden make me nervous. Bring your son along.'

'You're paranoid,' she says, 'but I'll come, I've made a photo of figs for you, blown up, I thought it would amuse you, it's quite sexy.'

Mrs Robinson has no problems with labour. She is a practical woman. She drives a combi and issues orders in accordance with the prevailing rules. She leaves the house when the Northwest Breezes come to work for her because she doesn't like to see them, she says. The poor, she says, we'll always have with us. Then we almost quarrel. Then I say: 'They turn me into a liar and hypocrite, they make me feel guilty and alone. They immediately know everything about me without asking a single question. They ask if I have old clothes, an old mattress, a few sheets of corrugated iron. The flowers that I throw out they take home in newspaper, and the next time they come they're wearing the shoes that I put into the black bag, with their heels peering out like the mortal remains of my conscience.'

Then she says, 'Heavens, but do you ever sound like a writer again today. Have you taken your St John's Wort yet?'

Through a chink in the curtain I peep at them working. It's hard work.

They sweat copiously. I look at my watch, eleven o' clock, time for a break. I take out large beer mugs of Oros and ice.

'Just hang on, madam,' says Jan and removes his shirt ostentatiously.

'There we are,' he says and takes the mug from my hand, drinks with thirsty gulps so that the syrup runs down his chin. It's a spectacle put on just for my sake, I feel. I look at his body. On the soft part of his belly, just above his navel is tattooed: 'Fear not for the Angel of the Lord is with thee'. I know I shouldn't say anything, but I nevertheless say: 'Geez, didn't that hurt?'

'Madam,' he says, 'what could I do? I had it written so that I could feel I was still alive.'

I refrain from comment, go into the house again, peer through the curtain. Simon also takes off his shirt. They say something I can't make out and laugh salaciously. I'm convinced it's about me. Perhaps they suspect that I'm standing here behind the ostentatiously drawn curtain. And why am I peeping? I think, if I really want to see anything I can just go and look. What is it that I don't want to meet face to face?

There where I'm having the devil's grass taken out to construct a gravel garden to save water, they're loading the sods onto the wheelbarrow. They take turns to pack and cart away. The wheelbarrow is heavy. Hup! Jan strains over the furrow, hup! One more time to negotiate the edge of the garden path. The wheel blocks. I watch them devise a ramp up and a ramp down with bricks. Old hands with a blocked wheel. Tricks of the trade.

One o'clock. They dig a trench for the picket fence for the herbaceous border. Their muscles wrench with the effort of the pickaxe in the clay soil. The skin over the ribs ripples and tenses. The gullets jump up and down with the effort and with the swallowing down and scraping away of old slimes, of years of smoking cheap tobacco in newspaper, of TB probably. Of harsh whooping coughs as a child. Five-days-a-week bodies. Now and again resting on the spade, on the pickaxe, they survey their progress. Fifty rand's worth of progress, a week's supply of wine and cigarettes. Spit, spit in the trench. Only this liquid curse has remained. They grab, grasp the spade again, the spade by its handle, the pickaxe by its shaft, and fling their bodies at the herbaceous border trench. Both work up a disconcerting cough. The progress slows down as the afternoon moves on. I bring strong coffee with lots of sugar.

'You mustn't over-exert yourselves,' I say, and hear my own voice sounding in my ears. 'You must say if you want to knock off,' I try to correct myself.

'No, we're holding out, madam, we're holding out, we're going to beat it, this little ditch.'

My friend comes to visit with her still life of figs in a cellophane wrapping.

'My, but you're energetic, aren't you!' she says as she walks up the garden path.

I get a hug and a kiss and have to inspect the figs before we go through the front door.

'Don't be like that with me in front of these people,' I say. 'I don't want them to know my whole story.'

'Oh nonsense, what do they know?' she says.

'They know everything. They look right through you.'

'You're imagining things again.' She looks at me. 'That's why I like you so much, because you have such an active imagination.'

She has taken a photo of me with a chameleon on my shoulder. She tends to think we are in paradise. She persists in thinking this even though a saucepan of stewed quinces is stolen from her stove while she is hanging out the washing. Now she has made photocopies of my snake warnings and put them up all over her house. 'So, is that the madam's sister, then?' asks Jan when she has left.

'Yes,' I say, 'that is my sister.'

'No, I'm asking because it feels half-and-half like family but it doesn't look like family. Me too, I just feel like family, the madam knows, there where I come from I wasn't my mother's child or my father's child, I was a throw-away. So they took me in. Didn't treat me nice, my father. So when I was sixteen I took him by the chest and thrashed him good and proper and from then on it was downhill all the way with me. But now I'm in the shelter and that helps. We support each other a bit there.'

I pack food for Jan and Simon to take with them – cooked sausage, a tin of beans each, fruit, bread. I praise them for their labour. I'm very satisfied, I say. I ask if they're satisfied. They nod politely.

The next day I collect Jan in Vryburger Street again. Simon can't come because Beauty needs him for a removal in town. With him Jan has a small toothless yellow woman wearing a scarf. I have seen her before with him in the neighbourhood, and now, like then, she waves at me exuberantly as if she knows me well. I try to remember, but I don't know her. It's impossible, I've only been back for a few months in the town where I spent my youth. Perhaps she remembers me from way back, I think. It happens to me all the time, that people greet me whose faces I recognise but whose names I've forgotten. Just before Jan bends down to get into the Volkswagen, she taps him on the shoulder from behind and pouts her little mouth at him, her eyes shut tight. I can't believe what I see. Jan from the night shelter with the angel of the Lord carved on his stomach turns to her, takes her face between his hands, and plants a tender kiss on her mouth.

'So who's that, Jan?' I ask when I can no longer contain myself.

'No, how shall I say to madam, she's also from the shelter, I'm half-and-half very fond of that one but how shall I say, actually I'm sorry for her because you know she's been deaf and dumb from birth.'

Jan speaks freely, it doesn't seem to bother him that I interrogate him.

'And it's a nuisance because everybody uses her as they like, she can't scream, you know. Just the other day I had to shovel someone off her with a garden fork. But then it's her own fault too, because let me tell madam this, now there's a girl who can knock it back. I've told her I'm going to leave her if she carries on like that.'

'Heavens, Jan, what are you telling me now?'

'No, madam knows, I give her just one look like this then she knows which way the wind's blowing, but I understand her when she shows me like this.' He shows me how she shows him.

'I think I have, how shall I say? I think I have a how do they say? A talent for that girl.'

He tells me of his own accord how they found each other. There were three of them at first. Her husband was dying of TB and then he died. And because she couldn't talk he took mercy on her, interpreted for her to the doctor and the priest and the undertaker. And spoke the words at the grave as he understood them from her. Since then they've been together.

The work on the new garden is halfway when the first winter rains fall. The pergola is halfway up, the furrow for the picket hedge is full of rain water.

My sister calls to have a look.

'Lord, it looks as if you're building a sheep pen here,' she says.

My brother calls to have a look. 'Yes, well,' he says, 'you and your sister can never let well enough alone, always have to dig everything up and change it.'

My father phones. 'How is your gardening coming along, my child? Are you healthy? Just look well after your safety.'

July. It is snowing in Jonkershoek. I drive into the kloof to go and look at the snowfall from close by, come upon a little steenbok standing with a wet snout trembling against the wall of the pump station. She leaps away in confusion as I come around the corner. In her wake the silver-speckled fynbos branches swing back in a spray of drops. Away, away on delicate hooves. Why do I have such a need for a garden? I think. Here, here in front of me, scarcely ten minutes from my house, is the whole mountain in which I can walk to my heart's content. And what lives and grows there hasn't been collected, hasn't been woven, cultivated or irrigated. It is what it is, the ten thousand joys and sorrows, and it is good.

Back at home I find Simon standing in front of my door. I say but we didn't have an appointment I say I don't have work it's raining I say he mustn't come when we don't have an appointment and I only work through Beauty I say he knows she will say if I need someone that's the only way how it works I don't want people standing on my stoep at all times and any time.

He lets me have my say. He listens and looks at his shoes. Am I imagining it, or does he rock gently on his feet, forwards and back, like somebody in a high position listening to a long story from a subordinate?

Suddenly he looks at me straight on. His voice is also straightforward. 'I'm hungry,' he says. 'It's cold and I haven't eaten anything for three days.'

I smell the alcohol on his breath.

'Sorry,' I say. 'Sorry, there's nothing I can do about that. Where do you find money to drink?' He grins. I realise I've made a mistake. Pronounced the greatest cliché in the Boland. He gets his own back on me, changes his tone to the obsequious, pleading vernacular. He advances with the leverage of three centuries.

'Ag Lord madam,' he says, 'it's cold. Just give me a little piece of bread then please. Does the madam think I'll walk all the way from the shelter just to make a joke? They say it's going to rain for weeks, and then we garden boys can't find jobs. What am I supposed to eat?'

'I'm not your madam,' I say. 'My name is Marlene and if you want to be a boy that's your business.'

Why do you pick on me? I want to say. Why the fuck do you think I'm your customer? What exactly makes me look like a soft target to you? Why don't you go and ask Beauty?

But I don't say anything. Beauty is but skin deep, Beauty is as Beauty does. Or something like that.

I give him bread, I give him R30, I enforce parity, I want to make it into a formal arrangement, an agreement between equals.

'This is an advance,' I say. 'You owe me a few hours of work. Is that clear? Do we have a deal?'

'We have a deal,' he says.

I shake his hand. How else do you make a deal as woman alone? I see his shoes. The toes gape open. How does one make a deal with a shoeless person? What is the meaning of a handshake between somebody with an empty stomach and somebody who gets off on snow-covered peaks?

'Do you want a lift back to the shelter?' I ask. My voice sounds hollow.

He only nods. 'Fasten your safety belt,' I tell him as he gets into the car.

Then I have to laugh. Safety belt. I ask you. I laugh and I laugh.

He grins.

I say nothing. I laugh like a clockwork gadget that's running down, less and less, till I've run down.

'If Jan had been here,' says Simon, 'Marlene knows what he would've said? He'd have said: "Now what is now so half-and-half funny, madam?"'

EBEN VENTER

Tinktinkie

Translated from the Afrikaans by Mariëtte Postma.

Rose at the crack of dawn on the Sabbath Day to prevent Ouma from nagging him for going out to potter about with his pigs. Shorts, Adidas, same shirt from last night. His keys. He did not use the toilet. Ouma would be lying awake already. Lying there, closed eyes, thinking of the end awaiting her around the corner.

In the kitchen Patience and Kasi were busily at work. They were watching the mealie porridge and peeling the apples to be stewed for the afternoon. The peels fell neatly into a small basin. Always keeping everything neat as a pin. He greeted them and they greeted him back. Tinktinkie noticed a pudding bowl with prunes below a net and nicked one for himself. Took care that the screen door did not slam shut behind him.

The women in the kitchen liked the little man. He never got in their way. He just followed his own path. He was different. Once he grew up, he would get the farm back into shape, they were saying.

The morning was cold against his bare legs. He started to run. The dog didn't understand why she had to stay behind in the yard the last few weeks when he went to the pigs. But Tinktinkie didn't want him sniffing and yapping close to his two young sows, they were both almost in farrow. Besides, the Landrace pig was already carrying the stress gene.

He heard Oom Dries saying that. Oom Dries allowed him to bring his two sows to his Chester White boar. Oom Dries said this cross-breeding would stand the heat better.

'You can start fattening up a little sucking-pig for your Tante Rebecca, ready for this Christmas.' And then Oom Dries touched him softly behind his neck. He only reached Oom Dries's belt as yet.

This was all Oom Dries wanted in return for the favour. Tinktinkie knew people cared for him a little bit more because he had lost his dad. He was only little and he already had his own farm going. He had five pigs altogether. He knew too what power this gave him. He could get what an ordinary farmer would have to dish out lots and lots of money for. Oom

Dries imported the Chester White seed from America. Tinktinkie wondered if what he was doing could perhaps be sinful.

He kept all along the water furrow below the willows that were just starting to bud. It was not really quite summer yet. Over the bare patch between the house and the pig sties a little wind was scattering past. A tattered rag, broken brick, pebbles and glass splinters. Some wire. He never managed walking across the bareness; it made him feel too poor.

The water furrow was barely going. No longer overflowing, day and night, down to the lucerne fields, the way he could remember from the time when he was still very young. Ouma said they should all pray for the fountain to last, for when it dried up, they could just as well start packing their bags and leave Koppiesfontein. At night Ouma sometimes smelled a little sour.

The pigs heard him coming. Three in a paddock close to the lucerne fields, each of the sows in her own farrow-pen. Aaida and Lolla were their names. When Oom Dries drove up there yesterday, taking stock of the two sows' condition he said: 'Upon my word, 'Tinkie, you can count on farrows of twelve or more.' His eyes started twinkling. 'There are young farmers in our district who should actually come and learn from you.'

Oom Dries pressed against the wall of the pigsty, supported himself with his huge male hands. He was a heavy man, this Oom Dries. One could hear it from his breathing.

'Have you heard about the pigs in Malaysia, 'Tinkie?' he asked while he was watching the sows.

'Nee, Oom Dries.'

'They had to kill off the whole country's pig population. Encephalitis. Transmitted to humans by the culex mosquito. It must have been a terrible massacre. Well yes, 'Tinkie, I should be going now. Fresh air, clean water and a balanced diet. But you know that already. Otherwise your pigs would not be looking the way they do.'

Tinktinkie scraped all the remaining bits from Aaida's feeding-trough, scrubbed the sides clean and watered it down with a hose. Then he washed the water trough and filled it up. He came to his feet when he heard people passing by along the road. They came to visit Patience and Kasi on foot and on bicycles. Dressed up in their Sunday best. Should he shove off? He didn't want to draw any attention to the pigs. He'd rather scram himself. The pig's snout was all around him. They knew him very well.

The sky was a dirty blue. It wasn't going to be hot today. 'My little children,' he said when he touched Aaida's swollen teats. She started eating the mealies and bone meal greedily. They should never be unnecessarily fat when with young; it could cause problems when birthing.

The corners of his eyes were still foggily covered in sleep. When he walked away he took a last look at the pigsty behind him: 'My little children,' he said once more. He quickly went to the tap outside to wash before he entered. Even though he knew it wasn't quite possible to rinse off everything that was clinging to him after having been with the pigs, that didn't put him off.

His mother was standing inside in her dressing gown with a Stuyvesant, looking out onto the flower garden. Would she have seen him at the tap?

'Morning, Mummy.'

'Morning,' she replied.

He waited for her to go on talking, but she'd turned back to the window. He went to sit at the table and reached for the toast with his hand. The kitchen door opened and swung shut behind Patience's buttocks and she placed his bowl of mealie porridge in front of him. Her hand touched his on the plastic table cloth. He looked her in the eye and gave her a smile. A lump of butter, sugar, milk. The radio was playing morning hymns. The culex mosquito. There were always mosquitoes around the farrow-pens once summer had started. What kept mosquitoes at bay?

Ouma came in, wearing her outfit for church. A mauve dress with mauve lace at the seam and high up against her bosom. With her she had her hymn book, Bible, mauve gloves and handbag with the peppermints and stuff. She placed her precious little bundle on the sideboard. Came and kissed him on the forehead. Scent and smell of bread dough.

'Did you ask the Lord for His grace on your porridge before you started to eat, Sonnie?'

'Yes, Ouma,' he lied. No need to pray on Sundays when you were going to church anyway.

'Aren't you sitting down to eat, Hendrien?' she asked in his mother's direction.

'I'll have something later, Mummy. I won't be going to church with you today.'

'You must let Kris be, Hendrien. He won't get up out of his grave. It was the Lord's will.'

'It's not that, Mummy,' she bit back. Tinktinkie sat there without touching the spoon of porridge at his mouth.

'You won't fool me, Hendrien. You are not leaving Kris alone there where he is now. You are being unfair to him. The Word says, leave the dead to the dead.'

'Ma, you are not going to tell me what to do in my own house.' Her hand fluttered. She wouldn't say anything else, Tinktinkie knew that already.

'I'm only trying to help,' Ouma said very softly and slowly buttered half a slice of toast.

His mom became funny after Daddy had been taken away. Chin on her chest. Two empty packets of Stuyvesant on the small table in front of the television, mornings when he came in. She never asked a thing about his pigs anymore.

With the two litters he should be able to buy himself a computer.

* * *

Remarkable, was the word that came to the Revd Tertius when he thought about this morning's sermon while sitting down at the table for breakfast. Words given unto him by the Higher Hand. But there was also a touch of nerves that he couldn't hide.

'What's wrong with you now, Tertius?' asked his wife when she put the bacon and eggs, mushrooms fried in garlic and scones down in front of him. Bes read him like a book.

'You must stick to the biblical text, Tertius. That's why the Lord has given you good brains. Don't drag politics into your sermon.'

Bes was irritated. In the living room the children, dressed in their Sunday best, were fighting over the new Nintendo. She felt that Tertius did not assert himself properly in this house.

Bes was a charming woman. She had grown up in Oranjezicht. 'You are cut out for modelling,' she had always been told in the Cape. Because of her slender waist. Legs up to her chin. Then she fell in love with the student minister. Must have been his legs that turned her head those days. His total unawareness of his own body. Now she was stuck here in the bloody sticks. And Tertius, who never said a thing about politics, was now off on a dangerous tangent.

Once, when he was balancing on the windowsill to cut his toenails, he turned to her in bed: 'They are going to kill off the last one of us. Nothing has changed. We're back to the days of the border wars. And these days the church is absolutely useless. Even here, Bes, you have to admit to it, the members of the congregation are bolting one after the other. Antjie Krog was spot-on with her remark: the Afrikaners have become totally irrelevant, politically and culturally.'

Head on her arm she lay there, looking at him. Shifted her bosom, grimaced. The tyre hanging over his underpants. Black body-hair creeping from his buttocks up his back. Never used to be there before. And what happened to his faith? His lovely smile?

'Small wonder they're bolting if their minister carries on like this.' She jumped up from the bed and opened the shower taps. She no longer wanted to hear him around her.

The church was not too empty. The weather offered no excuses for not attending.

Bes bent down to her children just before they started filing into the minister's pew: 'Behave yourselves now, or you can forget about your ice-cream today.'

Tinktinkie and Ouma sat in their usual spot in the western wing. Ouma's mauve glove rested lightly on his leg. He sucked a peppermint without anybody seeing or hearing him. If only the long prayer he had to stand for were over.

Since the carnage in the Kenilworth church a few years ago, they started locking the doors. Nobody even mentioned it anymore. Ouma always used to nudge him on the leg and wink when Oom Dries went out in the middle of the sermon for some fresh air under the privets. Now he was caged in. Behind them Tinktinkie could hear him having trouble breathing properly.

Matthew 8 verses 28 to 34 was the biblical passage that was read out from the old translation, from the pulpit. Where Jesus came upon the devil-possessed in Gergesa.

'And suddenly they shouted and said: what do we have to do with you, Jesus, Son of God?' And then followed the passage of the big herd of swine grazing close by. Tinktinkie listened. He heard how the devils had begged the Lord if He could please allow them to possess the swinery when He drove them out. And then the whole swinery stormed off the cliff – into the sea – and drowned.

'This is where the reading ends, brothers and sisters. Let us pray.'

Tinktinkie planted his little legs. The heat was fortunately not too bad yet. During the long prayer in summer spots and curls started swimming behind his eyelids because of having to stand so long. He tried to see them: they looked like the sea-horses at East London's aquarium.

'And Lord, we entrust our children to you, those who are working, but especially those who are struggling to find work …'

His pigs. He trusted the Koppiesfontein people, but he didn't really know about the visitors who came to see Patience and Kasi. They could break open his tiny little locks like nothing. That was what frightened him the most when he had to attend church: that one of his pigs would be missing when he came home. Please just let them spare Aaida, and Lolla's lives, he prayed silently during the prayer of the Revd Tertius.

'As Bible text, brothers and sisters, verse 29 was imprinted onto my heart: "and suddenly they shouted and said …" "Suddenly" is expressed here by the Greek word *idoù*. A strong word in the original text, a word demanding an exclamation mark. These people, these devil-possessed people, were therefore terribly frightened when they were confronted by Jesus.

'The Greek here refers to *légontes* which means a great number, rather like a sea of people. We can surely conclude that although only two devil-possessed are mentioned in Matthew, and only one in Mark and Luke, there were a multitude of devils present in these human beings or being. *Légontes!*' The Revd Tertius made his voice fly high. He reached the essence of his sermon. Beneath his jacket and waistcoat and shirt and vest he was wet through. He had anticipated this and used extra deodorant.

'And this great crowd of people shouted against Jesus. It has been written that they had shouted so loudly that it sounded like a croaking. This devilish sound came from the crowd, so that we can assume that the underworldly croaking sound straight from hell echoed over the beautiful meadow right next to the sea.'

Then the Revd Tertius came to the Greek sentence which he had understood as having special significance. He made a fist above the pulpit. 'What do we have to do with you, Jesus, Son of God?' And then, once more: 'What do we have to do with you, Son of God?'

Tinktinkie started fidgeting. And Ouma pressed another peppermint into his sweaty little palm.

'Brothers and sisters, we are here confronted with the powerful clash between the children of the devil and Jesus himself. Terrifying for the devils, this day, this moment when, despite their own devilish power, they face their own downfall.

'There is today in southern Africa – and more specifically in this beautiful and afflicted country of ours – an equally powerful manifestation of the devil himself. Brothers and sisters, I am talking here about AIDS. It is a virus that is decimating thousands, no, thousands upon thousands.'

Bes blushed and touched her cheeks, hoping that nobody noticed her reddening. Tertius was totally losing it. She knew where he was heading with this. He was going to distort the biblical text with his interpretation. And these fools were going to swallow every word of it. Dammit, the day would come, and that day was just around the corner, when she was going to pack her bags. Back to the Cape. Turn Ennio Morricone's music up just as loud as she wanted to. Tertius should be subjected to the process of censure by the Theological Council or whatever that lot of old fossils in Potchefstroom called themselves.

'The *Afrikaner* of 23 July 1999 reports that, according to the latest survey of UNAIDS, 8,9% of Swaziland's population have been contaminated with the HI-virus; 3,9% of Lesotho's just over two million people have been infected; and 6,5% of our country's population have been affected by the HI-virus. One hundred and forty thousand casualties caused by this virus have been reported in South Africa.

'Brothers and sisters, God does not sit still. We know today which population group here at the Southern Point of Africa is hit the hardest by this virus. God does not slumber or sleep, brothers and sisters.' The Revd Tertius's voice broke as he strove for an even higher tone of voice.

'This devilish virus shouted it out when it came into contact with the Almighty. "Go!" Jesus commanded the enormous number of devils. We know which part of South African society is affected most severely, brothers and sisters. The battle is not in vain, even though that is how it may seem. The end is near. Look out over the meadow and see who are spilling over the cliff into the sea. By the thousands.

'"Go!" Jesus ordered the devils. And the devils took possession of the swinery, the Greek refers here to *boskoméné*, pigs that have been fattened to the point of revulsion. And by the thousands these devilish swines are storming into the depths of the sea.'

Tinktinkie sat up straight as a ramrod. Kicked with his feet against the floor. His heart inside his shirt was going crazy, crazy with these things. He jumped off the pew and raised his hand high as if at school.

'Heavens, child,' hissed Ouma and pulled him down.

But Tinktinkie flared up again, threw his hand high into the air and yelled before anyone could stop him: 'But what about the little ones, Reverend, what about the little children?'

IVAN VLADISLAVIĆ

The WHITES ONLY Bench

Yesterday our visitors' book, which Portia has covered in zebra-skin wrapping-paper and shiny plastic, recorded the name of another important person: Coretta King. When Mrs King had finished her tour, with Strickland herself playing the guide, she was treated to tea and cakes in the cafeteria. The photographers, who had been trailing around after her trying to sniff out interesting angles and ironic juxtapositions against the exhibits, tucked in as well, I'm told, and made pigs of themselves.

After the snacks Mrs King popped into the gift shop for a few mementoes, and bought generously – soapstone hippopotami with sly expressions, coffee-table catalogues, little wire bicycles and riot-control vehicles, garish place mats and beaded fly-whisks, among other things. Her aide had to chip in to make up the cost of a set of mugs in the popular 'Leaders Past and Present' range.

The honoured guests were making their way back to the bus when Mrs King spotted the bench in the courtyard and suggested that she pose there for a few shots. I happened to be watching from the workshop window, and I had a feeling the photographs would be exceptional. A spring shower had just fallen, out of the blue, and the courtyard was a well of clear light. Tendrils of fragrant steam coiled up evocatively from a windfall of blossoms on the flagstones. The scene had been set by chance. Perhaps the photographers had something to prove, too, having failed to notice a photo opportunity so steeped in ironic significance.

The *Star* carried one of the pictures on its front page this morning. Charmaine picked up a copy on her way to work and she couldn't wait to show it to me.

The interest of the composition derives – if I may make the obvious analysis – from a lively dispute of horizontals and verticals. The bench is a syllogism of horizontal lines, flatly contradicted by the vertical bars of the legs at either end (these legs are shaped like h's, actually, but from the front they look like l's). Three other verticals assert their position: on the left – our left, that is – the concrete stalk of the Black Sash drinking fountain; in the middle, thrusting up behind the bench, the trunk of the controversial kaffirboom; and on the right, perched on the very end of her seat, our subject: Mrs King.

Mrs King has her left thigh crossed over her right, her left foot crooked around her right ankle, her left arm coiled to clutch one of our glossy brochures to her breast. The wooden slats are slickly varnished with sunlight, and she sits upon them gingerly, as if the last slat's not quite dry. Yet her right arm reposes along the backrest with the careless grace of a stem. There's an odd ambiguity in her body, and it's reflected in her face too, in an expression which superimposes the past upon the present: she looks both timorous and audacious. The WHITES ONLY sign under her dangling thumb in the very middle of the picture might be taken up the wrong way as an irreverent reference to her eyes, which she opens wide in an expression of mock alarm – or is it outrage? The rest of her features are more prudently composed, the lips quilted with bitterness, but tucked in mockingly at one corner.

The photographer was wise to choose black and white. These stark contrasts, coupled with Mrs King's old-fashioned suit and hairdo, confound the period entirely. The photograph might have been taken thirty years ago, or yesterday.

Charmaine was tickled pink. She says her bench is finally avenged for being upstaged by that impostor from the Municipal Bus Drivers' Association. I doubt that Strickland has even noticed.

There seems to be a tacit agreement around here that Mrs King is an acceptable form, although it won't do for anyone else. When I pointed this out, Charmaine said it's a special case because Mr King, rest his soul, is no more. I fail to see what difference that makes, and I said so. Then Reddy, whose ears were flapping, said that 'Mrs King' is tolerated precisely because it preserves the memory of the absent Mr King, like it or not. He said it's like a dead metaphor.

I can't make up my mind. Aren't we reading too much into it?

* * *

Charmaine has sliced the photograph out of the unread newspaper with a Stanley knife and pinned the cutting up on the notice board in Reception. She says her bench has been immortalised. 'Immortality' is easy to bandy about, but for a while it was touch and go whether Charmaine's bench would make it to the end of the week.

We were working late one evening, as usual, when the little drama began. The Museum was due to open in six weeks' time but the whole place was still upside down. It wasn't clear yet who was in charge, if anyone, and we were all in a state.

Charmaine was putting the finishing touches to her bench, I was knocking together a couple of rostra for the Congress of the People, when Strickland came in. She had been with us for less than a week and it was the first time she had set foot in the workshop. We weren't sure at all then what to make of our new director, and so we both greeted her politely and went on with our work.

She waved a right hand as limp as a kid glove to show that we shouldn't mind her, and then clasped it behind her back. She began to wander around on tiptoe, even though I was hammering in nails, swivelling her head from side to side, peering into boxes, scanning the photographs and diagrams pinned to chipboard display stands, taking stock of the contents of tables and desks. She never touched a thing, but there was something grossly intrusive about the inspection. Strickland wears large, rimless spectacles, double glazed and tinted pink, and they sometimes make her look like a pair of television monitors.

After a soundless, interrogative circuit of the room she stopped behind Charmaine and looked over her shoulder. Charmaine had just finished the 'I', and now she laid her brush across the top of the paint tin, peeled off the stencil and flourished it in the air to dry the excess paint.

I put down my hammer – the racket had become unbearable – and took up some sandpaper instead. The people here will tell you that I don't miss a thing.

Strickland looked at the half-formed word. Then she unclasped her hands and slid them smoothly into the pockets of her linen suit. The cloth was fresh cream with a dab of butter in it, richly textured, the pockets cool as arum lilies.

'What are you doing?' Strickland asked, in a tone that bristled like a new broom.

Charmaine stood back with the stencil in her hand and Strickland had to step hastily aside to preserve a decent distance between her suit and the grubby overall. Unnoticed by anyone but myself, a drop of white paint fell from the end of the brush resting across the tin onto the shapely beige toe of Strickland's shoe.

The answer to Strickland's question was so plain to see that it hardly needed voicing, but she blinked her enlarged eyes expectantly, and so Charmaine said, 'It's the WHITES ONLY bench.' When Strickland showed no sign of recognition, Charmaine added, 'You remember the benches. For whites only?'

Silence. What on earth did she want? My sandpaper was doing nothing to smooth the ragged edges of our nerves, and so I put it down. We all looked at the bench.

It was a beautiful bench – as a useful object, I mean, rather than a symbol of injustice. The wooden slats were tomato-sauce red. The arms and legs were made of iron, but cleverly moulded to resemble branches, and painted brown to enhance a rustic illusion. The bench looked well used, which is often a sign that a thing has been loved. But when you looked closer, as Strickland was doing now, you saw that all these signs of wear and tear were no more than skin-deep. Charmaine had applied all of them in the workshop. The bruised hollows on the seat, where the surface had been abraded by decades of white thighs and buttocks, were really patches of brown and purple paint. The flashes of raw metal on the armrests, where the paint had been worn away by countless white palms and elbows, turned out to be mere discs of silver paint themselves. Charmaine had even smeared the city's grimy shadows into the grain.

Strickland pored over these special effects with an expression of amazed distaste, and then stared for a minute on end at the letters WHI on the uppermost slat of the backrest. The silence congealed around us, slowing us down, making us slur our movements, until the absence of sound was as tangible as a crinkly skin on the surface of the air. 'Forgive me,' she said at last, with an awakening toss of her head. 'You're manufacturing a WHITES ONLY bench?'

'Ja. For Room 27.'

Strickland went to the floor plan taped to one of the walls and looked for Room 27: Petty Apartheid. Then she gazed at the calendar next to the plan, but whether she was mulling over the dates, or studying the photograph – children with stones in their hands, riot policemen with rifles, between the lines a misplaced reporter with a camera – or simply lost in thought, I couldn't tell. Did she realise that the calendar was ten years old?

Charmaine and I exchanged glances behind her back.

'Surely we should have the real thing,' Strickland said, turning.

'Of course – if only we could find it.'

'You can't find a genuine WHITES ONLY bench?'

'No.'

'That's very hard to believe.'

'We've looked everywhere. It's not as easy as you'd think. This kind of thing was frowned upon, you know, in the end. Discrimination I mean. The municipalities were given instructions to paint them over. There wasn't much point in hunting for something that doesn't exist, so we decided at our last meeting – this was before your time, I'm afraid – that it would be better if I recreated one.'

'Recreated one,' Strickland echoed.

'Faithfully. I researched it and everything. I've got the sources here somewhere.' Charmaine scratched together some photocopies splattered with paint and dusted with fingerprints and tread-marks from her running shoes. 'The bench itself is a genuine 1960s one, I'm glad to say, from the darkest decade of repression. Donated by Reddy's father-in-law, who stole it from a bus stop for use in the garden. It was a long time ago, mind you, the family is very respectable. From a black bus stop – for Indians. Interestingly, the Indian benches didn't have INDIANS ONLY on them – not in Natal anyway, according to Mr Mookadam. Or even ASIATICS. Not that it matters.'

'It matters to me,' Strickland said curtly – Charmaine does go on sometimes – and pushed her glasses up on her nose so that her eyes were doubly magnified. 'This is a museum, not some high-school operetta. It is our historical duty to be authentic.'

I must say that made me feel bad, when I thought about all the effort Charmaine and I had put into everything from the Sharpeville Massacre to the Soweto Uprising, trying to get the details right, every abandoned shoe, every spent cartridge, every bloodied stitch of clothing, only to have this jenny-come-lately (as Charmaine puts it) give us a lecture about authenticity. What about our professional duty? (Charmaine again.)

'Have we advertised?' Strickland asked, and I could tell by her voice that she meant to argue the issue out. But at that moment she glanced down and saw the blob of paint on the toe of her shoe.

I had the fantastic notion to venture an excuse on Charmaine's behalf: to tell Strickland that she had dripped ice cream on her shoe. Vanilla ice cream! I actually saw her hand grasping the cone, her sharp tongue curling around the white cupola, the droplet plummeting. Fortunately I came to my senses before I opened my big mouth.

★ ★ ★

It was the first proper meeting of the Steering Committee with the new director. We hadn't had a meeting for a month. When Charlie Sibeko left in a huff after the fiasco with the wooden AK47s, we all heaved a sigh of relief. We were sick to death of meetings: the man's appetite for circular discussion was insatiable.

Strickland sat down at the head of the table, and having captured that coveted chair laid claim to another by declaring the meeting open. She seemed to assume that this was her prerogative as director, and no one had the nerve to challenge her.

The report-backs were straightforward: we were all behind schedule and over budget. I might add that we were almost past caring. It seemed impossible that we'd be finished in time for the official opening. The builders were still knocking down walls left, right and centre, and establishing piles of rubble in every room. Pincus joked that the only exhibit sure to be ready on time was the row of concrete bunks – they were part of the original compound in which the Museum is housed and we had decided to leave them exactly as we found them. He suggested that we think seriously about delaying the opening, which was Portia's cue to produce the invitations, just back from the printers. Everyone groaned (excluding Strickland and me) and breathed in the chastening scent of fresh ink.

'As far as we're concerned, this date is written in stone,' Strickland said, snapping one of the copperplate cards shut. 'We will be ready on time. People will have to learn to take their deadlines seriously.' At that point Charmaine began to doodle on her agenda – a hand with a stiff index finger, emerging from a lacy cuff, pointing at Item 4: Bench.

Item 2: Posters, which followed the reports, was an interesting one. Pincus had had a letter from a man in Bethlehem, a former town clerk and electoral officer, who had collected copies of every election poster displayed in the town since it was founded. He was prepared to entrust the collection to us if it was kept intact. Barbara said she could probably use a couple in the Birth of Apartheid exhibit. We agreed that Pincus would write to the donor, care of the Bethlehem Old Age Home, offering to house the entire collection and display selected items on a rotating basis.

Item 3: Poetry, was Portia's. Ernest Dladla, she informed us, had declined our invitation to read a poem at the opening ceremony, on the perfectly reasonable grounds that he was not a poet. 'I have poetic impulses,' he said in his charming note, 'but I do not act upon them.' Should she go ahead, Portia wanted to know, and approach Alfred Qabula instead, as Ernie suggested?

Then Strickland asked in an acerbic tone whether an issue this trivial needed to be tabled at an important meeting. But Portia responded magnificently, pointing out that she knew nothing about poetry, not having had the benefit of a decent education, had embarrassed herself once in the performance of her duties and did not wish to do so again. All she wanted was an answer to a simple question: Is Alfred Qabula a poet? Yes or no?

No sooner was that settled, than Strickland announced Item 4: Bench, and stood up. Perhaps this was a technique she had read about in the business pages somewhere, calculated to intimidate the opposition. 'It has come to my attention,' she said, 'that our workshop personnel are busily recreating beautiful replicas of apartheid memorabilia, when the ugly originals could be ours for the asking. I do not know what Mr Sibeko's policy on this question was, although the saga of the wooden AK47s is full of suggestion, but as far as I'm concerned it's an appalling waste of time and money. It's also dishonest. This is a museum, not an amusement arcade.

'My immediate concern is the WHITES ONLY bench, which is taking up so much of Charmaine's time and talent. I find it hard to believe that there is not a genuine example of a bench of this nature somewhere in the country.'

'Petty apartheid went out ages ago,' said Charmaine, 'even in the Free State.'

'The first Indian townships in the Orange Free State were established way back in October 1986,' said Reddy, who had been unusually quiet so far, 'in Harrismith, Virginia and Odendaalsrus. Not many people know that. I remember hearing the glad tidings from my father-in-law, Mr Mookadam, who confessed that ever since he was a boy it had been a dream of his to visit that forbidden province.'

'I'll wager that there are at least a dozen real WHITES ONLY benches in this city alone, in private collections,' Strickland insisted, erasing Reddy's tangent with the back of her hand. 'People are fascinated by the bizarre.'

'We asked everyone we know,' said Charmaine. 'And we asked them to ask everyone they know, and so on. Like a chain letter – except that we didn't say they would have a terrible accident if they broke the chain. And we couldn't find a single bench. Not one.'

'Have we advertised?'

'No commercials,' said Reddy, and there was a murmur of assenting voices.

'Why ever not?'

'It just causes more headache.'

'Oh nonsense!'

Reddy held up his right hand, with the palm out, and batted the air with it, as if he was bouncing a ball off Strickland's forehead. This gesture had a peculiarly mollifying effect on her, and she put her hand over her eyes and sat down. Reddy stood up in his ponderous way and padded out of the room.

Pincus, who has a very low tolerance for silence, said, 'Wouldn't it be funny if Charmaine's bench turned out to be the whites' only bench?'

No one laughed, so he said 'whites' only' again, and drew the apostrophe in the air with his forefinger.

Reddy came back, carrying a photograph, a Tupperware lunch-box and a paperknife. He put the photograph in the middle of the table, facing Strickland. She had to lean forward in her chair to see what it was. I wondered whether she fully appreciated the havoc her outsize spectacles wreaked on her face, how they disjointed her features. She looked like a composite portrait in a magazine competition, in which some cartoon character's eyes had been mismatched with the jaw of a real-life heroine.

Everyone at the table, with the exception of our director, had seen this routine before. Some of us had sat through it half a dozen times, with a range of donors, do-gooders, interest groups. For some reason, it never failed to involve me. I also leant forward to view the eight-by-ten. No one else moved.

I looked first at the pinprick stigmata in the four corners. Then I looked, as I always did, at the girl's outflung hand.

Her hand is a jagged speech-bubble filled with disbelief. It casts a shadow shaped like a howling mouth on her body, and that mouth takes up the cry of outrage. The palm Reddy had waved in Strickland's face was a much more distant echo.

I looked next at the right hand of the boy who is carrying Hector Peterson. His fingers press into the flesh of a thigh that is still warm, willing it to live, prompting the muscle, animating it. Hector Peterson's right hand, by contrast, lolling numbly on his belly, knows that it is dead, and it expresses that certainty in dark tones of shadow and blood.

These hands are still moving, they still speak to me.

Reddy jabbed the photograph with the point of his paperknife. 'This is a photograph of Hector Peterson, in the hour of his death,' he said. Strickland nodded her head impatiently. 'The day was 16 June 1976.' She nodded again, urging him to skip the common knowledge and come to the point. A Wednesday. As it happened, it was fine and mild. The sun rose that morning at 6.53 and set that evening at 5.25. The shot was taken at 10.15 on the dot. It was the third in a series of six. Hector Peterson was the first fatality of what we would come to call the Soweto Riots – the first in a series of seven hundred odd. The photographer was Sam Nzima, then in the employ of the *World*. The subject, according to the tombstone that now marks his grave, was Zolile Hector Pietersen, P-I-E-T-E-R-S-E-N, but the newspapers called him Hector Peterson and it stuck. We struck out the "I", we put it to rout in the alphabet of the oppressor. We bore the hero's body from the uneven field of battle and anointed it with English. According to the tombstone he was thirteen years old, but as you can see he looked no more than half that age … Or is it just the angle? If only we had some other pictures of the subject to compare this one with, we might feel able to speak with more authority.'

This welter of detail, and the offhand tone of the delivery, produced in Strickland the usual baffled silence.

'Not many people know these things.' Reddy slid the point of the knife onto the girl. 'This is Hector's sister Margot, a.k.a. Tiny, now living in Soweto.' The knife slid again. 'And this is Mbuyisa Makhubu, whereabouts your guess is as good as mine. Not many people know them either. We have come to the conclusion, here at the Museum, that the living are seldom as famous as the dead.'

The knife moved again. It creased Mbuyisa Makhubu's lips, which are bent into a bow of pain, like the grimace of a tragic mask, it rasped the brick wall of the matchbox house which we see over his shoulder, skipped along the top of a wire gate, and came to rest on the small figure of a woman in the background. 'And who on earth do you suppose this is?'

Strickland gazed at the little figure as if it was someone famous she should be able to recognise in an instant, some household name. In fact, the features of this woman – she is wearing a skirt and doek – are no more than a grey smudge, continuous with the shadowed wall behind her.

I looked at Hector Peterson's left arm, floating on air, and the shadow of his hand on Mbuyisa Makhubu's knee, a shadow so hard-edged and muscular it could trip the bearer up.

The child is dead. With his rumpled sock around his ankle, his grazed knee, his jersey stuck with dry grass, you would think he had taken a tumble in the playground, if it were not for the gout of blood from his mouth. The jersey is a bit too big for him: it was meant to last another year at least. Or is it just that he was small for his age? Or is it the angle? In his hair is a stalk of grass shaped like a praying mantis.

'Nobody knows.'

Strickland sat back with a sigh, but Reddy went on relentlessly.

'Nevertheless, theories were advanced: some people said that this woman, this apparent bystander, was holding Hector Peterson in her arms when he died. She was a mother herself. She cradled him in her lap – you can see the bloodstains here – and when Makhubu took the body from her and carried it away, she found a bullet caught in the folds of her skirt. She is holding that fatal bullet in her right hand, here.

'Other people said that it didn't happen like that at all. Lies and fantasies. When Nzima took this photograph, Hector Peterson was still alive! What you see here, according to one reliable caption, is a critically wounded youth. The police open fire, Hector falls at Mbuyisa's feet. The boy picks him up and runs towards the nearest car, which happens to belong to Sam Nzima and Sophie Tema, a journalist on the *World*, Nzima's partner that day. Sam takes his photographs. Then Mbuyisa and Tiny pile into the back of the Volkswagen – did I mention that it was a Volkswagen? – they pile into the back with Hector; Sam and Sophie pile into the front with their driver, Thomas Khoza. They rush to the Orlando Clinic, but Hector

Peterson is certified dead on arrival. And that's the real story. You can look it up for yourself.

'But the theories persisted. So we thought we would try to lay the ghost – we have a duty after all to tell the truth. This is a museum, not a paperback novel. We advertised. We called on this woman to come forward and tell her story. We said it would be nice – although it wasn't essential – if she brought the bullet with her.'

'Anyone respond?'

'I'll say.'

Reddy opened his lunch-box and pushed it over to Strickland with the edge of his palm, like a croupier. She looked at the contents: there were .38 Magnum slugs, 9 mm and AK cartridges, shiny .22 bullets, a .357 hollow-point that had blossomed on impact into a perfect corolla. There were even a couple of doppies and a misshapen ball from an old voorlaaier. Strickland zoomed in for a close-up. She still didn't get it.

'If you'll allow me a poetic licence,' Reddy said, as if poetic licence was a certificate you could stick on a page in your Book of Life, 'this is the bullet that killed Hector Peterson.'

* * *

So we didn't advertise. But Strickland stuck to her guns about the WHITES ONLY bench: we would have the real thing or nothing at all. She made a few inquiries of her own, and wouldn't you know it, before the week was out she turned up the genuine article.

The chosen bench belonged to the Municipal Bus Drivers' Association, and in exchange for a small contribution to their coffers – the replacement costs plus ten per cent – they were happy to part with it. The honour of fetching the trophy from their clubhouse in Marshall Street fell to Pincus. Unbeknown to us, the treasurer of the MBDA had decided that there was a bit of publicity to be gained from his association's public-spirited gesture, and when our representative arrived he found a photographer ready to record the event for posterity. Pincus was never the most politic member of our committee. With his enthusiastic cooperation the photographer was able to produce an entire essay, which subsequently appeared, without a by-line, in the *Saturday Star*. It showed the bench in its original quarters (weighed down by a squad of bus drivers of all races, pin-up girls – whites only – looking over the drivers' shoulders, all of them, whether flesh and blood or paper, saying cheese); the bench on its way out of the door (Pincus steering, the treasurer pushing); being loaded onto the back of our bakkie (Pincus and the treasurer shaking hands and stretching the cheque between them like a Christmas cracker); and finally driven away (Pincus hanging out of the window to give us a thumbs-up, the treasurer waving goodbye, the treasurer waving back at himself from the rear-view mirror). These pictures caused exactly the kind of headache Reddy had tried so hard to avoid. Offers of benches poured in from far and wide. Pincus was made to write the polite letters of thanks but no thanks. For our purposes, one bench is quite enough, thank you.

You can see the WHITES ONLY bench now, if you like, in Room 27. Just follow the arrows. I may as well warn you that it says EUROPEANS ONLY, to be precise. There's a second prohibition too, an entirely non-racial one, strung on a chain between the armrests: PLEASE DO NOT SIT ON THIS BENCH. That little sign is Charmaine's work, and making her paint it was Strickland's way of rubbing turpentine in her wounds.

When the genuine bench came to light, Charmaine received instructions to get rid of 'the fake'. But she refused to part with it. I was persuaded to help her carry it into the storeroom, where it remained for a month or so. As the deadline for the opening neared, Charmaine would take refuge in there from time to time, whenever things got too much for her, and put the finishing touches to her creation. At first, she was furious about all the publicity given to the impostor. But once the offers began to roll in, and it became apparent that WHITES ONLY benches were not nearly as scarce as we'd thought, she saw an opportunity to bring her own bench out of the closet. The night before the grand opening, in the early hours, when the sky was already going grey behind the mine-dump on the far side of the parking lot, we carried her bench outside and put it in the arbour under the controversial kaffirboom.

'When Strickland asks about it,' said Charmaine, 'you can tell her it was a foundling, left on our doorstep, and we just had to take it in.' Funny thing is, Strickland never made a peep.

I can see Charmaine's WHITES ONLY bench now, from my window. The kaffirboom, relocated here fully grown from a Nelspruit nursery, has acclimatised wonderfully well. '*Erythrina caffra*, a sensible choice,' said Reddy, 'deciduous, patulous, and umbrageous.' And he was quite right, it casts a welcome shade. Charmaine's faithful copy reclines in the dapple below, and its ability to attract and repel our visitors never ceases to impress me.

Take Mrs King. And talking about Mrs King, *Mr* King is a total misnomer, of course. I must point it out to Reddy. The Revd King, yes, and Dr King, yes, and possibly even the Revd Dr King. But Mr King? No ways.

It seems unfair, but Charmaine's bench has the edge on that old museum piece in Room 27. Occasionally I look up from my workbench, and see a white man sitting there, a history teacher say. While the schoolchildren he has brought here on an outing hunt in the grass for lucky beans, he sits down on our bench to rest his back. And after a while he pulls up his long socks, crosses one pink leg over the other, laces his fingers behind his head and closes his eyes.

Then again, I'll look up to see a black woman shuffling resolutely past, casting a resentful eye on the bench and muttering a protest under her breath, while the flame-red blossoms of the kaffirboom detonate beneath her aching feet.

ZOË WICOMB

Another Story

Approaching DF Malan airport. The view from the window on the right, that is, as you enter the aircraft: it falls out of the blue, suddenly, even with your eyes fixed on the ground rising towards you – a perfect miniature plane, a razor-edged shadow in the last of the sunlight, earthborne, yet flying alongside where before there had been nothing. And then it grows. Because the sun is low and because nothing, no nothing will remain a little toy-thing. (A darling little toy-thing, but that sort of word has no place here and must be excised.) Yes, flying across the earth, it gradually grows larger. Still wonderful while its outline remains sharp, until an ungainly leap in size when overblown, with edges grown soft and arrowed wings blunted, the once-lovely little thing spreads and is swallowed. A simple multiplication and division sum, a working out of velocity, height, angle of the sun etc. could have foreseen that moment. But she didn't. Or perhaps couldn't. So that was that. And the plane landed with the usual bump and the ping of the pilot's intercom.

To tell the truth, Miss Kleinhans was scared. And Dollie's voice as she leaned over the wild-with-morning-glory fence, rang in her ears.

'If you asking my advice, Deborah Kleinhans, I say stay right here where you belong. You not young, man, and there's no need to go gallivanting after family you don't know from Adam. I mean, family is now family, but the whole point is that family is family because you know them. It's not a stranger who gets to know you through ink and how-do-you-do on paper. And remember Cape Town is full of troubles with people throwing stones and getting shot. And what with you being a stranger in town. Have you listened to the wireless today?'

Deborah's head spun in an attempt to work out how knowing or not knowing blood relations affected the claims that such people could legitimately make on her, for she had come to see the visit as a duty. Also, the morning-glory trumpets had started yawning and she watched the first fold up neatly, spiralling into a tight spear that betrayed nothing of its fulsome blue.

'Dollie, this thing will take some thinking about. But it's too cold out here for me.' She had not asked for Dollie's advice; she had merely spoken of her indecision. But if only she had listened to Doll who was after all a sensible person, a neighbour she could rely on, even if that husband of hers was a good-for-nothing dronklap. I should have been a spinster like you, hey, Dollie sometimes said in exasperation, but Deborah could tell how the word spinster cut into her heart, for Doll would swirl the remains of her coffee and gulp down the lot as she rose with just that hint of hoarseness in her voice, I'll have to go and get ready the old man's bredie. Or his socks, or boots, or ironing, and even she, the spinster, knew that that was not the worst a woman had to do. She who had worked for years in white households knew more about things than people thought.

There had been two letters. The first simply a matter of introduction. A certain Miss Sarah Lindse from a wayward branch had traced her, a great-aunt, wishing to check the family connection and with Old Testament precision had untangled the lines of begetting into a neat tree which Deborah found hard to follow. Coloured people didn't have much schooling in her day but she knew her Bible and there was no better education in the world than knowing the Bible from cover to cover. Still, enough names on those heavy branches looked familiar, although so many children, dear Lord, why ever did her people have so many children. Family tree! It was a thicket, a blooming forest in which the grandest of persons would get lost. And she pursed her mouth fastidiously; she had a lot to be thankful for.

There were times when you had to face the truth; times like this when you'd made a wrong decision and the good Lord allowed you the opportunity to say, I have been guided by vanity. And in the same breath she found her vindication: for a woman who had worked as a respectable housekeeper all her life, but in service all the same, the connection with this grand young woman was only what she deserved. A history teacher at the university in Cape Town. The drop of white blood, no doubt, and she sighed as she thought of that blood, pink and thin and pure trouble. Ag, that was a long time ago and now she had a niece, a lovely girl who was educated and rich and who wrote in the second letter, I'll send you a plane ticket. Come and have a holiday in Cape Town. To her, an old woman whom the child had never even met. And Deborah, who had been timid all her life, who had kept her feet firmly on the ground and kept her eyes modestly fixed on those feet, for once looked up to see the serpent of adventure wink through the foliage of the family tree. And she was undone. And at her age too, but she replied, keeping to the lines of her Croxley pad with a steady hand, although these modern pens behaved as if light upward strokes and bold downward strokes were the last thing they hoped to achieve: I have always wanted to fly and would like to look around Cape Town. But I don't need a holiday so you can save up the darning and mending and of course I could do the cooking while you get on with bookwork. Thank you for the offer.

It was also that nonsense of Dollie's. She had managed to think it through and it simply did not make sense. Family is family and the whole point of such an unnecessary statement was that you didn't have to know the person. Vanity again: she had proven her ability to reason things out for herself and in showing off to Dollie had brought upon herself this business – this anxiety.

If only she had someone to talk to on the flight. Silence was something still when you were on your own but here with a flesh and blood person sitting right by your side, the silence fidgets between you, monitors your breathing, stiffens the body and makes you fearful of moving. So many new things cannot become part of you unless you could say to the person sitting right there, My what a business this is, without of course letting on that you've never flown before. But the red-faced woman next to her had swung round to the aisle as if she, Deborah Kleinhans, freshly bathed and in her best crimplene two-piece, as if she had BO. Ag, it's the way of the world, she consoled herself, these whites don't know how to work things out, can't even run their own blooming homes. If she were in charge she'd have apartheid to serve the decent and god-fearing – that was a more sensible basis for separating the sheep from the goats, but she sighed, for how would one know, how could one tell the virtuous from the hypocrites, the pharisees. These days people grew more and more like jackals and the education business only helped to cover up sorcery and fornication.

And here Miss Kleinhans felt once more a twinge of regret, a tugging at her intestines that happily could be diverted from the new niece to the wonderful South African Airways lunch. All nicely separated in little compartments that Dollie could well be alerted to, her with the eternal bredies, day after day everything mixed together, meat, potatoes, tinned peas and veg and then, on the plate, that man of hers would stir in the rice, pounding, as if it were mortar to be shovelled into the cracks of his soul. But it would've been nice just to say to the red-faced woman, Isn't it oulik these little brown dishes like housie-housie things. Last time I flew they were orange you know. Just in case. And she lifted her head high; no one could accuse her of being ignorant, green and verskrik as a young farm-girl. The Goodlord she felt sure would forgive her. Especially after the temptation, the terrible desire to put one in her bag, only the little SAA pudding dish of cream and brown plastic and with the white woman's back virtually turned to her, nothing could be easier. But she didn't. And she praised Dearjesus who resisted forty days in the Wilderness and felt sure that He would not expect her to fast just because He had, not on this her first flight with food so prettily packed.

That was before she thought of the order of eating. She knew that one did not just start any old where you liked. Her De Villiers household always had fish or soup to begin with but how was she to determine the order of things that in fact were the same? A test that would have made the woman, if her back had not mercifully been turned, giggle at her ignorance, for there in the little compartments was tomato and lettuce alone and again tomato and lettuce with meat, and how was she to decide which came first? More than likely the two halves of the same tomato turned into different names on different plates, which only went to show how silly all this blinking business was, but she was grateful all the same for the disdain of the woman who had swung round into the aisle. At what point was she to eat the round bread? Only poor people, her father had always said, ate bread with their dinner, so she would look upon it as a test, like in the fairy tale of a round red apple or something to tempt and catch the heroine out. Why else would the two large black berries have been hidden under the lettuce? She would have arranged it on top to set off the green and red; she had always paid attention to presenting food attractively and Mrs de Villiers never had anything but praise for her dishes.

The pip of the foul-tasting berry proved yet another trap. How was she to get the damned thing out of her mouth and back onto the plate? Would she have to pretend that she was not hungry, that she could only just pick at her food? What nonsense, she admonished herself. This was no boiled sweet destined to dissolve; she could not very well keep a pip hidden in her cheek until god knows when, so she spat it into a paper napkin under cover of wiping her mouth, and niftily tucked it into her sleeve. There was no one watching her; she would tuck in and not waste the poor girl's money; this food – never mind if it didn't live up to the cute containers – was expensive and, what's more, paid for. How could she, a grown person, be so silly and she chuckled audibly so that the red-faced woman took the opportunity to adjust her discomfort, to straighten her spine and allow herself ten degrees that would bring Miss Kleinhans's fork just within her line of vision.

The girl must have been relying on a family resemblance; why else had she not suggested ways of identifying herself? Perhaps she should wave a white handkerchief or something. That was what people did in *Rooi Rose,* which only went to show that *Rooi Rose* then was not for people like her. She could never do such a thing, make a spectacle of herself. It must have been the flight through high air that made her think such unusual thoughts. As if she had taken a feather duster to her head so that those stories, she now clearly saw, were for white people. Which did not mean that she couldn't read them: she was used to wearing white people's clothes and eating their leftovers, so what difference did it make reading their stories. As long as she knew and did not expect to behave like a *Rooi Rose* woman. It was difficult enough just sitting there, waiting, with so many idle eyes roving about. She lifted her head to concentrate on the lights flashing their instructions about smoking and seatbelts until they finally clicked off, the messages exhausted, and felt herself adrift midst empty seats and the purposeful shuffling of people anxious to go.

Deborah looked about and caught sight of the red-faced woman who flashed her a warm smile. What on earth could the person mean? She was not to be lured by a smile of falsehood, here where there was no danger of striking up a conversation. As far as she was concerned it just was too bladdy late. Haai, what a cheek, but then, not keeping track of things, a smile leaked from her lips all the same and she had no choice but to incline her head to nod a greeting.

The usual Cape Town wind awaited her, just as Dollie had said, and Deborah smoothed her skirt and patted her head to check that the doekie was still in place. Crossing that space was not simply a question of putting one foot before another. The tarmac felt sticky underfoot; the wind snapped like a mongrel; and her ankles wobbled unreliably above the Sunday shoes. Ahead, through the glass, a tinted crowd waited, waved, and what would she do if the girl was not there? That she could not allow herself to think about. The Goodlord would provide. Although the Goodlord so often got His messages mixed up, like telephone party lines, so that good fortune would rain into the unsuspecting lap of that heathenish husband of Dollie's, when it was she, Deborah Kleinhans, who had spent the holy hours on arthritic knees, praying. If red-face walking purposefully just ahead of her was expecting no one, you could be sure that some thoughtful niece on the spur of the moment had decided to meet her after all, while she, a stranger in this town ... But this time, and Deborah was careful to smile inwardly, this time, He got it just right.

⋆ ⋆ ⋆

Sarah was confident that she would recognise her great-aunt by the family resemblance and indeed the woman walking unsteadily across the tarmac could be no other than Deborah Kleinhans. Who, incidentally, was the only elderly coloured woman on the flight. Sarah corrected herself: so-called coloured, for she did not think that the qualifier should be reserved for speech. It grieved her that she so often had to haul up the 'so-called' from some distant recess where it slunk around with foul terms like half-caste and half-breed and she stamped her foot (which had gone to sleep in the long wait) as if to shake down the unsummoned words. Lexical vigilance was a matter of mental hygiene: a regular rethinking of words in common use, like cleaning out rotten food from the back of a refrigerator where no one expects food to rot and poison the rest.

The old woman was stronger, sturdier than she imagined, with the posture of someone much younger. But she was tugging at the navy-blue suit which had got nipped, or so it seemed, by her roll-on, so that her hemline dipped severely to the right. Also, threatening to slip off, was the doekie that had to be hauled back over the grey head as she struggled with a carrier bag in the wind. But they met without difficulty.

'So we found each other. Something to be grateful for these days when you lose and search for things that disappear under your very nose ...'

'And people going missing by the dozens,' Sarah interjected. Deborah looked alarmed. Whatever was the child talking about; not her, she had to get back home; Dollie would be expecting her in precisely one week.

'Ag, they say big cities swallow you up but we're old enough to look after ourselves. Dollie's people,' she added, 'even in Kimberley, you know, after the riots. Clean disappeared. But one never knows with these children. Dollie is now Mrs Lategan who's been my neighbour for twenty years.' Then she chuckled, 'But what if we are not the people we think we are, or no, that's not what I mean. Let's sit down, child, I get so deurmekaar and I need to take a good look at you.'

They sat down and looked at each other, surrounded by squeals and hugs and arm-waving reunions. In the two pairs of eyes, the flecked hazel eyes derived from the same sockets of a long-dead European missionary, there was nothing to report. The improbable eyes, set generations ago into brown faces, betrayed nothing, as eyes rarely do, but both claimed to read in the other signs and traces so that they held each other as firmly as the rough and wrinkled hand gripped the young and smooth. Deborah wondered for the first time why the girl had brought her all that way. Sarah thought of her father who in his last years had kept a miscellany of rare physical complaints. A man who knew his viscera like the back of his hand and could identify a feeling of discomfort with self-claimed accuracy – his liver, or pancreas, or lower section of the colon – an unnecessary refinement since the remedy of Buchu Essence served them all. She hoped that her great-aunt would not get ill; those were surely the eyes of a hypochondriac.

The girl was rather disappointing: untidily dressed in denim without a dash of lipstick to brighten her up. There was something impenetrable about her face, a density of the flesh that thwarted Deborah who prided herself on looking right into the souls of strangers. Also, her car was not at all what Deborah had expected but then she did not think any car smart except for a black one. The house that they pulled up at was very nice, but modest, she thought, for a learned person. With so much rain here in Cape Town it seemed a pity not to have a proper garden. Just a little patch of untrimmed grass and a line of flowers sagging against the wall. Yellow and orange marigolds, their heads like torches, so that she turned to look back at the dark mountain and saw the last light gathered in the flaming peak of a cloud.

The medicinal scent of marigolds followed them into the house. Through the passage lined with old photographs. So many people with nothing better to do than stand around and wait for the click of a camera. And right into the kitchen until the marigolds submitted to the smell of coffee. From a blue enamel pot like her very own the girl poured large cupfuls and her heart leapt, for city people, she thought, only drank instant coffee, didn't have time, Dollie said, for Koffiehuis. Washed in a caffeine-induced wellbeing she felt her feet throb all the more painfully so that she eased off her shoes to find two risen loaves straining under the nylon stockings. Why feeling good should have reminded her of feeling bad she did not know, but oh, she felt like a queen being led to her room with a bowl of hot water in which to soak those feet. But queens get their heads chopped off, so it was not too surprising that in that dream-wake state as she rested before dinner, Deborah orbited wildly in a marigold-round, her eyes chasing the pinpoints of light where orange turned to fire, and her head threatening to fly off. She rose clutching her throat.

At table Sarah talked too much. Deborah, used to turning her own thoughts slowly round, this way and that, and then putting them away safely for another inspection day, found the girl's insistent ways too exhausting. Like Mr de Villiers's office with rows and rows of narrow drawers packed with papers – the girl's head was like that. And she spoke fast, whirring like a treadle-machine that made her own head, still delicate from dreaming, spin once again. And all these things from the past, the bad old days that Sarah wanted to talk about. Stories folded and packed in mothballs right at the bottom of Deborah's head. To disturb those was just plain foolish, just asking for things to come toppling down.

'Perhaps later this year I'll come to Kimberley. To look around all those places. The old farm, Brakvlei, all those places where the Kleinhanse lived,' Sarah said.

But the old woman would not be roused. 'Nothing there to see. Not a coloured person left in those parts. You won't find a riempie or a rusty nail.

No, it's years since I left and soon after that the others trekked. The drought, you know. Girlie, this is a lovely bobotie. I haven't had any for so long; being on your own you can't really make such elaborate food.'

The girl was not a bad cook. And the bobotie was good although Deborah liked it just a little bit sweeter. Just a spoonful of apricot jam to set off the sharpness of the dried apricots. That's what she liked about bobotie – the layers, different things packed on top of one another. She always did it in a pyrex dish so that you could see the separate layers of curried mince, apricots and then the thick custard just trying to trickle down to the dried fruit. Almost a pity to eat it.

'No really,' she said through slipping dentures, 'there's nothing like a good bobotie. Bananas are also good you know, but to contrast with the custard, apricot is best.'

In the tall, frosted glass of Fanta, the orange bubbles broke merrily at the brim, almost too pretty to drink. On the same principle Deborah's good clothes remained unworn at the back of the cupboard, but today, in her Sunday wear, eating and drinking the beauty of it all, her old heart was content and this Sarah was a girl to be proud of. She would bring Dollie along next time; my, what a time they could have.

Then Sarah said in a preacher's voice, '... nothing but an untidiness on God's earth – a mixture of degenerate brown peoples, rotten with sickness, an affront against Nature ... So that was the farm.'

They had slipped into comfortable Afrikaans, a relief to Deborah whose English pinched like the Lycra roll-on that Dollie insisted had to be worn for the visit. And now the girl had switched to English once again so that she groped and grunted, for syllables from the two languages flew to each other to make wild words; because she did not understand about the sickness and death and because she felt a great weariness, a cloud settling around her head. The girl was surely mad. Everybody gets sick and dies, but Brakvlei was never rotten. Oh no, theirs was the cleanest of farmyards, the stony veld swept for hundreds of yards and even the fowls knew not to shit near the house. In that swept yard a young man rested his brown arms on the latched lower door, leant well into the dark but spotless kitchen with the sun behind him lighting the outline of his tightly curled hair. And Deborah, sick with shyness, packed more wood into the full stove and felt her hem a hot hoop below her knees, for she had outgrown that dress, and she had never been looked at in that way. Even when he offered to cleave a log that refused to go into the stove, his eyes burned and then her Pa came, to see his favourite daughter, his miracle late-lamb, younger than the grandchild, tug at her skirt and he ordered Andries away. That day she tore the dress into rags and braved a beating for she knew that a strip of plain cotton could simply have been sewn on to lengthen the skirt. But a beating has never done anyone any harm and she could thank her Pa now for sitting here where the girl's strong hands came to rest on her shoulders.

'Auntie feeling alright? Perhaps a drop of Buchu Essence?' she inquired, once again in Afrikaans.

'No, I'm alright. Just put a little bit of bobotie on my plate.' Then Deborah remembered the libel. 'Cleanliness is next to godliness. That's what my mother always said. And it was my job every morning to sweep all around the house. Really, it was just rearranging the veld, making our own patterns of earth and stone with the grass broom, but Ma said, The veld will swallow us up if we don't sweep. No, you can ask anyone; Brakvlei was the tidiest little place you've ever seen. If your people thought otherwise, well, then they just don't know what tidy means. All my life I have kept that motto: Tidiness is next to godliness.' And then her anger subsided: her mother would not have quoted the adage in English as she just had, not at home. What had she in fact said? How unreliable words were, lodging themselves comfortably in the memory where they pretended to have a rightful place. Deborah did not hold her memory responsible.

'No, no,' Sarah soothed, 'I'm sure you're right. I have no doubt that Brakvlei was well kept. But I wasn't really talking of Brakvlei; it was just something I remembered. From a story.' But the young woman's eyes burned so brightly, so busy-bodily, oh Deborah just knew that passion for probing deep into other people's affairs. Who did this child think she was, wanting to pry into her life and she who had never said a word to anyone about Andries, the tall young man whom she saw just once more before her father waving the old shotgun told him not to set foot in that swept yard again.

'People come and go and in the end it's no bad thing. No point in brooding over things that happened a long time ago. I haven't got time for those old stories,' she said firmly.

'A pity really; it's an interesting story that needs to be told by ...'

'And what would you know about it?' Deborah interrupted. 'It's never been interesting. Dreary as dung it was, sitting day after day waiting for something to happen; listening for hooves or the roll of cartwheels.' But she checked herself. Hearing only the wind howl through the bushes and the ewes bleat, she had made up stories. Of driving through streets lined with whitewashed houses; of friends, girls in frilled print frocks who whispered secrets under the breath of the wind; and of Andries on horseback galloping across the swept yard right up to the kitchen door. But she said, 'You know I have my books – *Rooi Rose* every fortnight, I haven't missed a book since I started working for the De Villierses and when I retired I kept it up. Every fortnight. Good stories that seem to be about real life, but well, when you think about it, you won't recognise anyone you know. They'll give you no useful tips. They're no better than the nonsense I used to make up in my own head to kill the time. My advice, child, is to stick to your business and forget about stories of old times.'

'It depends surely on who tells the story. Auntie Deborah, that's what I must ask you about. Do you know if someone has written the story of our family, from the beginning, right from the European missionary? Do you by any chance remember a woman, a white woman speaking to your mother or brothers or yourself about those days? A woman who then wrote a book? Have you ever heard of the book, of ...'

'No, I don't believe it. What nonsense, of course there was no such woman. A book for all to read with our dirty washing spread out on snow-white pages! Ag, man, don't worry; it wouldn't be our story; it's everyone's story. All coloured people have the same old story.' And then Deborah slumped in her chair.

Sarah knew it, just her luck, the old woman travelling all this way to put down her head and die at her table. She held a bottle of brandy to the lifeless lips. The eyelids fluttered and Deborah sat up with remarkable agility as if the laying of her head on the table had been a deliberate gesture of exasperation.

'Just tired child. Don't worry, I'm not going to die here; I'll die respectably in my own house and that not for some time yet.'

Sarah helped her to bed. 'Tomorrow evening,' she said, as she tucked her in, 'I have to go to a meeting. But in the morning we'll go out. Somewhere exciting, but let's talk about that tomorrow.'

'To the Gardens, girlie; that's where one should go first. I've heard so much about the Gardens in Cape Town. Where the fine ladies parade.' And she giggled for she knew it could not be as her mother had described so many years ago. And even then it was a second-hand account, told by her grown-up sister Elmira whom she had never known.

* * *

Deborah was not surprised by the knock. Her heart had swollen, filling her chest with a thunderous beat and rocking her entire body as she heard the footsteps steal past her window, round to the back of the house. Skollies with armfuls of stones, just as Dollie had warned her. Then a low, barking voice – Quick. Here. Slowly, she twisted her head to look at the clock. Then Deborah leapt out of bed. She would not await death lying prone in her bed. Oh no, if skollies planned to kill her, well, they would meet her standing up straight, ready to meet her Maker. Her hands groped for the dressing gown but the old arms shook too violently to guide them through the sleeves. She crept out to the hall; she could at least telephone the police. But they were already at the door. What kind of cheeky skollies were these who thought she would open the door to her own death? Why did the girl not wake up? She pulled on the dressing gown. The knock grew louder and someone shouted, 'Open up; it's the police.' They had come for Sarah.

* * *

Deborah waited for Dollie in the Lategans' kitchen. Mr Lategan put the kettle on for coffee, making an elaborate display of not knowing where to find things, so that she suggested that he put on his shoes while she made the coffee. That the man should be told to make himself decent, as if she would divulge a word to someone sitting in his socks. And she thought of the folly of having expectations, of how she had imagined sitting at that table with Dollie, telling her story.

But there they sat drinking the coffee she made and Mr Lategan knew exactly where to find Dollie's buttermilk rusks which they dunked. And so she told him, for she could not expect the man to ask again. About the police who came for Sarah at 5.30 in the morning, pointing their guns as if they were in a play on the TV. And how they turned the house upside down and even looked in her suitcase. But they were very polite, especially the big one in command who apologised nicely and said to her, 'You should have kept an eye on the girl,' so that she turned to him triumphantly and said, 'So you don't know everything like you said you did. I've known this girl for less than a day.' Mr Lategan interrupted to say that if they didn't know that, they could so easily have got the whole thing wrong, the wrong house, the wrong woman, everything. Which was exactly what Deborah was about to say, but it was so nice to be back and because she could have added, also the wrong Deborah Kleinhans, for she felt as if the story had been playing on the TV, she allowed him to be the author of the observation.

There was also Cape Town to tell about even though she knew that he had been twice. But the city was so big that he could not possibly have been to the same places and he certainly listened with great interest. Sarah had written a letter to her neighbours, the Arendses, and even then Deborah marvelled at the girl's skill, how she wrote like lightning, her hand flying across the paper in such straight lines, even though the big policeman leant over her, checking every word. Busybodies, that's what they were, going through people's things and reading their letters. Mrs Arendse took her to the Gardens but her heart was not in it.

Someone else, a young woman whose name she could not recall, took her to a museum to see what the girl called her ancestors. Hottentots in a big glass box, squatting around an unlit fire of all things, so that she left in disgust. But she said nothing to him of the large protruding buttocks and the shameful loincloths of animal skin. No, her heart was not in it and Mrs Arendse arranged an early return flight for there was no point in waiting to see Sarah again. They telephoned many times but there was no point, everyone said.

When Dollie came she told it all again and she did not mind Mr Lategan sitting there until he tried to correct her. If things were slightly different the second time round, well, she was telling it to someone different and he should have had the decency to keep quiet. So she went, taking her bag, for she had not yet been home and Dollie shouted after her, 'I'll come with,' just as she unlocked her door.

Dollie lay across her bed while she unpacked. The frock for parading in the Gardens, a bold print of yellow daisies on white, she folded away into a bottom drawer for the nights were drawing in and really it was perhaps too bright for someone of her age. And then she told Dollie. Of how she had offered to make a nice pot of coffee because it was so early and that's just what you needed in order to think clearly. If the policemen burst rudely into the house, well, she was brought up decently. Sarah shouted at her but she knew how a civilised person should behave. And she paused in an attempt to trace the moment when things became muddled but all she recalled was an unmistakable smell of marigold, a weariness and the precise timbre of the sergeant's voice as she finished pouring the coffee: 'Milk and sugar for the other two but just black and bitter for me.' Then without thinking, without anticipating the violence of the act, Deborah Kleinhans took each cup in turn and before his very eyes poured the coffee into the sink. Together they watched the liquid splash, a curiously transparent brown against the stainless steel.

ACKNOWLEDGEMENTS

The publisher and editor acknowledge the writers or estates and/or publishers who have permitted stories to be included in this anthology. (Translators are acknowledged at the beginning of the relevant story.) Every effort has been made to contact the copyright holder. Those copyright holders whom we have been unable to contact are requested to contact the publisher.

Hennie Aucamp, Tafelberg-Uitgewers, for 'The Coat without End'. (Tr. from *Dalk gaan niks verlore nie en ander tekste*, 1992.) Selection of English translations, *House Visits* (1983).

Chris Barnard, Tafelberg-Uitgewers, for 'Bush'. (Tr. from *Duiwel-in-die-Bos,* 1968.)

Ken Barris, Jonathan Ball [Ad Donker], for 'The Questioning' from *Small Change* (1988).

Herman Charles Bosman Estate, Human & Rousseau, for 'Funeral Earth' from *Unto Dust and other Stories* (1963; 2002), a collection compiled, posthumously, by Lionel Abrahams. A later 'Oom Schalk' story – the first 'Oom Schalk' stories appeared in periodicals of the 1930s and were collected by Bosman in *Mafeking Road* (1947) – 'Funeral Earth' was published initially in *Vista* (1950).

Abraham H de Vries, Tafelberg-Uitgewers, Jonathan Ball [Ad Donker], for 'The Girl with the Bra-pistol' in M Trump, ed., *Armed Vision: Afrikaans Writers in English* (1987). (Tr. from *Vliegoog*, 1965.)

De Vries, Human & Rousseau, for 'Ruins'. (Tr. from *Om tot verhaal te kom*, 2003.)

HIE Dhlomo Estate, Ravan Press, for 'The Barren Woman' from the unpublished manuscript 'When Evening Falls' [1940s]; published in *HIE Dhlomo: Collected Works* (1985).

RRR Dhlomo Estate for 'The Death of Masaba', first published in *The Sjambok* in 1929, and collected with other stories by Dhlomo in *English in Africa* 2.1 (1975).

Ahmed Essop, Ravan Press, for 'Hajji Musa and the Hindu Fire-walker' from *The Hajji and other Stories* (1978).

Nadine Gordimer and, on behalf of Gordimer, AP Watt Ltd for 'The Credibility Gap' from *Livingstone's Companions* (Jonathan Cape, 1972), 'The Termitary' from *A Soldier's Embrace* (Jonathan Cape, 1980) and 'Once upon a Time' from *Jump and other Stories* (Bloomsbury Publishing, 1991).

Stephen Gray for 'The Building-site', previously published in literary magazines and B Goldstein, ed., *More Like Minds* (1991).

Liz Gunner for 'Cattle Passing' (2002).

PJ Haasbroek, Human & Rousseau, Jonathan Ball [Ad Donker], for 'Departure' in M Trump, ed., *Armed Vision: Afrikaans Writers in English* (1987). (Tr. from *Verby die vlakte*, 1982.)

Bessie Head Estate, Heinemann, for 'The Wind and a Boy' from *The Collector of Treasures* (1977).

Christopher Hope, Bateleur Press, for 'The Fall of the British Empire' from *Private Parts & other Tales* (1981).

Maureen Isaacson, COSAW, for 'I Could Have Loved Gold' from *Holding Back Midnight and other Stories* (1992).

Ashraf Jamal, Brevitas Publishers, for 'The Beggar-guest' from *The Shades* (2002).

//Kabbo for his contribution to the Bleek and Lloyd Collection (UCT): extracts from Bleek and Lloyd's *Specimens of Bushman Folklore* (1911).

Antjie Krog (Samuel), Lekotse, TRC transcripts, Random House, for 'The Shepherd's Tale' and extracts from *Country of My Skull* (1998).

Alex La Guma Estate, Heinemann, for 'A Matter of Taste' from *A Walk in the Night: Seven Stories from the Streets of Cape Town* (1962).

C Louis Leipoldt Estate, Tafelberg-Uitgewers, for 'The Tree' from H Aucamp (comp.), *Wys my waar is Timboektoe: 'n persoonlike reis deur Afrika* (1997).

Sindiwe Magone, New Africa Books [David Philip], for 'The Sacrificial Lamb' from *Push-Push! & other Stories* (1996).

Eugène N Marais Estate, Nasionale Pers Beperk, for 'The Grey Pippit'. (Tr. from *Dwaal-stories*, 1927.)

John Matshikiza, Mail & Guardian Books, for 'Of Renaissance and Rhino Stew' from *With the Lid Off: South African Insights from Home and Abroad, 1959-2000* (2000) by John Matshikiza and Todd Matshika. 'There's a Purple Man in my Bantustan' from the *Mail & Guardian*.

Sarah Gertrude Millin Estate for 'Up from Gilgal' from *Legion Book* (1924). Selection of stories in *Two Bucks without Hair* (1957).

Rosemary H Moeketsi, Vivlia, for 'Guilty as Charged' from N Raselotsa & L Molema, eds, *Women Creating the Future: An Anthology of Women's Writing in South Africa* (1998).

Maud Motinyana, Pandora Press, for 'Two Minutes' from A Oosthuizen, ed., *Sometimes When it Rains* (1987).

Casey Motsisi Estate, Ravan Press, for 'Kid Playboy', first published in the column 'On the Beat', *Drum* (February 1959), and republished in *Casey & Co: Selected Writings* (1983).

Es'kia Mphahlele, Ravan Press, for 'Down the Quiet Street', first published in *Drum* (January 1956) under the pseudonym Bruno Esekie, and republished in *The Unbroken Song: Selected Writings* (1981).

PT Mtuze, Skotaville, Shuter & Shooter, for 'The Way to Madam' from DBZ Ntuli & R Finlayson, eds, *The Rainbow Flute: A Selection of Short Stories Translated from Indigenous African Languages* (1997). (Tr. from *Ungakhe uxelele mntu*, 1990.)

HW Nevinson Estate, John Murray, for 'Vae Victis' from *Between the Acts* (1904).

Njabulo S Ndebele, Northwestern University, for 'Death of a Son' from D Bunn & J Taylor, eds, *From South Africa: New Writings, Photographs & Art* [Special Issue of *TriQuarterly* 60, 1989]. (First published in variant form as 'At Last We Got the Body', *Tribute*, September 1989.) Selection in *Fools and other Stories* (1983).

Oral Past. Acknowledgements to tellers, transcribers and translators.

WHI Bleek & Lucy C Lloyd for the San/Bushmen texts from *Specimens of Bushmen Folklore* (1911).

Henry Callaway for 'The Man who Threw Away his Bread' from *Nursery Tales, Traditions and Histories of the Zulus* (1868).

SM Guma for 'The Child with a Moon on his Chest' from *The Form, Content and Technique of Oral Traditional Literature in Southern Sotho* (1980).

CLS Nyembezi, for the isiZulu texts of 'Nkulukulu', 'How Death Entered the World' and 'Maqinase, the Wily One' in *Igoda* [a school reader series] and reprinted with dual isiZulu-English selections in NN Canonici, *Izinganekwane: An Anthology of Zulu Folktales* (1993).

George McCall Theal for 'The Bird that Made Milk' from *Kaffir Folklore* (1882).

For a useful selection of oral tales in translation see AC Partridge, ed., *Folklore of Southern Africa* (1973).

Marguerite Poland, David Philip, for 'The Wood-ash Stars' from *The Wood-ash Stars* (1983).

Pulvermacher [JD du Toit Estate], Human & Rousseau, for 'Prayer of Titus Tokaan', Cape-Dutch periodical piece (± 1893) republished in AH de Vries, ed., *Die Afrikaans kortverhaalboek* (1978; 2001).

Jan Rabie Estate, Nasionale Boekhandel, for 'Maiden Outing to Rondebosch', from FV Lategan, BA Mackenzie & MW Smuts, eds, *More Afrikaans Short Stories* (1969). (Tr. from *Nooiensrit*, 1965.)

Jayapraga Reddy Estate, Skotaville, for 'The Spirit of Two Worlds' from *On the Fringe of Dreamtime and other Stories* (1987).

Sheila Roberts, Justified Press, for 'Carlotta's Vinyl Skin' from *Coming In and other Stories* (1993).

Riana Scheepers, Human & Rousseau, for 'Book'. (Tr. from *Feeks*, 1999.)

Karel Schoeman, Tafelberg-Uitgewers, Nasionale Boekhandel, for 'Seed in a New Earth', from FV Lategan, BA Mackenzie & MW Smuts, eds, *More Afrikaans Short Stories* (1969). (Tr. from *Die saad in die nuwe aarde*, 1967.)

Pauline Smith Estate, Library of the University of Cape Town, for 'The Sisters' from *The Little Karoo* (1925).

Can Themba Estate, Heinemann, for 'Crepuscule' from *The Will to Die* (1972). Reminiscent of his last years as a journalist on *Drum*, Themba's story in its manuscript form was written probably in the early 1960s. It was published in South Africa for the first time in the local reprint of *The Will to Die* (1982).

Marlene van Niekerk, Litnet, for 'Labour'.

Eben Venter, Queillerie, for 'Tinktinkie'. (Tr. from *Twaalf*, 2000.)

Ivan Vladislavić, New Africa Books [David Philip], for 'The WHITES ONLY Bench' from *Propaganda by Monuments and other Stories* (1996).

Zoë Wicomb, Ravan Press, for 'Another Story' from S Lefanu & S Haywood, eds, *Colours of a New Day: Writing from South Africa* (1990). Selection of stories in *You Can't Get Lost in Cape Town* (1987).

Peter Wilhelm, Ravan Press, Jonathan Ball [Ad Donker], for 'Jazz' from *At the End of a War* (1981) and *The Bayonet Field* (2000).